### Praise for Wendy Lee's novel *Happy Family*

"[Lee] deals with a hot-button issue in a manner neither shy nor didactic, and she invests her characters with humanity when they might easily become sociological types. *Happy Family* is worth reading for those reasons alone, and serves as the debut of a writer who may well do great work later on." —*San Francisco Chronicle*

"Rich and multilayered, Lee's novel explores what it means to be a part of something, whether it's a family or a culture. Told in Hua's sparse, somber voice, the story grabs readers from the start and doesn't let go until the final page. A truly memorable first outing." —*Booklist* (starred review)

"First novelist Lee's craftsmanship is evident in sparse but expressive prose. She carefully and insightfully handles the contentious issue of the adoption of Chinese children. . . . This debut delivers on the promise of Lee's interesting premise." —*Library Journal*

"This first novel uncoils slyly, then strikes with startling yet inevitable plot developments that unfold before the reader sees them coming. . . . A powerful debut." —*Kirkus Reviews*

"Wendy Lee's sure-footed debut locates the raw nerve connecting two social phenomena—China's one-child law and the adoption of Chinese babies by American parents. Hua, Lee's stranger in a strange land, speaks in a soft but firm voice from the ineradicable margin." —Ed Park, author of *Personal Days*

"Wendy Lee debuts with a quietly dangerous novel of domestic life . . . The story moves among some of the new taboos in American life as we live it now, sure-footed and unflinching, fun and smart—a remarkable first novel." —Alexander Chee, author of *Edinburgh*

# ACROSS

## *A*

# GREEN OCEAN

# WENDY LEE

*Wendy Lee*

**KENSINGTON BOOKS**
www.kensingtonbooks.com

*For my sister*

# CHAPTER 1

Ling Tang sat on the back porch, waiting for the right time to come. It wouldn't be long now; the late-afternoon sunshine had already crested the fence between her house and the next-door neighbors', stretching across the lawn like strands of honey. Since her husband, Han, had died last year, Ling had not gone out into her own backyard. With no one to cut the grass, it had grown lush and thick, full of bugs that rose in a haze over the greenness. During the time her husband was alive, he'd cut the lawn every two weeks in the summer, pushing a mower through the grass with a firm hand. Dandelions, evening primrose, and clover would fall evenly in his wake.

Once, Ling had looked out the kitchen window to see Han standing still in the middle of the lawn, the spring air ruffling the hair around his ears. He bent so swiftly to the ground that she'd run outside, alarmed that he had hurt himself. When she reached him, he motioned for her to crouch down. He parted the grass around a nest of what appeared to be mice that had frozen in the cold. They were larger than mice, though, with soft brown fur and tiny, pointed ears. As if suddenly recognizing a face, Ling realized they were baby rabbits. An inexplicable sadness came over her, and she looked at her husband for some response, some guidance for what to do. But Han covered the nest as quickly as he had discovered it with the cut grass, where it lay like a secret.

Underneath that luxuriant wave of grass lay other memories. Ling recalled how her daughter, Emily, then fourteen years old and newly impressed by a home-economics class, had tried to plant a vegetable garden next to the fence one year. For weeks Ling fixed salads with lettuce leaves that looked like pieces of lace, tomatoes riddled with holes, cucumbers that tasted like water. Ling tried to tell her daughter that it was okay, nobody was perfect at everything, but Emily had yanked out the plants. All that remained of that horticultural experiment was a slight depression in the earth.

Ling remembered another time when Han had shouted at their son, Michael, when he had been twelve, for something he had done in the backyard. Michael had been balanced on the weathered gray fence that separated them from their neighbors on the right, the Bradleys, trying to see—what, Ling wondered, the Bradley girl hanging out by the pool?—and Han, arriving home from work, had caught him. He'd yelled something that she couldn't hear through the kitchen window, something she imagined to be worse than a reprimand, because Michael had jumped down onto the lawn so quickly that he'd twisted his ankle. As Ling had wrapped a bandage around his foot, she'd noticed how Michael bit his lower lip, trying not to make a sound.

The Bradleys had lived in their house almost as long as Ling and Han had lived in theirs, and they were about the same age, in their late fifties. Their children, also a son and daughter, had known Emily and Michael in school, but aside from one time when Ling had asked Mrs. Bradley to babysit, the parents had not interacted much. There were none of the neighborly activities that she had seen on television or read in books, no borrowing of eggs to make a cake, requests to take in the newspaper during vacation, or the necessity of jumper cables to start a car. Neither she nor Han had ever been invited over to the Bradleys' house or to so much as dip a toe in their pool. At Han's funeral, Mrs. Bradley had brought over a pot of chili that was so spicy that it made Ling's eyes water. Which was odd, because she hadn't even cried over her husband yet.

Since the funeral, though, Ling had watched the Bradleys with renewed interest. She wanted to see their lives unfurl before her eyes, as hers with Han should have. She wanted to see the bare bones of what it meant to take care of and comfort someone; the way a husband might reach down to pick up something his wife had dropped, or how a wife might place a sweater around her husband's shoulders. But the Bradleys were private folk and kept their blinds drawn; the trees on the other side of the fence remained untrimmed, hiding their daily existence behind a scrim of leaves. Ling couldn't help but feel cheated, deprived of not only an experience that should have been hers, but even of being able to witness it secondhand.

If the Bradleys were an alternate future of the Tangs, Ling's neighbors on the left were a version from more than thirty years ago: a young couple named Jerry and Marta Katz, and their baby son whose thin, wailing cry could often be heard from next door. When the Katzes first moved in nine months ago, Ling had watched Marta walk around in the backyard, raking leaves until she could barely bend over the swell of her stomach. She reminded Ling of herself when she and Han had first moved to New Jersey from New York City, Emily just a bump beneath Ling's knitted poncho. Ling wondered if Marta had felt the same queasy blend of anticipation and fear that she'd had years ago, the sense that her life was finally starting.

Today, Jerry Katz must have come home early from work, for he was out inspecting his own lawn. He took a few steps, plucked a blade of Kentucky bluegrass, and held it up to the light. He seemed displeased, although compared to the veritable jungle next door, his lawn looked like it had been ordered from a nursery catalog, each blade straight as a solider in a battle against overgrowth and disorder. He mowed once a month with a huge power mower that would have both impressed and mortified Han Tang.

"Hello, Jerry," Ling called out. She was careful to pronounce his name clearly. Her command of English was excellent, but she sometimes found herself stumbling over certain vowels or forgetting common phrases at the most inconvenient times. The other day she had forgotten how to say *stamp* at the post office and instead the word in Mandarin Chinese, *youpiao,* radiated in her mind.

"Hey there, Mrs. Tang," Jerry said, pronouncing her last name like the drink favored by astronauts. "Hot enough for you?" He lifted his baseball cap, leaving a fringe of hair dark with sweat over his forehead.

"Yes, very hot," Ling agreed, and fanned herself for emphasis, although she did not find it particularly warm. In fact, she wasn't even perspiring. But sometimes she found it easier to go along with other people in these matters, to be agreeable for the sake of being agreeable. If she wasn't careful, these little moments of acquiescence would build up, but she figured talking about the weather was harmless. "How is the baby?" she asked.

"He's doing fine," Jerry said. "Hope he isn't keeping you up at night."

"Oh, no," Ling assured him.

Another acquiescence. But she didn't think it was appropriate to say that she actually enjoyed being woken up in the middle of the night by the baby's cry. Sometimes when that happened, Ling thought it was one of her own children—Michael had had colic; Emily, bad dreams—and she would half-rise to go to the next room. It was probably even less appropriate to admit that she sometimes sat at Emily's old bedroom window and watched Marta's shadow as she paced with the baby slung over her shoulder like a little sack of rice, her hair backlit so that it formed a halo against the curtain.

"Hey, Mrs. Tang," Jerry said, looking over the fence that separated their property, "why don't you let me mow your lawn for you? It'll take twenty, thirty minutes, tops—"

"No!"

Jerry tugged confusedly at the bill of his cap.

"I mean," Ling said, "it's too hot right now. Maybe later, when it's cooler."

"Okay, when it's cooler," Jerry agreed. "Marta and I owe you for those baby clothes you brought over for Ephraim."

Ling waved that away. "Old clothes, they go to waste if not for Ephraim."

"Well, thank you, anyway," Jerry said, and moved away as he continued his lawn inspection.

Ling had been saving the clothes for her own grandchildren,

but when she had heard that Marta had had the baby, she had gone down into the basement and looked through her children's infant clothes, most of which were spit-stained beyond possible reuse. Ever practical, Ling had dressed Michael in some of Emily's more neutral onesies and jumpers, although occasionally a pastel or flowered garment slipped through. One of the items she had bought especially for him was a tiny blue sailor suit, and he had outgrown it at once. Since it was almost new, she decided to give it to Ephraim.

What an odd name the Katzes had chosen for their child, Ling thought. It was a Jewish name, Marta had told her, that of her maternal grandfather; she herself had been named after her grandmother, who was of German ancestry. Ling didn't know how Marta's grandparents had possibly gotten together. It was what an old aunt of hers had said of a second cousin who had married a Japanese man: *impossible.*

Although, Ling supposed, it was a more valid reason than those behind her own children's names. She and Han had decided that their children would grow up with only English names, so as to better fit in the country that would be their home for the rest of their lives, but they did not know what the popular names were at the time. In the end Ling had named their daughter after Emily Brontë, her favorite English author when she was a student in Taiwan, and their son Michael because it was from the Bible. Ephraim, she had an inkling, was a biblical name as well, so maybe that was okay. She hoped Emily and Michael would be similarly inspired when it came to naming their own children, although who knew when that would be.

Ling still had hope for Emily, who was thirty-two and had been married for seven years. The trouble was, Emily worked long hours as an immigration lawyer, and there was little sign that she intended to slow down. Ling couldn't understand why her daughter chose to work in Chinatown, the very place from which Ling and Han had escaped, alongside the kind of people they had tried to distance themselves from. There was something about her selflessness that troubled Ling. It reminded her of when Emily was a child and she would bring home stray cats and dogs, whether they needed saving or not. But at least Emily was married, whereas Ling did not know whether Michael was dating anyone. She wasn't even sure what his exact address in the city was anymore, since he moved around a lot; who his roommates were; or what he did at his job. She only knew he was a graphic designer at an ad agency, which meant, she suspected, that he drew pictures on the computer all day in the same way he had drawn pictures as a child.

Michael had always been secretive, especially as a teenager. He'd spend hours next door with the Bradley girl, hardly speaking to his parents, until one day Ling decided to go through his room. It was, she had a faint suspicion, something that was not considered acceptable in this culture; you were supposed to trust your children and give them privacy. Whereas, when she had been growing up in Taiwan, Ling would have never thought to hide anything about her life from her sisters, let alone her parents. She didn't know what she expected to find—cigarettes or dirty magazines, she assumed—but instead discovered some drawings in the bottom of a desk drawer. Most were abstract, but some were sketches of people whom she assumed were classmates. Then, to her surprise, she discovered a picture of herself at the kitchen sink; Michael must have been sitting at the table, watching her, without her fully realizing it. And another, a more detailed portrait of his father, a disembodied head in charcoal. But, somehow, Michael had managed to capture exactly the droop of Han's right eyebrow, the weary curve of his chin, so that Ling could imagine the way these features felt in real life as she traced the line on the paper with a fingertip. How was it that Michael had been able to observe his father so closely? How could he have known, if only instinctively, what his father had been feeling? Suddenly, as if she were an intruder, she put the drawings back into a folder and shut the desk drawer.

These days, whenever Ling asked Emily about Michael, Emily's reply would be, *Oh, cut him some slack. He's only twenty-six. He lives in a city where women vastly outnumber men. It makes sense he's not going to settle down. Besides, people his age don't really date anymore, they just hook up.* What did that mean, anyway—to hook up? Ling thought of two trains, the back of a dress. All she could think of was one of the first voices she had heard after she had moved into her house. She had been in the middle of unpacking boxes in the kitchen when she heard a tinny, disembodied voice, which for a second she thought was that of someone calling through the window. She followed the sound to a receiver that had been accidentally knocked off the wall, where the voice told her that the phone was off the hook. But you did not hook up a phone, you hung it up.

The truth, Ling realized, was that Emily knew as little about Michael's personal life as she did. She had always wanted her children to grow up close, as she had with her own sisters, but was afraid that the six-year interval between her two children forever doomed them to older sibling–younger sibling rivalry or worse, indifference. She just wanted them to be happy, that was all. And for them to be happy, they had to have families, spouses, children. These things were what had made Ling happy, although, as her own children were growing up, she had never considered the question of whether she was happy or not.

Jerry Katz had gone back into his house, and the sunlight had traveled clear across the lawn now. Due to how it reached halfway up the fence, Ling figured it was around seven o'clock and finally the right time to try calling Michael. It was late enough so that he would have left work, but early enough so that he wouldn't have gone out yet. Calling her children could be such an ordeal. Emily didn't want Ling to call her cell phone since she also used it for work, but if Ling called Emily's home number, she almost always reached her husband, Julian, instead. She didn't mind making small talk with her son-in-law. In fact, she enjoyed discussing with him the improvements he was making to the house, or, more recently, what late-season vegetables were growing in the backyard (unlike the teenage Emily, Julian appeared to be an adept gardener). At first she had thought it strange that he always was at home, but now she had come to accept it as just another aspect of her daughter's marriage she didn't understand.

Julian had a profession. He was a documentary filmmaker who, as far as Ling could tell, worked sporadically on other people's projects and occasionally on his own. So far he had made a ten-minute piece about a bunch of trust-fund artists who scorned their parents' support, that had been in a minor festival. It was, Ling suspected, based on his own life, except that Julian did use his family's money; that was the only way he and Emily could afford their house in Westchester. Ling had been so excited when Emily had announced just before her thirtieth birthday that they were buying their own place, although she was slightly disappointed that it was so far away from her—about equidistant from the city, but in the wrong direction. It would be very inconvenient for Ling to help out with the baby she was certain Emily would shortly announce she and Julian were expecting. But two years had passed, Han had passed away, and still no sign of a grandchild.

Julian wasn't a bad son-in-law, Ling acknowledged. In fact, she quite liked him. Yes, he had once brought her white roses, not knowing that white was the color of mourning in most Asian cultures, but that was forgivable. He and Emily looked good together as a couple, and would provide her with adorable mixed-race grandchildren. But Ling was afraid that Emily gave too much to everyone but those closest to her and that one day her husband would ask her for something she was not able to provide.

Now, Michael was just as hard to reach but for a different reason. He only had a cell phone, which Ling supposed was the trend among young people nowadays, but it caused more problems than if he had a landline. Strange how the more convenient technology made it to talk to people, the more difficult it was to find them. Ling had been trying to reach Michael for the past week; since Monday. She wanted his advice on what it meant when you went to a restaurant with a man and he paid, when you had long conversations with him and he listened intently, when at the end of your outings together, he gazed into your eyes and said he looked forward to seeing you again soon. In short, she wanted to know about dating.

Ling didn't know how much of an expert Michael was on this subject. Of course, in high school he had been oddly close to the Bradley girl, and once he had brought home a girl from college who wore a bowler hat. But certainly he was a better option for a confidante than Emily, and not only because Emily was so loyal to her father's memory. Ling was afraid that Emily might start asking uncomfortable questions, or worse, think that her mother's real motivation for calling was to ask when she and Julian were planning to have a baby. Children could be so selfish, thinking the world revolved around them.

Every day this past week, when Ling had dialed Michael's number, the message had gone to voice mail. She supposed he must be terribly busy, or else he would have called her back by now. *Cut him some slack,* Emily had said, and Ling had spent the past few days cutting it, whatever slack was. But now she picked up the kitchen phone and pressed the buttons, willing a human to pick up on the other end. *We're sorry, the mailbox is full,* answered a voice that could never have belonged to a real person. The messages couldn't all be from her, as she'd just called once a day. And besides, she had not actually left messages. She never liked hearing the sound of her own voice being played back, with its accented English even after almost thirty-five years of living in this country. The one good thing about cell phones, she supposed, was that she didn't have to leave a message for someone to know she had called.

She hung up and sat for a while in the kitchen, her fingertips cold. It was not unusual for Michael to let his phone go to voice mail or to not call her back for a few days, but for his mailbox to be full? This must mean other people were trying to reach him without success, that he wasn't calling *anybody* back. To make sure she had heard right, she called again, and once more received the same, disembodied message. As if on their own, her fingers punched in the number again and again, until she forced herself to stop. She sat there clutching the receiver, as though it was the only thing grounding her.

The last time she had felt this way was almost a year ago, when the hospital had called to tell her that her husband had had a heart attack.

Han's death had occurred quite suddenly at work. He had been a laboratory technician at a pharmaceuticals company in Trenton. Ling did not know exactly what he did—whenever he had tried to explain it, her mind felt overstuffed, like when she was first learning English—but she knew he cared enough about it to the point that he rarely took a day off. She remembered noticing the strain of his back through his shirts, worn thin from too much washing. He had been fifty-seven years old.

By the time Ling had gotten to the hospital, he was already gone. *It was heart failure,* the doctors had said. She hadn't believed them at first. Wasn't heart failure caused by too much weight, too much food, too much drink, too much of everything? Her husband was as slim as the day she had set eyes on him, and he never touched alcohol or smoked a cigarette. He was the kind of person who got up at dawn to take a brisk walk around the block, and he went to bed at ten thirty every night, without a minute or two's deviation. She wanted to tell the doctors this, as proof that there had been some mistake, but for some reason her English came out all twisted, and they were more interested in whether she needed to be sedated.

When Ling called Emily's cell phone to tell her what had happened, she added that she and Michael shouldn't hurry to the hospital. *Don't you want us to be with you as soon as possible?* Emily had asked. There was no point, Ling had said, since it was too late to say good-bye to their father, surprising even herself with her calmness. When Emily did arrive, Ling thought that her daughter looked like she was working too hard. There were dark smudges under her eyes, and her shoulder-length hair badly needed a trim. It also didn't help that she had inherited her father's dusky complexion, his wide-set eyes and generous mouth. Ling knew her daughter had more important things to worry about than her appearance, but surely a little makeup wouldn't hurt. However, she knew if she mentioned this, Emily would respond tartly that she shouldn't think all lawyers looked like those on television.

Michael, however, took after his mother—tall and thin and pale, with delicate features and long, sensitive hands and feet. When he was young—perhaps because she knew there would be no more children after him—Ling treated him like a piece of porcelain. She picked him up whenever he cried, chose the best bits from her own plate to feed him, took care to leave on a night-light in his room. This irked Han, who thought she babied him, and he insisted that his son should grow up tough, as he had. How tough, Ling didn't know, although she was aware that life in 1960s Beijing must have been difficult.

At the hospital Michael sat with her quietly, holding her hand, while Emily flew about interrogating doctors, browbeating nurses, commandeering cups of coffee that no one wanted to drink. In that way she was her father's daughter, capable and methodical, even to the point of lacking an imagination, Ling sometimes thought. But Ling could not be more grateful for her daughter's help. Emily was the one who had made the funeral arrangements, organized the gathering at the house afterward, picked out a black silk dress from Ling's closet for her to put on, even though she herself was wearing an old black knit thing that made her look like she was wearing a tube.

After the funeral, most of the people who had come to pay their last respects were Chinese families from church or Han's coworkers, the majority who were also Asian. The only white people in the room besides Han's old boss and his wife were the Bradleys from next door—Mr. and Mrs. Bradley and their daughter, who now lived in Boston—and Emily's husband, Julian.

Most notable among the guests was the lack of relatives. Ling's family still lived in Taiwan, and Han had no living relatives that Ling knew of. For the eulogy, Pastor Liu had only been able to say, *Han Tang, beloved husband to Ling Tang, beloved father to Emily Tang and Michael Tang.* Of course, Han had also been someone's son and someone's brother, but he rarely talked of his parents or siblings in Beijing, and Ling assumed that he chose not to tell her about his past. She knew her own childhood in Taiwan could not compare, where she had grown up the middle daughter out of three girls. The family had been a political one that had come over from the mainland in 1949, and so had been spared the twin ravages of famine and fanaticism. The children were cared for by housekeepers and maids rather than Ling's beautiful, indolent mother. Because none of them were boys, their father largely ignored them. Occasionally, Ling felt the sting of her parents' disinterest, but she had never known the pain of separation or persecution, like her husband must have.

Not that you would have been able to tell what Han had suffered by looking at his picture at the funeral. Sitting on the mantelpiece in the living room, the framed photograph, which had been taken at Emily's wedding, depicted a close-lipped, square-jawed man whose eyelids were beginning to sag with age, but whose stiff-bristled hair was still black. It occurred to Ling that if you looked around the room at its occupants, most of them immigrants, you would not be able to discern beneath their smooth façades what their previous lives had been like.

Every time someone came up to offer their condolences to Ling, she grew more irritated, even sarcastic.

*He was a dedicated employee. . . .* This was from Han's old boss, whom Ling hadn't seen in nearly ten years. Standing next to his faded wife, he didn't look as imposing as she'd remembered, or maybe he'd been diminished with age.

*He was a wonderful person to work with. . . .* A female colleague, who appeared to be past retirement age but who was probably still working because she had no husband or children to support her.

*May God watch over him. . . .* From one of the newest members of the First Baptist congregation, a young woman just arrived from mainland China, the cheap, shiny material of her clothes screaming fresh off the boat.

*We'll miss having him next door. . . .* Mr. and Mrs. Bradley, unctuous in their carefully pressed clothes. Mrs. Bradley had a green casserole dish tucked under her arm like a football.

Ling directed Mrs. Bradley toward the kitchen, thinking fiercely all the while, *You will not miss him. You never knew him. I never even knew him.*

She walked through the living room, making sure that drinks were topped and plates were full. The food laid out was a mixture of Chinese comfort foods—sticky rice with sweet sausage, lion's head meatballs, soy-sauce chicken—mixed with more mundane meat loafs and salads. She'd never be able to eat it all, even if she made her children take some back home with them.

Emily and Michael were in the kitchen, where the dishes that couldn't fit on the dining room table had been placed. They were looking at one item in particular, Mrs. Bradley's casserole dish.

Michael lifted the lid, and he and Emily and Ling peered inside to see a lumpy red-brown concoction of beef and beans. At the same time, something wafted forth that stung the insides of Ling's nose. An unaccustomed sensation overcame her, and it was a few moments before she realized that tears were forming in the corners of her eyes. She turned aside so that her children wouldn't see her cry. Judging by the crinkled look on their faces, they felt it too. *Phew,* Emily said, and dumped the contents of the pot in the trash.

Both of her children had offered to stay a few days after the funeral, but Ling knew that Emily was itching to return to work, and Michael probably wanted to be back in the city, too. They promised to visit more often, to take turns calling her so that she would hear from someone every day. To her surprise, they actually did this, at least for the first month or so, and then went back to their usual rare calls. During this time Emily also made several trips back to put her father's finances in order. Once again, Ling was grateful for her daughter's ableness. As far as she was able to understand these matters, there was no mortgage or debt that Han had left her to pay off, and there seemed to be enough in his pension plan so that she would be taken care of for the rest of her life. If she lived the way they always had, without a penny or a second wasted, she wouldn't have to worry about a thing, or so Emily told her.

Before they left, Ling had asked her children to take whatever they wanted of their father's. Emily asked for the photograph that had been on the mantelpiece. She didn't seem to recognize it until Ling told her that it was from her and Julian's wedding. Ling had cut herself out of it, so maybe that was why it looked so strange. What Michael took Ling wasn't sure, although he had spent hours looking through his father's papers. Ling didn't know why he was so interested, as most of them were legal documents. There was very little writing that had been personal, as Han was the kind of man who hadn't seen the point of putting anything down on paper. His legacy was in the house he had paid for with his hard work, in the funds he had left his widow, in his children, and what they would accomplish with their lives.

After Emily and Michael had left, Ling had packed her husband's clothes and few possessions—the black comb he had used every morning, the alarm clock he had always set at night, even on weekends—into boxes in the basement. She was surprised by how little impact he had made within the house itself. She'd never noticed how much the rooms had been filled by her own things and the children's. The hallway had rung with the sounds of their voices; the walls had shook when they'd slammed shut the doors to their bedrooms. Han had always been more of an afterthought, the kind of man who never made much of an impression when he entered a room, not even a room in his own house.

The following year had passed quietly, and Ling was surprised by how much she missed her husband. Now she was too aware of herself, how it took longer for her to climb the stairs at night, the strange little pains that greeted her in the morning, the way her very bones ached after drinking a cold glass of water. Maybe things would have been different had she been in Taiwan, surrounded by relatives, but this was the path she had chosen. Han was the man she had chosen, and she would stay by her decision, and its consequences, even after his death, for the rest of her life.

Outside the kitchen window the sun was setting, casting shadows that reached into the farthest corners of the backyard. With cold fingers Ling dialed Emily's cell phone. Her daughter answered on the first ring.

"Hi, Mom," Emily said. "Is everything okay?"

Ling was silent.

"Mom." Emily's voice was worried now. "What's happened?"

Ling realized that the last time she had called Emily's cell had been a year ago to tell her about her father. "Have you heard from your brother?" she asked.

"Michael?" Emily almost sounded relieved.

*As if you had another brother,* Ling thought.

"I haven't talked to him in a while," Emily continued. "But you know how he is. It's impossible to get ahold of him."

"He doesn't pick up when I call him."

"Do you leave a message?"

"No."

"Mom!" Now Emily was getting that exasperated tone to her

voice. It usually happened whenever she talked to her mother, just not so early in the conversation. "It's really annoying when you do that. Why don't you just say you want him to call you back?"

It would be impossible to explain to her daughter the different tightropes she walked with each of them when it came to calling them on the phone. "I never leave a message. He knows it's me."

"Yes, who else would call multiple times without leaving a message?"

"Well, today I could not leave a message, even if I wanted, because the mailbox is full. I have tried to call him all week, and he doesn't answer. What does it mean?"

"I think," Emily said, "it means that he's been busy at work all week and doesn't want to be disturbed. I think it means he hasn't had time to check his messages. I think it means he's living a normal life."

"What if something's happened to him?"

"Like what? Mom, I know you think the city is a dangerous place, but it's different from when you and Dad lived here."

"He could have an accident, and no one will know," Ling persisted.

"He must have friends who check up on him." At this, Emily sounded a bit dubious. Not that Michael wouldn't have friends; it was just that neither she nor her mother knew who they were.

"I don't know," Ling said. "I have this feeling."

"Describe this feeling for me." It was the lawyer coming out in Emily, thought Ling, in which she made everyone feel like they were on trial.

"It's a feeling that a mother knows when something is not right with her child. You will know someday when you have children of your own." Emily's pause told Ling that she had overstepped her bounds. She could picture her daughter on the other end of the line, probably still at work, her brow furrowed impatiently.

"Mom, this isn't about me. It's about Michael."

"But it is about you. You're his older sister. You should be looking out for him." Even though she had come to realize her children were not that involved in each other's lives, Ling hoped to appeal to her daughter's sense of responsibility.

"Fine," Emily said. "If it makes you feel any better, I'll stop by his apartment after work, just to make sure he's okay."

This was more than Ling had hoped for. "You will do that?"

"How long can it take? Twenty minutes to get to the East Village, one minute for him to answer the door. Done."

Ling tried to hide her relief. "That would be a big help."

Emily's voice softened. "Don't worry, Mom. It's probably nothing."

With all her heart, Ling hoped she was right.

# CHAPTER 2

When her mother had called her, Emily Tang was still in her tiny office in Chinatown, a Styrofoam container of takeout sitting in the semicircle she had managed to clear on her desk. After she hung up, she regarded her dinner with a jaundiced eye. She'd had the same pan-fried noodles in a brown sauce from the greasy restaurant down the street almost every night this past week, but had ceased to taste it. Once upon a time, when she'd first come to the city from the suburbs as a wide-eyed college student, she'd thought Chinese takeout was charming, the stuff of a thousand romantic comedies involving single women in their well-decorated loft spaces. At home her parents had never allowed takeout, their reasoning being why buy Chinese food when you could cook it yourself? So she ate it in mall food courts with her teenage friends, after hours of trying on clothes and deciding everything made her look fat. Now, all she saw when she looked at takeout was monosodium glutamate and cheap immigrant labor, packaged in a nonbiodegradable container. She dumped it in the trash.

There were few things more pathetic than someone sitting in their office after seven on a Friday night and eating bad takeout, but Emily had good reason to be working late. For the past month she had been involved in a case that would validate the choice she had made six years ago to give up a judicial clerkship in favor of a junior associate position at the immigration law firm of Lazar and Jenkins. Although immigration law had been part of Emily's coursework at school, the first image it conjured up for her was the subway ads in which mustachioed male lawyers promised superherolike vengeance, or at least a few thousand dollars in damages. At the time, she was putting in twelve-hour days at the civil courthouse downtown, depressed by the parade of drug addicts, drunks, squatters, wife beaters, homeless people, and plain old crazies. She figured she would be better off dealing with immigrants, although she knew from her parents that they could be just as crazy.

When she talked about it with her husband—she and Julian had just been married for a year—he had told her to take the job, that she shouldn't think about the pay cut but what great things she could accomplish for the people who needed it the most. Fired up by his encouragement, Emily had promptly sent in her resignation. Of course, Julian had also seen how she'd come home grumpy and irritable from each day's events, too exhausted to do more than remove her clothes and slide into bed. She knew she couldn't have been easy to live with. It wasn't the first time that she reminded herself how lucky she was to have a husband who supported her decisions, who saw the best in her even if she had trouble seeing it in herself.

The fifty-year-old firm of Lazar and Jenkins had recently moved to Chinatown for the cheaper rents and had, by default, taken up the causes common to many of its inhabitants. Usually, that meant expired visas and green card applications, but occasionally something interesting would come up: a fire that exposed a landlord who crammed more than ten tenants into windowless six-by-eight-foot rooms; a garment worker who had lost her arm up to the elbow by working faulty equipment. Cases like these reminded Emily of how she'd felt participating in protests in college, only this time everything was happening in real life, to real people, as opposed to some distant cause. She was the only person at her firm who spoke any form of Chinese, although because it was the

Mandarin she had learned from her parents, and not the Cantonese or Fujianese that the majority of her clients spoke, she still needed a translator most of the time. Still, she knew that her face often made it easier for them to open up to her. In return, she often searched the faces of the people she represented, hoping to see traces of her parents in them. This had especially been true since her father had died.

She had received the call on a Tuesday afternoon last summer—*Daddy's gone,* her mother had said, just like that. Emily had been hurt by her mother's insistence that she not hurry to the hospital, until she realized this was the way her mother was coping with the irrevocability of her father's death. It was final; there was no point in trying to get there any sooner. Her mother had also asked Emily to tell her brother. Emily couldn't remember exactly what she had said to Michael, only that she would meet him at the train station and they could go home together. She also couldn't remember what Michael's reaction had been; she thought he had been oddly silent, although it was hard to gauge someone's feelings over the phone. All she could recall was that it had been a hot day, and the air conditioner had been broken, so that tears mixed with the perspiration trickling down her cheeks.

After she had ended the call to her brother, she saw her colleague, Rick Farina, standing in the doorway, a concerned look on his face. Rick was the other associate Lazar and Jenkins had hired at around the same time as she had started. At first Emily hadn't thought much of him, knowing that he and his wife and three kids lived in a two-family house with his parents in the Bronx. But after working on several cases together, and commiserating over the ineptitude of their bosses, they became close without any hint of petty workplace competition. Sometimes Emily even dared to think that they were friends. Certainly, it felt like it the time Rick invited her and Julian to his house for a barbecue a couple of summers ago. She had always admired the calm, even-handed, respectful way he treated his clients, and seeing where he came from gave her insight into the source of his stability. His Italian parents seemed to be a heartier breed of immigrant than her own, proud of their son and his accomplishments without expecting anything more from him. His wife, Lisa, was a blond, friendly woman who had no qualms about displaying her impressive bosom when she nursed her youngest, a baby girl. Rick's two boys, with varying degrees of his flashing smile, asked Julian to join them in a game of touch football. To Emily's surprise, Julian gave in and appeared to actually enjoy himself while she stood on the sidelines and watched the various members of the Farina family mill about in the backyard.

Perhaps what Emily appreciated most about Rick, though, was what he had done that afternoon last summer. As she had sat frozen in her chair after hanging up the phone, he turned off her computer, handed her purse to her, marched her out of the office, and put her in a cab. Afterward, he had sent flowers, offered to come to the funeral, but she refused. It was enough that he had understood, in those first blinding minutes, how she'd needed to be treated— not to be asked questions, not even to be comforted, but to be told what to do.

Now, as Emily was getting ready to leave her office, she heard Rick's measured footsteps in the hallway before he knocked on her door and came in.

"Still here?" she said, although she knew he stayed at work as long as she did.

"I just heard from the doctors."

Emily knew she'd be at work a while longer. "Sit down."

She and Rick had both been assigned to the case of a thirty-eight-year-old man named Gao Hu, who had legally come to the States as a student and overstayed his visa. Since then, he had graduated from technical college, worked for over ten years at the same computer-support company, married a naturalized American citizen, purchased a house in Queens, and had a son, who was now eight years old. He had been applying for a green card through his wife when a red flag went up with Homeland Security. His name had been matched with a years-old notice to appear in immigration court for a deportation hearing, which had followed him around for years from one old address to the next, always a step behind until now. This infraction was enough for him to be arrested, and he had been taken to a detention center upstate, where he had been held for the past three months.

It was during this period, when it became clear he wasn't going to be released, that Gao's wife, Jean, had sought legal help. Emily and Rick had periodically gone to the detention center to see him, and two weeks ago, when Emily had gone alone, Gao had complained of leg pain. After some back and forth with the authorities, who claimed he was making it up in the hopes of being pardoned on medical leave, he was examined by an independent doctor, whose results Rick had just obtained.

"His leg is fractured," Rick said. "It isn't clear how it happened."

"The bastards," Emily said. "They kept saying he was faking."

Rick held up his hands. "Wait, it gets worse. When the doctor did the MRI on his leg, they discovered a defect in his heart. He's probably had it for years and never felt any symptoms, or thought they weren't worth checking out. It's possible it's been exacerbated by his current situation."

Emily briefly thought of her own father and his aversion to doctors, then tamped it down. "Are they allowing him medication?"

"He's been prescribed painkillers, but when medication's distributed at the center, the inmate has to be able to stand in line to receive it. Of course, Gao's leg has gotten so bad that he can't stand. And they won't give him a wheelchair."

Emily exhaled a breath. "Okay, what do we do?"

"First, we have to file a report. It's a criminal case now. Willful neglect, obstruction of justice, whatever we can throw at them. Next, Gao has to be allowed to get immediate treatment, for his heart as well as his leg. Once that's done, we have to find a way to get him out of that place. Maybe move him closer to the city, so we can monitor his condition."

"We should make some phone calls," Emily said, beginning to turn her computer back on. "Every single freaking congressperson. They should all know about this."

Rick reached across the desk and placed his hand on her arm. "It's late, there's no point in doing that now. We'll start drawing up the lists tomorrow, so we can make the calls first thing on Monday."

Emily grinned, adrenaline beginning to replace outrage. "Another working weekend." She enjoyed this about her job most of all, when it made any other problem in her life seemed petty in comparison. Suddenly contrite, she asked, "Did you have any plans?"

"The boys have a soccer game, but no matter—Lisa can go without me. How about you?"

"Julian wants to see some new documentary, but he'll have to do that by himself." She gave an exaggerated sigh. "Our poor spouses."

"Indeed." Rick paused and removed his hand quickly, as if he'd just realized he was still touching her. "Well, since we're going to be working all weekend, how about getting a drink?"

Emily glanced at her watch. "I'd love to, but I promised my mother I'd stop by my brother's apartment. He hasn't returned her calls in a week, so she thinks he's been kidnapped or mugged or something. Of course, he's probably just ignoring her."

Rick laughed. "Oh, to be young and without responsibilities."

They said good night, and Emily finally left work.

Outside, the sidewalks were littered with the detritus of the day: wadded-up newspapers, peanut shells, plastic bags. A few men were outside smoking cigarettes; a pair of tourists stopped in front of a lit store display and then strolled on. She passed a café in which a young Asian couple in the window dreamily split a shaved ice. In the distance, the Manhattan Bridge shimmered like a faraway promise. To Emily, these things were more romantic than any image of New York that her teenage, suburban imagination could have conjured up. She knew most people would think she was delusional, but what she enjoyed most about working in Chinatown was the way it smelled. Sure, in the summer the odors could get overwhelming, but she liked how the moment she got off the subway, even if she were blindfolded, she could tell where she was from the redolent mix of dead fish, rotting vegetables, and other assorted trash. There was a distinctly human element to it. She liked to think it was the blood and sweat of the thousands of immigrants who had passed through its streets. Whereas now it was probably the blood and sweat of tourists looking for the right knockoff bag, but she still liked to think of it that way.

Since she was running late, Emily decided to take a cab to Michael's apartment. It took her several more minutes to dig the unfamiliar address out of her phone's memory and flag down a vehicle. As the cab wound through the festively decorated tenements of Little Italy, across Houston Street, and up First Avenue, she tried to think of the last time she had been in this part of the city—possibly not since her twenties. Occasionally, Julian came in for his work, but for her, the city had been telescoped to Chinatown. She got in at seven in the morning on the train and left at seven at night, leaving no opportunity for anything else. She hadn't gone for a drink in ages. Maybe she should have taken Rick up on his offer. She absently touched her arm where his hand had been.

Looking out the window at the restaurants and bars and the young people strolling down the streets, Emily remembered when she and Julian had gone to a screening almost every weekend, something by one of his old film school buddies, or by a filmmaker he hoped to network with. She had sat through endless question-and-answer sessions, desultory after-parties with bad wine. When Julian introduced her to other people as a lawyer, they would give her a cool nod and then turn away, as if she came from a different world. *Look, assholes,* she'd think. *My work has more influence on the real world than your five-minute films about someone's antique camera collection or some guy who makes sculptures out of trash.* Later, she and Julian would laugh about the earnestness of some of these people, but she couldn't help wondering if he preferred that she be like one those red-lipsticked grad students who hung on to his every word if he so much as mentioned that he knew a distributor.

For the most part, though, she remained the supportive girlfriend, and subsequently, supportive wife. Then, since they had moved to the suburbs, these social events had gradually tapered off. Julian would go to some of them alone, and Emily would beg off, saying she'd had a long week and couldn't bear going back into the city again. She said she'd prefer to stay at home and work on legal briefs. In reality, she sat on the couch, ordered in dinner, and watched bad movies late into the night until she heard a car in the driveway, and then she'd switch off the television and snatch up a book, or at least a serious-looking magazine, for when Julian entered the house.

As the streets signs for Alphabet City flashed by, Emily wondered if her brother enjoyed where he lived. Unlike her, Michael had gone to a small liberal arts college in Massachusetts, although he'd returned to the city after graduation. He seemed to like his job as a graphic designer well enough, although, he didn't seem to be driven by any particular purpose. Emily supposed she could be full of advice, and, in fact, should be, but she was too busy doling it out to her clients every day. Besides, she'd done her time. When they were children, her parents had impressed upon her that her main responsibility was to look after her little brother. On the rare occasions her parents went out, she had to babysit. She was expected to help Michael with his homework and provide a good example in school. In a way, since she spoke English fluently and understood things like what should packed in an American child's lunchbox (definitely not pickled vegetables) or that American children received allowances for doing the simplest household chores (and more than a quarter per chore), it was as if she were another parent.

The cab stopped, and Emily got out into the warm, humid night. She stood in front of a building that must have once been peach-colored brick underneath the layer of grime. The tree-lined street was more pleasant than she had expected, the metal-gated storefronts only lightly adorned with graffiti. The skeleton of a luxury apartment building at the corner indicated better things to come.

By the side of the front door was a row of buzzers. The name next to Michael's was something undecipherable, apparently having been scratched out multiple times. She rang it, anyway. The intercom did not crackle to life, nor did the door release. She rang it again, still nothing. For the first time, she felt a twinge of apprehension. Maybe her mother wasn't so off base. But Emily knew she was getting ahead of herself. Michael could be out, or perhaps the buzzer didn't work. Then she noticed the door was slightly ajar, probably to let a breath of air into the stifling hallway that she now entered.

The apartment was on the fifth floor but seemed much farther. As Emily climbed the steep stairs, the temperature appeared to increase by a degree with each step. It didn't help that she was wearing a high-necked blouse and slacks, her approximation of business casual. When she reached the top, she paused to catch her breath from what air was left up there. The ceiling was very low; if she reached up, she could touch the skylight, which was dingy with pollution and pigeon droppings. It hardly seemed possible that there was a livable space behind the single door at the end of the landing. There was a buzzer, but unlike the one downstairs, it hung by a frayed electrical wire, like an eye from a socket, indicating its uselessness. She figured if anyone was inside, they must have heard her approach by now.

Emily lifted her hand to knock, but before she could make contact, the door opened. Behind it was a young blond man with glasses. For an instant she thought she had the wrong address. But she had the uncanny feeling that the look on his face reflected her own. Both of them had been expecting to see the same person: Michael.

Then the young man rearranged his features and extended his hand. "You must be Emily."

Emily took it. "And you are . . . ?"

"David?" He spoke as if he was unsure of his own name. When it didn't seem to register with her, he said, "I'm guessing Michael never told you. I'm his boyfriend."

They sat across from each other at the table, Emily and David, glasses of water sweating condensation onto the surface. A single fan idly pushed air around the tiny studio and out a window, but it didn't seem to help. Even the walls looked sticky in the heat.

Some people—under the age of thirty, Emily thought—might find the space delightfully bohemian. It was small and low-ceilinged, full of odd angles in which no furniture could possibly fit. A scarred strip of linoleum, upon which sat a metal sink, a half fridge, and a camp stove, indicated the beginning and end of the kitchen. The half-open cupboard above the stove contained two cereal bowls and two plates, two glasses, and a commemorative mug. A pilled green futon that looked like it had been salvaged from the street, covered in a tangle of sheets, was pushed up against the wall. Besides that, there was no furniture other than the table and chairs that were being used to sit in.

Having surveyed the room, Emily now turned her attention to her brother's boyfriend. Judging by the faint crinkles at the corners of his blue eyes, she guessed he was older than she had initially thought, possibly in his early thirties. She supposed he was good-looking enough, in a bland sort of way. Conservative haircut, weirdly old-fashioned but expensive-looking wire-rimmed frames. Despite the heat, he was nicely dressed in a pale-colored linen suit. When she glanced down, she saw that his shoes shone a rich chestnut brown. He must have also come from work, except that he was better dressed than she was.

"Are you okay?" David asked.

Emily jerked her head up, embarrassed at being caught giving him the once-over. "I'm just worn out from the stairs."

"I mean," he said pointedly, "are you okay with Michael being who he is? What he is?"

She was suddenly defensive. "What makes you think I didn't know?" She looked away. "All right, I didn't know. My parents definitely didn't. He never said anything about it. But it doesn't matter. It's fine with me if he's gay."

There, she had said it. "How did you two meet?"

David smiled nervously, the creases at the corners of his eyes deepening. "I know this sounds like a cliché, but we met at the Pride parade about a year ago. Not to worry, we weren't actually *in* the parade. We were both stuck on the same side of the street, trying to cross over—we were supposed to meet friends for lunch. We decided to give up and just have lunch together."

"Very cute," Emily allowed. "So you've been seeing each other for about a year? You must have known him when . . ."

"Your father passed away? Yes. Actually, I was with him when he found out."

Emily shook her head, trying to recast her memory of telling

Michael to involve another person in the same room. The scene was getting too crowded.

"I didn't expect to go to the funeral or anything," David said. "I knew we hadn't known each other long enough for that. And I understood why he wouldn't want me to meet his family."

*And still doesn't,* Emily thought. She tried to be charitable. "Well, it makes me feel better to know that he's had someone this past year to help him deal with everything."

The look on David's face made her wish she hadn't jumped to conclusions. "To be honest," he said, "we haven't been together the entire year. It's been sort of off and on. I've been pushing for more commitment from him. Even asked him to move in with me." He nodded at the walls around them. "As you might have noticed, this place isn't the most comfortable. I have an apartment uptown, where we spend most of our time together—that is, when we *are* together. I'm away during the day, so he'd have the space all to himself."

"And what is it that you do?" Emily asked politely.

"I'm a lawyer."

"Huh," Emily said, without volunteering more information. Her mother would love that.

"I'm afraid I pushed him too far about moving in, and we argued about it. Michael's very independent. You probably know that."

Emily nodded, not wanting to dispel his belief that they were close siblings. Not that David would have believed her, anyway, if she hadn't even known that her own brother was gay. She wondered just how much Michael had told David about her or their parents.

"It just seemed like a good idea, since he was laid off last month," David added.

"What? He never mentioned that he'd lost his job."

"Guess he didn't tell you a lot."

Emily tried to ignore that jab. "Tell me more about your argument."

"Months ago I made him give me a key to his place, though he never wanted one to mine." David gave a short laugh. "Earlier this week I tried to give him a key, and we argued about it, and he left my place in a huff. I've tried calling him since then, don't know how many messages I left. Then this morning when I called, the mailbox was—"

"Full," Emily finished for him.

"So I came over here after work and got into his apartment with my key. There was this note." David handed her a square of paper from his pocket, and she unfolded it. Her brother's writing, which she hadn't seen for a long time, possibly not even in an adult hand, wavered before her eyes. The paper had started soaking up droplets of water from the tabletop, blurring the ink.

Emily forced herself to concentrate and read out loud: " 'Gone away to take a break. Am fine.' What's that supposed to mean?"

"Don't know. Whenever we fight, I tend to let him go off on his own. We don't contact each other for a while, and I wait for him to call me. I don't ask any questions." David shrugged, as if acknowledging how one-sided it sounded. "That's just the way it works. But he's never left a note before."

"It's not a very disturbing note," Emily said, somewhat relieved. It almost sounded like Michael had gone down the street to pick up something at the store.

"You think we should report him missing?" David asked.

"When did you last talk to him?"

"Tuesday night."

Emily could feel herself going into work mode, the easiest way for her to handle the situation. "The police aren't going to find it a very compelling argument. This note suggests that he walked of his own free will. Plus, I'm sorry to say, but the fact that you two had a fight indicates that he might not want to be found. At least by you."

"We've got to do something," David said.

"I'm not sure there's anything we can do, except to wait for him to contact us. Where do you think he went?"

"No clue. He can't have gone very far. He doesn't have the money. He was going to have trouble making this month's rent. I've offered to help him out before, but he wouldn't take it."

Emily glanced around the room. "I wonder if there's anything else he left behind that could tell us where he's gone."

"Well..." Reluctantly, David handed her another scrap of paper. "I also found this."

On it was written the name "Edison Ng," a telephone number, and what appeared to be the name of a restaurant. Emily knew why David hadn't shown this to her before. "You think he's cheating on you?"

"I don't know what to think."

"There's only one way to find out." Emily picked up her phone, and before David could do anything to stop her, dialed the number. "Voice mail," she mouthed to David before saying, "Hi, this is Emily Tang. I'm looking for my brother, Michael Tang. He's been missing for a few days, and no one knows where he is. Please give me a call back as soon as you get this—it doesn't matter how late."

Then, attempting positivity, she said to David, "I don't think you have anything to worry about from this Edison Ng. From his voice, he sounded kind of like a high school kid. And 'Edison'? The ultimate nerd name."

She was rewarded with a half smile. "Thanks for doing that," David said. "You'll let me know if you hear anything?"

Emily promised she would, and they exchanged contact information. She slung her purse over her shoulder in preparation to leave, but David didn't make a move.

"I'm staying in this apartment tonight," he said. "Maybe tomorrow, too. I know it sounds silly, but it makes me feel closer to him somehow." He paused. "I really care about your brother. No matter what he does, to me or our relationship, I'm going to see this through."

"Good luck," Emily said softly. If David wanted to stay in the fires of hell, or what felt like it, he was welcome to.

On the train, Emily called her mother to report that Michael wasn't home, but she had talked to his roommate, who thought he had gone on some kind of trip. No, the roommate didn't know where, but he didn't seem to be that concerned.

The silence on the other end of the phone suggested to Emily that this had not alleviated her mother's worry. However, her mother only said, "I didn't know Michael had a roommate."

"Neither did I," Emily replied grimly before she hung up.

She supposed it shouldn't come as a surprise that her brother was gay. She tried to think back to any indications when they were growing up, but she didn't know what to look for. Insisting on carrying a doll around wherever he went? Wanting to dress up as a princess on Halloween? Trying on their mother's dusky rose lipstick, which looked more Pepto-Bismol than pink? *She* hadn't even done that as a child, and plus, all these things were stereotypes that meant nothing. True, Michael hadn't ever had a girlfriend that she knew about. But even if he had, there was no reason why he would have told her. Her parents had not allowed Emily to date in high school, and she doubted they would have lessened their restrictions for a son. Michael had been twelve when she'd gone off to college, hardly formed yet, and by the time they were both adults in the city, he was almost unrecognizable to her. Even before she and Julian had moved away, they'd mostly only seen each other during the holidays back at their parents' home.

She did understand why Michael hadn't said anything to their parents. Their mother might be more accepting, but she always presented a united front with their father, and under no circumstances could Emily imagine their strict, unyielding father comprehending what it meant to have a child who was gay. It probably wasn't even in his vocabulary. It was hard enough for her father to accept that Emily had married someone who wasn't Chinese or even Asian, most evident during uncomfortable holiday dinners. For some reason, her father's English grew even worse around Julian, and when he asked Julian about his work, he made everything sound like an accusation. Her father didn't understand why Julian wanted to make films that would never get shown at the local Cineplex. He didn't understand why Julian never spoke to his parents or preferred to spend the holidays with the Tangs, who could never celebrate properly, anyway, basting their turkeys with soy sauce, using sticky rice and red dates for the stuffing. How unfilial, he'd probably thought.

Emily knew her husband would never be fully accepted into her family, but she wasn't sure if it was the kind of family that anyone would want to be accepted into. Her parents were such *immigrants*—putting mothballs in their closets, keeping furniture covered in plastic, refusing to drink tap water unless it had been boiled, not trusting the dishwasher to get the dishes clean. This was true in every one of the client households she visited. Funny how what she couldn't accept in her parents she accepted without comment or criticism in her job. But she worked with these people; she didn't have to live with them.

Part of what had attracted her to Julian in the first place had been the differentness of his family background. He had grown up an only child in Los Angeles, in a multi-roomed ranch house appointed with expensive southwestern pottery and handloomed Mexican rugs. When he was eight, his parents had divorced. His father, a film company executive, had a string of girlfriends, all progressively younger and thinner and tinier, like nesting dolls. His mother was a former catalog model and spent most of her second husband's money on preserving her looks. The one time Emily met her, at her and Julian's wedding, she thought that the former Mrs. Yeager resembled an animated corpse.

After his parents' divorce, Julian had been sent to boarding schools at which he acted out in various but, he assured Emily, creative ways—performing dirty spoofs of the school song, showing subversive films on various methods of corporal punishment. For a time, it seemed like he wouldn't be able to get into any decent college, and he was thinking about taking the year off and traveling around Asia, but his father had pulled some connections, and here he was, all the way across the country from his parents, but still attempting to do everything he could to put as much ideological distance between the way they had brought him up and his present life.

The fact of it was that Julian was set to inherit a great deal of money, was already inheriting it, but it seemed to Emily that it weighed more heavily on him than if he had none. Sometimes she had thought he would be better off with someone who understood that particular problem of growing up with active, but lucrative, disinterest, rather than Emily, whose parents had achieved a comfortable middle-class existence but who had behaved every day as though a single wrong move would send them headfirst into the abyss shared by so many other immigrants.

When Julian asked Emily to marry him, the enormity of the ring overwhelmed her; not just the size of the diamond and how much it must have cost, but what it meant to make such a decision so early in her life. After all, her mother had gotten married at twenty-five, but look at what the following years had brought her: the suburbs, children, picking up her husband's socks every night. She had never known her mother to have the kind of job that could be called a career. Everyone was afraid of being like their parents, Julian had told her—look at himself. But he promised her that things would be different. She could follow whatever career she wanted, for as long or as short as she wanted. They'd never move out of the city. And, most importantly, they would not have children.

Julian had made it clear from the beginning of their relationship that his own childhood had been so miserable that he wouldn't wish it on anyone else. Not that he would lead the kind of life his parents had—of course not—but to him, it was too big of a chance to take. The last time they'd had a serious conversation about having kids, Emily had been studying for the bar, and she couldn't imagine what it would be like to worry about another human being in addition to the trajectory of her own career. Besides, Julian himself required considerable taking care of; she had always been the one who assured him that he could do good work, that he was different from his parents.

Well, Emily thought, he'd certainly reneged on his promise about where they would live. Back then, there was no way for either of them to predict what would happen, that Julian's filmmaking career wouldn't take off, so that he would need some other project to keep himself busy; or that every year he'd allow himself to spend more and more of his parents' money, until one day he surprised her by suggesting they move out of the city. *We could have a garden and grow heirloom tomatoes,* he'd said, with a gleam in his eye that was usually reserved in other men for high-end golf clubs or a luxury car (that, too, would come later).

This prospect had not frightened Emily as much as she once thought it would. By that time she was so firmly ensconced in her work that she didn't see how where she commuted from would make much of a difference. She would always have Chinatown, to anchor herself to not only her previous life, but her parents'. But she could see that with their renovated eighteenth-century farmhouse, with its sentinel evergreens that framed the front door exactly, Julian was creating a kind of familial history that she, too, had craved in her youth. So she went along with it, leaving all of the furnishing and landscaping to Julian, and privately storing this little concession away in the back of her mind, like a get-out-of-jail card, to be used when she really needed it. What Emily didn't expect was that she would need it sooner than expected, for she was beginning to suspect her husband had also changed his mind about having kids.

She could pinpoint this change as taking place shortly after her thirty-first birthday. Her actual birthday had been on a weekday, and since she had been working late on a case, it would have been impossible to plan anything. So instead Julian had made a reservation for the following Saturday night at a small Italian restaurant they had frequented when they had begun dating. It was located on the first floor of a brownstone in the West Village, so hidden by vines that you could walk by without knowing where it was, but even parents had discovered it by now.

The waiter had seated Emily and Julian next to a table with a couple who looked to be in their mid-thirties. They were extremely attractive; the man appeared to be Asian, and the woman, Scandinavian. Normally, Emily disliked being seated next to an interracial couple (out of the entire restaurant, she and Julian had to be seated next to *them?* It was like a practical joke). However, this couple was different, for they were with their infant daughter. She had fine hair the color of honey, but her eyes were undeniably Asian—small, dark, tipped up at the corners.

As if noticing her stare, the child smiled at her. Lest she come across as a curmudgeon, Emily smiled back. The child squealed with laughter, and Emily looked away, made uncomfortable by this miniature attention.

"Awfully late for kids to be up," she muttered to Julian.

"Come on, she's cute."

"Sure, but do you really think it's a good idea for her parents to take her out to a place like this?"

Julian shrugged. "Why not? The French do it."

"The French let their dogs eat at the table."

"A child isn't a dog, Emily."

"No, a dog's more fun."

Then Emily noticed a look of yearning, almost determination, on Julian's face, something she hadn't seen since they'd first met and he talked about the kind of films he wanted to make. *A child isn't a project,* she thought. But she knew that when Julian saw that little girl—or any half-Asian child, of which there seemed to be more and more, whenever she looked—he was imagining what their own child would look like.

It was as if, in a cruel twist of fate, her biological clock had been transferred to her husband. Emily had never felt anything in her own stomach other than a churning ball of fire over a deposition, quickly soothed by an antacid. She did know she did not like children. If she was being honest with herself, she was scared of them. She avoided lines with mothers and their screaming kids at the grocery store, switched seats on the plane if she was sitting in front of a child who kicked, tried not to gag when a woman nursed in a public place. Whenever her friends foisted a newborn into her arms, she held it gingerly, as if holding a ticking bomb.

Perhaps what she was most scared of was what children represented: the lack of a dream. She had always maintained that people had children because they didn't know what to with the rest of their lives. Even though she knew plenty of women had both careers and children, and that it was possible to get outside help, she also knew Julian disapproved of nannies, having basically been brought up by one. Even if he didn't expect her to give up her job to take care of a baby, he'd probably want her to cut back to spend more time at home. He, on the other hand, would make an excellent stay-at-home dad since he was there almost all the time now, anyway.

Since the night of her birthday dinner, Emily had watched Julian carefully for further signs, wondering if they'd always been present. Was this what moving to the suburbs had been all about, not just the wish to be able to have a garden, as he'd assured her? Had all the care he'd taken in decorating the house been more than just a sign of good taste? Was this the real reason behind the uncharacteristic purchase of his latest car, a silver Bimmer? Then her father passed away, and she felt as if the question of having children was not only hanging over her head, it threatened to stifle her. This time the pressure was coming from her mother, although it had always been there in some form. Ever since she had gotten married, Emily knew her parents had wanted her and Julian to have a baby. Announcing that she and Julian were planning to buy a house had almost seemed cruel, a false hope. Emily knew that the promise of a grandchild would greatly assuage her mother's grief.

If her mother were to know that Michael was gay, it would be even more important that Emily have a child. Her mother must be aware that plenty of gays and lesbians had children; they adopted, they used sperm donors, they hired surrogates. There was pretty much no excuse for anyone not to have a kid these days. But her mother was a traditionalist, and while it might not matter in the end, that she would love a grandchild no matter where it came from or how it had come into being, she would still depend on Emily to be the one who would do it properly, just as Emily had done everything else in her life. At some point, as skillful as she had been over the past few years at avoiding the subject of having children, Emily knew she would have to have an answer for both her husband and her mother.

The train had reached the station, and Emily disembarked along with a few other late commuters. Everyone else was heading in the other direction, into the city for a night out. Just the thought of it was exhausting to her; she wanted nothing more than to get into bed. She had little difficulty in locating her car in the lot, a Buick in an unfashionable shade of maroon that was older than she was. It was her mother's first car and had been handed down to her when she was old enough to drive, then transferred to Michael when he got his license, and then reclaimed when she'd moved to the suburbs. When she started using it again, she found that it was like a time capsule. Wedged in the backseat was the cushion her mother had sat on because she was too short to see over the wheel; the glove compartment was stuffed with mangled cassette tapes from Emily's teenage years; and underneath the floor mats were mummified French fries that must have come from Michael's tenure. In a fit of perversity, Emily decided to keep everything the way it was. She felt driving a car like that was the equivalent of giving the finger to all the SUVs she encountered on her neighborhood streets.

As she pulled into the driveway and parked behind the Bimmer, she saw a light on in one of the upstairs windows. She hadn't realized it was so late; Julian must have gone to bed. She opened the front door and walked softly into the kitchen, which gleamed with stainless steel and polished tiles. Emily herself never spent much time in here beyond brewing a cup of coffee for her travel mug, but this was Julian's domain. He had chosen the ecologically sustainable bamboo for the cabinetry, and the recycled glass for the backsplash. The meals he cooked were elaborate, requiring visits to multiple farmers' markets, even trips into the city for specialty items.

When she checked the bottom oven, she saw that Julian had left dinner for her, as was his habit. She knew that most people would appreciate this gesture from a spouse, but she was starting to feel oppressed by Julian's culinary zeal. Tonight appeared to be some kind of Moroccan stew, judging from the colorful blend of chickpeas and peppers. To prove that she had tried it, Emily dipped a finger into the sauce and licked it; it was rich with tomatoes and saffron. She covered the dish and put it in the refrigerator. Maybe she'd have it for dinner tomorrow, provided she got back early enough.

She passed through the living room with its massive fireplace at one end, the ceiling crisscrossed with rough-hewn beams that dated, the real estate agent had assured them, from the original structure built in the late 1700s. The aesthetic in this room was more appropriate to that time period: a pine Dutch Colonial sideboard, straight-backed Shaker chairs whose very angles spoke of openness and honesty. Julian had spent days at yard sales and local antique stores, looking for this kind of stuff, usually on weekdays when Emily was at work. He had loved the idea of buying a house that had a history, although Emily was quick to point out that it was a history that belonged to neither of them, hers being Chinese and his a mix of German and French. If it bothered her so much, Julian had said, why didn't she get one of those scrolled and lacquered cabinets or a delicately carved rose-wood table from an Asian import store in the city? Yeah, Emily had replied, that would go over real nice with the cherry end tables and Windsor chairs. Instead, she insisted on buying their couch, which was large and shapeless and upholstered in soft gray corduroy, and was absolutely brand-new.

Upstairs, Julian was already in bed, a book lying facedown on the comforter. For a minute, Emily gazed fondly at him, the shape of his biceps beneath the worn T-shirt he liked to sleep in; the tufts of light brown hair sticking up all over his head. His hair was starting to thin on top, which endeared him to her further. It was at these times that she was so overcome with love for her husband that it seemed impossible that she could refuse him anything.

When she slid the book out from under his hands, he stirred.

"Don't worry," she said. "I saved your place." Behind her back she inserted a coaster into the middle of the book, approximately where she thought it had been open to. Then she slipped under the covers, snuggling up to him.

Julian made a face.

"What? You used to like the way I smell," she said.

"You smell like the train."

She brought a sleeve to her nose. "True." She began to unbutton her shirt.

"That's more like it," he said, and buried his nose in the damp cleft of her bra. "Mmmm. Emily sweat."

"Gross," she said, and pulled away from him.

"How was your day?" he asked.

"Hectic. Oh, get this." She told him about Gao Hu's medical report. "Can you believe this kind of thing happens, in this country? Sure, maybe the gulags of Russia or Chinese labor camps or something, but in America?"

"Em," Julian said. "You're starting to sound scary. Right-wing scary."

"You know what I mean."

He put a hand on her thigh but appeared too tired to move it up any farther. "It's almost midnight. You don't want to work yourself up about this, or else you'll never sleep."

"I guess you're right. I need to go into the office tomorrow, too."

"One of those weekends, huh?"

"Sorry, baby." She threaded one hand through his hair and gave an experimental tug.

"Don't," he said. "There isn't any more where that came from."

She bent and kissed the top of his head. "There'll always be enough for me."

After a moment, he asked, yawning, "Anything else happen today?"

"I found out that my brother's gay and has gone off without telling anyone where." She paused. "Those two things are not related."

Julian looked more awake. "Really? Maybe he's at some gay retreat."

Punching his arm, she said, "I'm serious. He went away without telling anyone who cares about him—my mom, me, his boyfriend. . . ." She hugged her elbows to herself. "I met his boyfriend for the first time today. I can't believe my little brother has a boyfriend."

"How old is he now?"

"Twenty-six."

"That's old enough to be in a relationship. But given my memory of a certain someone's reluctance to get married, I would say that settling down early doesn't run in your family."

"I did too want to get married," Emily protested. "I just didn't like the way you went about asking me."

"What did you want, for me to do it in public?"

"Oh God, no. You know my coworker, Rick? He proposed to his wife by sending a singing telegram to her workplace when they were like twenty-two or something."

Julian laughed. "I guess it turned out all right for him."

"How so?"

"He has three kids, right? Sounds like she eventually forgave him."

She shook her head. "Three kids. It sounds so . . . archaic. I can't imagine what that must be like."

"Can you imagine what *one* would be like?" Julian asked quietly.

Another step, and she would be falling into the very thing she had dreaded for so long; a discussion that would have plenty of emotions and heated words, but no right or wrong answers, and possibly no final decision. She tried to speak slowly, rationally.

"Julian, I thought we decided on this a long time ago. When we first got married."

"People change, Emily."

"Only if they don't have the guts to stand for what they believe in. Do you remember how you used to say that population growth was out of control, and you were the last person who wanted to contribute to it?"

"Emily," he said. "I was nineteen when I said that."

"Have you even asked yourself why you've changed your mind? Maybe this is some kind of midlife crisis you're having. Maybe you're just looking for something you can finally be good at." She regretted the words as soon as she had spoken them, wished she could draw them back to where her darkest, and most truthful, feelings lurked. When she was tired, it was harder for her to keep them from slipping out, especially in front of her husband. She knew that their fourteen years together wasn't an excuse, as well as the fact that Julian would probably forgive her. She just couldn't help it.

"I know that you don't think much of what I do," Julian finally said, "but I'm not going to fail at being a parent."

"Julian." She put her hands against the sides of his face. "You're not a failure. You make all this"—she indicated the large, comfortable bed they were in; the solid oak furniture; the house and the yard beyond—"possible. Isn't that enough for you?"

"Most days it is. Most days I don't think about it at all. But other days, I drive down this street, I open this door, and I think, what does it all mean? Why bother having all this, of coming here in the first place, if this is all we're ever going to have?"

"That was your decision, not mine. I never asked to move out here."

"You're hardly here, anyway."

She got up from the bed, bracing herself. "I can't talk about this with you. Not now."

"There's never a good time for you to talk. You're always at work. I come home, and there's a message saying that you're going to be late again. Now you're not even here on the weekends. You probably spend more time with Rick than with me."

He had started to raise his voice. "Hush," she said.

"Who's going to hear, the neighbors?" This was impossible. They lived a half acre away from the next house, which sometimes worried Emily, who had always lived within shouting distance of neighbors, even if she didn't care to associate with them. "Even if they could, I don't care. What I care about is what's going to happen to us."

"Nothing's going to happen to us."

"Right," Julian said, and there was an edge to his voice that she had never heard before. "Nothing's going to happen."

They stared at each other across the expanse of the bed, neither of them speaking or even moving. Emily grasped for words, but for the first time, she didn't know what to say to her husband that would bring them back to an equilibrium, to where they were supposed to be. Then, as if surfacing from underwater, she heard her phone going off in her purse. Julian heard it too.

"If you get that . . ." He left the threat unfinished.

Emily grabbed her purse and went downstairs, briefly glancing at the unfamiliar number before picking up. "Hello?"

"Hey," came a young man's voice against a thumping backdrop of party music. "This is Edison Ng. I think I know where your brother might be."

# CHAPTER 3

Every travel website Michael Tang had looked at that summer had advised him not to go to Qinghai Province.

*One of the poorest and least populated provinces in the country, where political prisoners are sent to work in labor camps.*

*The provincial capital typifies the worst of modern China: polluted, industrial, without aesthetic merit. You are better off going straight to Tibet.*

*Qinghai isn't the armpit of China—that distinction most likely goes to Hubei—but it certainly comes close.*

Still, this is his destination, as he sits on a hard sleeper train from Beijing to Xining, the capital of Qinghai Province, in the northwest of China. It would have been much quicker to have taken a flight, but Michael wants to save money, and besides, he thinks that this way, he can see some of the country.

It turns out to be the most mind-numbing twenty-four hours he has ever experienced; physically numbing as well, for although the dark-green bunks are sparsely padded, they still feel like concrete to sleep on. Michael has the top bunk and feels like the main attraction in a hearse. During the day, the people who sleep on the upper bunks come down and sit on the bottom bunk, three per side, staring at one another like participants in a bad expressionist play. There are tiny hunched grandmothers, mothers holding infants, men in cheap rayon suits. People's Liberation Army soldiers, dressed in olive-colored uniforms, sit at small tables beneath windows on the other side of the aisle, playing cards. Despite the signs that indicate no smoking, every male seems to have a lit cigarette, so the train car is filled with a faint bluish smoke that smells like burning trash.

When Michael looks at the other people on the train, he sees nothing in their faces that reminds him of himself, or his parents, or even the recent immigrants he has seen on the streets in Chinatown. Most of those immigrants are from coastal areas and not the interior of the country, but still, these seem like a difference species of people—blunt, impassive, totally devoid of hope for a better life. They are, in a word, peasants.

Dressed in a T-shirt, shorts, and sneakers, he realizes that he stands out as a foreigner, even if his facial features more or less resemble those of the people around him. None of the other men, even though their clothes are of poor quality, are so casually attired. Also, no one else seems to have a backpack, although many do have large, square red-and-blue-striped plastic bags stuffed with everything from melons to DVDs. Michael recognizes these bags, filled with fake designer purses and sunglasses, from the vendors on the street corners in New York City. They must be the internationally designated receptacle for pirated consumer goods.

Despite his appearance, or perhaps because of it, no one speaks to Michael. He supposes it is just as well. Like Emily, he does not know how to read or write in Chinese; unlike her, he also does not know how to speak it, although he understands some of the phrases his parents used to toss around, usually having to do with it being time to eat, time to sleep, or time to go outside. Things that a five-year-old, or a dog, might understand. Periodically, he catches someone staring at him unabashedly, as if trying to read a fortune told on his face instead of his palm. At first, Michael looks away, but when he gets tired of it, he returns the stare until the other person drops their eyes. They seem to exhibit no embarrassment in doing this, and Michael comes to understand that staring is not considered rude in this culture. He also realizes that it doesn't mean the person is interested in whatever they are looking at. It's just something to see, to pass the time.

There's nowhere else to go on the train, other than the stinking latrine with its metal squat toilet. Once, Michael thought to stand in-between the cars, to try and get some fresh air, but came upon a woman holding her infant son over the gap, with his pants pulled down. She was whistling a tuneless song, and as she did so, the child began to urinate, not only into the gap but also all over the corridor. Michael turned around and went straight back to his seat.

So, still jet-lagged, he sits next to the window and looks out of it, the landscape passing by as if in a dream. It seems like days, but, in fact, has been just one since he's left the bustle of the modern airport in Beijing, stayed overnight in a nondescript hotel, and made his way to the crowded railway station where it appeared as if refugees were trying to get on the last train out of the city, but which he suspected was simply an ordinary day in the Chinese capital.

Since then, fields of grasses topped with yellow blossoms have given way to some of the most inhospitable-looking vistas he has ever seen: slopes covered with dun-colored rock, dry riverbeds that appeared as if they have been without water for the last hundred years. Sometimes the train track runs alongside a road, upon which an ox, followed by a farmer, trudge, both so covered with dust that they are nearly indistinguishable from the ground they walk on. Mud houses the same color as the landscape appear and disappear back into their surroundings. When there are more than several houses, apparently they are enough to be considered a village, and then the train stops. People open their windows and buy packages of dry noodles, tea eggs, bottles of water, and cigarettes from the vendors outside. When they are done with their purchases, they throw the wrappers and bottles back out the window. The sides of the tracks are littered with trash, often providing the only spot of color in the otherwise monochromatic scenery.

Also, along the whitewashed mud walls, are large Chinese characters written in red, sometimes ending with an exclamation point.

They look as if they are out of another time period, probably some kind of propaganda. *Go back!* Michael imagines them saying, in a private message just for him. *This is a mistake! You won't find what you're looking for!*

What, or rather who, Michael is hoping to find at the end of his trip is a man named Liao Weishu. This is the name signed at the end of a letter that Michael discovered among his father's things after the funeral. At that time, he had no idea what of his father's he should take. His mother had been so hopeful, offering old clothes that would never fit him, since he was taller and skinnier than his father had been; or accessories, such as cufflinks and tiepins, that could only be worn ironically. He recognized a navy-blue suit jacket that was the only one he remembered his father ever wearing, the collar stiff with hair oil, and the lining in the armpits discolored from perspiration. The jacket was so narrow that Michael imagined any-one who wore it must have perpetually hunched shoulders, con-stricted by fabric as well as other things.

Finally, he asked to go through his father's papers and chanced upon the one item that didn't look like it was some kind of financial document (these he'd leave to Emily to sort out): an envelope that was addressed to his father. The postmark indicated it had been sent about a month before his father's death, from someplace in China that he had never heard of and didn't think he knew how to pronounce. Then his mother had come into the room, and he had put the letter in his pants pocket, where it stayed unopened for an-other nine months. Sometimes he would think about it, and be sat-isfied enough to simply know it was there, and then he forgot about it altogether. The only reason he'd rediscovered the letter that fol-lowing June was because David had wanted Michael to go with him to the wedding of one of his closest female friends. Michael had taken out his sole good pair of pants and had come across the letter again.

Unfortunately, it was written in Chinese, except for one sen-tence toward the end of the letter—*Everything has been forgiven*—in neat but spiky handwriting, as if a crab had crawled over the page. Michael wondered if his father had racked up some kind of debt. He could ask his mother to translate, but that would bring up questions and uncomfortable memories. So instead he put an ad online for a translator, and it was answered by someone named Edison Ng, whom he arranged to meet at a coffee shop downtown. At first, he was skeptical of this skinny college kid wearing a backward baseball cap, but Edison assured him that he was fluent in both languages and could translate the letter for fifty dollars by the end of the week.

"Heavy stuff, right?" Edison commented after he'd delivered the translation. "Who do you think this Liao Weishu guy is?"

Michael was still trying to digest its contents. "Other than a friend of my father's, I don't know."

"For another fifty bucks I can track him down for you online. . . ."

Michael had to admire the kid's entrepreneurial drive. "Thanks, but I think this requires more than an Internet search. I'm going to have to go to China to find him."

As soon as Michael spoke those words, it seemed like the most logical solution in the world. Of course he had to go to China and meet this Liao Weishu. Liao did not know that his father had passed away, and it was up to Michael to break the news to him. You didn't write someone after forty years and just receive a letter in return. No, a personal visit was in order. Without telling anyone, he applied for a visa.

He wasn't running away, Michael assured himself. Although there were other, very good reasons for him to get out of the city. The heat, which made his apartment feel crappier than usual. The fact that the lease on his apartment would soon be up, and he might not be able to afford to renew it. His inability to find a new job—no one wanted a graphic designer who had once accidentally turned in a report with rude drawings doodled in the corners. That it would soon be a year since his father died, and his mother would probably want him to come home and commemorate it somehow. He imagined what it would be like—an uncomfortable dinner at home with Emily, who would be preoccupied with her latest case; and Julian, who would hover awkwardly on the periphery; and his mother, who would try to fill the silence with chatter, answering questions no one asked. Also, there was David. By that time, he and Michael would have known each other for around ten months, on and off, but if you counted the times they were on, it would only be around seven months. Not that anyone was counting.

After Michael found out what the letter had said, he told David that he had changed his mind about accompanying him to the wedding of his friend, Laurel.

"I don't understand," David said. "You have female friends too. Like that girl who lived next door, Annie."

"Amy. And we never dated."

Michael found it amusing that in high school, David had played straight, captaining a couple of sports teams and dating the daughter of one of the oldest families in town. Laurel's wedding was on the grounds of an organic farm, and Michael was sure he would be the only Asian person in attendance, aside from a couple of trophy girlfriends. Or maybe he would be the trophy boyfriend.

"This isn't what I signed up for," he told David. "Being your plus one."

"Fine," David said. "But you'll be missing out on some amazing grass-fed beef. Or is it free-range beef? Anyway, you know, beef that's so fresh it talks back to you." His tone was playful, but clearly he was troubled by Michael's reluctance to be considered a couple.

Therefore, David went alone to the wedding, which took place on a beautifully sunny day in late June, a day on which Michael stayed inside his crappy apartment and only ventured outside in the evening to get something to eat. When he came back, David was waiting for him, sitting on the top step underneath the skylight that was plastered darkly with pigeon droppings.

"How was it?" Michael asked.

"Wholesome and bourgeois," David said. Then, after a pause, "If you were there, we could have made fun of the flower arrangements. Fucking modernist sculptures, they were."

"I missed you, too," Michael admitted, before realizing a moment later that David had not actually said that he'd missed him.

But it didn't matter, because then they were kissing, and somehow Michael managed to unlock his door, and they moved as if in a choreographed dance the few feet across the room from the door to the futon that David always swore he would catch something from, and things were all right again.

That is, until a few weeks later, when David suggested Michael move in with him. By that time Michael had received his visa and was close to maxing out his credit card after purchasing a plane ticket, among other travel preparations. It was almost too easy to become upset at David and accuse him of things that were only partially true, before storming out of David's apartment and ignoring his calls. This way he didn't have to tell David anything about what he was intending to do, to explain himself when he didn't even know why he was taking this trip.

Michael realizes, though, as the train winds its way through the plateaus of northwestern China, this trip has everything to do with David Wheeler, and it was set in motion over a year before.

That summer morning, Michael had made plans to meet a friend at a restaurant in Chelsea, a place that guaranteed a wait of about an hour, followed by awful service. Thus, he was already not in a very good mood when he came to Fifth Avenue and found his way blocked by hordes of shirtless young men, cheering on a street full of more shirtless young men elevated in gaudily decorated floats. He had forgotten about the Gay Pride Parade.

Normally, Michael scorned this kind of event. Was there really a need to emphasize your otherness, to flaunt it in other people's faces? He had spent so much of his life hiding—hiding where his parents had come from in high school, hiding his boring suburban upbringing in college, hiding his lack of corporate ambition at work—that it was second nature to hide a less visible aspect of himself as well.

After struggling through the crowd for several minutes, he couldn't find a way to cross the street. He gave up and was about to call his friend to cancel when he heard a voice behind him say, "This sucks, doesn't it?"

Michael turned to see a young man, somewhat preppy-looking in a polo shirt and khaki pants, blond hair gleaming in the sun. "It does," he replied. "I'm supposed to meet someone on Seventh Avenue, but I guess I won't make it."

"Me too," the man said. "But I'm getting hungry. You want to grab a bite on this side of the street?"

Michael only looked at him for a few more seconds before agreeing. He wondered how long this man had been following him before picking him out among so many fine, shirtless specimens. It felt good to have been chosen.

Over lunch, at a fancy place he'd walked by many times but had never gone into, he found out that David was a lawyer and had grown up in Connecticut, and that his father, now retired, had also been a lawyer. Michael didn't say anything about his family, not even his sister's profession (Emily's work was such that he didn't think she and David were of the same tribe). By the end, when David took out his wallet, Michael let him pay.

On the street outside, when David turned to him, Michael expected him to say he'd had a good time, maybe even suggest that they do it again sometime. Instead, David said, "You want to go back to my place?"

In the cab, Michael reflected that this wasn't so different from a normal hookup, of which he'd had a few—in college, when it had been new and exhilarating, and then after he'd moved to the city, where it seemed like a cliché. It was a bit strange, though, to be doing it not after an evening of drinking, to be seeing the other person's face clearly, to be removing your clothes in the light rather than the dark. It was stranger still to wake up in that other person's apartment, not in the middle of the night or in the grainy regret of morning, but with late-afternoon sunshine stippling both your naked bodies.

David was still sleeping, and Michael looked at him more closely. Without his glasses, his face looked younger, and he slept with one hand curled under his cheek, like a child. His body was long and concave in the middle, where the smattering of fair hair on his chest turned thicker and curlier. His penis was somewhat unremarkable, except for how quickly it had lengthened in Michael's hand; now it was curled up against the inside of his thigh like a snail.

Michael got up to get a drink of water, but it was really a pretext to examine the rest of the situation he had found himself in. The apartment was several times the size of his own, and appointed sparsely with modern-looking furniture. What looked like actual art, rather than prints, hung on the walls. More significantly, the place looked like it belonged to an adult, an adult with money. At twenty-five, Michael was still used to secondhand furniture and multiple roommates, buying expired items and day-old bread from the grocery store in order to make the next rent check. He had only just started living without a roommate, because more than one person in the space in which he lived would be considered a fire hazard.

When he opened David's refrigerator, he found little food, but a great deal of condiments and individual glass bottles of sparkling water. He opened one of the bottles and took it back into the bedroom, where David was awake and smiling lazily at him. Without asking, David took the bottle from him and drank long and hard. It struck Michael as a more intimate act than any of the ones they had experienced with each other.

In the month that followed, he found himself spending most nights with David, or on rare occasions, if they were downtown, back at Michael's place. At first, Michael was ashamed of his apartment, its cramped size and lack of air-conditioning, the unscrubbable stains in the bathroom. There was nowhere to sit except on the frameless futon, as if it were a life raft. So, they usually ended up at David's, and if Michael came over early, he'd hang out in the bar next door, because he didn't have a key to David's place and he thought the doorman looked at him funny.

One day, Michael had just finished sucking David off, David's taste still in the back of his mouth, when his cell phone rang. He wasn't going to pick up, but he saw that it was Emily. Clearing his throat, he answered. Her voice was strangely calm, as if she were reporting something that had happened in another country. Although he comprehended what she was saying, his eyes were fixated on his own hand, lying on David's hipbone, like a long, pale lizard. It was impossible that in one moment he should feel so complete, and then in the next, absolutely empty.

Without telling David what was wrong, he dressed and left the apartment, walked twenty blocks downtown in a daze before remembering he had told Emily that he would meet her at the train station. That night, at his mother's house, after his mother and sister had gone to sleep, he finally called David to tell him what had happened. He did not say he would see David when he got back. As if an outsider to the situation, he listened to David struggle to find the right words to say and give up, a pattern that he would later recognize with other friends, coworkers, and people he didn't know at his father's funeral.

After ending the call with David, Michael sat in his old bedroom, still trying to feel something. He thought of his mother and sister in their own rooms, the efficient walls of silence that surrounded them all. Finally, he was able to dredge up an old hurt that had long since scabbed over but would twinge if he prodded it hard enough. It was much easier to feel anger at his father, and something his father had done years ago, than at the randomness of his father's death.

Michael had seen his father two weekends earlier, one of the rare times he'd gone back home that summer—partly to escape the heat in the city and partly to get some perspective on his relationship with David, which was turning out to be much more intense than he'd expected. At the time, David's closeness had been part of everything that had felt too close about the city; simply another thing that he needed to get away from. His father had been his usual taciturn self, glowering over something as minor as a creaky door hinge or a dead patch of grass on the lawn. He'd also been particularly concerned about a crape myrtle tree in the backyard that had caught a disease and had consequently lost all of its leaves, appearing as though it were in the dead of winter. Michael's father talked to him about what to do with the tree and finally announced he was going to cut it down; Michael had agreed. That was the essence of the last, illuminating conversation he had with his father.

At the funeral, since he didn't speak Chinese, most of the people there bypassed him. Emily seemed to be handling everything in her usual, capable manner, and he felt unnecessary, like an uninvited guest. So instead he snuck away early on with Amy Bradley, who had come in from Boston, where she attended design school. They went out and sat on the back porch.

"How're you holding up?" Amy asked.

"Could be better," Michael replied. "Any chance you got a cigarette on you?"

Amy grinned. "I have something better." She extracted a neatly rolled joint from her pocket. "I thought you might need this."

For a moment, Michael hesitated, knowing it wouldn't look good if he were caught smoking pot at his father's funeral. What would his mother think? But what the hell—next to Emily, he looked like a delinquent, anyway.

Passing the joint back and forth reminded him of when he and Amy were teenagers, parked in the woods in her parents' car, or up in her room. They spent afternoons at her house with pads of heavy Manila paper, Amy sketching clothing designs and Michael sketching her as she sketched. She was already into fashion then, making clothes on her own sewing machine and using Michael as a dress form. *You make the perfect model,* she gushed, which he interpreted to mean that he had the figure of an anorexic, prepubescent girl, and wasn't sure if he should take it as a compliment or not. Still, he stood motionless for hours as she pinned and re-pinned.

You would not have known Amy was talented in that arena from the way she dressed at school: torn black shirts, ripped black jeans, boots that looked like she would kick someone's head in if they looked at her wrong. She convinced Michael to join her in a social experiment, in which they wore their clothes inside out for a week. No one noticed, which Amy said was the whole point. When Amy cut her hair and dyed it black, people said they looked like twins, which they did not bother to dignify with an answer. Aside from the fact that Amy wasn't Chinese, she was short and her body full of curves that she tried to hide beneath her shapeless dark outfits. She decreed that she and Michael should kiss each other on the cheek, twice, whenever they ran into each other in the halls (*So European,* Amy had said). No one seemed to notice that either.

Early in their junior year in high school, Michael discovered that Amy was in love with him. She had kissed him on the mouth one night, when her parents were out and they'd broken into her father's liquor cabinet. One moment they'd been laughing about Courtney Snell's ridiculous answer in social studies class ("Where do Chicanos come from, Courtney?" "Um, Chicago?"), and then

Amy pressed her lips so fleetingly to his that he thought he had imagined it.

"Did you feel anything?" Amy asked hopefully.

Michael shook his head, although he *had* felt something, besides the burn of bourbon from Amy's lips. What he had felt was disappointment. He had been disappointed that it had been Amy who had kissed him, not Peter Lawrence, the slender, brown-haired boy who sat in front of him in math class and smelled not only like gym socks, but something that made his very skin tingle. The other time he'd felt that sensation, like an itch somewhere that couldn't be scratched, was when he was twelve and had been spying over the fence next door. Scott Bradley, Amy's brother, who was Emily's age, was swimming in the pool. His body looked long and tantalizing beneath the surface, the points of his shoulder blades glinting through the water. Just then Michael's father, coming home from work, saw Michael at the top of the fence—although not what he was looking at—and yelled at him for doing something so dangerous. Michael had jumped down from the fence, twisting his ankle in the process.

After the kissing fiasco, Amy became obsessed with boys at school who would prove to be just as unattainable: guys who had girlfriends, jocks who would never look twice at her. Michael would accompany her to dances where she'd hope to steal some boy away from his date, but it would go off badly, and she'd drink too much spiked punch, and the evening would end with her in the girls' room, throwing up, with Michael holding back her hair. *Why are you so nice to me?* she'd say in between sobs. *Because I can't be anything else to you,* he'd wanted to reply.

Amy was the only person from that part of his life who knew he was gay. She'd known from that night when he was sixteen, when he'd had nowhere else to go and no one else to turn to. She hadn't treated him any differently since then, except to get a little jealous of the female friends he made when he went away to college; especially Shannon Krist, whom he'd brought home once, even though he told her that Shannon thought she might be a lesbian. Over the years, Amy grew into herself, letting her hair return to its regular strawberry blond, although it was still spiky and short; keeping only a few tasteful piercings; dressing in her own geometric, angular designs that would cause people to stop her in the street and ask her where she bought her clothes.

Now, Amy asked, her eyes half-lidded from the pot, "Do you wish you'd ever talked to your father about what happened that night?"

"That was almost ten years ago. He probably forgot about it."

"But *you* haven't."

"Doesn't make any difference. Maybe it wouldn't have if I'd reminded him while he was around. He would never have admitted that what he said was wrong."

"But it *was* wrong."

Michael shrugged. "Not in his mind it wasn't. I'm sure he's said a lot worse. Done a lot worse, too, but that's beside the point."

"Do you think you'll ever tell your mom and sister?"

"Which part of it?"

"All of it."

He sighed. "Not right now. They have too much to deal with."

After a pause, Amy said, "I'm seeing someone. Don't judge. He's one of my teachers and—*don't judge*—he says I have a lot of talent. What do you think?"

"I think," Michael said, "that you're still going after the wrong men."

"That's probably true."

"I'm seeing someone too. His name is David. He pays for everything."

Amy arched a brow. "So you feel like a kept woman?"

"I don't know how I feel about it. Sometimes I think things are going well, and I don't know how I lucked out, and other times I feel like something bad is going to happen. Like this."

Amy said softly, "Your father didn't die because you were enjoying yourself with a man."

Michael considered this for a moment. Amy spoke so plainly, with such conviction, yet he couldn't quite disassociate what Emily had told him over the phone a few days ago with the feeling of David's skin, the salty essence of him.

"I think I'm going to break up with David when I get back," he said.

"You do that," Amy replied. "Maybe I'll break up with my guy too."

They looked at each other, as if daring the other to look away first, and then started laughing. Both of them knew that this was easier said than done.

Michael left Amy on the porch and went upstairs to use the bathroom. He was passing his sister's bedroom door, which was slightly open, when he saw something inside that made him pause: Emily and Julian, going at it like horny teenagers. He stepped away, and then chuckled to himself. So Emily wasn't that perfectly behaved after all.

After he got back to the city, he did break up with David. Then he couldn't stay away, and they got back together. This pattern repeated itself over the following year, with little variation. When they were apart, Michael didn't call for days, went out with other friends. During this time, he imagined David sitting in his tasteful apartment, sipping his mineral water, alone. David gave Michael expensive presents for his birthday and the holidays. Michael gave David nothing, unless you counted grief.

It was pretty childish behavior, he had to admit. It was as if by not committing to David, he didn't have to tell his mother and sister he was dating anyone, or that he was gay. He wasn't even sure if it mattered now. The person in his family who would have been most upset by it would have been his father, who was gone; and besides, his father already knew he was gay, had known for years, even if he didn't care to acknowledge it. But Michael had spent so long acting this way, it was as if he didn't know how else to be. If he cared to admit more, there were things he resented about David, the least being that everything seemed to have come so easily to him, especially when it came to his identity. Well, there had been that incident with his high-school girlfriend, Laurel, but the fact that she had invited David to her wedding said something about how easy it was to forgive him. He was on good terms with his parents and his younger brother, and he doted on his twin three-year-old nephews. He had been in several long-term relationships, all which had ended amicably, and he had never been desperate enough to pick someone off the street, before Michael. And even then, with his luck, Michael had gone right along with him.

David didn't make things easy, though. *Passive aggressive,* Michael thought. At the same time as David allowed Michael his space, he also insisted Michael give him a key to his apartment, in case Michael were locked out or something happened to him (yeah, right). Michael finally made him a spare key in order to shut him up, but refused to accept one to David's apartment. He was afraid of how easy it would be to stay there when David was away, and what that would lead to.

David's suggestion that they move in together came about quite innocently. It was on one of those late-summer evenings that had cooled down enough that they'd dared to open the windows, and sounds from the street below drifted in on the balmy air: murmurings from the bar next door, the distant wail of a siren. David lived in a neighborhood that seemed designed for young professionals with too little time to spend in their apartments and too much money to spend on food and drink. Although only a few dozen blocks away from where Michael lived, it might as well be in a different city. But, Michael reflected, this was the kind of life someone his age, or a little older, was supposed to live. And with someone like David.

He turned away from the window to see David holding out a glittering object in the palm of his hand.

"I made you a key," David said.

"I don't want a key. I don't want to be coming in and out all the time. Your doorman gives me enough suspicious looks as it is, like I'm a stranger."

"But you wouldn't be. Not if you lived here."

"Who says I want to live here?"

David laughed. "Come on. That place you live in is a dump. You need a tetanus shot to use the shower. Besides, didn't you say that your lease was up soon and your landlord was going to raise the rent? You can't afford that."

"How do you know what I can afford?"

"You know what I mean. You could live here for free. That is, until you find a new job."

"You'd like that, wouldn't you? So that I'd be completely dependent on you for everything?"

David paused. "I wasn't aware you depended on me for anything."

"Well, I don't want anything from you," Michael told him. "Not your charity, and not your money, and definitely not your key."

It was almost as if he were watching himself get up, walk past David and his still-outstretched hand, and out the door. Instead of waiting for the elevator, he took the stairs, and each step jolted him back into his own body, so that by the time he got to the lobby, he was aware of how theatrical he was being. He walked past the doorman, who always seemed to have a smirk in the corner of his mouth when he saw Michael and David together, and managed to exit the building before his cell phone rang for the first time.

Outside, people spilled out from the bar and onto the sidewalk, young men with their collars unbuttoned, young women barely able to stand erect after a day in heels. Still, no one wanted to go home, because that would mean being alone. Looking at these beautiful young people, Michael felt a sense of relief—comfort, even—in the knowledge that life was proceeding as it should; unattached, free.

There were three messages from David on his phone by the time Michael got back home, as well as a hang up from his mother. Briefly, he wondered what she wanted to talk to him about, but concluded that whatever it was, it couldn't be that serious. He hadn't spoken to his mother since he had lost his job a month earlier, afraid that she'd ask questions, offer to send him money, or even worse, suggest that he move home. Plus, he didn't want to have to relive that morning when his boss called him into his office to tell him that he'd been laid off. Although he'd been expecting it for weeks, and never cared very much for his work or the people he worked with, he had still felt an inexplicable void. Now he understood why people called both losing a job and a death in the family *life-altering events*. Maybe the trip he was about to take would be life altering as well.

So, ignoring the calls from both David and his mother, Michael put some things in a backpack. There wasn't much—some clothes and toiletries, and, of course, Liao Weishu's letter and its translation. He had an early morning flight to Beijing to catch. In a fit of conscience, he wrote a hasty note and left it on the table. He figured that after not hearing from him for a while, David would come over and use his key to get into his apartment, and he didn't want David to think the worst about him. Michael was already doing a good job of that himself.

The train finally pulls into the station in Xining, Qinghai Province, the morning of Michael's third day in China, to the strain of schmaltzy elevator music that comes on overhead at every stop. Michael slings his backpack over his shoulder and disembarks, whereupon he is beset by a dozen or so hotel touts, shouting things at him in Chinese. When that doesn't work, they switch to Japanese.

"Hotel?" Michael says in English.

"Hotel!" one of the men replies, and Michael goes with him.

He gets into a red taxi while the driver continues to chatter at him in English, some of which makes sense. Michael gathers that the man is telling him about the tourist attractions in the city and its environs, including something that sounds like a big lake. At least he remembers seeing a lake on one of the travel websites, which advised him that it isn't worth visiting.

The taxi stops in front of what must be the grandest hotel in town, a concrete square with an automatic glass door. Behind the front desk is a row of clocks and their corresponding times in international cities, in an imitation of a more cosmopolitan place, except *Losangeles* and *Saopaulo* are single words. The clerk stammers when Michael speaks to him in English. Michael obtains a hotel room for the equivalent of twenty US dollars. He paid the taxi driver two dollars.

"Should I put my passport in your safe?" he asks the hotel clerk, remembering something he read on a travel website.

"No need," the clerk says. "No minorities here."

"Excuse me?" Michael wonders if he has heard correctly, or if something has been missed in the translation.

"No Uighur people here."

Michael has no idea what kind of people that means, but goes along with it.

His room is decent enough, with a Western-style toilet and a washcloth the size and texture of a paper towel. Michael lies down on the scratchy orange coverlet on the bed. It's marginally softer than the hard seat of the train, but, for the first time since he's left Beijing, he is totally, blessedly, alone. He closes his eyes, and when he opens them again, several hours have passed and it is already afternoon.

Downstairs, he finds the clerk who speaks English and asks, "Can you tell me how to get to the normal university?"

If the clerk is surprised that Michael wants to go there rather than one of the usual tourist attractions, he doesn't show it. He marks the location on a map, and since it looks like a straight shot north, Michael decides to walk there and see if his first impression of the city will be changed any. It isn't. The heat has dissipated somewhat, but there is still a haze over everything. Even the leaves on the trees appear to be covered with a light film of dust. Rising in the background, barely visible through the pollution, are the outlines of mountains.

He walks by buildings that look like they have been recently constructed, or at least in the last fifty years: gray Soviet-style apartment blocks, stores fronted by blue glass, buildings covered in white tile, as if the entire outdoors were a bathroom. At the same time, amid the trucks and motorcycles, donkeys pull carts down the street. Michael spies a group of men waiting at a bus stop, looking unlike anyone he's seen in China until now. They're wearing robes peeled down over their torsos, with the sleeves tied around their waists, their faces flat and chiseled, the color of beef jerky. He realizes they must be Tibetans. He's definitely not in the China he'd imagined, a land of rice paddies, where everyone is either a farmer or a Communist cadre, or both.

As the sun appears to be poised directly overhead, Michael realizes he hasn't eaten that day. Not wanting to stop, and not feeling confident enough to enter one of the stores, he buys an ice cream bar from a cart. The shrewd vendor gives him one look and charges him as much as his taxi ride, but Michael doesn't have the language or the inclination to argue. He figures that two dollars are what he'd pay for a bad ice cream back in the States. Then he looks around and realizes something else that has given him away as a foreigner: The only people eating ice cream at this time of day are children. They are also, he thinks, looking down at his own bare legs, the only ones who are wearing shorts. Being in China so far has made him feel like a large baby, unable to express himself, eating the wrong foods, wearing inappropriate clothes.

Uncannily, Michael feels someone staring at him. Standing in front of him is a dirty-faced, bare-footed child, tattered clothes hanging off a skinny frame that indicates he's probably older than he looks. The child points at the ice cream and then at his mouth. Michael isn't used to beggars like this—panhandlers on New York streets, sure, but there is something about this boy that strikes him as more depressing. He hesitates, but then decides this isn't his country, or his problem. He shakes his head and turns his attention back to his ice cream, but before he can take a bite, the child shoots out a hand and plunges two grimy fingers into the ice cream bar so that it crumples into a sticky mess before he runs away.

Michael stares at the smashed ice cream, not quite sure what has just happened. Did that kid decide that if Michael wasn't going to give him his ice cream, then no one was going to have it? Was he even capable of such a devious thought? Shaking his head in disgust, though he isn't sure whether it is at himself or the child, Michael throws the dirty ice cream into the gutter. He isn't sure what kind of welcome this is, but he forces himself to move past it.

Thankfully, the farther he progresses down the street, the more pleasant it becomes, bordered by trees that are still spindly and stunted and dusty, but there are more of them, so they create some shade. Finally, on his right, are two open gates, signaling an institution of some kind. Just beyond, surrounded by a scraggly flower bed, is a statue of Mao with his right hand held up, as if in a benediction. Unlike other statues of Mao that Michael has seen in history books— where they're located in squares and parks—this version is only one and a half times the size of a regular person, and not as intimidating.

Michael checks the lettering over the gate against the characters the hotel clerk thoughtfully wrote down for him, and after confirming that this is indeed the normal university, walks in under Mao's watchful eye. Since he can't read any of the signs, he asks two female students where the English department is. One of them giggles and hides behind her textbook, but the other, bolder one, who appears to understand some English, points out a building to the left. Fortunately, it is not a large campus.

The severe-looking woman sitting behind the desk in the concrete-floored office gives a single nod when Michael asks her if she speaks English.

"Professor Liao does not teach here anymore," she responds to his query.

"But I have this letter. . . ." Michael holds it out to her as if in proof.

She coolly turns it over in her hands and taps the postmark. "It is an old letter. Sent over a year ago."

"Does he have a forwarding address?" Michael asks, desperate.

The woman shrugs. "I am sorry."

She looks at a spot in the distance behind his head, and Michael guesses that he has taken up enough of her time, although no one else appears to be in need of her attention. There's nothing else he can do but turn around and leave the building.

He sits down on a stone bench, still holding the letter, wondering what his next step should be. He can't believe that his journey might end here. There has to be someone on campus who knows where Liao Weishu has gone, but the odds of Michael finding that person, especially without knowing the language, is slim. Maybe the clerk back at the hotel can help him. Is there some kind of Chinese White Pages?

He's just about to stand when a soft voice calls out to him, "Hello!"

He looks up to see a girl in a blue-and-white gym uniform. She appears to be about twelve years old, although he guesses she must be a college student.

"You are looking for Professor Liao?" she asks. "I hear you talking to Miss Wang in the office."

"Yes, she said he doesn't work here anymore?"

"He is—retired." The girl looks proud for remembering how to say that word in English.

Michael leans forward so eagerly that she takes an involuntary step back. "Do you know where he is?"

She nods. "He lives on campus."

"Can you take me there?" Her startled look makes him think he's said something inappropriate, so he quickly amends, "I mean, can you deliver a message to him from me?"

The girl looks much more comfortable with that idea. Michael hastily scribbles a note with the name of his hotel. "It's okay," he assures her. "I'm an old friend." *Or at least my father was.* After he hands over the note, he grins. "I guess Miss Wang thinks I look dangerous."

She responds with a small smile. "Miss Wang does not like outsiders."

Michael thanks the girl and watches as she walks across the campus and disappears behind a row of buildings, resisting the urge to follow her. He's never considered that Liao Weishu might not be pleased he's come all the way from America to find him, that perhaps the man might not even want to be found. But Michael has done everything possible; all he can do now is to wait for Liao Weishu to get in touch with him, to come to him of his own accord. He just hopes that Liao will do so in the next two days, before he has to return to Beijing.

Back at the hotel, Michael orders overpriced and tasteless fried rice from the establishment's rundown dining room, the only familiar item on a badly translated menu of *sweat-and-sour pork balls* and *drunken hen in its own sauce.* He passes the evening in his room flipping through several state-run channels on the television and catches snippets of a news program on the growth of China's economy, a theatrical extravaganza of women dressed in shiny costumes, an old English-language Western dubbed in Chinese. The telephone rings, and he leaps for it, thinking it might be Liao Weishu.

"Hello?" he says into the receiver, then remembering where he is, *"Wei?"*

The voice that replies in Chinese, though, is female. He figures she must have the wrong number. "I don't understand," he mutters in English and puts down the receiver.

It rings again, and when he answers, it's the same female voice. This time she says an English word, impatiently: "Massage?"

"No, thank you," Michael says, and hangs up.

The phone rings a third time. Not caring whether he'll miss Liao Weishu's call, he unplugs it before going to bed and falls into a deep, dreamless sleep.

# CHAPTER 4

Earlier that summer, a Chinese woman stepped into Emily's office. She appeared to be in her late thirties, was nicely dressed in a linen pantsuit, and carried a handbag that even Emily could tell was made of an expensive leather by the way it softly gleamed. When she spoke, her Mandarin Chinese had a slight but unmistakable Southern tinge—a Cantonese accent. Her name was Jean Hu, and she wanted Emily to take on the case of her husband, Gao, whom she said had been wrongfully imprisoned.

"He's never been in any trouble with the law before," Jean assured Emily. "He's a good husband and father, a good citizen. Never any trouble," she repeated.

Emily didn't doubt it. Like her father, Gao probably didn't drink or smoke or cause public disturbances. It was likely that he mowed his lawn at regular intervals and kept his gutters clean. The worst transgression he could make was not putting up decorations on the holidays, not even Christmas. When she did a thorough search of Gao's police and tax records, looking for anything that might be a red flag, everything was impeccable. Ironically, she thought, the taxes Gao had paid throughout his life were now being used to keep him in detention.

"We have an eight-year-old son named Sam," Jean said at their meeting.

As if appealing to Emily's maternal instincts, she pulled a photograph from her purse, which Emily glanced at cursorily. It was just like any awkward school photo of a little boy, his grin lopsided due to two of his bottom teeth growing in. She wondered what you told an eight-year-old when his father was arrested one morning. "Does he know what's going on?"

"He knows a little. I explained it was a mistake, that his father would be back home soon."

"And that's what I'm going to do," Emily told her. "I'm going to bring Sam's father back home to him."

Jean had nearly cried, thanking Emily profusely for agreeing to help her husband. But really, it was Gao Hu who was doing Emily a favor. This was the kind of case that could make the hours she put in to her job worth it. It was an added bonus that this particular situation happened to involve a Chinese immigrant. She'd been slightly disappointed when one of her bosses, Mitch Jenkins, assigned Rick Farina to work with her. But Rick, she found, added some much-needed gravity to the meetings they held with various immigration enforcement officials, almost all of whom were uniformly middle-aged, balding white men. As much as Emily made herself act like a white man around them—swearing with them, laughing at their jokes, preemptively making comments that bordered on racism, even changing the way she walked and sat in her chair—she was incontrovertibly beneath them.

She was aware of this attitude in the law office every day. Despite her advantages in terms of her language ability, she knew she had to work harder than Rick to prove to her bosses that she was good at her job. Thus, she kept her office free from any family photos or personal details. She dressed in professional but nondescript outfits, eschewed makeup, so that in no way could she be compared to the paralegals and first-year associates who were constantly tugging on the hemlines of their skirts or reapplying their lipstick in the ladies' room. She considered her greatest achievement thus far to be the time she'd been having a heated debate with one of the partners, Joseph Lazar, and he'd walked into the men's room, fully expecting her to follow him in. Careful not to look down, Emily continued to argue with her boss as he did his business at the urinal, shook himself dry, and left the bathroom without washing his hands. This, she considered, was proof that she had truly been accepted into the inner circle. Although, it could also be due to the fact that Joseph was nearly eighty and beginning to lose his mind.

The rumor this summer was that Joseph Lazar was going to be forcibly retired and that Mitch Jenkins would be looking for a new partner come fall. Emily knew both she and Rick were in the running, despite the fact that they were still comparatively young. In a corporate law firm, it would have been unthinkable, but in an outfit as old-fashioned and offbeat as Lazar and Jenkins, stranger things had happened. If Emily made partner, her mother would be overjoyed to have something to brag to her church friends about. As for Michael, this would just make him look directionless in comparison, but she couldn't help that.

She wasn't sure how Julian would feel about it. After all, they didn't need the money, and this would mean she'd have to work even longer hours. She hoped he would be happy for her, as he was the one who had encouraged her to change jobs all those years ago, but privately she wondered if it would make him feel like, well, less of a man. From what she could tell, he didn't mind that, at least to an outsider, it looked like she was the successful one, the provider of the family. But since it was only still a dim possibility, she didn't mention it to him. In fact, the only person she'd discussed it with was Rick, at the party Lazar and Jenkins held every year on Bastille Day.

Who knew why Bastille Day instead of the Fourth of July—it was some tradition Joseph Lazar had started when he had founded the practice way back when—but it was an occasion that everyone in the company looked forward to. Booze that was normally hidden in bottom desk drawers came out; cigars that were snuck into bathroom stalls were puffed openly. The receptionist, Doreen, draped red, white, and blue bunting in the break room. *What?* she'd said. *It was on sale.* Someone had laid out a squishy wheel of brie on the table, along with some crackers and cheap red wine. This was the centerpiece around which the thirty or so members of the staff gathered, talking about the summer heat, whether it meant a long or cold winter; and then, as the spirits flowed more freely, who was hooking up with whom in the legal documents room after hours.

"You look lovely, Emma," said Joseph Lazar, waving vaguely in the direction of her chest with his wineglass.

"So do you," Emily replied with a straight face. She held her glass of wine, a precise two-thirds full, at an exact angle from her body. She never drank more than one glass of anything at these events, preferring to observe her colleagues as they got sloshed.

Joseph looked down at himself as to verify her comment, and nearly spilled wine across his seersucker suit; he often dressed and acted as if it were still the era in which the practice had been founded. "How is that case you're working on, the . . . the . . ."

"The Gao Hu case," she reminded him.

"You know, that case reminds me of my father. He came over from Hungary in the early nineteen hundreds. . . ."

Just as Joseph began to lean toward her again, ready to unspool a long story, Rick came by, put a hand beneath Emily's elbow, and ushered her into an unoccupied office.

"So, think he's going to be out by September?" He jerked his thumb at the doorway, through which Joseph's voice could now be heard chatting up one of the paralegals without skipping a beat.

"If he doesn't get sued for sexual harassment first." Emily paused. "You know, I'd be very happy for you if Mitch named you as his replacement."

"What makes you think it'd be me? You've been here just as long."

"Yes, but, you know . . . You're the kind that they go for."

"What do you mean?" Rick appeared genuinely confused.

"Do I really have to spell it out for you? Take a look in the mirror sometime, Farina."

"You should too," he said. "You're young, smart, beautiful—and not a bad lawyer either. They'd be crazy not to pick you."

Emily could feel her face flush, although maybe it was just the wine. She stared into her glass to avoid looking at Rick, but she could still feel his gaze on her.

"How're the kids?" she asked.

"Lisa's starting to wean Cleo." Rick made a face. "She wants to put it off as long as possible but, I mean, Cleo's three. She can't be going to preschool attached to the tit."

Emily gave a murmur that she hoped sounded supportive.

"So when are you and Julian going to . . . you know . . ." The unaccustomed hesitancy in his words suggested to Emily that Rick also had had a bit too much to drink.

"Procreate? Oh, that's not in the cards for us."

"You'll feel differently about it later. You're how old now, thirty-two?"

Emily knew Rick was perfectly aware of how old she was, because he always sent her a joke card on her birthday. This past one had a bunch of paper balloons that popped out when she opened it and said *Happy 2nd Birthday!* with a three inked in before the *2nd*—she suspected the card had originally been given to Cleo.

"Yes, but there's still plenty of time."

He wagged a finger at her. "That's what Lisa said, and look what happened. As soon as one was born, she was itching for another. Had to get back to work at it right away. Which is okay if you're me, but I don't know about that husband of yours."

Emily didn't know where he'd come up with that idea, since he hadn't interacted very much with Julian aside from firm dinners and the barbecue. She decided to let it slide.

"The thing is," Rick said quietly, "it's like your wife, who used to want you all the time, who couldn't get enough of you, suddenly stops wanting you. And then you realize you were just the means to an end."

Emily thought briefly of how she'd caught Rick and Lisa looking at each other over the heads of their children at the barbecue and how she'd assumed a certain kind of contentment that came from years of marriage in that glance. "I didn't know it was like that," she said.

Rick shook his head. "Never mind. I didn't mean to put any of my personal problems onto you. Let's talk about us." He raised his glass to hers. "Let's promise that no matter what happens, we'll still be friends."

"Friends," she said, clunking plastic glasses with him. But she knew that the person who wasn't chosen as partner would have to leave the firm. There would be no way that you could stay at a place that had effectively snubbed you. And after that happened, she and Rick could probably never be friends again.

So in a way she treasured what she thought of as her and Rick's last summer together. She grew to appreciate their late nights, that they were able to share the same frustrations and minor breakthroughs. She was reminded of all the hours they had spent together over the past six years, knowing he was toiling away in the office down the hall, eating the same terrible takeout, turning off the lights long after the janitors had cleaned the floors.

She also knew why Mitch Jenkins had added Rick to the case. This was a test, to see who was worthy of having their last name added to the signboard downstairs in the lobby of a decrepit Chinatown building, next to the names of an employment agency, a tax accountant, and a driving school. While outwardly, Emily was every bit as competitive as she'd always been, she couldn't help thinking that the promotion would help Rick much more than it would help her. She had seen where he lived; he had three children to support, and he probably helped out with his parents, too. He needed this more than she did.

Sometimes Emily thought about what would happen if she walked away from the case and let Rick have all the credit. But he knew her too well to not suspect something was up, and he'd never accept that kind of behavior from her. Also, this would mean that she would have to leave the firm, and that frightened her. As arcane as Lazar and Jenkins was, as outdated as some of its practices, she didn't know how to work anywhere else. She didn't have the experience or knowledge for corporate law, and public defense had no more appeal to her than it had immediately after law school. What would she do, open her own one-woman operation? Run it out of her house, so that both she and Julian worked from home? How easy it would be then to give up her career altogether, give in to Julian's wish for children, and become the dreaded suburban stay-at-home mom.

She didn't know what the future held, but the one thing she was aware of was that she would miss Rick, miss him awfully, and the Gao Hu case would likely be the last time she'd work with him. If it had been any other case, she would have wished it would last longer. After the medical report findings, though, it was even more important that they move swiftly.

Emily awoke the morning after Rick had delivered the report with a premonition, a bad taste not only in her mouth but in her mind, as if she had dreamed something too awful to be remembered. Gradually, she remembered the events of the night before, her fight with Julian, the phone call from Edison Ng, who'd said that he thought Michael was in China, in a place called Qinghai Province, which Emily had never heard of before. Something to do with visiting an old family friend? It had been hard to hear Edison over the background noise on his end. Emily would have to ask her mother if she knew anything about a friend from Qinghai.

Then she focused on the sunlight streaming in through the windows, and, turning to her alarm clock, which she had forgotten to set, realized how late it was. Cursing, she got up and threw on some clothes. The covers on the side of the bed next to her had been pulled up, and she couldn't hear any sound from below. Julian must have left the house. The night before, after she'd finished her call with Edison, she'd gone back into the bedroom only to find him asleep—or pretending to be asleep—which was a relief. Downstairs in the kitchen, the cupboards and tiles were as polished as they'd been the night before. Sometimes, when Julian got up earlier than she did, he'd brew her some coffee, but the countertop was bare. So that was how it was going to be from now on, she thought. She took a quick glance out the kitchen window and saw that her car was missing, although Julian's remained in the driveway. Of course, she'd unintentionally boxed him in last night. She rummaged through a drawer for his keys, thinking that she might as well drive into the city with all the time she'd lost.

Just then, her cell phone rang. Emily reached for the bag that she'd deposited on a chair the night before. It must be Rick, wondering where she was. Indeed, she could see that she'd missed several calls from him.

"Hey," she said. "I overslept. I'll be there as soon as possible."

Rick's pause was so long that she thought the connection had been dropped.

"Is everything okay?" she asked. "What's happened?"

"Emily," Rick said, "Gao Hu's dead."

As she drove southeast to Queens, to be with the Hu family, Emily listened as Rick told her the details. What the medical report hadn't revealed was how serious Gao Hu's heart defect was: a pulmonary stenosis that severely limited the flow of blood. Who could say whether the condition had been worsened by recent events, but essentially he had been on death row since he'd been arrested. Sometime in the dawn of his ninety-sixth day of his incarceration, he'd had a heart attack. He'd been discovered in his bunk by his cellmate. The detention center claimed to have been unaware of any health issues and maintained that the inmate had exaggerated the pain in his leg. They hadn't treated him any worse or any better than anyone else in their care.

Jean Hu had been informed earlier that morning, and Emily and Rick now needed to decide how to proceed with the case. Actually, the case was much stronger now, Emily thought. Since this was a wrongful death while in the care of the state, they could potentially achieve millions of dollars in damages. It was easier for her to focus on these things rather than think about what Jean and her son, Sam, must be feeling; the shock that would give way to a numbness that settled in like a long winter.

Emily turned down the Hus' street, a neat line of virtually identical, two-story brick houses. She'd visited the homes of previous clients, some of whom weren't comfortable talking to her in her office or even in a public setting, such as a restaurant. She'd encountered everything from a tiny walk-up apartment that housed several generations to a boardinghouse where people lived in cell-like rooms only a few feet wide. But when she'd first visited the Hus' earlier that summer, there had been a whiff of something like home. Maybe it was the smell of pickled vegetables, stir-fried scallions and garlic, or the underlying bitter tinge of Chinese herbs that Jean brewed for Sam, who suffered from allergies. Whatever it was, it made Emily think of a place that was the opposite of her own large, empty, suburban house.

She had visited the Hus' many times over the past couple of months, and not just for work. At first, she'd told Rick that she'd wanted to get a picture of what Gao's family life was like, so that she could present a human interest angle to the case. But she hadn't expected Jean to welcome her in, invite her to stay for dinner, where she sat at the table next to small, serious-faced Sam, as if she were a daughter. Jean's cooking was much better than her mother's, and she made traditional dishes such as winter melon and red bean soup. The interior of the house felt comfortingly familiar: the pile of shoes outside the front door, brush paintings jostling for space on the walls with generic watercolor prints, the piano on which Sam was probably forced to practice on at least an hour a day.

Throughout the house, Emily had the sense that Gao was there and he wasn't there. This was familiar to her, for it reminded her of her own father, away at work. Sometimes she wondered what Jean must feel at night when she went to bed, not knowing whether or not her husband would return. She felt she understood why her mother had wanted to get rid of her father's things so soon after he had died. Perhaps it was easier to know what had happened, to accept it, rather than be kept in a state of false hope.

Today the front door to the house was open, so Emily went through it and into a living room packed with Chinese people. The atmosphere was akin to that of a party, with people eating and chattering away. She caught snippets of conversation in English and Mandarin, about mundane topics such as which college whose son was going to, or whose daughter was having another baby. It was strangely like being at a family reunion rather than a wake.

She tapped an elderly man on the shoulder and asked him if he knew where Jean was. He pointed up the stairs. Emily stepped into a bedroom that seemed almost entirely filled with women. Jean sat on the bed, her face strained, exposing lines that hadn't been evident before. But Emily noticed she was as impeccably dressed as when she'd first met her, and she'd made an attempt to put some color on her lips and cheeks. No matter what happened, you had to look good in front of other people. She remembered going through her mother's closet, looking for something appropriate for her mother to wear to the funeral, and finding a black silk dress that she had never remembered seeing her mother wear before.

Noticing that she was a stranger, the other women made way for Emily to approach Jean. Not knowing how else to react, Emily ended up saying "I'm sorry, I'm so sorry" over and over to Jean, who began to parrot it back to her; "I'm so sorry," as if apologizing for her husband being late to an appointment. There was a delayed reaction to her movements that Emily had seen in her own mother when her father had died, probably from a sedative.

The crowd parted again, and Sam came in to lean against his mother's shoulder. His lips were clamped shut, so you couldn't see that his teeth had grown in straight.

"Sam," Emily said softly, reaching a hand out to him, but he looked away, as if he didn't know her. She wondered again what he had been told—how did a child grow up knowing that his father had been tortured to death?

Suddenly, she couldn't breathe anymore; the presence of all these people in this room was suffocating her. With a mumbled apology, she got up and went downstairs into the hallway, where she leaned against the wall. She remembered her father's funeral, the kind of people who had come, the church families who had said the same nauseating things to her about her father being in heaven (not if he had anything to do with it, she thought, since he had been clear that he didn't believe in it), and the coworkers who had seemed surprised to get a glimpse into the private life of someone they only had ever seen in a lab coat.

There had also been the neighbors, Mr. and Mrs. Bradley. Their son, Scott, Emily remembered as being a bit of a creep. Once, when they were children, he had given her a dead butterfly. In high school, he had been one of those kids that Emily frowned upon, who cut classes to smoke in strip-mall parking lots. She didn't know what had happened to him, although she figured he must have straightened out by now, and the last she'd heard was that he'd moved out west. The daughter, Amy, had been too young for Emily to know much about, but she recalled that she and Michael had been friends. Amy had been there that day at the funeral too, her reddish-blond hair long and sleek against her elegantly asymmetrical, all-black outfit. The last time she'd seen Amy, as a teenager, she'd had spiky hair dyed electric blue and wore combat boots, and a stud that flashed silvery in her tongue as she spoke.

Emily saw that Amy still sported that piercing as she came forward and hugged her, said something comforting. Then Amy went over to Michael, and Emily watched as she linked arms with her brother, and they went out of the room together. Something akin to jealousy pricked at her skin, at the sight of a woman who was closer to her brother than she was.

Emily looked around for her mother and saw that she appeared to be holding her own among the guests. So she went and collected Julian from where he had been chatting with some church lady about the merits of compost, and pulled him up the stairs and into her bedroom. It looked the same as when she'd left thirteen years before to go to college: the dresser whose top was laminated with stickers, the shelf of trophies she'd won in debate and mock trial, the four-poster bed with its white quilted bedspread. Tacked above the bed, completely unironically, was a poster that said: EVERY JOB IS A SELF-PORTRAIT OF THE PERSON WHO DID IT. AUTOGRAPH YOUR WORK WITH EXCELLENCE!

Julian, who was flipping through one of her yearbooks, started to laugh.

"What's so funny?"

"I'm not laughing at you, just with your glasses."

"Let me see that." Emily grabbed the book away from him.

Of course he'd had it open to her senior year high school picture. She'd been so earnest in her thick, plastic, tortoiseshell-framed glasses and flowered turtleneck, the amount of coolness she exuded in inverse proportion to the number of clubs listed below her name.

She'd been able to turn that gawky seriousness into something more purposeful in college. Although she ended up going to school in the city, less than an hour-long train ride away from the suburban town where she'd grown up, she felt like she had entered a glittering new world, where people stayed up late to talk about obscure forms of poetry, foreign philosophers, and failed social experiments. She became an activist, marching for sweatshop-free sneakers and cruelty-free meat in the dining halls. This intersected nicely with the campus AV club, whose members were looking for demonstrations to film, which was how she had met Julian.

It had been in Washington Square Park, in the middle of winter, when she had been participating in a demonstration advocating equal opportunity in tenure, and he had been filming. *Female professors are half as likely to gain tenure as their male counterparts,* she told him as the snow fell around their heads. *Women with children are a quarter less likely as men with children to achieve tenure in the sciences.* She had thought he was cute, despite the scruffy long hair that poked out from beneath his knit cap. He had thought she was a lesbian.

She disproved that one evening, a few weeks later, when she came over to see the final cut of the video he'd put together. She'd watched with horror as the camera focused on her wildly gesticulating hands and then on her face until it filled nearly the entire screen, zooming in on her flared nostrils. Nobody looked good on amateur video, especially a video of a demonstration, but this was too much. She had felt so disgusted that she promptly offered to sleep with Julian, who appeared to accept out of pure surprise.

When she had first brought Julian home from college, she had been acutely embarrassed of her family; the way her father blew his nose so loudly it could be heard down the hall; how her mother shuffled around in her house slippers and plastic apron; her weird little brother, who wore vintage black T-shirts with the names of bands that sounded like things you might find in a hardware store: Anthrax, Black Flag, Nine Inch Nails. Then she found that Julian had been ignored for so long by his own parents that he welcomed the attention, her father's gruff questions about what he planned to do with his future, her mother's insistence that he was too thin and should eat more. Things that would drive any normal person crazy, but Julian seemed to appreciate them so much that in the beginning she wondered whether he liked her family better than he liked her.

During those visits, Emily slept up in her room while Julian was expected to stay on the couch. At around midnight, when her parents were in bed, she'd steal down and they'd have sex on the nubby brown sofa, cautious of her parents and brother one floor above, and then she'd go back to her bed. But they'd never actually done it in her bed. The closest that bed had ever come to seeing any action was when Emily and Alvin Wang, her partner in mock trial and equally bespectacled, had necked for two hours on one of the rare occasions her parents were out.

"Come here," she said to Julian, and when he did, she pulled him down on the bed next to her.

"Ouch," Julian said as his elbow hit the headboard.

She started wrestling playfully with him, trying to provoke him with little jabs, and somehow she started crying. It was as if she couldn't stop, as she continued to hit him softly with her clenched fists. He simply absorbed the blows, holding her wrists, until it appeared she was worn out. Then, in one fluid movement, she shifted so that she was straddling him, pinning him down.

At first he tried to return her kisses, but she was moving so fast, darting back and forth so quickly, that he kept missing her mouth, and they landed on her jaw, her ear, the corner of her eye. His hands moved down her back, beneath her ugly, black knit dress, where he pressed the palm of one hand between her legs. She gave a cry, almost as if she were begging something of him, and her fingers worked to pull down his zipper. Then they both froze in place, her dress worked up around her hips, his fly undone. The bedroom door was ajar, just as they had left it, but there had been a flicker of movement beyond, accompanied by the faint sound of footsteps.

"Did you hear something?" Emily asked.

He shrugged. She tried to get back into their rhythm, but the moment had passed. He sat up, extricating himself from her, stuffing himself back into his pants.

"Please," she said.

"Em, I don't think we should be doing this."

"You're right." She rose from the bed, drawing her dress down over her knees, and peered into the mirror over the dresser, where she tucked her hair behind her ears so that two precise curlicues fell over her shoulders. "I'm going downstairs," she announced, and left him among her old trophies.

That night, when they were lying on the brown foldout sofa in the den, which they had been allowed to sleep on together since they had gotten married, they did not reach for each other, and the next day, Julian returned home while Emily stayed to help her mother. She'd been surprised at the quickness with which her mother had bundled her father's things down into the basement. At first, she thought her mother might be considering moving into an apartment or a smaller house near where her church friend Beatrice Ma lived, but that wasn't the case. Then on subsequent visits, she'd been alarmed at how it almost seemed as if her father had not lived there at all.

When her mother had asked her to take whatever she wanted of her father's, she'd hesitated. Nothing seemed appropriate; not the belts nor ties nor a single pair of cuff links that her mother pushed on her to take home to Julian. For one thing, none of it was anything Julian would wear, and what about Michael? Wouldn't he want any of this to remember their father by? Apparently, her mother had made that suggestion, and Michael had refused. So she'd selected the photograph of her father from the funeral, which her mother told her had been taken at her wedding, but Emily didn't remember it. *He was very happy at your wedding,* her mother had told her, but Emily certainly didn't think her father looked very happy; tight-lipped, with his bushy eyebrows making him appear even more stern than he really was. Where had she been when this picture was taken? Probably worrying about the flower arrangements or the seating plan. She had not been thinking about him at all.

She put the photo in the living room when she got home, the only picture that showed her father because in all her other family photos—a Christmas from a few years ago, her graduation from law school, a childhood vacation to Florida—he was the one taking the picture. She couldn't afford not to display it. Since there was nothing from Julian's side of the family, this was all she had.

"Hey."
Emily looked up to see Rick's broad, familiar face.
"I've been looking for you everywhere," he said.

"Did you see Jean?" she asked.

"Just briefly. I can't imagine what she's going through. What's with all these people, though?"

She shrugged. "Relatives, I think." That, she belatedly realized, was the biggest difference between her father's funeral and today. "I feel like we're in the way here."

"We definitely can't discuss anything. Maybe we should go get that drink we were talking about yesterday?"

Emily glanced at the clock. "Now? It's, like, three."

"I know a place." Rick offered his hand to her, and she took it as he led her through the crowd.

Emily followed Rick in her car until they came to what she thought must be the sorriest bar this side of the Triborough Bridge. Every surface appeared to be covered with a sticky film, and half the lights twinkling on the walls had burned out. A gray-haired, itinerant-looking man was nursing a drink at the counter, while two kids who appeared to be underage were shooting pool.

Emily found a table while Rick got their beers. For a moment she wondered if it was wise of her to be drinking with her colleague in the afternoon. But when Rick came back and sat down beside her, he immediately started talking business. Emily tried to concentrate on what he was saying, but her mind was fuzzing over quickly from alcohol and the events of the day.

"We've got a lot of work ahead of us," he was saying. "We're going to have to go back to the detention center, question the other inmates. We're fighting the whole system now."

"What about Jean?" Emily asked. "She'll need time. She has Sam to think about."

"The sooner we can get her talking, the better. We'll just have to be careful about what media she speaks to."

"How long do you think this could take?"

"To win the case? Years. But consider what could happen at the end of it. I don't mean just getting a settlement for Jean and Sam. I mean changing legislation, changing the way illegals are treated. That could be huge."

Emily looked into her beer. "I don't think I can do it." It came out plainer than she had intended, flattened by the dank atmosphere of the bar, but in truth she had been thinking this ever since she had received Rick's call that morning. In her shiny, perfectly appointed kitchen, she felt the very walls drop away from her for a moment before she willed them, and herself, upright again. It wasn't entirely unlike what she had felt the year before, sitting in her office, listening to her mother tell her that her father had died. She couldn't go through it all again.

"What did you say?" Rick was asking.

"I said, I can't do it," Emily repeated, with more certainty. "As of now, I'm off this case."

"What do you mean? We've only just started. I can understand that you're intimidated by what's ahead. I am too. But we can do it, if we work together."

"I can't put Jean and Sam through this. I just can't. They've already endured enough. If you or someone else wants to remind them every day how their husband and father died, then go ahead. But I, for one, don't have the stomach for it."

"Emily," Rick said. "This is the kind of case you've always dreamed of. What's happened to that?"

She shrugged. "I guess I've changed."

He regarded her warily. "Is this about something else? Is there something going on at home that you want to tell me?"

"No," she said. "Everything's fine. I guess I've just been working too hard lately. I need a break." Until that point, she hadn't even considered taking time off her job. But how easy it would be to take a day or two off, to let those days stretch to a week, maybe to leave her work and Chinatown itself. To walk away from everything that had ever been expected of her.

"Emily." Rick sounded very concerned now. He placed his hands on her shoulders, turning her to look at him. "I know you don't mean that. You love your work. That's what I've always loved about you. Besides"—here he stopped for a second, before continuing—"I don't know what I would do without you."

She tried to smile. "That's nice of you to say that, but you'll be fine. You'll make partner, Lisa will be so proud of you—"

His exhalation cut her off. "Lisa and I might be spending some time apart."

"Really?" She was incredulous, but for a second also wondered if Rick was lying, to try and get her to change her mind. She hadn't recalled him mentioning any kind of marital strife lately, and she liked to think that he felt comfortable by now to confide in her about such things. Then again, the case had taken over both their lives lately.

"Things haven't been good between us since . . . well, since around the time the baby was born. We've tried a lot of things since then—couples' therapy, individual therapy. Nothing's helped."

"What about the kids?"

"They'd be fine, I guess. Lisa would have them during the week, and I'd get them every other weekend. That how it works, right? It seems like half the parents we know are divorced, so they'd fit right in. Anyway, it appears that my marriage may be on its way out. And if you leave me too, Em, I don't know what I would do. . . ."

He turned to her, and it was the most natural thing in the world to put her arms around his neck. She was aware of his breath against her cheek, the way his hands felt flat against her back. Their mouths met, sloppily, tasting of sour beer and bitter desire, for so long that the two teenagers on the other side of the room took notice and hooted.

"Get a room!" one of them shouted.

"Should we?" Rick asked softly, his tone joking, but his eyes were serious. He held her hand, his thumb tracing circles in her palm.

That would be easy, too. They'd get into their respective cars and go to a motel even seedier than this bar. They'd undress each other slowly underneath the fluorescent lights, and she was sure that the sex would be good, but the whole time he'd be thinking about the wife he might not love anymore, and she would be thinking about the husband who might not love her, and in the middle there would be the kids he and his wife had, and the kids that she and her husband didn't have. It was entirely too messy.

"Emily?" Rick asked.

Emily forced herself to focus back to the present, Rick's hand that remained on hers although now it was still, as if he was holding his breath for her answer. "I'm sorry," she said.

She got up and walked out of the bar. She thought she heard Rick call her name again, but she didn't look back. Once she had gotten in her car, closed and locked the door, she felt safer, although she wasn't sure from who or what. She had told Rick that she was off the case, and she meant it. Jean would be all right; she had those relatives to help her. In time Sam, too, would be fine. People got over these tragedies every day, of spouses dying, of parents dying, no matter how young or how tragic. She wasn't dropping the case because of what she was afraid it might do to Jean and Sam. She was afraid of what it might do to herself.

She began to drive without really knowing where she was going. All she could think of was how much she detested Julian's car, this innocent hunk of lustrous chrome, how it moved so effortlessly that you could barely sense the road beneath you. You'd need to get in a crash in order to feel anything.

Then she had an idea of where she could go. When she reached the Belt Parkway she took it west, toward the Verrazano Bridge and New Jersey. She took out her phone and pressed her mother's number.

"Emily, where are you?" her mother asked. "It sounds like you're in a wind channel."

"Wind tunnel," Emily corrected.

"Are you in a car? You know it's not safe to talk and drive at the same time."

"I'll make it quick. I just wanted to tell you that I'm coming over to stay the night." She would think up a suitable explanation for her lack of an overnight bag later.

"Is Julian with you?" was her mother's immediate response. It occurred to Emily that her mother might actually enjoy her son-in-law's company.

"No," Emily said. "He's, um, going into the city tonight."

"You should go with him," her mother said. "Have some fun together. I heard all about it on television. It's called *date night*. I think it is very important."

That was laughable, the closest her parents had ever gotten to a date night was sitting next to each other on the sofa, watching television. "I don't mind, Mom," Emily said. "I think it'll be nice for you and me to spend some time alone together."

"You think so?"

"I know it's been almost a year since Dad died."

"Yes," her mother said finally. "A visit would be good. Even better if Michael were there too."

"About Michael . . ." Emily conveniently left out Edison Ng and just told her mother that Michael's roommate had remembered him saying something about going to China. "Dad didn't know anyone from Qinghai Province, did he?"

"No," her mother replied. "Your father never mentioned that place before."

Next, Emily called her home number. The answering machine came on, and she imagined her voice filling the silent, empty kitchen. "Hey," she said, "it's me. I'm staying at my mother's house tonight. I think that after last night, it might be the best for both of us to take some time to think. Also"—she inhaled a breath—"you know that coworker of mine, Rick? Well, I just kissed him."

She threw the phone on the seat next to her. Then she thought better of it and retrieved it, about to call again. But there was nothing she could do to change what she had just said, or what she had done back in the bar. From the moment she had woken up this morning, something had been driving her to act in direct opposition to who she thought herself to be, and she was powerless to stop its smooth, irrevocable trajectory.

# CHAPTER 5

Ling didn't know what the real reason was behind her daughter's coming home—she hoped she and Julian hadn't had a fight—but she was glad nonetheless. Emily hadn't been back all summer due to some case that was too big for her to talk about, and before that not since Christmas. There had been something in her voice just now that Ling had distrusted, although maybe it was due to the poor connection. She suspected her daughter was talking on the phone while driving, which was very dangerous, not to mention illegal where they lived. There were all those stories in the news about people who had gotten into accidents because they couldn't take the time to stop and make a phone call. Maybe Ling should mention it, but she knew her daughter would probably take offense at being told what to do.

Over Christmas, the last time she had seen her children together, both Emily and Michael had been listless. Ling had attributed it to its being their first holiday without their father, although Han had never been one for celebrations. He refused to put up decorations of any kind, so that theirs was the only house on the block without a blow-up reindeer on the front lawn or even a wreath on the door. Instead, they'd gone to the mall, where the idea of Christmas, represented by a twenty-foot-tall tree and fake pine-scented spray and free candy canes, was as aggressively pushed as any other item on sale.

On Christmas Eve, Ling had tried to entice her children with hot chocolate and board games, but even Scrabble, which used to be a surefire method of invoking Emily's competitiveness, had no effect. Usually, Emily would be racking up the triple-scores and fifty-pointers, but now she didn't even blink an eye when Michael put down the word *Kleenex,* which even Ling knew was a proper noun.

Then they'd opened their presents the next morning. Emily and Julian had given Ling a red cashmere sweater so soft that she knew her son-in-law must have picked it out; Emily didn't have the time nor the taste. Michael, bizarrely, had given everyone souvenirs—clear crystal paperweights with the Empire State Building or the Statue of Liberty laser-cut into them—that looked like he had picked them out from a street corner vendor in about five minutes.

Not knowing what her children wanted or needed, Ling had been convinced by a saleslady at a home goods store to get a lemon zester that was actually in the shape of a lemon. Emily had turned it over in her hands, as if she expected it to transform into some other gadget, but Julian had thanked her and said it would be very useful. Ling had gotten Michael some gloves, having noticed on a previous visit that there was a hole in his old pair. He'd seemed pleased by them, and she'd congratulated herself on her good sense, until she noticed later that he was already wearing new gloves and that these were made of expensive-looking leather. She doubted he could afford to spend money on such things, and wondered if they had been a present, and if so, from whom.

Afterward, Ling had announced she was going to the late-morning service at the church, and did anyone want to come along? Emily and Michael had declined, but to her surprise, Julian said he would go with her. Ling had been both touched and slightly appalled by this prospect. She hadn't wanted to go alone, but she knew everyone's eyes would be drawn to her when she walked along the pews with her non-Asian son-in-law. That had indeed happened, but as they passed those rows of intact families, Ling holding her head high, she felt a confidence that she didn't think she had felt since she'd last entered this building with her husband.

Pastor Liu delivered a lovely service, and then she and Julian had taken a walk around the chilly grounds of the church. Then Julian had said, "Ling, I need to talk to you about something." Her son-in-law saying her name still startled Ling after so many years. She almost wished that he would call her *Mom*. When the children had been little, her husband had even called her that when he was speaking in front of them. It was as if it were her given name in English.

"What is it, Julian?" she asked.

"I think it's important for a family to have some kind of spiritual anchor, no matter what kind of religion it involves. I hope this will be true for my kids someday."

Ling felt hope bloom in her chest. "Yours and Emily's?"

"That's what I wanted to speak to you about." Julian took a deep breath. "Emily doesn't want to have kids."

"Emily," Ling said after a while, trying to explain her daughter's lack of a maternal instinct, "does not like children. She does not even like dolls. I know, from when she was little. But it's not her fault, it's mine."

Julian stared at her, confused, then continued. "The thing is, she doesn't want to talk about it with me. She won't even try. I can't say that I understand why she feels the way she does about having a family, but I certainly can't try to understand if she doesn't talk to me."

Again, Ling thought to mention that it was her fault, hers and Han's, why Emily was the way she was; that Emily was her father's daughter through and through when it came to someone trying to understand her, but she didn't think it would help.

"I know there's nothing you can do," Julian said, "but I wanted to let you know what was going on. Just in case she mentioned it to you."

Ling shook her head. "She does not say anything to me."

She realized that neither she nor Julian, supposedly the people who were closest to Emily, had any idea what was going on with her anymore. But Ling was sure her daughter's lack of a desire for children was her fault.

Up until the age of five, Emily had at least tolerated dolls, although she never had more than one or two at one time, and in comparison to her increasing stuffed-animal collection, they were second-class citizens. They were always served last at tea parties, left at home during car trips, and remained uncuddled at night. Worst of all, they were simply forgotten, lying for days under the bed, limbs splayed and hair tangled. But one incident, Ling felt, had forever turned Emily against them. Emily must have just started kindergarten, and it appeared as if she might never have a sibling. Ling had conscientiously prayed as Pastor Liu had instructed her, eaten all the right foods, even turned to Chinese medicine in the hopes of conceiving. But every time she had been given reason to hope, allowed herself to retrieve Emily's old baby clothes from the basement, it had ended in a miscarriage. She'd take a deep breath, fold up the clothes with quiet hands, and put them away.

The push and pull of expectations, the rise and fall of desires, had taken its toll on Ling. She argued with Han almost every night, downstairs and with Emily's bedroom door shut, so that their daughter couldn't hear. But sometimes she grew careless and forgot to completely close Emily's door, let her voice rise higher than was prudent. What intensified her anger was that Han did not respond to her. Looking back, she realized he probably didn't know what to say. But back then she interpreted his silence as stubbornness, as a refusal to take some of the blame. They hadn't quarreled like this since they had first moved to the suburbs.

One night, Ling had gotten so angry that she grabbed the first thing she could lay her hands on—unfortunately, Emily's doll, abandoned on the sofa—and thrown it across the room. It had been, she reflected later, an incredibly childish thing to do. The doll hit the wall and landed on the floor, its head separated from the body, and the dress torn down the front. But it had done the trick; Ling's breathing slowed and the color receded from her face. Then she looked up and saw her daughter watching her from the landing. Her face not betraying anything, Emily went back to her room. Ling turned to Han for his reaction, but he did exactly the same thing. At the time, Ling had not recognized that both her husband's and daughter's faces bore the same expression, a blankness upon which nothing could be written.

Ling almost wished Emily had cried and Han had shouted at her. Rather, their lack of reaction to her behavior was confounding and disturbing. The next morning, she presented Emily with the mended doll as an apology. She had worried the head back on and spent the night fixing the dress, but she was a bad sewer, so the stitches were puckered, like an ugly scar. Emily took back the doll, but Ling noticed that the corners of her mouth only curved up for a second, hardly a smile. She never saw Emily play with a doll again.

As for her fights with Han, these too decreased in number, and then Ling discovered that she was pregnant, and this time it took. It seemed as if their periods of strife were behind them, but Ling couldn't help wondering when the next time would be and what effect it would have on their children. All parents argued, she knew, but it was as if she had to fill the void of Han's silence, to provoke him into revealing something about himself. She almost wished he would strike her, so that she would know how he really felt. Sometimes she wondered if it had to do with the way they had met, both recent transplants to New York City, although they had both emigrated a few years before that. They hadn't known each other very long before they'd gotten married. But that was the way it was back then. If a woman wasn't married by the age of twenty-five, there was something seriously wrong with her.

It wasn't like when Emily got married. Nowadays, twenty-five was considered young, and an early marriage led to divorce. Ling remembered Emily announcing her engagement to her parents, how almost apologetic she seemed, nervously twisting the monstrous carbuncle of a ring on her finger. She had not consulted her parents beforehand, nor had Julian asked Han and Ling for their permission. But sometimes Ling caught a look on her daughter's face that weekend, an expression of doubt that never tipped over the edge into a question. She wondered what Emily was feeling. Did she think she was making a mistake? She wished she was close enough to her daughter that Emily would confide in her, so much like the American mothers and daughters she saw on television, who spilled secrets the moment they stepped together into a coffee shop or nail salon.

Han's reaction to Emily's engagement was simply to say that he did not think they could pay for the wedding if she insisted on marrying this *laowai*. Emily shot back that they didn't need his money; Julian had plenty from his parents, even though he didn't talk to them. And besides, they planned to go to city hall, *so there*. She had been so young, her quivering lower lip contradicting the certainty of her words.

Ling had wanted to tell her daughter that her own misgivings weren't because Julian wasn't Chinese. For her, it was more whether Emily really felt she could be happy with this man. There was nothing she wanted more than for her daughter to learn from her own mistakes.

Ling Chu had met Han Tang at a dance in Chinatown, not long after she had moved to New York. Before that, she had been a graduate student at a small Christian college in Connecticut, sponsored by her church in Taiwan. Her first year there had been spent in a bewilderment of unfamiliar food, cold weather, and spoken English, which none of the classic British novels she had read could have prepared her for. Also, there were few Chinese people at her school, making the possibility of her finding a husband that much less likely. Back home, her older sister had married a banker who had lost his first wife, while her younger sister had married a college classmate. To be the only unmarried daughter, and living overseas no less, was a burden she couldn't possibly place on her family. So, not long after she turned twenty-four, Ling abandoned her pursuit of a degree and decided to move to the city with her friend Felicia Lam.

At the dance, Felicia was partnered with a slim young man in a closely cut gray suit. Ling had seen him arrive late, wearing a dove-gray fedora that matched the shade of his suit, as if he were a Chinese mobster. As the couple turned in the sway of the music, she willed him to look at her, and to her amazement he did, with eyes as dark as wells, over Felicia's unsuspecting shoulder. After a few moments, he left Felicia and introduced himself to her with a formal bow. He was not that much taller than Ling and had floppy black hair that had been slicked back, but strands still fell forward to frame his wide but handsome face. He danced a bit stiffly, as if following an internal metronome. He told her his name was Han Tang. He was a chemistry student, but in his spare time he enjoyed reading the classical poets: Du Fu, Wang Wei, and Li Bai; the last he thought was too sentimental. To her astonishment, he also considered Mao Zedong a poet.

*How can you call Mao a poet?* she had asked, incredulous.

*"Let a hundred flowers bloom,"* he replied. *How can you not consider that poetry?*

This young man astonished her. She was convinced he was the one who had the heart of a poet.

Han had also told her, over the course of the night, that he had emigrated from mainland China the previous year through the sponsorship of a distant relative in San Francisco. He had worked as a dishwasher when he first arrived and, wishing for something better out of life, had recently come to the East Coast to start over. His immediate family back home had all passed on, so in effect he was the last of his line. Ling was not intimidated by this grand statement. Rather, she was impressed by this revelation; it gave height to his slight stature and, perhaps most significantly, it told her that he was ready to start a family soon. She was even willing to overlook the fact that he was from the mainland, which to a girl from Taiwan was tantamount to being Japanese.

Ling Chu and Han Tang went ice-skating at Rockefeller Center. They slurped noodles in Chinatown restaurants and watched movies uptown at the Thalia. Six months after they had met at the dance, he proposed, and they moved into an apartment on the Upper West Side. When she got married, Ling quit her job selling gloves at a department store downtown and furnished the place, purchasing green and gold dinnerware, persuading her husband to buy a television, although all they could afford was black-and-white. Sometimes she sat alone in the apartment during the day, on their recently acquired brown sleeper sofa, and marveled that she had managed to get married at all.

She wanted to start having children immediately, but Han had just received his biochemistry degree and was looking for a job. Ling understood the need for the delay, but by the time he announced that he had been offered a job in New Jersey, she had an announcement of her own—she was pregnant with their first child. Although she had been upset to leave her friends, Ling looked forward to a new life in which she could live in a house and drive a car as large as a boat, and in which she and her husband would have no one else but each other to depend on.

The house they had moved into, located in a recently developed suburb, was nothing like their apartment. Everything they did here was like taking the first steps in a foreign country. The lawn, which had been transported piece by piece and patched together like a quilt, was so fresh that their shoes left dimples on the surface. The bushes barely made indentations against the walls, and there were paint flecks on the windows that looked next door and onto the raw beams of another house in early stages of construction. Inside, the water gushing from the faucets unexpectedly turned reddish brown and an earthy smell would fill the bathroom.

The first thing the Tangs discovered about their house was that it was plagued with mice, due to the new houses constantly springing up around them. The mice left what Ling liked to think of as *little presents* behind the toaster, and at night when she padded awkwardly downstairs to the kitchen, she would find half a dozen of them scurrying away into the corners when she flipped on the light. Determined to get rid of them, Han bought traps baited with peanut butter, because he said it had been scientifically proven that mice preferred peanut butter to cheese. One night when Ling had gone to the kitchen to get a glass of water, she discovered a mouse caught in a trap, its eyes bulging like grains of black rice. It had managed to pull itself a few inches across the linoleum, and its right hind leg paddled uselessly. *I know how you feel,* she wanted to tell it. Then she decided to let her husband deal with it in the morning, turned off the light, and went back to bed.

Ling knew no one in this town, if it could be called a town; the houses were situated so far apart from the shops. While her husband was at work, she learned how to drive the maroon Buick that

Han had purchased for her. She was terrible at it. When she pulled out of the driveway, she often ran over their mailbox, flattening it as if it were a pin and her car, a bowling ball. She practiced in empty parking lots, worrying about jolting the baby as she awkwardly shifted gears. She was also concerned that she and Han were arguing too much and that this would also hurt the baby, that the emotions that surged through her would make the baby anxious. She could feel the baby restlessly turning somersaults in her stomach, giving fretful little kicks. The sensitivity with which it seemed to pick up on all her moods indicated to her that it would be a girl.

Ling and Han seemed to argue about everything and nothing: the mice that continued to wreak havoc in the kitchen; the cost of gasoline since Ling practiced driving so much; the fact that even though she practiced she could still not drive on the highway, so that she was limited to buying groceries from the local stores and could not easily make a trip into the city to get the Chinese vegetables to make the dishes that he wanted. They also argued about church. Han had grown up considering religion to be a liability, something that could cause you to be thrown into jail if so much as a Bible, given to you years before by a well-meaning missionary, was discovered in your house. So Ling often ended up going to church alone, especially after arguments with her husband.

Then one evening they had a particularly bad fight, something that had started innocently enough, with Han faulting her for buying an old piece of meat, slimy and inedible, from the butcher's. Ling had known this from the moment the butcher had placed it on the scale, but she had not trusted her English enough to demand something different. She had meant it to be a funny story, and an explanation why they were having eggs-and-tomato for dinner again instead of a dish with meat. But Han turned it into an accusation: *Don't you know you have to stand up for yourself in this country? Can't you even learn that?*

Ling spun around and left the house. She didn't trust herself to drive, so instead she walked down the street, turned the corner, and continued to walk without being aware of where she was going. She knew she must look odd, an eight-months' pregnant woman on foot. Gradually, the houses on either side, with their trim front yards and neatly cornered gables, thinned out. The street sign she came to was unfamiliar, and when she looked behind her, it was as if the landscape she had passed through had magically rearranged itself. To her dismay, the sidewalk ended altogether, and beyond it stretched fields that she had never seen before. Then a strange sense of calm spread through her body at the sight, the unending green-ness in the waning light. Even on all her drives around town, she had never known she'd been so close to escape.

She stood on the concrete that made up the edge of the side-walk and let the warm summer wind ruffle her hair. If she closed her eyes, it was almost as if she were floating in an amniotic sac, not unlike what her own baby must be experiencing. By now her stom-ach was so big that she carried it like a basket of laundry in front of her. Ling wondered what would happen if she went into labor at that very moment. Would she give birth in the fields like a cow? The baby kicked gently, as if to reassure her that everything was going to be okay. Then it kicked harder, against her bladder.

Ling looked around her to make sure no cars were approaching. Usually, the idea of urinating in public would be enough to make her face heat up with shame, but now she stepped a few feet into the grass, squatted, and relieved herself without even hiding be-hind a tree. When she was done, she smoothed down her maternity smock and turned around. She must have been gone at least a half hour by now, and Han would be worried. But finding her way back was more difficult than she'd thought. When she got to an unfamil-iar intersection, she hesitated. She could knock on someone's door, but she didn't know how to ask for directions. So, for the first time in her life, she decided to let a higher power—God, or whatever you wanted to call it—take over. She continued to walk, and within ten minutes saw a street sign that she recognized. Along with her relief was a slight tinge of disappointment. She couldn't have got-ten lost even if she'd wanted to.

It was dark by the time she got back, and the dinner she'd pre-pared earlier lay cold and congealed on the table, even more unap-petizing. Ling sank into a chair, suddenly aware of how tired she was.

*I was just about to go look for you,* Han said. *Where did you go?*

*Nowhere,* Ling replied.

*I knew you couldn't have gone very far.* Han's words made him appear unconcerned, but Ling caught the tone in his voice. This was the closest he would come to apologizing for what he'd said.

The only other person who knew where Ling had gone that night was the baby, who did turn out to be a girl. When Ling discovered she hadn't given birth to a boy, she turned away from her husband. She was afraid he would once again find fault with her. But Han held her and said not to worry, there was plenty of time, all the time in the world.

For much of Ling's married life, her husband had been an enigma to her. Aside from the first outpouring of his family history, she didn't know much about where he had come from, aside that his parents and siblings—two sisters and a brother—were city folks. He did not seem to have kept any connections from his previous life in China, unlike Ling, who received any number of letters from her friends and relatives. She remembered only one personal letter received by her husband in recent years, about a month before his death. It was on similar airmail paper as the letters that normally arrived for Ling, but it had been postmarked from mainland China, not Taiwan. That was all she could discern of it before Han whisked it away, the expression on his face preventing her from asking any questions.

Sure, she knew many things about her husband: how delicate his stomach was; how loud his snores at night; how his discarded socks looked like cow dung, not unlike the ones in the fields she drove past in the daytime, down that road she'd fled before Emily was born. She adjusted her habits accordingly over the years, making sure the dishes she cooked weren't too spicy, waking him up when the snores got too loud, picking up after him. If knowing the most intimate details of someone's life wasn't really knowing that person, then what was?

Still, Ling couldn't help feeling that a person's family was their history. Certainly that was the way it had been thought of where her family originally came from, when people lived in their ancestral villages and you could look up the names of anyone's great-grandparents on the tablets that hung next to the shrine at the center of every compound. The fact that you were expected to visit this shrine regularly, to burn incense and bow before your ancestors, guaranteed that you never forgot them. But war, famine, revolution, persecution, and other random elements did much to divide families from one another. Ling's own family in Taiwan was far removed from its ancestral village near Shanghai, having been displaced by the Communists in 1949, but so many of their nationalist compatriots had also come over, and much of their former ways were able to be recreated. Han, she supposed, had not been so lucky. The ultimate break, she thought, must be moving to another country. The new language, the new customs, drove a wedge between the old life and the new that could never be removed.

Another mystery about her husband, Ling felt, was his lack of friends. He never associated with the husbands in the church congregation as she did with the wives. Sometimes a coworker would invite them to dinner, and on those rare occasions they would leave the children with a babysitter, later entrusting Emily to watch over Michael, until Michael was old enough to be left home by himself. Ling found these dinners to be awkward affairs, although she preferred it when the coworkers were Asian, as they often were. In the Indian or Malaysian households, she could taste something familiar in the foods, empathize with mothers' concerns over their children's schoolwork, recognize the way people displayed English magazines like *Time* and *Newsweek* on the coffee table, while the newspapers in the kitchen were in their native languages. She understood what it meant to try too hard.

One of the most awkward dinners she attended had been thrown by Han's boss. This was when Han had been working in a nearby town, when Emily was in college and Michael was sixteen, before his most recent job in Trenton which, Ling was convinced, had contributed to his heart disease with its hour-long commute. Han had worked at this particular company for over twenty years; it was why he and Ling had moved to New Jersey, and he considered this boss a friend; the man had even attended Han's funeral nine years later.

Ling had agonized over this event for days, whether she should get a new dress, what she should bring as a gift. She did not know how to choose wine, and it all seemed costly, so in the end she settled on what would traditionally be brought to a Chinese house, a box of clementines, tied with a bow. But the wife of Han's boss had not known how to react, taking the box from Ling with a bemused smile. *Look at what a thoughtful gift Han's wife has brought us,* she called out to her husband. She then made some comment on how you could never get enough vitamin C.

Indeed, Ling had felt drab next to this woman, who wore a bright floral dress that suggested a hothouse gone awry. Ling wore a black silk dress she had ended up buying specially for the occasion, thinking that black was sophisticated even though it was a color she did not usually wear. Since she did not drink, she sipped from a glass of water while the other wives spoke over and around her. They were all white, taller than her, and seemed to already know one another, and, as if they did not think she could speak English, they did not bother to include her in their conversations. During dinner, she kept her words to a minimum, praising the massive roast, which to her was too salty. She and Han ended up leaving early, the first out of all the guests. *Thank you for the oranges,* the boss's wife had added when they left, reminding Ling again of her dreadful mistake.

She thought this was why Han was so quiet on the drive home. As each mile passed, she could feel something simmering just beneath the surface, and she steeled herself for the inevitable confrontation as soon as they pulled into the driveway. She only hoped that he would confine it to the car, so that their son couldn't hear. But after he turned off the engine, he just got out of the car and went inside. Ling sat in the car for around ten minutes, glad for the reprieve. She collected herself and decided the evening hadn't been so bad after all.

After waiting a good amount of time, she unbuckled her seat belt and went into the house. The air in the hallway felt disturbed, as if someone had just rushed through it. But the kitchen and living room were empty, the lights blazing. Upstairs, Michael wasn't in his room, and in their room, Han was getting ready to go to bed. *He went out,* was all he said to Ling's question about where their son had gone. Ling watched him for a moment. Something about the way he removed his shoes and lined them up inside the closet made her heart ache.

She waited downstairs in the kitchen for Michael to come home, watching the second hand of the clock make its slow, quiet revolution. Maybe he had gone to the Bradleys' next door, to see that girl who wore what looked like safety pins in her ears. Finally, Ling went to bed, allowing herself to drift into an exhausted, restless sleep only after she heard the back door shut and footsteps come up the stairs. The next morning, after Han had left for work, and she was sitting across from her son at the kitchen table as he ate his breakfast, she did not ask Michael where he had gone. She didn't want to know; for now she was simply glad that he was safe, that he hadn't gotten into a car accident, or run away, or any of the number of things that could happen to a teenager these days.

As the spring wore on, Ling detected a rift between Han and Michael. She supposed it was a consequence of Michael being a teenager. He started going next door to the Bradley girl's more often, or stayed late after school, so that they barely saw him. Ling wasn't surprised when he announced that all of the colleges he had applied to were out of state, as if he couldn't get away from his parents fast enough. After he went away to school in Massachusetts—it could have been worse, Ling thought, he could have gone to California, but he hadn't gotten into that one—he rarely came back, refusing to let his parents pay for his plane or train fare or saying that he was spending the holidays with a roommate's family. Then he moved to the city, and Ling had been overjoyed to have both her children so close to her again, but the proximity did not mean that either of them visited any more often. There was little more that she could do other than drop hints, since she was too proud to go to them herself. Besides, it was their responsibility. This was what you had children *for,* so that they could visit you in your old age.

After Han passed away, Ling wondered if Michael regretted not having spent more time with him. Did a son ever get over his father's death? She wished she knew how to provide the kind of comfort that she could when he was a child, over a scraped knee or a harsh word from his father. But somehow she had lost her way with him, and now he was on the other side of the world, in China.

*Qinghai Province.* What in the world could Michael be doing there? Ling thought of the two characters that made up the ideogram for *Qinghai:* the character *qing,* which meant "clear" or "green," and *hai,* which was the word for ocean. Supposedly, it came from the province's vast grasslands. Wasn't there a folk song about a girl from Qinghai? Or had she been from Mongolia? She wasn't sure. Anyway, some place with a lot of grass.

Then Ling remembered something else—the letter that had come for Han the month before his death. She could picture the pale blue flash of it, the address from Xining, Qinghai Province, before Han had turned away from her with it. The letter must have ended up in his papers, and Michael must have discovered it after the funeral, when he was looking through his father's things. If only Ling had asked Han about it earlier when he'd received it, had not been deterred by the shield that had come down over his face. She was beginning to think that had been a mistake. Perhaps she should have been nosier with her children as well. Maybe she should have asked more questions, probed more deeply into things that they didn't want to talk about, or else she wouldn't be learning about their lives after the fact, as if they were strangers.

When Emily's car pulled into the driveway, Ling gave the silver Bimmer a double take. "Did you get a new car?" she asked as Emily came up the front walk. She'd always wondered why Emily continued to drive the old Buick.

"No," Emily said. "It's Julian's."

She didn't bother to explain further, and Ling followed her daughter into the house, where she told Emily about the letter from Qinghai Province.

"Do you know what it said?" Emily asked.

"I never asked your father," Ling admitted.

"How did Dad come to know someone way out there?"

"I don't know. Your father was originally from Beijing, but a lot of people from the cities were sent west in the sixties and seventies."

"That was during the Cultural Revolution, right?"

"Yes, but your father wasn't one of them," Ling assured her. "His family was always safe."

"Then why don't we know anything about them?"

Ling considered for a moment. "Well, they had all passed away before he came to the States." But she hadn't asked about this either, hadn't doubted her husband's word that he knew no one back in China. Obviously, this letter proved him wrong.

"It still doesn't explain why Michael went there," Emily said.

"Maybe his roommate has heard from him by now?" Ling ventured.

"Who?"

"The roommate you told me about on the phone."

"Oh, right." Emily looked shamefaced. "I should check in with him."

It was almost dinnertime, but Ling had not thought about what they would eat. Emily told her to order some takeout—*Just not Chinese,* she'd said—while she called Michael's roommate. Ling overheard her asking the roommate if he had gone back to his own apartment, which was confusing. Was he a roommate only some of the time? She really didn't understand the way young people lived now.

They ended up getting sushi from a Japanese restaurant Ling had never been to before, but whose circular was often, annoyingly, stuck in her mailbox. She didn't trust raw fish, let alone anything Japanese, but after Emily had urged her to try the cooked, less-frightening items, she had to admit it wasn't so bad.

She waited for her daughter to bring up what had caused her to pay an unexpected visit home, but Emily didn't say a word. So Ling prattled on about how Michael could get by in China without knowing the language, whether he knew to only drink water after it had been boiled, if he was being scammed by unscrupulous tour guides. She preferred to think Michael was just on a trip to the motherland rather than for whatever reason he had truly gone.

Finally, at a break in their conversation, Emily asked, "Did you and Dad fight a lot when we were kids?"

"All couples fight," Ling said vaguely, and then, taking this opportunity to deflect the question, asked, "Don't you and Julian fight?"

"Sure," Emily replied easily.

"What do you fight about?" She kept her tone carefully neutral.

"Oh, nothing. How I'm working too hard, as usual."

"Are you working too hard?"

"Actually, I'm thinking of taking some time off."

"That's good," Ling said. "Maybe you and Julian can go away together. Beatrice Ma's son and daughter-in-law just went on a cruise to Mexico for a whole month."

"How come you and Dad never went on vacation?"

"We did go on vacation."

"That doesn't count."

Ling knew Emily meant the educational trips she and Michael had been taken on as children, to Williamsburg in Virginia and Cape Canaveral in Florida. The children had fought in the backseat of the car about who got to hold the map, who got to choose the radio station, who had the stinkier feet.

"How come you and Dad never went anywhere by yourself, even after Michael and I left home?" Emily asked.

"Your father didn't like to take time off work unless it was for a good reason." Ling smiled. "Kind of like you."

"I do not—" Emily stopped herself. "Maybe we *will* take a vacation," she said. "Maybe all of us can take a vacation *together*. How does that sound, Mom? Want to go on a cruise?"

"No." Ling shuddered. "I think I will get seasick." She tried again. "Did you tell Julian where you were going before you left?"

"I left him a message. What did you and Dad fight about?"

Ling sighed. "All sorts of things. Most of the time I wanted your father to say he was sorry. But he couldn't do that."

"Why not? That's the easiest thing in the world to do."

"Emily," Ling said abruptly. "Do you remember what happened with Mr. Albertson's cat?"

Emily had been around twelve and in her animal-saving phase. She'd just done a pro-and-con paper on euthanasia in animal shelters for her debate class (why would *youth in Asia* be a bad thing?

Ling had thought, mishearing), spotted a white cat padding across the street one day, and brought it back home. Ling had been at a loss as to what to do with it. Emily refused to call the animal shelter, saying that it would probably be put to sleep, so they had to keep it. Michael, who was six and had recently lost his goldfish, was excited at the prospect of a real pet.

"That cat," Emily said now, "had no collar."

It was what she had said when an irate Mr. Albertson had gone knocking on every door on the street, demanding if anyone had seen his cat, which was named Genevieve, after his dead wife. Ling remembered Mr. Albertson calling that name over the neighbors' backyards at night, but she had not known he had been referring to a cat. The sound had been so plaintive that she had just assumed he was mourning the loss of his wife. Mr. Albertson had called Emily a "disingenuous little monkey," and Ling had made her apologize.

"Okay," Emily amended. "Maybe I should have been more sincere when I apologized to Mr. Albertson. What happened to him, anyway?"

"He passed away over ten years ago. He was still very much in love with his wife. Now he can finally be with her."

Emily rolled her eyes, which Ling chose to overlook.

"I don't know what happened to the cat," Ling added.

"What does the cat have to do with anything?"

"What I mean, Emily, is that sometimes it is hard for you to say that you're sorry."

"I say I'm sorry all the time."

"Not to the people who need to hear it, when they need to hear it the most."

Emily opened her mouth to say something and then closed it. Ling had never been so blunt with her daughter before. She decided to back off and let Emily tell her about her and Julian's fight when she was ready.

After dinner, Emily suggested they watch television, but Ling couldn't concentrate on the late-night news, in which it seemed like death and destruction were around every corner. She looked sideways at her daughter. Emily seemed completely engrossed in the glowing screen, but Ling could see that the skin under her eyes was sallow, and her brows were drawn together, creating a hieroglyphic on her fore-head. In a couple of years those lines would be permanent. Emily was also anxiously fingering a small rent in the knee of her jeans—*pick, pick, pick.* Ling wanted to put her hand on her daughter's, to tell her that no matter what was going on at work or at home, it wasn't worth it. But she couldn't tell her. There was no space in their relationship for this kind of conversation, and Ling didn't know how to change that.

Emily got ready for bed, putting on an old shirt that barely covered the tops of her thighs. With her hair pulled back in a ponytail, her daughter looked like she was a teenager again. Then, as she had often done at that age, she disappeared into her bedroom without saying anything to her mother and closed the door firmly behind her.

Ling went about preparing the house for the night, putting the leftovers into Tupperware containers, taking out the garbage, securing the trash cans against raccoons. After she was done, she walked out onto the lawn, where she'd prayed so many years ago that she'd have a son. The grass tickled her legs, the blades rustling in the night breeze, almost sounding like the murmur of voices. She imagined Michael in Qinghai Province, standing in a similar field, the green stalks reaching up to his waist. Whatever he was looking for out there, she hoped he would find it.

# CHAPTER 6

When Michael wakes up, he senses that something is very wrong. It's not that he's in another country, as he'd gotten over that after his first couple of nights in China—was forced to, what with the constant onslaught of noise and lights and smells. As he swings his legs over the side of the bed and his feet touch the steady floor, he realizes what it is: He's no longer on a train. He looks out the window to see the early morning sun shining weakly through a layer of smog that is punctuated by various high-rises, many in the middle of being built. He opens the window a crack, and the sounds of construction and traffic waft upward, along with the ubiquitous smell of burning trash.

After taking a shower with the lowest water pressure ever—barely more than a trickle—Michael goes downstairs into the lobby. The same clerk from the day before is there, his suit only slightly wilted. Michael wonders if he's stayed there overnight, maybe slept somewhere in the back. The telephone calls from last night, from the woman offering a massage and who knows what else, come back to him. How did she know what room he was in? Could the clerk have had something to do with it? Michael can't tell from the young man's impassive face as he walks up to him. He wonders if the man's bland expression would change if Michael explained to him exactly why these calls from women were misdirected.

Instead, Michael asks the clerk if anyone has left a message. No, there has been no message. Yes, he will let Michael know if there is a call. Yes, if he leaves, he will inform the new clerk. In the meantime, can he call Michael a car, so that he can see the sights that this fine city has to offer?

Although he's already seen a few sights from the day before, Michael thinks this isn't a bad idea. He knows he can't stay in the hotel all day waiting for Liao Weishu to contact him. He figures the best way to distract himself is to see some more of the city. Maybe he'll go in the opposite direction than he went the day before, as if the farther he gets from his father's friend, the more likely it is the man will call him; a form of reverse psychology. The clerk suggests the Muslim market and, thinking that it sounds like an appropriately exotic and exciting destination, Michael sets off on foot.

He feels like he blends in the crowd a little better today. He's wearing long pants that partially obscure his tennis shoes, ditched the baseball cap and the backpack so that the only thing he's carrying is his wallet in his pocket. Cutting through the air is the acrid smoke from makeshift food stalls set up along the side of the road, sometimes no more than a couple of wooden benches and a table alongside a brazier. It's almost uniformly men sitting at these benches, shoveling the contents of the bowls into their mouths with disposable chopsticks. Some of them, with their mud-spattered shoes and pants, are obviously construction workers, while others, dressed in thin rayon suits, appear to be more business types. No matter their vocation, they're all consuming bowls of noodles in clear broth flecked with cilantro, or hot bowls of soy milk accompanied by fried dough sticks that Michael knows by reputation, if not experience. He remembers his mother describing these airy golden batons as part of her childhood breakfasts, where they took on the sheen of a fairy tale, as well as oil. But here they are, years and miles away from where his mother grew up in Taiwan. Maybe his father and Liao Weishu ate these things as children too, in Beijing. Just thinking about it makes Michael feel strangely homesick; not for his own home but for places he has never seen.

As tempting as all these dishes are, their savory steam curling in the air, Michael knows he has to resist. A single contaminated bite of food could send him to the closest restroom, if not the hospital. As he watches a vendor clean a bowl by swirling hot water in it and then overturning it on the ground, he thinks that hot water appears to be the panacea for everything here, not just to sterilize dishes. On the train, his seatmates took turns refilling the berth's silver thermos from a spigot at the end of the car. They used it to make meals out of their instant noodles, fill their jars of tea, dampen their facecloths in the only gesture toward cleanliness during days of traveling. This morning at the hotel, Michael almost tripped over a similar thermos that was placed outside of the door, along with a Chinese newspaper that, since he couldn't read it, he left where it was. Now he's beginning to understand his parents' almost fanatical attitude toward hot water, as well as their equally fervent distrust of water straight and cold from the tap; if water isn't boiled, it's deadly.

As he walks, and the morning stretches toward noon, Michael examines the faces of the people he passes, but they're even more alien to him than the people on the train. He encounters a few more of the Tibetan herdsmen he saw the day before, as well as apple-cheeked women wearing small white caps. He spies two old men, also wearing white caps, with round smoked glasses and grizzled beards, playing what appears to be a form of checkers on the sidewalk. Michael wonders if these are the thieving Uighur people that the hotel clerk mentioned the day before, although all they seem to be doing at the moment is stealing each other's checker pieces.

He realizes that he's in the Muslim market only when he sees the green dome of a mosque rising above the walls at the end of a lane. Otherwise, the market does not look very Muslim to him. The tables and blankets spread out on the ground are covered with pirated DVDs, cell phone cases, plastic toys—anything you could get in New York City's Chinatown, and probably originating from the same factories in China. Halfway down the street, the wares on display change from electronics and gadgets to produce and other food items. Every vendor seems to be selling a combination of the same things: perfectly round heads of cabbage; jewel-toned eggplants; brown eggs with feathers still stuck to them; blocks of bean curd in tubs of water, sleek and white as koi.

Michael encounters more snack foods, like hard, fried braids of dough and sticks of what look like miniature candied apples drenched in a crimson glaze. He lingers by a table covered with trays of thick, round, dark-pink slabs, trying to figure out what they are. The seller offers Michael a sample piece, and despite the alarm bells of contamination ringing in his head, he takes it. The man is smiling and nodding at him so hard that Michael feels compelled to take a small, polite bite, and discovers that it's tangy and crumbles like sugar. He knows this flavor; these slabs are like a larger version of the haw flakes he used to eat like candy as a child. The seller looks so expectant, his nodding so enthusiastic, that Michael has to buy a brown paper sack full of them. He continues to walk down to the end of the market and then back, nibbling on the huge haw flakes until he's almost dizzy with the sweetness. He feels like Gulliver, or Alice in Wonderland, suddenly made small while the world around him has grown enormous.

When he and Emily were children, their parents would take them into Chinatown for the afternoon. Rarely venturing above Canal Street, they'd eat lunch in one of the restaurants that were virtually interchangeable, with their pink tablecloths and laminated menus, and then they'd stock up on the foods they couldn't get from the local grocery store, like barbecued pork, long beans, and dried shrimp. Michael was agog at everything, the live fish flopping in buckets, the twisted roots in the herbal medicine store. But then, he was only seven while Emily was thirteen, itching to come into the city with her friends and not with her lame parents and little brother. If they were good, Emily and Michael were allowed a treat; small cylinders of haw flakes, wrapped in pink paper with green lettering. Separated into disks they looked like pennies, or communion wafers. Later, at church, Michael would wonder if religion tasted a little bit like Chinatown.

On the ride home in the car, Emily tried to teach Michael how to play poker with the haw flakes as chips, but he got frustrated and started throwing them at her, and then their father yelled at them to quit it. In the fading afternoon light, with his father at the wheel, his mother asleep, and Emily absorbed in a book, Michael would look out the car window and play a game in his head that was based partly on boredom and partly on the desire to scare the shit out of himself. He'd place a haw flake on his tongue and slowly start counting, and if the flake didn't disintegrate before he reached a hundred, the car would crash.

There was one occasion when Michael counted up to a terrifying one hundred and twenty. He closed his eyes and held his breath, expecting the car to swerve at any moment into the guardrail, to be flung into the back of the seat before him. He imagined the tearing of metal and glass, the crunch and shatter of bone, the spray of blood like in the horror movies he wasn't allowed to watch. Nothing happened. Then he looked up to see the flash of his father's face in the rearview mirror, grainy but no different than it always was. Something about that steadfastness of his father's expression, its immovability, reassured him. Michael swallowed the sweet, sticky film in his mouth. Of course the car wouldn't crash; his father wouldn't let it.

It was, Michael remembers, as the sweet aftertaste lingers on his tongue, maybe one of the last times he had such conviction in his father's ability to keep him safe, to make everything right.

When he exits the Muslim market and turns onto a quieter side street, Michael feels strangely depleted. He's finished his snack and the blood sugar it provided. It's late afternoon now, and he considers taking one of the cream-colored, red-trimmed buses back to the hotel. But he doesn't know how much a ticket costs, and it appears to be rush hour, with crowds of people pushing and shoving at each stop. So instead he decides to fortify himself for the walk back with a soda. He pays the vendor and has just started to unscrew the cap when he feels a hand quickly dart in the pocket into which he has placed his wallet. He turns around to see a figure darting down the street ahead of him. Without thinking, Michael sprints after him. With an extra burst of speed, he reaches out and grabs the back of the thief's shirt and spins him around.

It is a teenage boy, red-cheeked and panting. Michael is both taller and stronger than him. He grasps the boy by his collar and shakes him, hard.

"Give me my wallet, you fucker!"

A confused look crosses the boy's face. Michael shakes him again, shouts more obscenities. The fact that the boy doesn't understand what he is saying makes him even angrier. Spit flies into the boy's eye, and he blinks it away. Now he is limp in Michael's grip, his shoulders sagging, his head lowered.

A crowd from a nearby bus stop has started to gather around them, including an older man who the boy looks toward. The man nods once, and the boy sheepishly hands the wallet back to Michael. Then the bus arrives, dispelling everyone's curiosity, and the two disappear into the throng of people that board it.

Still breathing hard, Michael checks his wallet with trembling fingers. A hundred kuai bill is missing. Somehow, between the time Michael caught him and got back his wallet, the boy managed to steal the note, which is worth fewer than twenty dollars. Everything else, though, is intact. Also, amazingly enough, Michael is still holding the soda, which is now warm. He throws it away.

Slowly, he starts on the endless walk back to the hotel. His nerves are still jangling with uncertainty and fear—fear over the theft, but also at the way he had acted. It was clear the pickpocket was young and much weaker than him. But Michael could have punched him, he had been that angry. He thinks about the man who the boy looked at for direction afterward. Were they some kind of father-and-son pickpocketing team? What kind of father would let his child steal? *Someone who has no choice.*

For the first time he feels the alienness of the city around him, the possible danger. The street kid yesterday who grabbed his ice cream momentarily rattled him, but now he's shaken. Suddenly, everyone looks untrustworthy. He wonders how many times he's been swindled since he's arrived, whether the student who offered to pass on his message to Liao Weishu the day before really will do so. She could just be another in a long line of locals out to make a fool of the American who looks like them, but otherwise could have come from a different planet. The afternoon has left a bad taste in his mouth, and he doesn't know how much longer he wants to stay in this city.

Furthermore, even if Liao gets in touch with him, how naïve is Michael to think that he has anything meaningful to say about his friendship with Michael's father? Michael is expecting Liao to shed some light on his father's life, to provide an explanation for what his father said to him one night when he was a teenager, which has forever divided the way Michael felt about him into a Before and an After. But Michael is beginning to think that everything he's done since he opened Liao's letter—buying a plane ticket on credit he can't repay, running off to a country whose language he doesn't speak, and walking around with his wallet practically in plain sight—has been a big mistake.

Tired, hungry, unsure of himself, Michael then encounters the most miraculous sight he has seen thus far on his trip: a fast-food restaurant.

Huge plate-glass windows frame an interior bright with fluorescent lights and molded plastic tables and chairs. Clusters of red and white balloons flank the doorway, along with two girls in striped uniforms and caps. The sole purpose of the girls appears to be to open the door and welcome people. *"Huanying guanglin!"* they chorus, and Michael finds himself drawn through the entrance as if hypnotized by their cheeriness. Inside, more uniformed girls are standing around aimlessly, save for one girl who sits in a corner, blowing up balloons while her boyfriend in a People's Liberation Army uniform holds them for her.

The menu, a colorful board of meal combinations, needs no translation. A hamburger costs twenty kuai, and Michael suspects that you could get about five bowls of noodles for that and be more full, but he orders one. He can't remember the last time he ate a hamburger—probably not since living in the city or in college, where it was considered seriously uncool—so it must have been when he was a teenager. When his burger comes, he notices that it contains shredded cabbage instead of lettuce. The French fries appear normal, although when he looks around he notices that people are dipping them not into ketchup squeezed out onto their placemats but one by one into the ketchup packet itself.

As he bites into his hamburger, ignoring the odd crunch of shredded cabbage, the familiar combination of bread and gristle and grease is comforting. So is the general atmosphere of the place, although it's a little like looking through a fun-house mirror. Most of the customers appear to be couples or families with single children and, unlike what might be expected back home, they appear to be solidly middle class. Then Michael notices he's the only person who's eating by himself. Everyone else has someone with whom they are sharing their meal, and that, he realizes, is what marks him as a foreigner and an outsider, not the way he's dressed or the way he's eating his fries.

He watches a mother encourage the wobbling steps of a toddler, who has a French fry clasped in each chubby hand, as the father records the occasion on camera. Strange this Chinese child is growing up with fast food so readily available. It wasn't until he was a teenager and had wheels of his own that Michael was able to eat fast food like all the other kids. His parents did not believe in eating out; his father said it was a waste of money and his mother said it was unhealthy, although now he wonders if it was really an unconscious act of cultural preservation rather than stinginess or a fear of the unknown. Whatever it was, he feels a little grateful now that he didn't grow up stuffing his face with fries like this kid.

Farther down from the family sit a boy and girl whose affected slouches in front of their fast food make them look like any young couple in the world. Something about their body language makes Michael think that maybe they aren't together, but friends in the way he and Amy Bradley were in high school. He wonders what Amy would think if she knew he was in China. Out of all the places they talked about escaping to when they were teenagers, they never considered going this far.

When he turned sixteen in the spring of his junior year and had gotten his permit, Michael was allowed to drive his mother's old car, which Emily had left behind when she'd gone to college. Compared to his better-off classmates' vehicles, the ancient Buick was so unhip that it might possibly come full circle and be hip; Michael wasn't sure. But in any case, it allowed him and Amy to go off campus for lunch, where they'd pick up greasy sacks of burgers and fries at the drive-thru and then park in the farthest corner of a strip mall's empty lot.

Their main topic of conversation was how to escape their hometown. It wasn't enough that the city was about an hour away, that sometimes they would go in for an afternoon to browse thrift stores for clothes that Amy could cut up for her designs. They both had strict curfews, and Michael's parents wouldn't let him drive that far, so they were bound by the train schedules. Also, Emily lived in the city, and even though he and his sister didn't talk much, just the fact that she was there made the place less exciting for Michael. So, as he plotted with Amy about which far-flung colleges to apply to, he pictured a green-lawned campus in California where he would have intellectual conversations while throwing a Frisbee and smoking pot, simultaneously. Funny that he ended up going to a small college in the middle of Massachusetts, and Amy to Boston, and although they promised to visit, they only saw each other during the holidays when they were back home.

Although outwardly it seemed like their relationship was the same, Michael sensed that things had changed ever since that night Amy had kissed him. They remained a duo at school, but he could see that his rejection continued to smart. Not that he didn't think she suspected he was gay. But he knew that she wanted him to tell her himself, that this was the only way he could make up for what he had done to her, and he wasn't sure he was ready to do that yet.

Amy did her best to try to extract a confession from him, usually by baiting him with Peter Lawrence, on whom Michael still had an unrequited crush. By this time, Peter no longer sat in front of him in math class, but as one of the school's preeminent jocks, he was everywhere: the center of pep rallies, the star of basketball games and swim meets. Michael would drag Amy with him to the sporting events, especially the swim meets—*Why the sudden interest in swimming?* Amy would ask with a sly smile. But she went along with him. Sitting in the stands, angling his head to catch a glimpse of Peter's smooth body breaking the surface of the water in the 200-meter butterfly, Michael was reminded of the time he had watched Amy's brother, Scott, swim in the pool next door and twisted his ankle.

One day when they were sitting in the car at lunch, Amy tossed a copy of the school newspaper into his lap. On the front page was a picture of Peter Lawrence with his arms raised high, exposing the perfect triangle of his torso, from the wide straight line of his shoulders to the point of his tight swim trunks.

"So?" Michael said, reading the headline. "The swim team won the regional meet."

"I heard he has a girlfriend now," Amy said.

Despite himself, Michael asked, "Who?"

"Lindsey Jensen."

Michael made a face.

"God, I know. It's disgusting."

Lindsey Jensen was not a peppy blond cheerleader, as might be expected, but a pretty Asian girl who had been adopted by white parents and was the head of the student council. Somehow, that made it even worse.

Michael looked up to see Amy grinning at him. "What? I don't care who he dates."

"Like hell you don't." Amy threw a French fry at him but missed, and it got lodged somewhere in the backseat.

When he got home that night, Michael tore out the picture. He wasn't quite sure what he was going to do with it, since he could hardly pin it up on his wall, so he put it under his mattress. It was, he thought, possibly the most contraband thing in the house.

Then one night his parents had done something they'd never done before, at least in Michael's memory: They'd gotten dressed up to go to a dinner hosted by his father's boss. There was something pathetic about the way they had prepared for this event, the care with which his father had ironed his navy-blue suit jacket, how his mother had tied a sad little bow onto a box of oranges. After they'd left, Michael finished his homework, and then with the rest of the evening stretching before him, called Amy.

"I'm painting my nails red," Amy informed him.

"Red?" Michael was puzzled, as Amy usually painted her nails the darkest color she could find.

"Yeah. Everyone expects me to have black fingernails so I'm doing the opposite."

Michael wondered who "everyone" was, besides himself, but he didn't comment further.

"You want to come over?" Amy asked. "I can make some popcorn. We can watch some stupid movie on TV."

"I thought your parents didn't let you watch movies on a school night."

"Okay, some stupid PBS special, then, on humpback whales or some other stupid endangered species."

Michael declined, so they talked about their trigonometry homework, which neither of them understood; and the horrible outfit that poor Courtney Snell had been wearing that day (a long-sleeved blouse paired with a very short skirt, so that she looked like an Amish hooker); and then they said good night.

Bored, Michael took out the picture of Peter Lawrence and began to masturbate to it. He had masturbated to magazines before but never the picture of someone he knew, which made it doubly exciting. After a while, the thrill started to wear off, and his room began to feel stuffy and closed in, so he decided to go downstairs. The best position was to put the picture on the coffee table while he stood in front of it. From the back it almost looked like he was watching television, except that the screen was blank.

This was how his father found him.

Michael had been concentrating so much that he hadn't heard the car pull into the driveway or the back door open. He was at the point where he was trying to orgasm, a white fog filling his head. It cleared when he heard his father enter the room, and then it was too late to hide the picture on the table or the fact that his pants were down. What his father said next, Michael would never forget.

*You are my punishment. You are what I deserve.*

What scared Michael most of all, even more than the words, was the look on his father's face, as if he'd seen a ghost, as if the very life were being sucked out of him. It was as if his father couldn't bear to look at him.

Michael yanked up his pants, turned, and ran down the hall, out the front door. Fueled by adrenaline, he climbed up the gutter of the neighboring house and knocked on Amy's window. She let him in and held him as he told her what had happened, and she didn't let go. He couldn't tell her the exact words his father had said—they were still too painful—but what he could get out was enough.

"How typical," Amy spat out.

He was surprised, touched even, that she was crying.

"Your father's a monster," she said.

"He isn't."

"Are you *defending* him?" She stared at him, her face shining with outrage and tears, reflecting everything that he should be feeling but couldn't. The only thing he could feel was guilt, that it was his fault for what had happened that night, for having the picture, for going downstairs, for even cutting it out of the paper in the first place. Although Amy had given him the paper, so maybe it was her fault too.

"No, but there has to be an explanation."

"Yeah, that he's a terrible person."

Later, Michael would remember this conversation and wish it were that simple, that his father was just that kind of person who would react in that way to his son's being gay. But, much later, when he took the time to recall what his father had said, it seemed to him that it was almost as if his father meant the words as much for himself as for Michael. It didn't lessen the hurt any, but it did offer a sliver of hope, that maybe what happened *wasn't* Michael's fault, that someday he might be able to ask his father what he meant and receive an answer that would absolve him of everything he had done wrong in his life. Of course, he thought he had years ahead of him to ask that question.

Amy was the one who convinced Michael that he had to go home that night, so that his mother wouldn't worry about him. *She has nothing to do with it,* Amy said, and Michael agreed, although he didn't think his mother had guessed the truth about him, or that his father would tell her. He never thought about asking his mother for help. As far as he could see, his mother backed up his father on all family matters; he wasn't even sure she had her own opinions on anything, except for going to church, maybe. He had never heard them fight before, not unlike Amy's parents, who, according to

Amy, quarreled at least once a week about her father's drinking, the way their daughter dressed, how poorly their son was doing in college. Michael didn't know whether this was a good sign or not about his parents' marriage; you just didn't think about that with parents like his.

But he did think it was unnecessary to make his mother worry about where he had been, even if his father obviously wouldn't care. So, in the middle of the night, he snuck back into his own house. He glanced briefly into the living room. The picture was gone from the coffee table; it had probably been torn up and thrown out. There was no indication of the words that had been spoken there a few hours earlier.

When Michael went downstairs the next morning, his mother was the only one in the kitchen. She looked worse than he did, as if she hadn't slept all night. But since she didn't ask where he had been, he figured she knew where he had gone.

"Where's Dad?" he asked.

"He went to work early."

"Did he say anything to you?"

"What kind of thing?"

Michael hesitated. For a second, he honestly considered telling his mother. Sure, he couldn't trust that she wouldn't react in the way his father had or that she would understand, and even if she did, there wasn't anything she could do to change his father's mind. But he needed someone other than Amy to know, someone in his family.

"About last night," he finally said.

"Oh, yes," his mother replied. For a moment his breath caught, only to be expelled when she continued, "He told me you had gone out." Then she turned to the sink and started to wash the dishes, destroying his resolve.

In the following days, Michael didn't see much of his father, and the next time they were together, at the dinner table, neither of them alluded to what had taken place. Michael almost wondered if he'd imagined what had happened, if he'd dreamed up that night. But if his father wasn't going to bring it up, then he wouldn't. He wondered if that was his father's way of apologizing, to pretend nothing had happened. Or perhaps that was generous thinking, and the truth was that his father preferred that that night had not occurred at all. Whatever it was, Michael was fine with letting things be. From that moment on he did his best to avoid his father, who felt that having the kind of son he had was his punishment in life.

Michael is dreaming that he's chasing after the teenage pickpocket at the bus stop. But instead of yelling and shaking the boy when he catches him, he pours the bottle of soda over his head. It streams down the boy's face, soaking his clothes, pooling at his feet. It's the most humiliating thing Michael can think of doing to him.

The telephone's ringing jerks him awake. He glances at the bedside clock and sees that it is almost midnight. It rings again and, mindful of who was on the other end the night before, he answers cautiously, *"Wei?"*

"Hello?" returns a voice in English that is tinged, weirdly enough, with a British accent. "Is this Michael?"

"Yes, this is he. I mean, that's me." Michael feels like he's the one speaking a foreign language.

"This is Liao Weishu. My former student said that you are looking for me?"

Michael doesn't know what to say. It's as if at the moment his wish has been granted, all thoughts have gone out of his head. He grasps at his manners. "Thank you for calling me back. You . . . you were a friend of my father's?"

"Is your father here with you?"

"No, he's . . . he's passed away."

There is such a long pause that Michael wonders if he has been understood.

"When did he pass away?" For the first time, Michael hears a hitch in Liao's flawless English; he can't tell whether it's a reaction to an unfamiliar phrase or something more.

"Last August."

"I am sorry to hear that. The rest of your family is here with you?"

"My sister and mother aren't here; I came alone. Because of your letter." Michael cringes at this last part, thinking how strange that must sound.

"Ah, that is how you know where I live."

"Yes." Michael gladly latches on to that explanation. He doesn't feel comfortable getting into the details of the letter over the phone, not when he hasn't met Liao in person yet.

"And you came all the way here, to Xining City?"

"Well, I wanted to visit China. . . . I didn't know where else to go."

"It is true that this city does not have as much to offer as Beijing or Shanghai or even Xi'an, but it is a good place to visit." Liao continues briskly, "Now that you are here, you must be my guest. I invite you to come over tomorrow and have dinner with my family."

This is more than Michael could have hoped for. "I'd really like that, thank you."

"But first, since you have come from so far away, my son and I will take you sightseeing. There is much to see here."

Michael thinks he has already seen most of what the city has to offer over the past two days, but he agrees and arranges with Liao to meet in the lobby of the hotel the following morning. Then he hangs up, alternately ecstatic that Liao has called him and also a little disappointed at their businesslike exchange. He supposes there will be time to get to know each other tomorrow.

Before he goes back to bed, Michael takes the two pages of Liao's letter and its translation from an inner pocket of his backpack and spreads them out before him. He rereads the translation, even though now he feels like he knows what it says by heart.

> *My dear friend Han,*
> *I am sure that you are surprised to hear from me. After all, it's been forty-five years since we were Red Guards together in Beijing. As you can imagine, not all of those years have treated me well, especially the first fifteen. But once I was released from the labor camp, after it had been determined that I had been sufficiently reeducated, I was allowed to stay on in Xining and*

*become what I always wanted to be, a professor. I taught English at the normal university here. My learning English did have some use after all.*

*So, as you can see, my life has turned out quite well. I am married and have a son, and a grandson. I hope the same has been true for you. I want you to know that I bear no ill will toward you. Everything has been forgiven. These are new times, and in order for a new China to flourish, we must forgive and forget.*

*Your old friend,*
*Liao Weishu*

# CHAPTER 7

Like she had the day before, Emily woke with the vestiges of a dream in her head, but this time she remembered it. Before she had gone to sleep last night, she had planned out a whole new life for herself. She'd take her savings and rent an apartment in the city and do all the things she hadn't done when she was in her twenties—go to galleries and museums, bars and nightclubs—because first she had been studying for law school, and then she had been too busy with work, and then she had moved away. That this new life might mean she would quit her marriage as well, she hadn't really thought about.

But she hadn't dreamed about this new exciting life. Instead, she dreamed she had been with her client, Gao Hu, who was now dead. In her dream, she had taken his wife's place, and she and Gao had been walking down the beach with Sam, their eight-year-old son. They were holding hands with Sam in between, their shadows spreading before them over the golden sand, the setting sun casting an ethereal glow over the water. It was, Emily reflected later, probably based on some commercial she had seen on television the night before, showing what your life would be like if you took a certain antidepressant.

At one point, Gao let go of their hands and walked into the sun-lit water as easily as if he were walking into a field of wheat. On the shore, Emily and Sam waved at him until the blinding reflection prevented them from seeing him anymore. The impression Emily had been left with was not one of sadness; rather, it felt like they were bidding him good-bye at the train station. Then she felt like she were both the wife and the son at once, and that underneath the calm of the adult, there was the slight tingling panic of the child, that she might never see her father again.

Lying in her childhood bed, Emily remembered a real instance when she had been waving good-bye to a parent, but it was to her mother, not her father. It had been the summer she was seven years old, and she had been standing in the driveway of the Bradleys' house next door. Her mother had left her and Michael, who was just an infant, with Mrs. Bradley as she went off to run some er-rand. Emily could recall seeing the maroon Buick turn the corner, her mother's hand extending from the window in a final wave, and then she was gone. Mrs. Bradley had returned to the house with the babies, Amy and Michael, but Emily remained outside.

Then Scott Bradley, whom Emily didn't like very much, came up to her. Scott was in her class at school and liked stealing things out of his classmates' lunches. Plus, whenever she saw him, his upper lip was gleaming with snot. He had sandy hair and a freckled face, which he scrunched up when he was asked a question in class, as if it were a great effort to think. Their third-grade teacher, Mrs. Mayer, spent a lot of time telling Scott to sit down, stop fidgeting, and keep his hands to himself. Nowadays, Emily realized, he would have been diagnosed with attention-deficit disorder.

In direct contrast, Emily was at the head of her class in every possible category: grades, attendance, poise, playing well with oth-ers. She sat up straight in her seat, her hands clasped together on top of her desk. Often she knew the answer to a question before the teacher asked it, and then she would sit on her hands to not raise one of them, so as to not look like a show-off. Every day her mother sent her to school in dresses, combed her long hair straight down her back, held her bangs away from her eyes with a bobby pin.

This was before Emily needed glasses, although already she was beginning to squint. She requested to sit up front, not because she was a goody-goody, as her classmates thought, but because she couldn't see the blackboard and didn't want to admit it to anyone. She was afraid that if she were made to wear glasses, she'd look like Janice Chang, her poor bug-eyed classmate who everyone made fun of. Besides, how would boys like her if she wore glasses? More than anything, she wanted Jonah Mason, who was Scott Bradley's best friend, to think she was pretty. She was even wondering, as she stood in the Bradleys' driveway that one morning, whether Jonah would be coming over that day to play with Scott.

"I have a present for you," Scott said. One of his hands was clenched in a fist, which he used to wipe his nose.

"What is it?" Emily asked.

"Hold out your hand and close your eyes."

Coming from a seven-year-old boy, this could only mean trouble, but Emily did as she was instructed. She felt something drop feather-light onto her palm. When she opened her eyes, she saw that he had given her a butterfly. It was the most beautiful thing she had ever seen, with wings of an iridescent blue and purple and green, outstretched like a miniature kite.

"See, it's pretty, just like you," Scott said, almost shyly.

"Thank you," Emily replied. When she looked at Scott, a little bit of the feeling she had for his friend Jonah crept up on her, and she almost liked him.

"Touch it," Scott said.

Emily thought she had read somewhere that butterflies were covered with tiny scales, and if you touched a butterfly, you could brush off these scales and hurt it. But this butterfly's wings looked so soft and shimmery that she couldn't resist. She touched the butterfly, but it didn't do anything. It just lay still in her palm.

"It's dead," she said in wonderment.

"You killed it! You killed it!" Scott shrieked, dancing around her spastically.

"I did not!" Emily cried, finally understanding that she had been tricked. Then she burst into tears. Although she knew Scott must have found the dead butterfly somewhere, she felt as if she were responsible for the death of this lovely, innocent creature.

"What are you two doing?" Mrs. Bradley had come out, having heard Scott's triumphant yelps.

"Nothing," Emily said. She quickly shook her hand, and the butterfly fell onto the ground, disappearing into the grass like a jewel.

"Well, come inside now, both of you," Mrs. Bradley said, putting a hand on Emily's back and guiding her toward the house. She extended her other hand toward her son, who continued to dance just out of reach.

That day just got worse and worse, especially in contrast to the day before, when Emily had spent the afternoon playing with her friend Josephine Crawford. Josie still played with dolls, which Emily considered babyish, but they were such interesting dolls, with historically accurate accessories, including a butter churn that really worked, for the pioneer doll, and hand-painted dishes, for the Victorian doll. Additionally, Mrs. Crawford had served them cucumber sandwiches and scones for lunch. English tea, she called it.

But today, Emily had to eat peanut-butter-and-jelly sandwiches that Mrs. Bradley had slapped together, with generic peanut butter and the kind of white bread that felt like a wad of gauze in her mouth. Emily was unusually clumsy and spilled her glass of milk, and Scott pointed and laughed at her. Later, instead of Jonah coming over to play, Scott went to Jonah's, but at least that gave Emily a respite. She had not brought a book to read, so instead she watched Michael and Amy toddle around on the living room floor while Mrs. Bradley did the laundry. She was amazed at how easily Michael and Amy played together, sharing toys and making friendly, inquisitive noises at each other, like dolphins. They even fell asleep at roughly the same time in Amy's playpen.

It was late afternoon by now, and Emily stood in the front window, waiting for the familiar car to drive up, but it never did. As the shadows of the trees lengthened across the street, she began to suck on her thumb, something she hadn't done since she was three.

"It won't be long now," Mrs. Bradley told her.

Emily tried desperately to remember what her mother looked like that morning, but all she could recall was the disembodied hand fluttering from the car window, as if it had belonged to a stranger. Lights flickered on up and down the street, casting unnaturally long shadows in the front yard. Emily heard a door close and guessed that Mr. Bradley must have come home. She tiptoed into the hall just beyond the kitchen door and overheard snippets of Mrs. Bradley talking to her husband. *She left at nine this morning. . . . She said it would only be a few hours. . . . No one's home next door. . . . She didn't leave a number. . . .*

Mr. Bradley looked up and spotted Emily behind the door. He asked her to come into the kitchen, but Emily refused. She did not trust him, his bulbous red nose, the way he held his hand out to her. Mrs. Bradley was beginning to dish up supper, the smell of it suggesting that it wouldn't be much more appetizing than lunch. She invited Emily to join them at the table, but Emily refused. After a while she went to sit on the sofa, although in a position that still gave her a good view of the street. She sat in the dark, as no one had bothered to turn on a light, and listened to the Bradleys having dinner. She hoped that she would hear further discussion of her mother, but Mrs. Bradley only told Scott to wipe his hands on his napkin instead of his shirt. With the warm, lit room behind her, Emily felt like the Bradleys' kitchen was the real world while she herself was stuck somewhere else.

She must have fallen asleep, because she woke to lamplight and her father standing over her. He apologized to the Bradleys, saying that his wife had been held up and asked him to go get the children, but the traffic had been bad, and so he had been late. Emily listened to her father's accented English and realized that everything he said was a lie. Her father did not know where her mother was either.

At home, her father deposited Michael in his high chair and asked Emily to set the table. She could tell that he was trying to be positive. He opened a couple of cans of soup for their dinner, which

Emily knew her mother would disapprove of because there were no fresh vegetables involved, but she didn't have the heart to tell him.

"This is really good soup, Dad," she said, and he gave her a tired smile.

Emily wondered if it was going to be like this from now on, just the three of them, eating out of cans for the rest of their lives. She'd probably have to quit going to school to take care of her little brother, since her father had to work. This thought terrified her. She didn't know what to do with a baby. Besides, Michael was sickly, often going to the doctor and even once by ambulance to the hospital, just last month, because he had stopped breathing during a particularly serious bout of colic.

Emily had been woken that particular night by the sound of sirens and a flashing light coming through her window. She ran downstairs to see that her mother and brother had left in the ambulance. Her father told her to put on a jacket over her nightgown and get into the car; they were going to drive to the hospital. Her feet were cold as she sat in the waiting room, since she only wore slippers. As if to make up for forgetting her shoes, her father bought her a cup of chalky hot chocolate that came from a vending machine. She sipped it cautiously, feeling grateful but guilty for taking comfort in its sweetness and warmth when something very serious was happening to her little brother.

Her father sat on the cracked vinyl seat next to her. She could tell that he wanted to get up and go into the other room, but she was too young to be left alone. She wanted to tell him that it was okay, she would be fine if he did. Even if something did happen to her brother, she would still be there.

Finally, she asked in a small voice, "Is Michael going to be okay?"

Her father replied, "Yes, your *didi* is going to get better. The doctors know what to do. No need to worry."

Emily could tell that last bit was for his benefit as much as hers. As soon as he had been born, her parents had told her Michael was her *didi*, her younger brother; and she was his *jiejie*, his older sister. This was the relationship between them, and it would never change.

"Dad," she asked, slipping her free hand into his, "did you have a brother?"

"I had two sisters and one brother," he replied. "All much older than me. I also had a friend who was like a brother to me."

"Where is he?"

"Very far away, in China. This is what happens when you grow up, you don't see your brothers and sisters anymore. That's why you and Michael have to take care of each other, while you can."

Emily didn't see how Michael could help her, but she thought she was a good *jiejie* to him. She played with him and carried him around; the neighbors, looking up from their porches, smiled when she pushed him down the street in his stroller, like a doll. Okay, sometimes when he cried she felt like smacking him, but he never stayed upset for long.

You wouldn't have known that Michael had almost died a month ago by looking at him now, in the Tangs' kitchen. He sat in his high chair, banging his spoon happily against the tray. Emily reached over and wiped some drool from his chin with her finger. He was a pain, grabbing her hair, screaming when she had barely touched him, but he was *her* pain. She decided she was ready to look after him for the rest of her life, if need be.

Just then a car pulled into the driveway. Emily jumped up from her chair, but her father was faster, opening the back door before her mother could even put her key in the lock. Emily expected her father to demand, for all of them, where she had been, but instead he just embraced her. Emily stared; she had never seen any display of physical affection between her parents before. As for herself, she was so overcome with relief that she could hardly stand. Her mother picked up Michael from his high chair and held him, stroked Emily's hair with her other hand. She did not say anything about the empty soup cans in the sink. Emily did not remember her mother leaving her family alone for such a long time again.

A soft knock came at her bedroom door.

"Come in," Emily said, and when nothing happened, practically shouted, "It's okay, Mom, you can come in."

The door opened a crack. "Emily, look who's here."

Her mother threw open the door with a flourish, as if she were a magician, to reveal Julian standing behind her. Despite herself, Emily's heart hiccupped in her chest at the sight of her husband. Every detail of his appearance struck her as both familiar and new, as if he were someone she had known from another life. Then gradually the facts took over: the blue shirt he usually wore when he worked in the garden, the ink stain that came from his habit of carrying uncapped pens in his pants pocket, the stubble on his unshaven cheeks that would be rough, like a cat's tongue. The only thing she didn't recognize about him, had no understanding of its history or emotions, was the drained look on his face. She could only guess at what lay behind it.

Apparently, concerned that neither her daughter nor son-in-law had said anything to each other yet, her mother asked Julian, "Did Emily tell you about Michael?"

"That he's gay?"

Emily gave him a look.

"Oh, shit," he said, realizing too late that her mother didn't know. "I'm sorry."

Emily supposed there was no way that Michael's revelation, if he had been waiting for the right time to tell it to his family, was going to go as planned, since she'd already pried the truth out of David. "Mom," she said. "We'll talk about Michael later."

"Okay," her mother said, although the expression on her face suggested the opposite was true. "I will leave you two alone."

When she had left the room, Julian asked, "So what did your mom mean when she asked if I knew about Michael?"

"We figured out that he's in China."

"What's he doing there?"

Emily shrugged. "Finding someone else? Finding himself? Why do you do something like that, anyway?"

"Seems to me like he could have told someone, so that people he cared about wouldn't worry about him."

Emily suspected that Julian wasn't just talking about her

brother. She slid up against the headboard to make room for him at the foot of the bed. Her bedroom was the place she felt most secure in this house, where she still felt the remnants of who she had been. She thought she might find comfort in that, but instead she just felt very small, as if she were that seven-year-old girl whose mother had briefly disappeared.

"How did you sleep last night?" Julian asked.

"Awful. I had this dream in which I lost my husband. You weren't the husband in the dream," Emily was quick to clarify, but he looked even more confused. "It was just one of those dreams," she said. "How was your night?"

"What do you think? After you left that message about kissing Rick?"

"It was an accident. We'd both been drinking." Emily pressed her lips together after that, knowing it wasn't an excuse.

"How did you think that made me feel?"

"I'm sorry," she whispered. "I'm sorry that you want children and I don't."

Julian scrubbed a hand over his face. "I had a long time to think about it last night, and I decided that you don't need to explain why you don't want to have kids. That's just the way you feel, the same as I feel the way I do, and there doesn't need to be any reason for it."

Emily said slowly, "I understand if you want to leave me."

"Looks to me like you're the one who's doing the leaving."

"I wasn't thinking straight last night." She gave a rueful laugh. "I had this whole new life planned for myself in the city, where I'd go out every night and have the kind of exciting time that everyone thinks they will have when they move to New York. But I realized that I didn't want that either." She inhaled a shaky breath. "Julian, I'm really scared."

"Me too. This Rick guy. What's going on with him?"

"Nothing. Nothing happened, and nothing ever will. I probably won't be seeing him at all from now on since I'm quitting my job." Although the idea had been percolating in her head since she'd learned of Gao's death and told Rick she was off the case, this was the first time she had articulated it. But once she'd said it, she felt her shoulders loosen, her jaw unclench, in something like relief.

"You love your job."

"Not anymore."

"What about that case you've been working on?"

"The client died after the detention center refused to give him medical care. I just found out yesterday."

"Em, I'm so sorry." Julian tried to make a move toward her, but she couldn't help recoiling, and he stayed where he was. "But you can't quit. Your clients need you."

"No, they don't. They can find anyone who'll be willing to walk them through visa applications, if they have the money."

"Then what about you, what the job means to you?"

"I don't like the way it's been affecting our marriage or who I've become. I need some time to figure out what it is that I want." She hesitated. "So do you."

"I know what I want. It's you—us."

"It's not that simple. Maybe for you the answer is having children, becoming a parent. And if that's your answer, you deserve someone who's willing to give you that."

"Emily," he said. "What are you trying to say?"

"I think," she said, "that we need to spend some time apart."

"You mean more than we have been lately?"

She tried to ignore his implication. "Yes. I think that I need to move out. At least for now."

He sighed. "I knew it. You never liked that house."

"It isn't about the house." She forced herself to steady her voice. "It's never been about the house. It's how I never feel like I belong there. I mean"—she paused and then tried to laugh—"even the chairs fit the living room more than I do. I never feel like I can be myself there."

"You never tried. You aren't there half the time."

"And you're there all of the time," she couldn't help pointing out.

"Fine, you don't like the house. We'll find somewhere else to live. We can move back to the city if you want. . . ." He trailed off when he saw the look on her face and swallowed. "Okay, I get it. You need some space."

"My own space."

"But where?"

"I haven't thought about it. I can't stay here." The moment she said it, Emily knew it to be true. The day before she had turned to her childhood home, when she felt she had nowhere else to go, but in the light of morning she understood it was only a temporary solution.

"Emily, will you reconsider this? Can we talk—"

"We *are* talking." Emily looked down, picking at the comforter. "I don't know what else there is to say."

"Okay," Julian said. "We want different things. But most people find a way to work it out."

She shook her head. "I don't think we can. We don't know how. Maybe it's been too easy for us. We've never had to struggle for anything together, against anything, except our parents' expectations, maybe. And that's not enough to keep two people together."

"You may have given up, but you don't get to make that decision. This isn't a case you get to close."

She looked up. "What do you mean?"

"It's like you're treating our marriage like one of your cases. You've gathered all your evidence and you've made your argument, and you won't listen to anything the other side says. You've never listened to what I've had to say. But you know what? In real life, that's a pretty selfish way to behave and a pretty shitty way to treat someone."

She bowed her head, knowing that a lot of what he said was true. "I'm sorry," she said, and she meant it. She reached for him and pressed her face against his neck. Its scent reminded her of the last thirteen years of her life.

Automatically, his hands moved, warm, underneath her shirt, and she let him pull the shirt over her head, stroke her until her body rose to meet his. The places he touched her were all places that she had once, as a teenager in this very room, wondered if she would ever feel comfortable enough to show another person. They rocked back and forth on her narrow twin bed, but it was a desperate coupling, and when it was over, both of them knew it hadn't been enough.

As they lay there in her narrow twin bed, Emily remembered the first time they had slept together, in college, after the screening of his awful activist film. They lay tangled in his extra-long flannel sheets, listening for the sound of his roommate returning.

"What did you think?" Julian had asked.

"About what?" Emily panicked. She had nothing to compare the quality of the sex to, having only slept with precisely one other boy her freshman year.

Julian grinned. "About my film."

"I think," Emily said, "that you're going to be a great filmmaker."

It wasn't necessarily that she believed that was true, even if she could view the film objectively, without herself in it. It was more that she believed in him; maybe she was even beginning to believe in the two of them, together.

Now, in her childhood room, she turned away while Julian got dressed. At the door, he stopped, and for some inexplicable reason hope rose in her, although she didn't know for what. He pulled a set of keys from his pocket. "Can I switch these with you?"

She nodded toward the top of the dresser, where the keys to his car lay. Julian made the exchange, and then he was gone. In a moment, Emily went to the window, in time to see the silvery flash of the Bimmer as it pulled out of the driveway, turned the corner, and disappeared from sight.

While she took a shower, Emily thought about what she would say to her mother, who she knew must be waiting for her. She didn't know if her mother and Julian had exchanged words, if there was anything he could say that would explain her behavior. She wasn't sure how to explain it herself, except that it had left her feeling so numb that she could barely feel the water against her skin.

As she headed downstairs, she could hear her mother on the phone with someone in the kitchen. She paused in the hallway to listen to the conversation.

"I don't care what people think about me and Pastor Liu," her mother was saying, probably to one of her church friends.

Pastor Liu? Ling thought of the slim, stooped man that she had always thought of as elderly, though she supposed he must be around her mother's age. The last time she'd seen him was at her father's funeral, and he had been exceedingly kind, although she didn't know how else someone in his position should behave. Was there something going on between her mother and the pastor?

Her mother had hung up, so she went into the kitchen. "Who was that?" she asked.

"Beatrice Ma. You remember her, the one with the four grand-children?"

"Yes, Mom."

"She was telling me what she heard at church this morning, how the Wang son—you remember him, right? He was in your mock trial class—has done something terrible, completely disgraced his family. . . ." Her mother finally seemed to catch on to Emily's mood. "Emily, what is going on? Are you and Julian still fighting? Is that why he came here this morning? Why did he leave so soon?"

Emily burst into tears.

They were sitting at the kitchen table, finishing up the leftovers from last night's takeout for lunch. Emily had cried until she felt so lightheaded, she'd had to hold on to the edges of her chair. Her mother had made her eat something, brewed some tea, but that offered little solace. Emily lowered her head and pressed the center of it against the slightly sticky tabletop. No amount of cleaning could remove the patina of spilled baby food, family dinners, and, lately, dust from disuse.

"Oh, Emily," her mother said. "What are you going to do?"

"I'm not going back."

"Emily," her mother said, "I don't know if that is a good idea. You know you can stay here as long as you want. And it is good to go away for a while, if you have to. Sometimes, after a fight, the only thing you can do is leave. I know this too. But, eventually, you have to go back. Because, no matter what, that is your home, and that is your family."

Emily recalled her mother's hand waving from the window, underneath the shadows of the trees as the car sped away down the street. Her mother, coming home without any explanation as to why she had been away for so many hours; her father, holding her for so long without a word.

"*You* came back," she said.

"Yes," her mother replied calmly. "I did."

"Where did you go that day?"

Her mother seemed to consider her question. "I went into the city, to Chinatown. I had lunch. Then I took the train back. That's it."

Emily knew something more must have happened, but she asked instead, "Why did you want to leave?"

"I was afraid."

"Of what?"

"That I was a bad mother to you and Michael. Your father and I fought about it the night before."

"I remember," Emily said, surprised to realize that she did. She could recall that she had been awakened that long-ago night by voices. She had thought it was a bad dream, as she'd had many of them as a child, and forgotten about it the next morning. "What did Dad say to you?"

"Nothing important. At least, nothing worth remembering now. What was important was that I felt like leaving, but I didn't."

"Was it because of us? Michael and me? If you didn't have us, would you have left Dad?"

"But I did have you two."

Emily sighed in frustration. "But what if, Mom? You can't tell me that you've never considered the alternatives to your life. What if?"

"*What if,*" her mother snapped, so uncharacteristically that Emily was taken aback. "What if I had never come to this country? If I had never met your father? Moved to this house? What if you or Michael had died when you were a baby? None of this happened, and now your father has left me."

"He didn't leave you," Emily pointed out, before realizing what her mother meant. Her mother wasn't talking about infidelities, of running away, but the ultimate betrayal of death, of being left behind to live the rest of her life alone.

"I don't want . . ." her mother said, as if struggling to find the words, "I don't want you to be like me."

"I won't be," Emily said, thinking, *Oh, if only you knew how much I try not to be like you.*

"What I want is for you and Michael to be happy, to have families of your own."

"We will."

"I don't think so, if you leave Julian. And what for? Just because he wants children and you don't."

"How did you know that?"

"Julian told me at Christmas, when you and Michael stayed home and we went to church together. He told me he was afraid you would not change your mind. That this would be a problem for you two."

Although she was a little disturbed that her husband had chosen to confide in her mother—as if her mother could do anything about it—Emily said, "Well, he was right."

"Are you sure?" her mother asked. "Emily, are you sure you don't want to have children?"

"Yes, Mom."

"How can you be sure?"

"I don't know. How can Michael be sure that he's gay?" It was a rhetorical question, but Emily regretted posing it when she saw the confused look on her mother's face.

"But now you will be alone," her mother persisted, "and so will Michael."

"Actually, Michael has a boyfriend." Emily figured she might as well come clean about everything she knew. "That's how I found out Michael was gay. When I went over to his apartment Friday night, his boyfriend answered the door."

"Michael and this boy live together? Is he the roommate?"

"What? There is no roommate." Too late, Emily recalled the lie she had told her mother. "His boyfriend lives uptown. His name is David. He's a lawyer."

"A lawyer?" her mother echoed.

"Yes, but the point is that Michael has someone who cares about him. He's going to be fine."

"Do you think," her mother said after a moment, "that maybe Michael is gay because I used to dress him in your clothes when he was a baby?"

"What? Mom, don't be ridiculous. Of course that has nothing to do with it."

"I just think," her mother said, "that it is somehow my fault. That you don't want children because of what happened to your doll."

"What doll?"

Her mother hesitated. "The one that I broke."

"I have no idea what you're talking about. Mom, did it ever occur to you that the way Michael and I turned out has nothing to do with the way we were raised? That we're now adults and responsible for our own thoughts and feelings?"

"Maybe," her mother replied, but she didn't sound too convinced. Perhaps, Emily thought, her mother wanted to know that she had some measure of influence in her children's lives, to keep them close to her.

"In any case, not wanting to have children has nothing to do with you or Dad. And really, it has nothing to do with Julian either. It has to do with me, and figuring out what it is I want. Can't you see that?"

Her mother nodded slowly, although Emily could tell that she hadn't changed her mind about what direction she felt her daughter's life was heading in—straight down, as far as she was concerned. But it looked like she wasn't going to argue with Emily about it anymore, at least for today. That was really all Emily could ask.

Just then, Emily heard the phone in her pocket beep. Taking it out, she saw that she'd missed a call. She glanced up to see her mother staring at her and could tell that her mother was dying to know who it was.

"It isn't Julian." The look on her mother's face shifted a little. "It isn't a secret boyfriend, either. There isn't anyone else, in case you were wondering."

"Oh." Her mother almost looked disappointed.

"I have to leave in a little bit, okay, Mom?"

"Where are you going? Aren't you going to stay here?"

"I can't. You have your own life, I don't want to get in the way. Like this morning, you didn't go to church because I was here, right? You could have gone without me."

"I didn't want to leave you by yourself."

"Then you could have woken me up and we could have gone together."

"You were too tired."

Emily felt like throwing up her hands. It was like arguing with a child; every excuse her mother was giving sounded like she was trying to hide something. Probably, judging by the snippet of conversation she had overheard that morning, that something had to do with Pastor Liu.

"Mom," she said gently, "I think it's good that you have a lot of friends from church. Even male friends. You do have male friends there, right?"

"Um, yes," her mother said. "There's Mr. Tsai, Mr. Chao . . ."

"If you wanted to be more than friends with one of them, I wouldn't be opposed to it."

A look of horror crossed her mother's face. "Oh, no! They are married."

"Well, if they weren't married. You keep on saying that you're afraid of Michael and me being alone. But it's been a year, Mom. You don't have to be alone, either."

"Emily, we are talking about *your* marriage," her mother said firmly, and Emily knew that was the extent to what she was going to get out of her mother about what was or wasn't happening at church. "Where are you going to stay?"

"In the city."

"With friends?"

"Maybe." Although as Emily said it, she had another, better idea. "I'll call you after Michael comes back, Mom. Maybe the both of us can plan to come out and spend a weekend with you?" She paused, recalling the three of them together in this house last year, quiet and slow-moving, as if shell-shocked.

"Yes," her mother said quietly. "I would like that."

Since she had brought so little with her, Emily was able to get ready to leave quickly. Up in her room, she made the bed so neatly that you couldn't tell someone had slept in it the night before, or that that morning it had been the site of whatever was the opposite of consummation. She picked up the keys, said good-bye to her mother, and pulled out of the driveway. Once on the road, she started to feel better and looked forward to getting back into the city. There were two people she needed to see before the day was over.

# CHAPTER 8

Ling stood in the driveway, her hand raised to wave good-bye to Emily. She only lowered it when the car had vanished around a curve. A couple of hours ago she had been surprised to hear a car pull up to the house and to look out the window to see that it was the maroon Buick she had driven so many years ago. For a moment she thought that time had been turned back, and she would see her younger self emerge from the car, in a pantsuit and permed hair. But it had been her son-in-law, and Ling realized that Julian and Emily must have switched cars. Apparently, they had switched back before he had left.

Although she knew there was still a lot that Emily hadn't told her, this was the most Ling had ever heard about her daughter's marriage. They were not much for discussing things in the Tang family, Ling had come to realize. Maybe if she'd told Emily what her own marriage had been like, her daughter would be more forthcoming. But now there was no point; Emily seemed to have made up her mind about leaving Julian. Perhaps someday she would reveal more, but for now, Ling would just have to have faith that her children would solve their own issues.

For example, Michael and his issue, if you could call it that. After she had left Emily and Julian to talk upstairs, Ling had gone down to the living room, where she'd had to sit down on the sofa to absorb the fact that her son, her sensitive little boy, liked other boys. How could that be? Michael had never showed any inclination for fashion or interior design, and his room had always been the picture of slovenliness. Wasn't that the opposite of what gay people were like? She had no idea, aside from what she saw on television. No family she knew had a gay son, or daughter, for that matter. There was that boy in church, Carl Cheung, whose voice soared higher than any of the sopranos; that was suspiciously feminine, wasn't it? But who knew what that meant?

As she was pondering this, Julian appeared in the doorway. He looked even more disheveled than when he had arrived, his shirt untucked, his face grim.

"I'm sorry, Mrs. Tang," he said. "I tried my best."

*Tried what?* she wanted to ask him, but sensed by the look on his face that she should pose this question to her daughter. Instead, she just nodded, and Julian left through the front door. She heard a car start and pull out of the driveway, and it was quiet. Then the pipes above her started to thrum as Emily turned on the water to take a shower. Ling wondered just what her daughter was trying to wash away from her life.

The stillness enveloped Ling again as soon as Emily's car turned the street corner and she could no longer hear its familiar sputter. She had thought she'd gotten used to being by herself, but Emily's unexpected visit was like a splotch of color on a black-and-white canvas. Afternoons were especially hard for Ling, and she had taken to watching talk shows on television, marveling in the ways that people managed to mess up their lives without half trying. Ling thought of how whenever her children visited after they had left home, it had seemed like part of herself was being wrenched away, no matter how much she convinced herself that they would come again. Han hadn't seemed to feel like this, reminding her of how close both of them lived, a mere train or car ride away, and that she could go visit them if she wanted to. But Michael had never invited her to see his various lodgings—for a good reason, she now knew—and Emily's house had always struck her as peculiar, filled with furniture that was old and worn down on purpose.

Then, in a time that should be one of crisis, near the anniversary of their father's death, Emily had suddenly come to her, only to leave just as abruptly, and Michael had done the opposite by going away as far as he possibly could by himself. If he had to go to China, why not take along his poor old mother, who could certainly help him with the language and the customs, even though she herself had never been to the mainland. Maybe they could have all gone—herself, Emily, and Michael—as a sort of family vacation, although it would have been different without Han.

She wondered what Han would think about his son being gay, and Ling was secretly glad he wasn't around to know. Han had always been hard on Michael for the slightest things—for leaving his bike on the lawn, or getting poor grades in math, or spending too much time next door with the Bradley girl. Then, when Michael was a teenager, this attitude intensified, until Ling thought it might be something more than just regular fatherly disapproval and teenage sullenness. After he left home, Michael rarely came back to visit, and his reasons seemed less like Emily's—that she was too busy—and more that he couldn't stand to be around his mother and father. Maybe it had something to do with his sexual orientation. Ling had to admit to herself that she secretly welcomed this explanation, as it had less to do with her own shortcomings as a mother. But still, she should have seen it, she should have found a way to help her son. Because she knew that his father would not have. She knew that above all, Han wouldn't have been able to hide his disappointment that his son was not who he had wanted him to be.

When Ling learned she was going to have a second child, she knew that it would be a boy. She craved meat—steaks so rare that they dripped blood—and the baby sat low and round above her pelvis. It wasn't that she didn't love her little girl, who was already more serious than a six-year-old had any right to be. Emily held hands with her mother when they walked down the street, helped her wash the dishes at night, announced she wanted to go to bed early so that the next school day would come faster. There was nothing Ling enjoyed more than combing tangles out of her daughter's long hair and tying the sashes of her dresses.

After Han came home from work each night, Ling would watch as her daughter immediately stopped what she was doing to run to her father. Emily craved his approval so desperately, as if she knew that she would soon be displaced by her brother. Ling knew how much having a boy meant to Han. It would be a validation of his passage to America, of the days he had spent working as a dishwasher, of his decision to move to a suburb where not many families looked like theirs. It would help with the fact that no matter how tidy he kept his lawn, waved to the neighbors, and subscribed to the right local paper so that it was delivered in the center of their doormat every morning, he would never quite be viewed with the same easygoing acceptance as, say, their neighbor Mr. Bradley, whom everyone knew was a closet alcoholic.

Indeed, after Michael was born, her husband showed a tenderness unfamiliar to Ling, even in the early days of their marriage and when Emily was born. He came home from work early to be present for the baby's evening feeding, allowed him to fall asleep in the crook of his arm. He insisted that Ling follow the Chinese traditions of not washing her hair or going outside for the month after she had given birth, in order to rebuild her strength. He bought a black-skinned chicken to make soup, since it was considered to be more nutritious, and red-dyed eggs to symbolize good luck when the baby turned a month old. Ling had renounced these kinds of superstitions when she had joined the church, but she went along with them for her husband's sake.

Michael turned out to be a difficult baby. He had colic, when he'd cry so long and hard that it sounded like he was choking on his own discomfort. Ling tried everything, feeding him, holding a heating pad to his back, walking circles around the room. They took him to the doctor, who only said that Michael would grow out of it. Until then, the entire family had to endure sleepless nights, and Ling felt at times that her child's sobbing would kill her.

Then there was the time Michael cried so hard that he stopped breathing. When that happened, Ling could literally feel his dead weight in her arms. She shook him, and his head flopped as if the string that had been holding it up had been cut. For a moment she felt as if her own heart had stopped. Then she screamed for Han to call an ambulance.

Until then she and Han had done their best to make their house look just like any other on the block. Han fixed loose shingles on the roof and mowed the lawn regularly; Ling tended flower beds and refrained from cooking anything that might result in strange smells wafting out the kitchen window and over fences. But after that night, it was apparent that something was not right with the Tangs. First, there had been that ambulance roaring down the street in the early morning, waking up everyone on the block. And then there was the day about a month later, when a strange car parked outside their house. From it emerged a no-nonsense-looking woman with a briefcase.

Ling went to answer the doorbell.

"Hello, Mrs. Tang?" the woman said, offering a large, capable hand. "My name is Gretchen Davis. May I come in?"

She went on to say something about herself that Ling couldn't quite understand but allowed the woman to pass through, wondering if she was selling something, like the rouged ladies who tried to get into the living room to set up their cases of makeup, or the ones who wore no makeup at all but carried pamphlets about how to achieve eternal life.

Gretchen Davis walked into the Tangs' living room, looking around in a manner that indicated more than idle curiosity. "I suppose your husband must be at work," she said to Ling. "Where are your children?"

Ling explained that Emily was at a friend's house for the afternoon, and that Michael was upstairs, napping.

"How is your daughter doing in school?" was the next question.

"She is doing okay," Ling replied. "Not the best in the class. She needs to work harder."

This was not true. Mrs. Mayer had told Ling at a parent-teacher conference that Emily was the brightest student she'd had in years, although she was concerned about the way Emily peered at the chalkboard and thought she might need glasses. But Ling did not want to say this to Gretchen Davis. She felt that it would be safer to be modest and pretend her child was ordinary, if not downright delinquent like the Bradley boy next door.

Judging by her visitor's raised eyebrows, Ling didn't think that her intentions had come across clearly enough. She noticed that the woman began to scribble some notes on a pad that she had extracted from her briefcase.

"Mrs. Tang, when does your daughter get up in the morning? What does she eat for breakfast?"

Ling replied eight o'clock and rice porridge. Sensing that her mothering skills were being evaluated, she wondered if she should have changed that last answer to something more appropriate and American-sounding—eggs, for example. Gretchen asked for permission to go into the kitchen, where she opened the refrigerator door and exposed the unruly heads of bok choy and napa cabbage. Gretchen glanced into the cupboards at the dishes Ling had bought to set up house with. She didn't run a finger along the counter to check for grime, but she might as well have.

Now Gretchen wanted to see their bedrooms. Ling tried to imagine the rooms through a stranger's eyes. Emily's room with its four-poster bed and white quilted coverlet was tidy. As far as Ling could tell, there were no unwholesome books or dangerous toys sticking out anywhere. In the other bedroom, Michael was awake and lying quietly in his crib. Ling picked him up and unwillingly handed him over to Gretchen, who examined his reflexes and unbuttoned his onesie to check his body.

"How did he get this?" she asked Ling, pointing to a bruise on his thigh, where the joint of his plump little leg met his body.

Ling stammered that maybe she had held him a bit too roughly when she tried to pin his diaper. Or perhaps she had been holding him when she turned and accidentally bumped into the edge of a door. She had no idea. Finally, Gretchen Davis made her way to the front door, handed Ling a business card, and said she would be in touch. Ling locked the door after her, feeling that she had just taken a test in which she had gotten every answer wrong.

That night in the kitchen, after Emily and Michael had been put to bed, Ling handed Han the card, which said *Social Services* on it. Maybe it was something routine, she suggested in a hesitant voice. Maybe they were doing this to all the families with school-age children in the area, and it just happened to be the Tangs' turn. Han said in a low, terrible voice, how could she not realize that Gretchen Davis thought that Michael had had to go to the hospital because the Tangs were abusing their children? How could she have let that woman into the house? Had the neighbors seen anything? Didn't she know what a huge shame this was to the family?

He stopped, veins bulging from his forehead as if they were strings to be plucked. He didn't say it, but Ling knew that he also blamed her for being the one who was holding Michael when he had stopped breathing. For being a bad mother. But wasn't it Han's fault, she said aloud, for leaving her alone with the children all the time? Why couldn't he admit that he was wrong to have left New York City, to have married her, to have come to America in the first place?

*Please,* Han said, *keep your voice down,* even though she was speaking in Mandarin Chinese and Emily probably wouldn't be able to understand. *I am tired of keeping my voice down,* Ling said, and went upstairs. She didn't care if Emily had heard. Actually, she hoped she had, so that someday when she had a husband of her own, she would know what to do when you were pushed so hard against the door that you couldn't just lean against it, you had to open it and go out into the dark night.

The next morning, Ling came downstairs at eight o'clock to find Emily already seated at the kitchen table. Ling asked her if she had slept all right, and Emily nodded with no indication of having heard her parents' fight the night before. While she fed Michael, Ling made a phone call to Mrs. Bradley next door. She said that she had to go to the city at the last minute, and would Mrs. Bradley be able to look after the children for a few hours? Mrs. Bradley hesitated, and in the background Ling could hear the Bradley boy acting up. Ling had never asked her neighbor anything like this before, but finally Mrs. Bradley agreed.

Ling got the children dressed and ready to go. She told Emily that she needed to run an errand and would be leaving her and Michael with the neighbors. Would Emily please look after her little brother? Emily looked back at her and nodded once, the solemn look on her face almost enough to change Ling's mind and take Emily with her. She couldn't manage two children, but she might be able to handle Emily, who was self-sufficient for her age. But where would that leave Michael? No, it was best if they stayed together.

Ling delivered both children to Mrs. Bradley. Then she drove to the nearest rail station, parked the car, and boarded the train that would take her into the city. As the landscape passed by her window, she thought about where she would go. She hadn't spoken to her old friends, like Felicia Lam, in years, and guessed they had all moved on by now. She just knew that she had to get out of her house, which still bore the taint of the social worker and her fight with her husband.

Inevitably, her steps led her to Chinatown. The intervening years in the suburbs had softened her, so that all she noticed now about it was the dirt, the odd smells, the uncouth people who spoke in a different dialect—already the neighborhood had started changing from Cantonese-speaking immigrants to Fujianese-speaking ones. Having heard that the crime rate was up in the city, she kept her purse hugged tightly to her. She found a dingy restaurant to have lunch in and lingered there over her tea until the bitterness was just a ghost on her tongue.

How easy it would be to disappear into the crowds here. She could change her name, get a job as a waitress or a garment worker, rent a room in a boardinghouse. No one would ask any questions. Hundreds of new people came to Chinatown every year under false names and with false papers, to start their lives over. In a way, she had done it nine years before when she had come to America from Taiwan, then again when she left her college town in Connecticut for the city; she could certainly do it again. She thought about the time she and Han had first moved to the suburbs, when she was pregnant with Emily and she had walked until she could go no farther. She had thought she was running away then, but there had been nowhere to run to. It would be much easier to run away in the city, where no one would recognize her.

Just then someone entered the restaurant, a tall man with a measured gait and a way of holding his head that she knew very well, having looked upon him almost every Sunday morning for the past eight years. Ling quickly looked down, hoping that Pastor Liu wouldn't see her, but there were few other people in the room, and he made his way straight to her table.

"Mrs. Tang," he said. "A pleasant surprise. What brings you to the city?"

"Just some shopping," she stammered. "And you?"

"I'm here to see some recent immigrants from the mainland. I'd appreciate it if you didn't tell any of the other parishioners about it. I'm afraid that some of them don't like it when I spend my time outside of the regular congregation, but these people need guidance and direction too."

"I won't," Ling promised. "Actually, I was just about to—" *Leave,* she meant to say, but Pastor Liu was already sitting down across from her.

"How is your family doing?" he asked.

"They are fine," Ling replied. To be polite, she added, "And yours?"

"Not too well, I'm afraid," she was surprised to hear him say. "You see, my wife was recently diagnosed with breast cancer. It's early yet, so we're hopeful."

"I'm sorry," Ling said, although she wasn't sure whether she meant she was sorry about his wife or for not thinking that her pastor was someone who could have a life outside of church. Certainly, she had met Mrs. Liu, a tiny woman a full two heads shorter than her husband, but had never thought very much about her, or about their life together. She knew that they did not have any children, and that while Pastor Liu had been born in the States, his wife was from Taiwan, like herself. "Is there anything we can do?" she asked.

"It helps to be needed by my congregation. You know, to feel like you're being useful to someone else, to have a purpose."

"That must be a wonderful feeling."

Pastor Liu looked at her keenly. "I'm guessing it's similar to how a wife feels with her husband and children?"

"My husband . . ." Ling hesitated, not knowing how much to reveal, but figured Pastor Liu had already taken her into his confidence. "He doesn't understand me."

"What makes you say that?"

"Recently, we have had some trouble. But I think that maybe he has never understood me."

"I think," Pastor Liu said slowly, "your husband might not understand you all of the time. But he will always care for you and the children." He paused. "I'm guessing that he is not a man given to showing his emotions?"

Ling shook her head.

"So you will have to do it for the both of you. Maybe he had a difficult time in his childhood. You will need to provide him with the family that he's never had. Are you able to do that?"

"Yes," Ling said. "Yes, I can."

"Good." Pastor Liu placed his hand on hers, lightly, but she drew more warmth from it than her cup of tea. Then he glanced at his watch. "Well, I must be going."

"Thank you," Ling said as he got up from the table.

After a while, Ling paid her bill and left the restaurant as well. Outside, on the street, the day was quickly winding down. Vendors were hauling in produce from the sidewalks; at the market, the fish had been removed so that only watery pink impressions were left on the ice. Ling wondered if she should buy something to bring back, to make it seem like she had indeed come to Chinatown to shop, but suddenly her urge to get back home was so strong that she almost broke into a run for the subway station.

From there, to the train, to retrieving her car from the parking lot, she couldn't help feeling that when she got home, the windows would be dark, that Social Services had come to collect her children, or that her family had left her instead of her leaving them. Or maybe she was in one of those fairy tales where years had passed while she was gone and another family was living in their house now.

The sight of the familiar lit windows as she pulled up in the driveway almost made her weep with joy. Before she had removed her keys from her purse, the door had opened and Han was standing just inside. Without a word he pulled her into his arms, and when they finally let each other go, she did not say where she had gone, for it did not matter. She was home now.

In the weeks that followed, the Tang household returned to normal. No one came to take the children away. Since that night in the hospital, Michael's colic seemed to get better, and then one day it miraculously stopped. Against her will, Emily had her eyes tested and was found to be farsighted. As if resigning herself to the inevitable, she chose pink plastic frames that made her dark eyes look huge, like something caught underneath a magnifying glass. Although Ling assured Emily that the glasses were becoming, privately she mourned the loss of her daughter's looks, and wondered what Emily would remember about the day her mother almost left her family.

As for Pastor Liu, his wife passed away the following year. Although she did not speak with him in private again for a long time, in her mind, Ling started to consider him not as just her pastor, but as someone who had loved and lost. And in the following years, whenever she and Han would take the children into Chinatown, she'd remember that afternoon and conversation with him and think fondly about who she had been back then, as if she had been a different person entirely.

*I don't care what people think of me and Pastor Liu,* she had said that morning on the phone to her friend Beatrice Ma, although that couldn't have been further from the truth.

Beatrice Ma had been full of the news that Ling had missed that morning by not going to church. From the way she talked, you would have thought that Sundays were not a time to reflect but for discussing other people's shortcomings. Apparently, the juiciest piece of news was that the Wangs' eldest son, Alvin, an investment banker, had blown his yearly bonus on an escort service. It was nice to know, Ling thought, that there were people out there whose children were even more confused about what they wanted out of life than hers.

"Where were you this morning?" Beatrice finally asked.

"My daughter came to visit."

"Oh? You didn't tell me she was coming."

*I don't always tell you everything,* Ling thought. In direct opposition, Beatrice seemed to tell Ling everything about herself, from the way her stomach felt after eating lunch to the latest style in which she planned to get her hair cut. Beatrice had always been talkative, but it seemed to have gotten worse after Han had passed away, as if she imagined Ling were starved for conversation. Many of her friends at church had acted the opposite. In the days after, they were reluctant to visit her, as if they were afraid that by sheer association their own husbands would drop dead as unexpectedly as Ling's had. Ling felt that this had become the most relevant thing about her; if she were living in a folktale, she'd be known as the Widow Tang.

"How is Emily?" Beatrice wanted to know.

"She's fine." Ling did not want her family problems to become more fodder for Beatrice's gossip mill.

"She's not pregnant yet?"

"No."

"That's too bad. How old is she now?"

"Thirty-two."

Beatrice made a clicking sound with her tongue. She herself had been blessed with four grandchildren, two each from her sons, and she was always complaining about them and her daughters-in-law. Sometimes, listening to Beatrice complain about how fat one grandson was getting or how one granddaughter had forgotten to send her a thank-you note for a gift, Ling wanted to take her oldest friend's nose between her thumb and forefinger and twist *hard.*

By now Beatrice had moved on to an entirely different subject. "You know, Pastor Liu asked about you today. He was wondering where you were."

"What did you tell him?"

"I reminded him that it was almost a year since . . . Well, that you probably needed some time alone," Beatrice finished.

Ling imagined her friend sitting in her kitchen, still dressed in her designer-label church clothes. Her husband had probably snuck off the moment they'd gotten home to join one of the card games that the men organized on Sunday afternoons; old habits die hard, even outside of Chinatown.

"That sounds about right," Ling replied.

"Pastor Liu seemed very concerned that you weren't there. If I hadn't told him that you wanted to be left alone, I think he might have paid a house call just to make sure you were okay. Wouldn't people have something to say then?"

As Ling told Beatrice that she didn't care what other people thought, she wondered if Pastor Liu would have indeed come to see her. Probably not, she decided, especially after their last conversation, which had taken place following church the week before. But Ling would never tell Beatrice what had happened then, not with that mouth of hers.

"How are you doing?" Beatrice asked. "Really?"

"I'm fine," Ling forced herself to say. "Thank you for asking. You're a good friend, Beatrice."

"Oh, nonsense," Beatrice said. She went on to talk a little more about the Wangs' son, how his wife had thrown him out of the house and demanded a divorce, and what a shame it was since they had two young children, and what a disgrace to the Wang family name. Then she made Ling promise that she would call her the next day to go shopping, which Ling automatically agreed to before she hung up.

Ling gazed out of the window at the backyard, wondering what exactly Pastor Liu had said to Beatrice. Had he sounded more concerned about her than, say, elderly Mrs. Yee who had broken her hip last week? Or had she just imagined that he'd wanted to ask her a very serious and rather awkward question the last time they had been together?

She certainly hadn't sought out any special attention from Pastor Liu. She had made that clear a year ago when her husband had passed away. At that time he had asked Ling if she needed someone to be with her, but Ling had refused, saying that she had her children. The only thing she asked him to do for her was to deliver the eulogy at Han's funeral. After Emily and Michael left, she sometimes considered taking Pastor Liu up on his offer, but thought it would be inappropriate.

Then, three months ago, in the parking lot after church, Pastor Liu asked Ling if she wanted to have lunch with him.

"There's this new vegetarian Indian place I've been meaning to try," he said.

Ling could feel her taste buds instinctively recoil. Not because she didn't like Indian food; she just had no idea what it was. Han's culinary preferences didn't extend to farther parts of Asia, and so neither did hers. Ling had an idea that Indian food involved curry, and curry was spicy, wasn't it? She remembered an ethnic meal that Julian had cooked when she and Han had visited him and Emily after they'd first moved to their house. It was made up of mashed vegetables that reminded her of weirdly flavored baby food, accompanied with what appeared to be pancakes. When Julian had said that they were supposed to use their hands to eat, Han had looked at him as though he were a barbarian.

"Not your favorite?" Pastor Liu asked, misinterpreting her silence.

"I've never had Indian food," Ling admitted.

"We should definitely go, then."

Ling agreed they would take his car, although as Pastor Liu carefully opened the door and closed it behind her, she wondered if that was a mistake. Maybe she should have driven her own car and followed him, in case some of the church ladies were watching. But she supposed that would make it look even more like they were doing something wrong. How unbecoming it was for someone her age to blush at the thought of going anywhere with a man, as if she were a teenager, a teenager who had never been on a date before. Of course it wasn't a date, since it was the middle of the day. Besides, even if they weren't exactly friends, she and Pastor Liu had known each other for more than thirty years.

Although it was bright outside, the restaurant was dimly lit, as if it were in a perpetual state of dusk, or maybe just some bulbs were missing from the fixtures overhead. The little light there was glinted off gold decorations on the walls, multiarmed dancing gods, and pagan masks. They made Ling feel a bit uncomfortable, having just come from a Christian church, but Pastor Liu didn't seem to care, so she figured it was all right.

Pastor Liu took a penlight from his pocket and trained it on the menu. "That's better," he said.

This gesture struck Ling as immensely practical but also something only an old person would do. In any case, better light wouldn't have helped her decipher any of the strange items on the menu, and she asked Pastor Liu to order for her. The dishes that arrived were not as strange as she'd feared, nor as spicy.

"Have you ever been to India, Ling?" Pastor Liu asked.

Ling almost choked on her food. She shook her head, then remembered that Pastor Liu had recently traveled to India on a mission. "What is it like there?" she asked.

"Very poor, more poor than places in China, even."

Ling nodded, not wanting to reveal that she had never even been to mainland China.

"But the people I've seen there appear to be happy, despite their simple lives. Or, rather, I don't think they're any less capable of happiness than many of the members of our congregation."

Ling thought about Mr. Tsai, who was rumored to be in serious debt; Mrs. Chao, who supposedly was cheating on her husband; her friend Beatrice, who complained about everything.

"Even the animals seem to be happier than they are here," Pastor Liu continued. "The cows walk wherever they want, the dogs don't have collars or leashes. They may not live as long, but I'd argue that they lead freer lives."

Looking across the table at Pastor Liu, Ling couldn't help but remember the last time the two of them had sat together in a restaurant, in Chinatown twenty-five years earlier. Ling wondered if he saw much change in herself. There was no question that there was physical change. Her body and the lines of her face had softened, her hair more coarse and thin, although she had given into vanity and dyed it black. But as for internal change, how young and naïve she had been then, thinking that she could leave her family. Also, she had never considered the possibility that she and her husband might not grow old together. Perhaps it was better that her younger self had not anticipated that prospect.

When it came time to leave, Pastor Liu took the check over Ling's protests. "You can pay next time," he said, and she subsided at the startling, yet not entirely unwelcome, thought that there might be a next time.

Over the next few months, this became Ling and Pastor Liu's routine after church, to take one of their cars to the Indian restaurant, where Ling became bold enough to try things with names like *saag paneer* and *malai kofta,* and return to the church parking lot, after which they would go their separate ways. Ling came to find that Sunday afternoons, which she used to dread above all others, with its quiet after the bustle of church, could pass quite quickly. She didn't doubt that she and Pastor Liu were the topic of conversation among the church ladies, but she didn't care. She was a widow; Pastor Liu was a widower. It was her right to call on her pastor if she needed help with the grieving process.

But when she and Pastor Liu met up, they did not talk about Han, although they did discuss her children. Ling described Emily as a lawyer who worked with immigrants and Michael as an artist, albeit on the computer.

"They both sound quite accomplished," Pastor Liu said.

"Not so accomplished. Emily is married but has no children. Michael has no girlfriend."

"But they have steady jobs."

"I don't think they are happy. When I call them, they say they are fine, fine, and act as if they can't wait to get off the phone. I wish that my children could be closer to each other. But I feel they live as far away from each other as I do from my sisters in Taiwan."

"I'm sure they talk without your knowing about it."

"I hope they do. I hope they are at least able to talk about their father."

Pastor Liu was quiet for a moment, and then said, "Ling, I understand what you must have gone through this past year. What happens when you lose a spouse."

As she watched him say these words, Ling thought about how much he had loved his wife, must still love her if he had never remarried more than twenty years after her death. "But," Ling said, "you have to move on." This was actually a line she had heard on one of those talk shows she watched in the afternoon. Who knew that so much could be learned from the ruins of other people's lives?

"Maybe," Pastor Liu said, "there is a way we can help each other move on."

His eyes held hers for an instant before she looked down. She knew that she was not ready yet for what he intended to ask her, for what their relationship was turning into, perhaps not this Sunday or the next.

So, the following Sunday, when Pastor Liu followed her into the parking lot, she turned around.

"I don't think we should be doing this," she said.

"Ling, all we're doing is having lunch."

"Still." She struggled to find the words. "I don't think it's correct. It is too soon."

She could not read his face now. "Maybe it is too soon," he acknowledged. "But when it is the right time—"

"I will call you, Frank," Ling said, without realizing that she had called him by his given name.

She went to her car and left the parking lot as fast as she could, causing more people to stare than during any of the times she and Pastor Liu had left the church grounds together.

This was the real reason why she hadn't gone to church in the morning. Worse, if Emily had gone with her, Pastor Liu would have come over to say something to her, and then Ling was sure that she'd blush, or say something inappropriate, that would reveal what she and Pastor Liu had been doing these past few weeks. Not that there was anything wrong with having lunch, as he had said, but Ling was afraid of what it might lead to. She had so carefully constructed her life this past year around the idea of herself as being alone, now that she had finally eased herself into it, she didn't think she knew how to be otherwise.

As she walked from the driveway into the house, Ling heard the telephone ring. She wondered if it was Beatrice again, calling about something else she had heard at church that morning, or maybe it was Pastor Liu. That second thought made her breath catch a little. She automatically put her hand to her hair, just before she picked up the receiver, and paused to laugh at herself. To still care about how she looked, as if she could be seen through the phone. Surely, that had to be a sign of something.

# CHAPTER 9

At eight o'clock the next morning, when Michael comes down to the hotel lobby, he sees a young man leaning against the front desk, talking to the clerk. Behind him is an older man who rises when he sees Michael, and then Michael is finally face-to-face with his father's childhood friend.

Michael knows Liao Weishu must be around his father's age, but he appears much older—a slight, stooped man with leathery skin and thinning hair. When he smiles, he is missing some of his bottom teeth. But his eyes shine, and his handshake is strong.

"You look like your father," Liao says, appraising Michael openly.

All his life Michael has been told that Emily looks like their father while he looks like their mother, but he just nods and smiles.

"This is my son, Liao Bin." Liao Weishu indicates the young man. Michael can see a resemblance between them, in the set of the mouth, the shape of the eyes.

"You can call me Ben," the son says. His English is just as proficient as Liao's, although it sounds more colloquial without his father's British accent.

Ben looks to be around Michael's age, with a head of close-cropped hair and a round face. Unlike most of the other young men Michael has seen so far in this city, he is informally dressed in a tracksuit that probably cost more than the cheap rayon suits he's seen other men wear. Around his neck is a plastic lanyard that holds some kind of laminated credential.

Ben gestures toward the clerk. "I told him that you are an old family friend and they should take good care of you."

"How do you know him?"

Ben lifts the plastic lanyard from his chest. "I'm a certified tour guide."

"He knows everyone in the hotel business," Liao says proudly.

For a moment the three of them stand there looking at one another, smiling, not sure of what to say next. Michael feels that he should be bursting with questions, but instead he thinks that these two people are almost as much strangers to him as if he had encountered them on the street. He feels disoriented somehow, as if they had been conversing in Chinese instead of in English.

Then Liao says, "We should get started. We have a lot to see today."

They exit the hotel to where a car is parked at the curb, and Michael realizes that he has no idea where the Liaos are taking him. Ben gets into the driver's seat, and Liao motions for Michael to take the passenger's, but he refuses, deferring to the older man. To Michael's relief, they seem to be heading out of the city. He recognizes the train station where he arrived a few mornings before and is amazed by how familiar this place already seems to him.

"Where are we going?" he ventures to ask.

"First," Liao says, "we will take you to Kumbum Monastery. In Chinese it is called Ta'er Si. It is one of the oldest and most important Buddhist monasteries in China. Then we will go see Qinghai Lake."

"Everyone who comes here has to see the lake," Ben adds. "It's the number-one tourist destination in the province, after the monastery."

"Do you get a lot of foreign tourists here?" Michael asks.

"Sometimes Americans or British, but mostly Japanese and Koreans," Ben answers. "There are also a lot of Chinese from the big cities in the east. They want to see what Tibet is like, but even though the train now goes to Lhasa, it's too far and the elevation is too high. It's not comfortable. So they come here instead. It's like, how do you call it, Little Tibet."

"Are there a lot of Tibetans here?"

"Yes, and Uighur people—they are Muslim; so are the Hui people. You will recognize the Hui women by the white caps they wear."

Michael thinks of the hotel clerk's cryptic comment when he checked in. "Does everyone get along? The minorities, I mean?"

"They are happy here," Ben replies. "They get preferential treatment in the schools and can have more than one child. There aren't any difficulties like there is between the black people and the white people in America."

Michael opens his mouth to say something, then thinks better of it and closes his mouth.

Liao corrects his son. "I have heard before of some difficulties in the far northwest, in Xinjiang Province, where the Uighur people live. But it was not that serious."

"Not like the problems you have with religion in your America," Ben adds.

Michael doesn't bother to clarify that, either.

Ben puts a cassette tape into the player on the dashboard, and some kind of Chinese pop music blares forth, stalling further conversation. Michael looks out the window to where the outskirts of the city give way to fields covered in delicate yellow flowers. The sky turns into a clear blue that has previously only peeked through the smog. However, the mountains look no closer; in fact, they appear to be getting farther away. The illusion makes it seem like they will be traveling forever.

Then the smooth landscape is broken by what appears to be a complex of concrete buildings with towers that rise above the barbed-wire fence at certain intervals. Michael thinks it's funny how, no matter what country you're in, an institution that looks like this is easily identifiable as only one thing. Still, he asks, "What is that?" and Ben turns the volume down.

"It is a labor camp," Liao says matter-of-factly.

"You were in a labor camp once?" Michael says, thinking of the letter and not of the propriety of his question. But once he says it, it remains hanging there like a dark cloud.

Fortunately, Liao does not appear to be offended. "Yes," he replies. "But it was not this camp. The one I was in was farther south, closer to the monastery. It was shut down because it was too small, and they built this new one in the 1980s. It was after I had been released, so I never got to see it. I am guessing that because it was more modern, it was more comfortable." Liao laughs a little.

Of course, Michael wants to ask Liao why he was in the camp, and for so long—did he say something political, did he kill someone—but he can't bring himself to ask. Instead, he just looks at the scenery passing by, thinking the fields have a tinge of desolation despite their bright blooms. He wonders if that is why Liao looks so aged, beyond what he imagines are the general harsh conditions of living in this part of the country.

They are traveling through a valley now, and then, in front of them, rises the monastery. It almost looks like something out of an amusement park; a group of buildings with high slanting walls and colorfully painted eaves. The roof of one appears to be made out of pure gold. Michael can't help thinking that the curve of the roofs, curled up like the ends of a mustache, look unmistakably Chinese.

The car pulls into a square surrounded by souvenir shops. A bus is parked there, and a group of Chinese people in matching baseball caps stand around a guide who is holding aloft a flag. They appear to belong to the tourist category Ben mentioned before, those from the eastern cities. Michael wonders if they feel this place is as exotic as he does, despite not having traveled out of the country.

When Michael, Liao, and Ben get out of their car, a group of rosy-cheeked children run up to them. Michael can't help but keep a hand on the wallet in his pocket, in case one of them decides to steal it. They seem to be repeating a word that sounds like English.

"What do they want?" Michael asks.

"Pens," Ben says. "A lot of foreign tourists give them pens instead of money." He shoos the children away with a few sharp words in Chinese. "You don't have to worry about them," he adds, noticing Michael's apprehension.

When Michael explains that he was pickpocketed the day before, Liao sighs. "There is a lot more crime in this city now. People come in from the countryside to look for work, and when they cannot find it, they steal."

"Can't the government do something about it?"

Liao lifts his hands. "*Mei banfa.* There is no solution."

In the monastery, they are able to wander around freely. Ben shows his credentials to anyone who comes up to them, and they are waved through halls hung with *thangkas* depicting the Buddha and what must be other holy figures. Michael never really paid attention in the one class he took in college on Eastern religions. He does recall the Free Tibet group; how once, a member—a white boy with ratty blond dreads—accosted him as he was walking across the lawn and demanded to know what he thought about China's human rights violations there, as if he had an opinion simply because of his appearance.

Ben, like a good tour guide, explains the history of the place, how the Yellow Hat sect of Tibetan Buddhism was founded there, something about a legendary tree on the grounds that sprouted from someone's blood, but Michael only half listens. He watches as the monks, with their gracefully draped maroon robes, walk on by. The older, graying ones wear spectacles; Michael thinks he sees the Dalai Lama everywhere. The younger ones, with their shaven heads, appear boyish and innocent. Some seem to be on their way to classes, with books tucked under their arms. Others are doing ordinary household chores, like sweeping the floor with twig brooms, dusting shrines upon which offerings of money and fruit have been laid. They are not chanting or meditating or doing anything monkish like that. They are behaving, Michael thinks, like ordinary human beings. He watches the monks as they carry on with their lives.

But most of all, Michael watches Liao Weishu. Liao stands a little apart from Ben and Michael, letting the two younger men walk together. His impassive face behind its round glasses reminds Michael a little of a turtle. Liao does not add anything to what Ben says, doesn't even indicate that he's listening. He hasn't asked Michael anything about his father or his family. It's almost as if he isn't interested. He nods occasionally to the monks as they pass him.

"Come," Ben calls. "Here is something I think you'll enjoy."

The moment they step into the cool, dark hall, Michael is accosted with a pungent smell, as if milk has been left out in the sun for days. Then, when his eyes adjust to the dim light, he sees before him an intricately carved scene of temples, floating deities, trees and flowers, in all the colors of the rainbow.

"Yak butter," Ben tells him. "The sculptures are made out of yak butter and then dyed. Do you like it?" He pauses expectantly.

"It's amazing," Michael says. "But it doesn't smell so nice."

"No," Liao agrees, wrinkling his nose. "Let us get some fresh air."

They have lunch at one of the outdoor restaurants in the square at the foot of the monastery. The main choice of meat appears to be mutton, which Liao orders in a dish of chewy but tasty noodles that are shaped like small squares. A man in the back is making them, tearing pieces from a length of dough and flicking them into a boiling pot of water with his thumb, as if he is dealing a deck of cards.

Ben also orders watery Chinese beer, and then, in what Michael secretly suspects is a diabolical move, Liao orders tea that comes with yak butter. The old man puts a hunk of the slimy yellow stuff in a bowl and pours the liquid over it, turning it into something the color of dishwater.

"Try it," Ben suggests, and Michael thinks he's in on the prank too. But when he does take a sip, he finds the tea to be salty and strangely satisfying.

"Do you visit the monastery often?" Michael asks Liao.

Liao shakes his head. "I first visited it about thirty years ago, after

I was released from the labor camp. You see, a monk here was my good friend. Later, I used to take my wife and son here to visit him."

Ben says, "I don't remember him."

"You were only a baby," Liao tells him. "My friend is dead now, and I haven't been back here since. This place looks very different compared to back then."

"How so?" Michael asks.

"It was not in the renovated form you see today. Everything needed painting and repairs. You also did not have the buses or begging children. That all came with the tourists. But it is still a very holy place. You can feel it when you are here."

Michael considers what he feels at the moment: the sunshine on his face, a soft breeze. Is that what Liao is talking about? Because otherwise, he feels nothing.

The look on his face must betray him, because Liao chuckles. "If your father had heard me say that, he would not believe me either."

"What do you mean?"

"When we were growing up, your father was very practical. In school, he wanted to study science, the way things worked. I was more interested in the languages and arts. He used to tease me for being able to speak English, when it could not be of any possible use to me. I have to admit," Liao continues, "for years your father was right. But things are different now. Look at my son."

"Yes," Ben interjects. "Now I depend on English for my job."

"When did you start learning English?" Michael asks him.

"In small school. In your country, that's what . . . ?"

"Elementary school?" Michael guesses.

Ben nods. "Of course, I also learned English from my father." Liao Jr. and Liao Sr. grin at each other.

"Ah," Liao finally says, waving his son's praise away. "My English has much to be desired."

Michael laughs at how archaic Liao's words sound and stops when he realizes the elderly man is being serious.

"Even your laugh sounds like your father's when he was young," Liao remarks.

"What was my father like back then?" Michael tries.

Liao pauses. "He was a good man. He was always a good man. He was just led astray, as many of us were back then."

Michael figures that if he doesn't ask now, he never will. "Can you tell me more about my father's childhood?"

After a long moment, Liao nods and sets down his tea bowl.

The part of Beijing that your father, Han, and I grew up in was called Houhai, meaning *the back sea,* near the Forbidden City. It was a series of *siheyuan*s, or four-walled compounds; lakes bordered by willows; and winding streets. They said it was where the ancient scholars lived, where they got the inspiration for their poetry. Even when things got bad, during the worst of the famines and the unrest, it was as if time stood still there. In other parts of the city, people had to take apart their furniture, even tear down the frames of their doors, to use as kindling in the winter to stay warm. But not us. We were untouched.

My family lived next door to Han's; maybe many years ago we were related. All the children played with one another and blended in, until you couldn't tell which family they belonged to. Han and I were both the youngest sons in our families, he of four siblings and I of five. Together, we faced down our older brothers, who were always beating up on us, and our older sisters, who were always scolding us for something we had done by accident, like muddying up the floors they had just cleaned. Whenever that happened, they blamed both of us equally, and we received the same amount of scolding and the same number of smacks. They called us two jumping beans, both halves of the same chestnut.

We did not look the same, though. Han had an open, inviting face and a mobile mouth that easily laughed. I was quieter, spoke less, and had ears that stuck out. Han was also taller and bigger than I was, and when he outgrew a jacket or a pair of dungarees, his mother would give them to my mother for me to wear. We all did this, so that by the time the clothes were passed down from the oldest to the youngest child, they were in disrepair. Han always tried to outgrow his clothes faster, so that they would be in better condition for me to wear.

We were the same age and in the same class at school, with me always sitting in the seat behind Han. I have to admit that Han was better at his schoolwork. He was quicker witted and always seemed to know what the teachers wanted to hear. At the same time, he could mock the teachers behind their backs, and they would never catch him. When we were ten years old, I made a special enemy of our history teacher, Teacher Mu. She was a spinster and looked about fifty years old, even though we all knew she must've been around thirty. But although she seemed ancient, she was strong. She would beat students with a paddle if they did not answer questions correctly or spoke out of turn. Other teachers used corporal punishment as well, but they were usually men. Somehow, being beaten by a female teacher was more of an insult.

One day, Teacher Mu was giving a lesson on the history of sanitation. According to the textbook, in 1952, Mao Zedong launched a patriotic sanitary campaign against the bacteriological warfare of the United States. People's homes were checked by a special sanitation committee to make sure they were adequately clean. Patriotic citizens had good hygiene, and they learned to brush their teeth twice a day and to wash their hands before meals and after using the toilet. Teacher Mu made it sound like before the 1950s, no one did this.

To show the importance of sanitation, Liu Shaoqi, who later became chairman and then was denounced as a traitor, paid a visit to a city in the interior of the country. He greeted people from all walks of life, from the mayor to the night soil collector. You know what night soil is, right? It's what's taken from the outhouses after people are done doing their business. The night soil collector puts it in a cart and dumps it outside of the city in the fields, where it is used as fertilizer. Then the vegetables that are grown in the fields are taken back into the city to be sold. That's why it's important to wash your vegetables carefully before you cook them. Collecting night soil is still done all over China today.

Anyhow, as the story goes, Liu Shaoqi walks up to the night soil collector and commends him for doing such an important job. He says that the lower and dirtier the work, the more patriotic a citizen is for doing it. Then he shakes the night soil collector's hand.

"I hope the night soil collector washed his hands first," Han whispered to me.

Without thinking, I laughed out loud. It might as well have been a clap of thunder for the way it rang out in the classroom.

Teacher Mu fixed her stern gaze on me. "Master Liao, what is so funny?" she demanded.

"N-nothing," I said.

"If you don't tell me what you were laughing at, you will stay after class."

I nodded, my head hanging down in defeat. We all knew what staying after class meant. With other teachers, you had to wash the blackboard or clap erasers. With Teacher Mu, it meant that she would get out her paddle, tell you to bend over, and let you have it.

When I looked over my shoulder, I saw that Han's face had gone pale. He had not meant to get me in trouble. But it was my fault—I didn't have to laugh at what he said. If I had told Teacher Mu what I was laughing at, she would have made him stay after class too. If he had spoken up and taken the blame for what had happened, she would have still punished me for being the one who laughed. There was no point in both of us being punished.

After class, Han hung around until Teacher Mu told him to leave unless he wanted a beating, too. I knew he would stand just outside the door, waiting until the ordeal was over. Knowing he was so close made me feel that I could better endure what was going to happen. Teacher Mu told me to pull down my pants and lean over my desk. Then she thwacked me twenty-five times with her paddle. At least Han told me it was twenty-five; after the first few I stopped counting. Those blows stung, but then it seemed that I got used to it and didn't feel anything. I knew the real pain would come later.

Han told me that when he was hiding outside the classroom door, every time he heard the paddle come down, he pinched himself on his arm. That's how he knew how many times I had been struck. Indeed, he later showed me the red welts that ran down his left arm, from his shoulder to his wrist. They were like miniatures of the welts that had now started to rise on my own skin. That was also the only apology he ever gave me for the part he had played in my punishment. He never said he was sorry. Maybe he didn't think words would be strong enough.

After I came out of the classroom, Han helped me walk home from school.

"Is it that bad?" he asked.

"No," I said, but I had to clench my teeth not to cry. It wasn't because my bottom hurt, but because, infinitely more shameful, I had wet myself.

When we got home, Han helped me change and snuck my soiled pants to his house. Perhaps he just threw the pants away, as they were likely ones I had inherited from him, anyway. After that, our relationship went back to the way it had been before, usually me getting into trouble for something that Han had instigated. But we were children then, and children do not think about the consequences of their actions. Besides, I had my chance to get revenge on Teacher Mu six years later, when our positions of power had changed. Until then, all I had thought was that someday, when I became a teacher, I would be much better and more understanding than that miserable Teacher Mu.

Even though our families lived next door to one another, Han's father and my father couldn't be more different. My father worked at an iron-smelting factory on the outskirts of Beijing, leaving home early in the morning and coming back late at night, his face blackened by the end of the day. He wanted something better for me and hoped that I would become a teacher, even though I was not particularly good at my schoolwork. Han's father owned a shop that traded some foreign goods, like cigarettes and face powder and even some books in English. There was also something that set him apart from the other fathers in the neighborhood: religion. I didn't understand what that meant until I was a teenager.

When I was thirteen, an American missionary named Mr. Frazier came to live in the neighborhood. He offered to teach English to the local children, but I was the only one, at the suggestion of my father, who took him up on it. I suppose that at the same time I was learning English, Mr. Frazier was teaching Han's father about Christianity. I liked my missionary teacher, especially compared to my Chinese instructors. He had an easy manner about him, and was patient with my frequent questions about America. He told me that he was from a place called the Ohio River Valley, and that he had left behind a wife and two sons. My mother felt sorry for him and often invited him over for dinner. And, strangely enough, I seemed to have an aptitude for this foreign language.

Mr. Frazier's method of teaching was not to sit in a classroom, but for us to take walks around the rambling back streets of Houhai. He would encourage me to describe what I saw in English, stepping in now and then to provide the necessary vocabulary word.

Once, he asked quite seriously, what I thought of the people I saw: Did they appear content?

I glanced at the small shops, the owners sitting outside on stools and fanning themselves, chatting with their customers or people walking by. No one looked like they were in want of anything. I remembered something my father had told me, about hundreds of people who had died from hunger and floods when I was a child. But that had mostly affected the peasants, not city folk. My father sounded sure that nothing horrible like that would happen to us.

"I guess they look happy?" I said.

Mr. Frazier smiled. "There is no right or wrong answer. Maybe they are happy, as you say. But I wouldn't be surprised if there was change afoot."

"What do you mean?" I asked.

"Just that there is something in the air. You can smell it." Mr. Frazier winked at me and walked on.

I sniffed the air, but all I could smell was the faint fishy odor coming from the lake. I still had no idea what Mr. Frazier was talking about. That evening I related our conversation to Han and asked what he thought of it.

"Your foreigner teacher sounds crazy," he said. "I would be careful around him if I were you, or you're going to start saying crazy things too."

In general, Han scoffed at my English lessons. He would mimic my tones and say that I would start looking like a foreigner, that my nose would become bigger and my face as pale as that of a ghost. But I think he was jealous of my lessons that didn't include him, that I knew something he didn't. That this was one subject in which I was better than him.

Then, in the summer of 1966, Mr. Frazier went back to America. He said he had been recalled by his church, but all of us knew that something else was going on, even if the adults never spoke of it. Of course, religion during this time was effectively banned. Although we were aware of the atrocities that were occurring in the rest of the country, even in Beijing, we were sheltered from most of it. Because my father worked with metals, he was considered useful to the state. Han's father cleared the foreign goods from the shelves in his shop and started selling Mao badges and commemorative plates. He replaced the cross that hung on the wall with a propaganda poster that featured the Great Helmsman's face.

Then one day Han confided his father had started stealing away in the middle of the night, only to come home in the early morning.

"What do you think he's doing?" I asked.

"Maybe he has a gambling problem," Han guessed. Gambling was also banned during this time, but people got around it, as they got around everything. "Maybe"—and his eyes grew wide—"he has a mistress!" I should add that we were sixteen years old and knew nothing about women.

"I don't think so," I said, more out of respect for Han's mother, who had always been kind to me, than knowing what a mistress did.

"I'm going to follow him the next time and see what he's up to," Han said. "Will you come with me?"

"I'm not sure." I hesitated. "What if my father catches me?"

"*Your* father sleeps like a log. He'll never wake up."

This was true; my father was so exhausted by his proletarian job that the house could come down around his ears and he wouldn't stir.

So one night I snuck out of our compound and met up with Han without anyone knowing. We followed his father's shadow at a safe distance, down streets and alleyways, until he entered what appeared to be an ordinary house like our own. Maybe he did have a mistress and another family, I thought. Han and I found a window, and through the glass we saw my father sitting among several other men I did not recognize. One man was standing in front, reading from a book.

A sudden intake of breath from Han. "They're *praying*."

I asked, "Is your father a *jidu tu?*" A Christian. "How can that be?" For some reason, I thought that religion had stopped when Mr. Frazier had returned to America.

"He isn't," Han said. "He wouldn't do that to our family. There must be some mistake."

He started to walk away, and I ran to keep up with him. At the time, neither of us knew that his father was in a house church and part of an underground network. Although these churches appeared after 1949, they proliferated during this time period when religion was illegal—some of them still exist today.

Even though Han and I didn't fully understand what we had just seen, we knew it was something serious. At one point on our way home, Han stopped and turned so abruptly that I almost ran into him.

"Promise me you won't tell anyone about this," he said. Even in the softening moonlight, his eyes were hard.

"I promise," I said.

"So my grandfather was a Christian?" Michael wonders aloud.

"Yes, are you surprised to hear that?" Liao asks.

"No, it's just funny. My mother's the one who's the Christian in our family. My dad never liked it."

"Well," Liao says, "now maybe you know why. It was dangerous back then to be religious. A little bit today, even."

Michael hopes Liao will continue with his reminiscing, but Ben taps his watch. "We should go if we want to see Qinghai Lake."

The three of them get back into the car and drive northwest. There are few vehicles on the road, just some motorcycles and trucks that are headed from the city to distant townships. The rolling green mountains are bleak, occasionally punctuated by a gleaming white stupa capped with gold. One distant hill is covered by what appears to be ants. Then, as they get closer, the dots morph into animals that look like a cross between a buffalo and a skunk, with white stripes down the backs of their dark, woolly hides. Michael realizes that these are yaks, the source of the smelly butter. A herdsman, dressed incongruously in a muddy-looking suit and cap, turns his head to watch the car pass.

The car dips, and when it rises again, a silver glint is discernable between two hills. It grows larger until it turns into an expanse of water that is a darker blue than the sky above. Ben stops the car by the side of the road, and he and Liao and Michael get out and walk. There is no sound but the wind whipping past them, over the flatness of the water and to the mountains beyond. Michael has never seen a lake this big before, where it looks like it'll never end. Waves lap softly against the sandy shore, as if they don't know this isn't really a beach.

"It's like an ocean," he murmurs.

Ben overhears him. "Yes," he says. "Qinghai Province gets its name from this lake. *Qinghai* means 'green lake.' Some people say it is because the water in the lake sometimes looks green. Others say it means the grasslands around the lake."

"It's beautiful," Michael says.

He means it. The vastness of the sky and water around him, the fields and the mountains, makes him feel wonderfully small and inconsequential. No matter what he does, what he says, it won't make a drop of difference. As time passes, and people come and go, this landscape will stay the same.

Michael is reminded of a vacation his family took many years ago, to the south of Florida. They'd made the trip down by car, and his mother had packed a huge amount of sandwiches into a cooler that rested in between the front and backseats. They took this cooler into motel rooms where the television never worked and a dripping faucet left a rusty streak in the sink like a bad memory. Emily and their mother would sleep in one double bed, and their father and Michael in the other. With his back turned, Michael could sense every rise and fall of his father's chest, and he'd try to synchronize himself to his father's breathing.

He was eight and Emily fourteen, and they had clamored for their parents to take them to Disney World. Even their mother had pleaded with their father that they had already come so far, that the children would never have this chance again, that it might actually be *fun*. But their father was unrelenting. Looking back, Michael wonders whether he felt it was too expensive, that you shouldn't pay so much for kids to have *fun* when they wouldn't even learn anything.

Instead, their father had insisted that they go to Cape Canaveral, to the park from which the public could watch the space shuttles launch. Of course, there were no shuttles in sight that day: just scantily clad beachgoers throwing Frisbees at one another or splashing about in the water. What a strange sight the Tangs must have been in comparison, like alien beings, their mother dressed all in flowing white, and a wide-brimmed hat to protect her skin, their father in his bug-eyed sunglasses to prevent cataracts. Emily, surreptitiously rolling up the sleeves of her T-shirt to try and get a tan; Michael in shorts that, ironically, had a Mickey Mouse patch on the back pocket.

They had picked their way over the sand and stopped where the water met the land, since not one of them was in a bathing suit, had not even thought to pack any. The places where they stayed didn't have swimming pools, or at least ones that you dared try. Their mother sat on the sand holding an umbrella, guarding their pile of shoes, while Emily, Michael, and their father waded into the surf. The ocean here was mild, gently tugging at their legs. Emily soon got tired of trying to keep from getting wet and went back to join their mother. Their father, however, waded in farther. Michael followed as far as he could, which wasn't very far, since he was so small. So he just stood and watched as his father headed toward the blurry line of the horizon.

A wave came up and hit Michael in the chest. Later, his mother would scold him for letting himself get soaked, but he couldn't turn around, couldn't tear his eyes from the figure before him. His father had stopped now, and was looking out toward the empty space where on other occasions there would be the cottony trail of smoke, the winking star of a shuttle hurtling toward space. Try as he might, Michael couldn't see what his father was looking at in the brilliant blue sky, whether it was something in the future or the past.

The touch of a hand on his shoulder brings Michael back into the present, to the shore of a lake, not an ocean; to a country located miles away from the scene in his head.

"Should we go back now?" Liao asks him.

"Yes," Michael says.

# CHAPTER 10

Emily figured that she'd left her mother's house early enough in the afternoon to escape the onslaught of people returning from their weekends away in the country or at the shore, but traffic was at a near standstill once she approached the city. She switched the radio from station to station, hoping to get a traffic update, but instead received a weather advisory. It was supposed to storm that night, breaking the heat wave, which Emily took as good news. The air felt about ten times hotter in the city than in the suburbs, what with all the concrete and glass, and the honking horns from the stalled cars didn't make things any better. Emily didn't know how people could stand it. Of course, she had once withstood it; it seemed like years ago, although it only had been two since she'd moved away.

Jean Hu had left a message earlier, and when Emily called her, they arranged to meet at a diner in the East 20s. Emily was surprised but glad to hear from Jean so soon, hoping this meant that she was ready to talk about the case. What Emily didn't want Jean to ask her about was the last time she had seen Gao, which had been two weeks before his death, when he'd first complained of leg pain. It was possible that Emily had been the last person to speak to him rather than his wife, as the pain had progressed so much that he had been unable to walk to a pay phone in his final days.

The detention center that Gao had been kept in was a turn-of-the-century redbrick building that looked as if it could be either an insane asylum or a boys' boarding school in another life. The only indication that it housed inmates were the fourteen-foot-high barbed-wire fences surrounding the compound, beyond which rose gently forested hills. Not the worst place to be held, Emily had thought when she first saw it, thinking of the grim processing center in downtown Manhattan that Gao had been held in before being shuttled upstate. Inside, however, the center was typically spare and utilitarian, its white walls only broken by displays of patriotism, such as a flag or a mural.

The last time Emily had seen Gao had been in the interview room. She observed that he looked thinner than when she had seen him last and that he noticeably winced when he sat down. "Is there something wrong?" she asked.

"My leg is bothering me." Although they could have conversed in Chinese, Gao seemed to be making a pointed effort to use English.

"Has anyone checked it out?"

"The nurse here thought nothing was wrong. Actually, they think I'm making it up. I have a top bunk and asked to switch bunks with my cell mate, but it was not allowed."

Emily made a note to herself to speak to the authorities about the bunk, as well as request an evaluation from an independent doctor. "You need to let me know if it gets any worse, okay? How are you doing otherwise?"

Gao attempted a wry smile. "It's not so bad here. There are some other Chinese-speaking detainees and I translate for them. A few have cases even worse than mine. But somehow, I feel less hopeful than them, that I have less of a chance." He paused. "That's why I want to drop the appeal."

"What?"

"I want to accept deportation."

"That's ridiculous," Emily said, before she realized that probably wasn't the most diplomatic or persuasive response. "Have you told Jean?"

"No." He bowed his head. "I was hoping you would."

Emily looked at Gao for a moment, the back of his neck where his hair had been unevenly shaved in a jagged bristle. She wished she could step inside his mind, to understand why a man would chose to leave his wife and child, everything he had worked for, even under such duress. There must be something else going on, beyond any physical pain, that had brought him to this decision.

"I know," she said, "that you're experiencing a lot of stress. You don't know whether we'll win this case. I'll be honest with you, I don't know either. But Rick and I are going to do the best we can. . . ." She stopped when she realized that the usual assurances she doled out to clients weren't going to make any difference. Also, Gao appeared to have stopped listening to her.

"Do you know the mural they have here?" he asked.

Emily nodded. A mural featuring the Statue of Liberty next to a bald eagle next to the American flag was the first thing anyone saw when they entered the detention center. Every time she walked by it, it made her want to gag.

"When I saw it, I finally understood what was going on. *You aren't wanted here. You don't belong here.* The message could not be clearer."

"I can see what you mean," Emily tried.

"You can't. You were born here, yes? I hear what my son faces. He comes home from school and says some kid made fun of him, asked him if he sees the world slanted because of what his eyes look like. That's nothing compared to being woken up by the police and taken away in front of your wife and child."

"What happened that morning?"

"Jean and I were asleep. Sam was watching cartoons. When the doorbell rang, he answered it, although we had told him never to do that, to open the door to strangers. He went upstairs to get me, saying, 'Daddy, they want you.' I didn't even get dressed. I thought they were those Jehovah's Witnesses. Who else would ring so early on a Saturday morning? I remember feeling annoyed as I went downstairs, annoyed at Sam for answering the door and already annoyed at the people at the door. I thought my morning was going to be ruined." He gave a short laugh. "I wish that were true. So, you see, even if I do get out, even if I become a citizen, I can never erase that morning. I'll always be afraid that this could happen again." Gao regarded her closely. "You don't understand because you could never imagine yourself in my place. It's not possible."

"No," Emily admitted. "But if you do decide to . . . accept deportation, where will you go?"

Gao shrugged. "I have some relatives back in China. Of course, they are strangers to me now."

"And Jean and Sam? What will they do without you?"

"There are savings, a retirement account. They will be provided for." Gao, Emily realized, had already disassociated himself from his family. "Sometimes I think they would be better off without me."

"Impossible. I've spent time with your family; I see how much they miss you. All they want is for you to come home."

"But can't you see? That is no longer home for me. America is no longer my home, and neither is China. I am somewhere in between."

Which, Emily thought, described the detention center exactly, a place of neither freedom nor definite incarceration, but a white-walled, white-floored limbo. This place, coupled with the uncertainty of his situation and physical pain, must be the reason why Gao was talking such nonsense about giving up. She refused to think it was anything else, not a despair that had burrowed deep inside him and wouldn't let go.

"Listen," she said, leaning forward and catching his eyes. "I'm not going to say anything to Jean about this. If you still feel this way in a couple of weeks, we can discuss it further. But first we have to get you some medical attention. Let's focus on that, okay?"

Gao nodded without much conviction. Emily figured he'd be feeling differently enough once some visible progress was being made on his case, and it was her job to make sure that happened.

As Emily drove away from the detention center, her mind was filled with what she needed to do. She hadn't been successful in arguing for Gao to be moved to a lower bunk, and getting an independent doctor in to evaluate him was going to be an uphill battle.

She thought about what Gao had said, about her inability to imagine herself in his place. Perhaps that was true, but she could imagine it for her father. She had never known exactly how he had come to the States. Her mother had said he had told her once that he had been sponsored by a distant relative, but that probably meant false papers. She wondered if he had walked the streets of New York City, even their New Jersey suburb, worried that he would be picked out. Perhaps that was why he had stayed in the background of his life, even after so much time had passed. This fear would become a natural reflex, a second nature. You could never feel at home in such a place.

But maybe her father had never felt at home anywhere. Aside from the time when she was seven and Michael had been in the hospital, she had never heard him talk about where he had come from or his family with any warmth. As she grew older, she learned not to ask about these subjects at all, instead getting any information she needed from her mother. But sometimes even her mother didn't know. Once, for a sixth-grade history class assignment on genealogy, she'd pulled out the encyclopedia set at home, which was among the only English books her parents owned. She'd written about the Tang dynasty and how it was a period when arts and culture flourished, especially poets like Du Fu and Li Bai. Her teacher had written on her paper, "Well researched, but what does this have to do with *you?*"

While China was no longer his home either, perhaps it wasn't so far-fetched to think that Gao might be able to forge a decent life there, with his knowledge of English and technology. But for Jean and Sam? He might as well be dead. Just knowing that Gao had considered leaving them would change the way Jean felt about him. So, Emily determined that she was never going to speak of Gao's decision to accept deportation to Jean, or to anyone else. She hadn't counted on what would happen two weeks later, when Gao was no longer alive, and she was to face Jean for the first time.

By the time Emily reached the diner where she was supposed to meet Jean, she was winded. She'd just run down ten blocks in the heat, after finally finding a parking space. She looked past a couple of elderly ladies splitting a dessert and an off-duty cop to see Jean sitting in a booth in the back. Jean looked better today, her hair combed and drawn back in a knot at the nape of her neck. Her face was freshly made up, its expression preternaturally calm. Her nails, resting against her coffee cup, looked as if they had just been done. You could not tell from looking at her that this was a woman whose husband had died two days ago.

"I'm sorry I'm late, the traffic was terrible," Emily said as she slid into the booth. The waiter arrived, and she ordered an iced coffee, then dabbed at the perspiration trickling down her neck with a paper napkin. "How is Sam?"

"He's okay. My sister's looking after him."

"Does he know?"

Jean sighed. "He doesn't know the whole story. I don't know how to tell him in a way that he'll understand. So for now he just knows that there was an accident and his father isn't coming back."

The almost dispassionate way in which Jean was talking about her husband's death was unnerving.

"How are you holding up?" Emily asked.

"They gave me something to help me sleep last night. Loraza, loraze something."

"Lorazepam." Emily remembered that this was what the doctor had given her mother too. Her mother had ended up sitting on the sofa with a dazed expression on her face, as though a disaster were unfolding in front of her on a television screen.

"I don't like it. I didn't want to take it, but they made me. It takes away all feeling, the good and the bad. I look at Sam, and I can't feel anything, not even love. But if I don't take it, I'll fall into pieces." Jean turned her coffee cup in a slow circle. "I appreciate your coming to see me today. I want to thank you for what you've done."

"There's no need." Her clients never blamed Emily outright for failing to win a case, but nevertheless she felt that she had let them down. After what had happened to her husband, it almost seemed like Jean was mocking her.

"There is. You tried. You did the best you could."

"I didn't do enough. I could have found a way to get those medical reports a little faster. Maybe we could have gotten doctors to Gao quicker, transferred him to somewhere closer. It's my fault."

"No," Jean said. "It's mine."

Emily stared at her. "How?"

"The green card that started all of this trouble—Gao didn't *want* to apply for it. I made him do it. I told him that he needed to become a citizen, for our son's sake, so that our son could hold his head high. I shamed him into doing it."

"But you didn't know what it would lead to."

"Maybe not, but Gao kept saying that he felt something bad was going to happen if we put in the application. He kept reminding me of the expired visa. I told him that it had happened so long ago that it couldn't be on the records anymore. But I didn't know what I was talking about. I should have trusted him. Our life was fine. Sam was fine. That is, most of the time. He told me that he was being picked on in school, for the way he looked, for being shorter than the other boys. I told him that his father was short too, and he turned away from me. So I wanted him to be able to be proud of himself and his father. I remembered how I was picked on when I came to America, for not being able to speak English. I didn't want him to feel different."

"Kids feel different for all kinds of reasons," Emily murmured. Jean didn't seem to hear her.

"But if Gao didn't think it was a problem that he wasn't a citizen, I shouldn't have either. If there was one more thing I could say to my husband, it would be that I'm sorry for not believing in him. For not believing that he was enough for our family." After a moment, Jean asked, "Did Gao ever tell you how we met?"

Emily shook her head.

"It was at a party for a mutual friend at a restaurant on Mott Street in Chinatown. Everyone was from the north of China except the two of us. We were the only ones who could speak Cantonese. Gao had grown up near Chaozhou. That's a little more than two hundred miles from Hong Kong, where I was born. But, you know, back then it would be almost impossible to go from one place to the other. They might as well have been two separate countries, divided by a huge sea. We never could have met each other except here in America."

Emily was reminded of how her mother had once said that she and her father had met at a Chinatown dance. They would also never have met had they stayed in their respective hometowns.

"Gao told me right away that his visa had expired. That's why he moved so often. He was afraid that he would be tracked down. He never left a forwarding address or told his landlord where he was going. But once he met me, he said he was ready to stop running."

Emily thought of the many couples she had encountered in her job; almost always one person was seeking citizenship through the other. She suspected more than one of them were false marriages, especially when the husband or wife had hastily been brought over from another country. But how was that different from any other marriage of necessity, a union forged from loneliness, unrealistic expectations, lack of choice? Emily sometimes wondered if that was true of her own parents. Hearing Jean speak, she knew that Jean and Gao's relationship had not been like that.

"What did you think when he told you about the visa?" she asked Jean.

"It didn't bother me. Almost everyone I knew back then had some kind of problem like this. You just didn't talk about it. I was one of the lucky ones. I had come to the States when I was ten and became a naturalized citizen. I never thought for one minute that Gao was interested in me for a green card. He even promised me, when we decided to get married, that he would never ask me to help him get one. It would be enough that our children would be full citizens. He always felt this way. If only I could have felt the same."

Tears were spilling down Jean's cheeks now, although her face was still impassive. It was eerie to behold, as if a waxen doll were crying. Silently, Emily handed her a napkin from the metal dispenser on the table.

"I just wish I had some sign that he had forgiven me, something he said." Jean blotted her face; the bow on her blouse was askew. "You saw him recently, didn't you? At the detention center?"

Reluctantly, Emily nodded.

"Did he say anything to you?"

Emily hesitated. Was there any point in telling Jean that Gao had talked about accepting deportation, about leaving her and Sam because he did not feel he could live in a country that no longer wanted him there? She wished she could say that he had talked about how much he loved his wife and son, but that would be disingenuous. "We mostly talked about his health. That's all."

"Oh." Jean looked down into her coffee cup, disappointed.

"Jean," Emily said softly, "you don't need Gao's forgiveness. You need to forgive yourself, for Sam's sake, if not your own. If you don't, he'll associate your guilt with his father's death for the rest of his life. Besides, blaming yourself doesn't make any sense. There's no way you could have known what would happen."

"If it's not my fault, then whose is it?"

"The immigration system's," Emily said firmly. "And we'll find a way to prove it. Well, Rick will." She stopped for a second. "I hate to tell you this, but I'm not going to be working on the case anymore."

"Why not?"

"It's too close to me, and I—well, I've been having a lot of problems, too. Personal problems."

"Like what?" For the first time that afternoon, Jean sounded intrigued.

"Well, my mother is starting to date again, my little brother's run away to China, and I've just left my husband."

"Those are a lot of problems," Jean observed.

"Yes," Emily said. "But even though I won't be on the case anymore, I'll be here for you, if you want to talk. I understand what you're going through."

A wrinkle appeared across Jean's smooth brow. "How so?"

Emily took a deep breath. "My father died a year ago of a heart attack."

"You never told me that."

"It wouldn't have helped." At least back then, Emily thought.

"Can I ask about your mother? Is she doing better now?"

"I think so. Of course, I haven't visited her as much as I should. But I was just home over the weekend, and she seemed to be doing okay. Maybe even better than I thought."

"I hope," Jean said, "that I will be strong like your mother."

Emily hadn't thought that her mother might be strong, or that she or Michael could be considered strong in the aftermath of their father's death. Certainly she didn't feel particularly strong at the moment, having just admitted to Jean everything that was currently going wrong with her life.

"I'll tell you what," she said to Jean. "Why don't we meet here in a year, at this very diner, and we'll see how you feel?"

Jean managed a faint smile. "I hope I'll feel differently."

"You will." Emily hoped this would be true of herself too.

The waiter stopped by to see if they wanted anything else, but they asked for the check. Jean had to return home soon, because she'd left her sister for too long with Sam, while Emily had another appointment to get to. At the street corner they said good-bye, Jean to take the subway back to Queens and Emily to head uptown. The next time they'd see each other would be at Gao's funeral, which was to take place next week. Emily promised she'd attend. No matter where she ended up living, no matter what state her career and marriage were in, she would be there.

# CHAPTER 11

After leaving Qinghai Lake, Michael, Liao, and Ben head back to Xining through the late-afternoon sunshine. Liao falls asleep in the car, his head lolling back against the headrest. With his mouth slightly open and the tendons ropy in his outstretched neck, he looks like a baby bird.

"There is a rug factory outside of town," Ben says to Michael. "We will pass by it soon. Should we go there?"

"Rug factory?" Michael repeats.

"Yes, they weave rugs out of yak wool. They're very warm. Maybe you can buy a rug for your family in America?"

Michael wonders who in his family would want a yak wool rug, which he guesses wouldn't smell much better than the yak butter. His mother would put it in the basement, while Emily would say that it didn't fit the décor in her house. Then he remembers something else he read on the travel website.

"Aren't the rugs made by prisoners?" Michael glances at Liao, who is still asleep; in fact, he is snoring a little.

"Yes," Ben replies pleasantly. "Do you want to go?"

"Um, no, thank you," Michael says. Then, feeling bold since Liao is clearly unable to hear him, adds, "Did your father ever talk about when he was in the labor camp? Like why he was sent there?"

"No," says Ben. "All I know is that he was in prison when he was a young man."

"You never asked him? I mean, you were never curious?"

Ben shrugs, keeping his eyes on the road. "Back then, you can accuse people of anything. It doesn't mean it isn't true or you are a bad person. Plenty of people were sent to the labor camps for doing nothing."

*They probably still are,* Michael thinks but doesn't say aloud. "So your father doesn't like to talk about the past?"

Another shrug. "There's nothing to talk about. But, no, he does not like to talk about it."

Michael sits back in his seat. "Neither did my father. Did your father ever mention mine before?"

"I don't remember him talking about your father, no. Only last night, when he says that you are here in Xining and wants to see us. He thought your father was with you, too. He was very sad that your father was not."

Michael considers and then dares to ask, "Do you feel you and your father are close?"

Ben glances briefly at his sleeping father, as if approximating physical distance. "What do you mean, close?"

Michael realizes that it isn't a language barrier, but maybe a cultural one that he's come up against. "I mean, do you feel you can tell him anything?"

"Of course I can tell him anything. He is my father. Also," Ben adds, "we live in the same house. He will hear anything I say."

Michael wonders at the nonchalance of Ben's statement, whether it's really true or Ben is just saying what he thinks Michael wants to hear. Or maybe he's misinterpreted the question, although Ben's English is good enough that Michael thinks otherwise. He has to admit that he's a little jealous of how Ben is able to speak so easily of his father.

The streets of the city flash by, and soon they are stopping at the familiar gate of the normal university with its statue of Mao. Ben drives onto the grounds and parks the car in front of one of the departmental buildings. As they're sitting there, Liao still asleep, Ben's cell phone rings. He takes out a device that looks much newer and more complicated than Michael's own from his tracksuit pocket.

"It is my mother," he explains to Michael after ending the call. "She wants to know when we will be home. There is a little time before dinner, though, to show you around."

Ben gently prods his father awake, and the three of them get out of the car and walk onto the college campus, which looks busier than when Michael was there two days ago. Students in their blue-and-white gym uniforms stroll about arm in arm, not couples, but girls with girls and boys with boys. Michael knows this doesn't mean anything, just that they're close friends. He saw two PLA soldiers walking around that way in the Muslim market the day before.

"They look very happy," Michael says of the students.

Liao makes a disapproving sound. "There are some problems. There are many things the students want to change."

"What kinds of things?" Michael asks, thinking about his own college experience and some of the most popular issues brought up then: protesting against anti-affirmative action bills, banning the Greek system, legalizing marijuana.

"They say there is bad service in the library. Also, the water they drink makes them sick if they do not boil it long enough. And they do not like how the lights go off at ten thirty every night."

"The lights go off at ten thirty?" Michael echoes.

"Yes, in the dormitories. The electricity is cut off. That way the students are sure to go to bed and get enough rest. Sometimes, though, they light candles to study, and then it is dangerous because they can burn down the dormitory."

Michael shakes his head behind Liao's back.

They pass by a clearing where strains of ballroom music issue from a boom box, and same-sex pairs of students and opposite-sex pairs of older couples dance together. They stop to watch as the dance pattern changes from a waltz to a foxtrot. A student switches disks on the boom box, and a synthesizer beat blares forth. The older couples move to the side, but the students break apart and began to sway to the music. They don't bop around in the way Michael expects, but move in perfect coordination, arms swinging together, hips swiveling in unison, like line dancing.

"What is this music called in English?" Liao asks.

"Disco?" Michael guesses. There is something very seventies about it.

"See," Liao observes. "Even when they dance disco, the Chinese like to be unified."

Michael nods, wondering if the man is trying to make some kind of discreet political statement, but Liao just walks on serenely.

Continuing the impromptu tour, Liao and Ben show Michael the canteen, where apparently the students' problem is that they want to conserve trees by using plastic spoons instead of wooden chopsticks, but the spoons cut their mouths. They walk by the field where the students do their morning exercises, like millions of other students all across China at exactly the same time. Then Michael is unintentionally taken past the students' restrooms, mainly identifiable by the deep, rank odor that he is beginning to associate with Chinese toilets. It is more than a stink; it seems to come from the very bowels of the earth itself. This, he thinks, is something the students should be complaining about.

Finally, they come to a square, five-story apartment building, all with glassed-in balconies in a row down the front. They climb three flights of stairs and enter a space that is about the size of Michael's apartment back home, except that it has concrete floors and walls whose upper half is painted white and the lower half, pale green, as if in a psych ward. A couple of scrolls, and a calendar showing a field of flowers, hang on the walls, but otherwise they are bare.

A young woman holding a chubby toddler comes forward to greet them. Liao introduces them as Ben's wife, whose English name is Mary, and his son, Rong Rong. Liao's wife, a smiling, round-faced woman, emerges from the kitchen. From what Michael can tell, the kitchen is the glassed-in balcony he saw from outside the apartment building. He can glimpse a two-burner stove on top of a low cupboard with a tank of propane next to it. The wall above the stove is peeling and streaked with black smoke from cooking. Above, criss-crossing the glassed-in space, is a line of drying laundry.

"Would you like to wash up?" Liao asks, pointing to a neon green plastic basin and matching water jug in a corner.

Michael declines, but asks to use the bathroom. It is a closet off the main room, and as he has suspected, contained a squat toilet. As spotless as it is, an inescapable whiff comes from it. He tries to pee quietly in the miniscule space so that his hosts won't be able to hear him. Where, Michael wonders, do the Liaos shower?

When he comes out of the bathroom, Ben suggests, "Do you want to see the rest of our apartment?"

"Yes, I'd like to take a tour," Michael replies, but Ben doesn't seem to get the joke.

The one room Michael hasn't seen so far is down a short hall-way. It is a bedroom with a single high bed covered with a bright pink coverlet and a matching honey-colored dresser, unlike the assorted furniture in the living room. There is a crib at the foot of the bed, and above the headboard hangs a huge framed wedding photograph of Ben and Mary, made to look like a painting. They are both in Western dress, Ben in a tuxedo and Mary in a frothy white gown and veil that seems to take up half the picture. She looks very different from the plain young woman Michael was introduced to, her face made up, her head tilted with her chin resting on one hand. Ben stands behind her, one hand on her shoulder and the other holding her free hand, in a pose that Michael recognizes from a thousand high school prom photos.

"Was this taken at your wedding?" he asks Ben.

"No," Ben says. "Chinese people don't have weddings like you Americans. This was taken in a photo studio after we got married. You can dress up in many different costumes, from the olden days, even the movies." He strikes a pose, arms outstretched as if he's at the prow of a boat, and adds when Michael looks confused, "*Titanic*. Are you married?"

"No," Michael says shortly. "Do you and Mary sleep here?" He figures that he can be just as nosy.

"Yes. Rong Rong sleeps in there." Ben points at the crib.

"Where do your parents sleep?"

"In the living room."

Michael marvels that a family of five lives in a space that is not much bigger than his own apartment in New York. He thinks about how if things had ended up differently for his father and Liao, he and Emily might have very well grown up like this, sharing a room. Actually, if that were true, he wouldn't have even been born; Emily would have been the one child his parents were allowed to have. As alarming as that thought is, he can't help but think that if that were the case, then his father wouldn't have had a son to be disappointed in.

"And where do you shower?" Michael finally asks the question he's been dying to know the answer to.

"There's a bathhouse on campus."

"Doesn't that get cold in the winter?"

"When it's cold," Ben says, "I run there and back." He grins. "It's good exercise."

After they return to the living room, Liao insists Michael sit down on a bed pushed against one wall, which Michael guesses is where he and his wife usually sleep. It is piled high with satin quilted blankets and pillows, and proves to be quite soft, if a bit slippery. Everyone else sits on chairs or stools around the low coffee table, and Michael realizes that the bed-couch is considered the place of honor.

The table is covered with food: a whole steamed fish with ginger, prawns encrusted in sea salt, sautéed greens with the bite of garlic, eggplant in black bean sauce, peppery egg mixed with tomato, sautéed corn with pine nuts. It is mind-boggling that so much food can have come out of that tiny kitchen. Michael knows that the Liaos must not eat so well every day, that it has all been prepared especially for him. He compliments the dishes and asks what makes them taste so good.

Ben whispers something to Mary, and she retrieves from the kitchen a small packet of what looks like baking soda. "This is gourmet powder," he says.

Michael inspects the packet, wondering if he should bring some back for his mother and sister. Then he sees the English letters on the side: *MSG.* He hastily thanks Ben and gives back the packet, and tries not to eat so much after that, but he supposes the damage is already done, and he doesn't want to offend his hosts, and the food is very, very good.

They don't talk much. Most of the sounds are made by chopsticks clinking against bowls, glasses against the tabletop, and Rong Rong's fussing when he is fed something he does not want to eat. Everyone seems to be feeding him, not only his grandmother and mother, but even Ben reaches over at times to put a tidbit into his son's mouth. It can't be so bad, Michael reflects, to have three generations sitting around the table like this. Despite what Liao has been through, no matter what conditions he lived in and currently lives in, he is able to enjoy his family now.

Now come the personal questions, mostly from the women. Michael is asked again if he is married. He replies that his sister, Emily, is. Mary wants to know if Emily is married to a Chinese or a *waiguo ren,* an "outside person," which he thinks is kind of funny because, obviously, Julian is not an "outside person" in America. When Michael says a *waiguo ren,* Mary nods sagely.

Michael asks how Ben and Mary met, and is told that Mary was a physical education teacher at the university while Ben was studying to be a tour guide. After they married, she quit her job and now spends her time taking care of Rong Rong and her in-laws. Liao was an English teacher until his retirement seven years before. He has a pension, but they mostly live off of Ben's income, which is quite good, Ben adds. He is not being immodest, it is just a fact.

They ask Michael what his job is and how much he makes, without any hint that these might be inappropriate questions to ask someone you just met. Michael supposes, like staring, these subjects are not considered forbidden here. He says he works with computers and that he doesn't know how to convert his salary into Chinese money. *It's probably so high you can't convert it,* Ben says, and Michael does not bother to correct him.

The women clear the table, and then Mary goes to put Rong

Rong to bed. Michael can hear Liao's wife in the kitchen and wonders if he should offer to help. But Liao and Ben just sit at the table, and he realizes that it is a time for men only. Liao goes to a cabinet and takes down a bottle of grain liquor and three tiny, thimble-sized cups. He pours some for each of them and raises his cup.

"*Ganbei,*" he says.

The liquor sears Michael's throat like firelight and doesn't taste like anything, it's so strong. But Michael nods when Liao lifts the bottle again. After a few rounds, everyone's tongues seem to be loosened, if not burned.

"Sometimes I think I'll try to work in America," Ben confides. "Do they need tour guides there?"

"Sure," Michael says, thinking of the people who work the tour buses in the city, although it is more likely, despite Ben's command of English, that he would end up one of those vendors in China-town hawking knock-off designer bags.

"It is very hard to go to America without a sponsor," Liao says. "Maybe you can sponsor my son?"

"Maybe," Michael replied vaguely.

Ben waves away his father's suggestion. "Sometimes I think there's no reason to go to America. I can make plenty of money here. There are more and more tourists every year. Look!" He extends his wrist. "A Rolex, made in China. You can get everything here."

Michael makes an agreeable sound.

"Besides, if I go to America," Ben continues, "I will have to be away from my family. Or maybe Mary can come, but we will leave Rong Rong here, and he will be raised by my parents. I've seen it happen. Your son grows up without you and does not know you."

"Things are different now," Liao says. "Back then, it was considered a good opportunity, even if it didn't always work out. It worked out for your father," he says to Michael, "but then he was lucky."

*Lucky?* Michael wonders. He isn't sure if his father was lucky or just worked hard. And then working hard became the purpose of his life, and sacrifice was all that he knew. But Michael doesn't know how to say this to his host. He suspects this kind of personal talk is more taboo than asking how much money you made.

"How did you find my father's address?" he asks Liao.

"My wife and I visited Beijing about a year and a half ago. We wanted to ever since I retired. I had not been back since I had left as a teenager. No one from my family is left there, but I wanted to see my old house, which I told you about before. Sometimes, you know, the place is more important than the people."

Michael nods.

"I found it is divided into many apartments, each around this size." Liao gestures around the room they are sitting in. "All the families are new to Beijing and do not follow the old customs. They throw trash everywhere and ruin the place. While I was there, I ran into a neighbor. Of course, now he is very old. He is the only person left there from before. He told me what happened to all the other neighbors, and that your father had gone to the States. Like I said before, he is lucky."

Michael thinks that immigrating to America must have been the hardest thing his father ever had to do in his life. And for what, to find a wife? To become a lab technician and buy a house in New Jersey? To send his two ungrateful children to college?

"This neighbor, he has a very old address for your father, but I thought I would take a chance and write a letter." Liao leans forward and pats Michael's arm. "I wondered why I had not heard from your father. I thought the address is too old. Now I know what happened. I was very sad to hear about your father passing away. But I am also glad that the letter brought you here, so that you can see Qinghai Province for yourself. Did you enjoy the monastery and the lake?"

"Yes, but most of all I enjoyed hearing about my father's childhood." Michael pauses. "Can you tell me more? What happened after you discovered that my grandfather was a Christian?"

Liao refills his cup as if to fortify himself for what's to come next.

\*　\*　\*

In the fall of 1966, everything changed. The schools were in a disarray. The classrooms had been taken over for political meetings, the schoolyards for public displays of humiliation, where people were made to wear dunce caps and kneel on broken glass. We weren't students anymore, we were Red Guards. You might have thought this would be an awful time to be a teenager. Actually, it felt like being on top of the world, to be sixteen years old and the most powerful beings around. Wherever we went, we were supposed to be able to knock on anyone's door and be given a place to stay and food to eat. In the beginning, people were hospitable and eager to do this, saying that the youth were the future of our country. Then, when the youth became more arrogant, grabbing whatever they wanted and making accusations if you tried to stop them, they became distrustful and afraid of us.

In groups of four or five boys, we went on raids through large houses abandoned by the bourgeoisie, smashing antique vases, paintings, figurines; things that would be considered quite valuable today. Back then, though, people believed you had to get rid of the old in order to make way for the new. These destructive acts were an attempt to obliterate our old selves, so that we could become new model citizens.

Han was in his element. He was a natural leader, charismatic and resourceful. He knew exactly when to draw back, when there was no point anymore to our wildness. Somehow, the destruction didn't seem so bad with him around. In addition to myself, our group usually included two other former classmates: Zhao, who had always been a bit of a bully, and Xiao Peng, who was quiet and bookish. Han was the sun around which we orbited, drawn in by his confidence, his surety that what we were doing was right.

Once, accompanied by Min—a girl whose revolutionary fervor scared us boys a little—we came upon a house that had already been ransacked to its very bones. It had belonged to a foreigner, judging by the English titles on the books that had been pulled from the shelves and half ripped apart: *Uncle Tom's Cabin, The Adventures of Tom Sawyer, Great Expectations.* In a different place and time, I would have taken those books for my own, although then it would have been stealing. But here I dared not show that the foreign words on the spines meant anything to me.

I think we were all impressed by the thoroughness of the Red Guards who had come before us. Sofa cushions had been slashed, the stuffing strewn around the floor like snow. Tables were missing legs and chairs, arms. Several picture frames had been ripped from the walls and dashed on the floor. Behind the broken glass of one I saw the image of a lady in Western dress. Irrationally, I thought about Mr. Frazier and wondered whether he had been reunited with his wife and children in the Ohio River Valley.

"This *yang guizi* got what he deserved," Han announced.

"I'll bet he had servants that he underpaid and exploited," Min chimed in.

"They should have strung him up—"

"—like the imperialistic pig he is!"

Xiao Peng and I just looked at each other as Han and Min took turns going on about the "foreign devil." I could tell that Xiao Peng felt uneasy about their ramblings but could do nothing but nod in agreement, like me. From somewhere upstairs came a crash; Zhao on a rampage, probably.

Then Zhao came down with a bottle of amber liquid. We all knew it was some kind of spirits, and that we should try it. Min found some glasses and did the honors of pouring.

"To the great Mao," Han said.

"To Jiang Qing," Min said, referring to Mao's actress wife.

"No!" Zhao yelled. "Her face is like the back of a horse!"

After a while, Zhao turned to Xiao Peng. "Little Peng," he said. "I've been watching you for a long time. I think there is something strange about you."

Xiao Peng smiled weakly. "What is that?"

Zhao went over and plucked the photograph of the lady in Western dress from the floor, swearing when he nicked his finger on a shard of glass. He shoved it in front of Xiao Peng's face. "Do you find this woman attractive?"

"Of course he doesn't," I said. "She's a foreigner." I turned to Xiao Peng. "Right?"

"I—I don't know."

"Aha," Zhao said as if this was some kind of proof. "I knew it. You don't like women."

"I do too," Xiao Peng protested.

"Then prove it"—Zhao looked around the room—"by kissing Min!"

Min squealed in protest and almost fell off her chair.

"Otherwise, you'll have to kiss old Liao here." Zhao laughed and pointed at me.

I scowled at him and looked toward Han to see if he would intervene, but he leaned forward, appearing interested. I doubted if any of us boys in the room had ever kissed a girl, but to me, Min was not a great prospect. She had rabbitty front teeth and slightly bulging eyes, which, when she was in the middle of a political tirade, seemed to threaten to pop from her head. But Han's eyes were fixed on her.

"Go on," he said.

Min giggled and minced up to Xiao Peng. She put her hands on his shoulders and touched her lips to his for barely a second. It was just a peck, but Xiao Peng looked like he was going to be ill.

"I *knew* it," Zhao said. The look he gave Xiao Peng was full of disgust and loathing. "You're nothing but a—"

"That's enough!" Han roared. "We're done here. Let's go."

As we quietly obeyed and filed out of the house, the glow gone from our adventure, I glanced at Han. He looked furious. I couldn't tell whether he was angry with Zhao for baiting Xiao Peng, or himself for letting things go too far. Or maybe, I thought, he liked Min and wished he had been on the receiving end of her thin, chapped lips. I started to look at my old friend in a new light. He was beginning to grow apart from me, desiring things that were beyond my comprehension.

As if he sensed our increasing distance, Han tried to include me more in the favorite activities of himself, Zhao, and the others, including struggle sessions. This was when people were put on trial for their crimes against the state and subsequently ridiculed, beaten, and stoned, because they were always found guilty. There were rumors that some people had even died afterward, although they had been old and had weak hearts, and by that time they had been dragged away, so no one saw their bodies anyhow. I didn't like such bloodthirsty spectacles and did my best to avoid them. I knew that if you did not go, you were considered weak by the other boys and that this might somehow make its way up to the authorities, but until that winter I managed to worm my way out of attendance.

Then one chilly day Han sought me out with a glint in his eyes. "There's a special struggle session tomorrow afternoon," he said. "Will you come?"

I tried to think of any excuse—that my mother needed me to help her with the washing, that I had promised my father to go to the store. Finally, I decided to be honest.

"I don't like attending those things," I told him.

He regarded me closely. "Those people are being punished for breaking the law, you know."

"But why do they have to be punished in public?"

"So that the people they have wronged can have the satisfaction of seeing justice done. If someone had cheated you, wouldn't you want to see them get what was coming to them?"

"I don't think so," I said.

Han sighed with impatience. "Just come tomorrow. You won't want to miss it."

I knew I had to go. If I didn't, Zhao and the other boys would never let me live it down. I had to go or else forever lose face.

So the next day, Han and I went to our old school, where many of the struggle sessions took place since it wasn't being used to teach students anymore. The yard had been transformed by big-letter posters denouncing the victim. When we got there, we could barely see what was going on because of the number of kids, all shouting and getting worked up. In earlier times, this crowd might have gathered because two boys were fist fighting. Now, it was a living, seething, mass of anger. To my surprise, the person that the fuss was being made over was our old teacher, Mu. She was kneeling in the middle of a circle, a board around her neck upon which the characters for "thief" had been painted. Apparently she had been caught stealing grain from a storehouse. It was obvious that she had done it because she was starving.

Teacher Mu had never been fat, but now she looked positively gaunt. Her glasses had been knocked from her face, so that you could see how sunken her eyes and hollow her cheeks were. Although she hadn't even been middle-aged when we had been her students, now she looked as old as a grandmother. For a moment I felt sorry for her. She probably hadn't held the position of teacher for years. Without a husband, children, any family members, she had likely suffered more than most. She was here now because she had no one to defend or protect her.

People were calling her names, from a thief to a whore to a capitalist roader, which didn't even make sense, because she was being punished for stealing like an ordinary criminal, not because of her ideology. Next to me, Han was starting to get worked up. He looked in my direction, and, when he sensed my discomfort, frowned. Then, as if giving up, he joined in with everyone else, hurling insults as if they were rocks.

Then a real rock flew out of nowhere and hit Teacher Mu on the forehead. Blood trickled down her face and into her eyes, making her look even more skeletal and ghastly. Another rock hit her on the back, propelling her forward and onto her face. This was a signal that the stoning could begin, since it was easier when the person couldn't look you in the eyes and reproach you for what you were about to do.

I felt Han pressing something into my hand. It was a sharp-edged stone that fit perfectly in my palm.

"Here," he said. "Do it."

I hesitated. But it seemed impossible that I should be suspended in motion. It seemed like my only choices were to go forward or to go back. And since I couldn't help Teacher Mu, I had to go forward. I threw the rock.

I guess you could say that my relationship with Han was never the same after that struggle session. Even though I had ended up throwing the rock (feebly, so that it hit Teacher Mu on the leg), he had witnessed my weakness. By the way, I never knew for certain what happened to Teacher Mu. I believe she was let go, but that she was crippled for the rest of her life. One of the milder outcomes.

Everyone who had been at the struggle session considered me a coward, especially Zhao. Until then, he had been remotely hostile to me, as he had been the night we were in the foreigner's house. But now he began to focus his attention on me and Xiao Peng, who seemed to be the only person who treated me the same as before. I felt that out of all the boys we knew, Xiao Peng was playing the part as much as I was. Although not considered an intellectual, and therefore not one of the "enemies of the people," his father was suspect because he had studied abroad in his youth. Therefore, it was of the utmost importance that Xiao Peng show that he was as devoted to the cause as everyone else. But he preferred to stay in the background, and I was content to join him there.

However, Zhao made it difficult. Sometimes, when he passed us in the street, he would mutter a derogatory word under his breath, and we would ignore him. But once, he pushed Xiao Peng into the mud. The funny thing was, while he did it, he was watching me for my reaction the whole time. He hardly looked at Xiao Peng, as if Xiao Peng were a tree or an inanimate object that just happened to be in his way. As he walked away from us, I realized he had pushed Xiao Peng to see what I would do. It was all incredibly like being in the schoolyard again when we were ten years old.

Eventually, Han noticed my defection. "What are you doing with Little Peng?" he asked. "You two sneak off in the evening for long periods of time. What are you doing together?"

"Nothing," I said. I didn't want to tell him that all Xiao Peng and I did was talk about books and his father's time abroad in England.

"I hope so. Because you don't want to be that closely associated with him. You know how he is."

I knew Han was talking about *tongxinglian*. You know what *tongxinglian* means, right? It means two people with hearts that are alike, being together. During this time, in addition to all the intellectuals and landowners who were persecuted, the authorities also went after people who were religious, and people who were considered sexual deviants. I knew these kinds of people existed, of course, but I never thought they could describe anyone I knew.

"Of course not." I looked for a way to shift his attention. "So how about you? What are you up to with Min these days? Or rather, what is she up to with Zhao?"

Han didn't reply, and I knew I had hit a sore spot with him. Anyone could tell that Min was playing Han and Zhao off each other, with her affections as the prize. I often saw one of them walking down the street with her, not touching, but still bound to her by the leash of attraction. I was still confounded by Min, the jaunty red bows tied to the ends of her braids, the smooth brown column of her throat rising from her man's shirt. If there was something that boys like Han and Zhao found attractive about her, it was lost on me.

"Actually," I said, "I'm worried about Zhao and what he might do to Xiao Peng." But when I told Han how Zhao had bullied Xiao Peng and that I thought he might take things too far one day, he merely laughed.

"You're just being paranoid," he said. "Zhao isn't that complicated. He doesn't have the brains."

"Still, I think he's dangerous," I said. "He could be dangerous to you, too. If he ever found out about your father—"

"He'll never find out," Han interrupted. "Don't worry, I can handle Zhao."

For a moment we regarded each other, the air between us uncertain. Then Han said, "Do you remember that day we went to the Summer Palace?"

It had been just a couple of years ago, when we were fourteen. We had ridden our bikes to the grounds of Empress Cixi's summer home on the outskirts of Beijing. The landscaped gardens and glimmering lake, over which stone bridges arched, were quiet and peaceful. We sat on the grass by the lake, watching the ducks swim by. Occasionally, a pebble thrown by Han broke the surface of the water.

At first, the things we talked about were silly. We played one of our favorite games, What You Would Be Willing to Pick Up in the Outhouse? Because the compounds where we lived had been built so long ago, there was no modern plumbing. Everyone in the neighborhood went to a public outhouse, which consisted of a building in which holes were dug in the ground with boards placed around them so you did not fall in. There were wooden partitions between the holes, and when Han and I went in there together, we would talk through the partitions. Often this annoyed one of our neighbors, Old Luo, who had indigestion and liked to defecate in peace.

Anyway, the premise of this game was to name something that you would be willing to go down into the hole to retrieve if you accidentally dropped it. The night soil collector would regularly come to take away the contents of the outhouse, but sometimes, especially in the summer, the piles would get pretty high and the stink was unbearable. It was better in the winter, because then the piles would be frozen, but it was much colder to hang around with your bottom uncovered.

"What if you dropped a schoolbook?" Han suggested.

I shook my head. You might get penalized by the teacher at school, but the book could be replaced. "A hundred kuai bill?" I tried. A hundred kuai may not sound like a lot to you now, but it was back then, especially to two boys.

"Not worth it," Han said. Then, "What if you dropped a passport?"

Neither of us had ever heard of anyone who had a passport. We only knew that they were very hard to get, maybe not even within your lifetime, and without it you would not be able to travel to other countries. It was like a magical key to other worlds.

"Summer or winter?" I asked.

Han considered. "Summer."

"After Old Luo has been in there or not?"

Han giggled. "After."

"Okay," I said. "I would do it."

After that, we discussed more serious things. We talked about what we wanted to do when we grew up. I wanted to be a teacher, of course, but first I wanted to see the world. I wanted to travel, to see places I had read about only in books.

"You don't have to go outside of China," Han pointed out. "There is plenty in this country that you haven't seen."

He was correct, since neither of us had been outside of Beijing at that time. Like most inhabitants of the capital, we did not feel the need to see how the rest of our compatriots lived. This was before young people from the cities were sent down for periods of time in the countryside, to learn how to work with their hands like peasants.

"Besides," Han added, "do you even know what you want to teach?"

"Not really," I had to admit.

"Do you even want to be a teacher, or is that something your father has put in your head?"

"I do," I said, and I meant it. "And whatever I end up teaching, I want it to be something that will help our country grow strong. Like, not the classics, but modern philosophy. Not Confucius, but Marx and Engels."

Han nodded his approval.

"How about you?" I challenged.

"Well, I want to help my country too, of course," he said slowly. "But I want to stay in China to do it. Maybe I will become a scientist and invent something that will help China become powerful again."

"That's specific," I commented, and he flushed.

"It doesn't really matter what I do, just so that my family will be provided for. You don't have to worry about that like I do."

I was aware that Han's father was often unwell, and his older brother had gone up north as a soldier, with no idea when he would return. His two sisters were unmarried, so there was no help there either.

"You're right," I said. "You should do whatever you need to do to help your family."

Han threw another pebble into the water. "Let's not talk about this anymore," he said. "You want to race home?" And before I could say anything, he jumped up, grabbed his bike, and began pedaling away. I hurried after him, but of course he'd had a head start and beat me.

"Yes," I said, when Han reminded me two years later of that trip we took to the Summer Palace. "I remember that day well."

"Good," he said. "I hope you will always remember it."

Only a few weeks after that, the local authorities paid me a call. My father welcomed them into the house, two policemen and a man who wasn't wearing a uniform but looked even more ominous because of it. My mother hastened to bring them tea, but the man in the plain suit held up a hand to stop her.

"We have come here to see your son," he said.

"Whatever he's done, it can't be that bad," my father said. He put his hand on my shoulder and gave it a quick, conspiratorial squeeze; I believe he thought I was going to be reprimanded for some kind of childish prank. That rare gesture of affection buoyed me through what was to come next.

Which was the police accusing me of engaging in "unnatural activities," in *tongxinglian*. And who with? Meek, inoffensive Xiao Peng. Immediately, I thought that Zhao must have been the one who had made this claim. He was the sole person who had ever cared to make insinuations about Xiao Peng. It was the kind of statement that in previous times was just an ugly rumor, but now had serious ramifications. I don't even know if Zhao knew how serious they were. It was like he had thrown a firecracker, expecting to make a spark, and had started an inferno instead. Why I had been dragged into it, I didn't know yet.

My mother began to weep as the policemen escorted me from the house. My father, sensing it was useless to protest at that moment, followed us to the gate and out onto the street. As we passed by the other compounds, our neighbors gathered at a wary distance on either side. Then I caught sight of Han running up behind us, trying to see who it was that the police were taking away. I will never forget the emotions that crossed his face: fear that his father was the one being arrested—relief that it was someone else—and then deep, profound guilt.

In an instant I understood that Zhao wasn't the one who had implicated me, it had been my oldest, dearest friend. They must have come sniffing around Han's family and, to protect his father, he must have offered up Xiao Peng. When pressured further by the police, he had to offer up me as well. It would have been easy to believe. Xiao Peng and I had been seen around together often, and were both known to be soft on ideology. Perhaps Han thought that we'd just spend a night in jail, be lightly beaten or fined. I like to think he was that naïve.

I don't remember much of what happened after that. I do know that I was sentenced to fifteen years of hard labor, in a re-education camp in the northwest of China. I might as well have been sentenced to the moon. Looking back, things could have been worse. I was not beaten, nor did I receive a public trial that would have humiliated my family. As far as I knew, my parents and siblings were not harmed. I don't know what happened to Xiao Peng, whether he had received a harsher or lighter sentence, whether he had been assigned to a labor camp too. There was no way of finding out. I don't know what happened to Zhao, either. Maybe he and Min finally got together, maybe he fell into the officials' good favor, maybe his throat was slit in an alley. I didn't really care.

The one person I wondered about was Han. How did he feel about the part he had played in it all? I wondered about it for the next fifteen years.

Liao stops to take a breath, as if it has exhausted him to tell this part of the story.

"Wait," Michael says. "My father sold you out?"

"There are some people who would think that."

Michael stares at Liao, not understanding how the man can sound so calm. Yes, it was forty-five years ago, but still . . . He wonders if he should apologize, somehow make amends. This whole time Liao and his family have taken him sightseeing, prepared dinner in his honor, and he hasn't done anything to reciprocate. He didn't even think to bring them something from the States. Then again, maybe there isn't anything he can do to make up for what his father did to his friend.

"Things like that happened all the time back then," Liao says. "Worse things. Neighbors turning in neighbors, children denouncing parents. You did what you had to, in order to survive. That was the only way."

"How did you survive being in the labor camps?"

"Ah," Liao says. "The thought of your father helped me."

Back then, the western part of China was very much unsettled. There were rumors of resources, oil and precious minerals, but no one knew how to extract them. The region's natural beauty was praised in tales and folk songs, but no one really wanted to go out there to see if it were true. You usually only went out west if you were a criminal and were sentenced to go there, and the alternative was death. This had been happening since the purges of the 1950s.

Xining City, the capital of Qinghai Province, was not the busy, modern Chinese city you see today. It was more like an outpost, inhabited by settlers the government had paid to move there. The railroad to Golmud, farther west, had not been built yet, so it was the last stop on the train. People there called the area Amdo, the old Tibetan name. The city was located on an extremely desolate plateau, the elevation so high that it would give you nosebleeds and headaches. Winds constantly blew sand from the desert, so that when you blew your nose, grit came out. It could snow nine months out of the year, from the ninth month to the fifth month. It was in this lonely place that I would spend the next fifteen years of my life.

The work we did at the labor camp seemed expressly designed to drive us insane with its pointlessness. We would be forced to dig a ditch, just to fill it up. We moved piles of stones from one quarry to another and then back again. The purpose was not to reeducate our minds through work, but to numb them until we couldn't feel anything other than thirst or hunger. Sometimes we were so thirsty, we would drink from the brackish water that collected in the ditches, and then spent the rest of the day shitting it back out. We ate corn cakes, which were made more filling by mixing the corn with ground husks. Some people tried to make their cakes last longer by crumbling them up and mixing them with dirt, but usually that just made your stomach hurt.

It's strange, but those corn cakes seem to be coming back into fashion now. They're called *wotou,* and I saw them in restaurants when I went to Beijing. There are some restaurants that deliberately re-create food eaten during the Communist era. All I can say is that the people who go to these restaurants must be too young to have actually lived during that time and tasted *wotou* for themselves. Otherwise, they would not eat them with such relish.

In the hottest days of summer, we would be allowed to work at night. I looked forward to these nights the most, especially when there was a full moon. In the moonlight, our surroundings looked less miserable than usual, the workers' backs and the trees looking as if they were covered in ice. It was a little like poetry. In fact, I would be reminded of the famous poem about the moon by Li Bai. He's the poet who drowned when he tried to embrace the reflection of the moon while drunk one night. Anyway, his relationship with the moon before that was much more innocent. Do you know this poem? Every child in China can recite it by heart. Even my grandson Rong Rong knows it:

> *Before my bed, the moonlight shone brightly*
> *I thought it was frost on the ground*
> *I lifted my head and looked at the moon*
> *I lowered my head and thought of home*

Of course, when children learn this poem, what do they know of longing for home? They *are* at home, with their families, maybe cradled in their mother's arms when they first hear it. What a waste of a poem on children. No, this poem is for a grown person who is far away from home, with little hope of returning. For me, when I tried to remember home, I could not picture it, not the shape of the gate or the height of the courtyard walls, the compound next door or the street just outside. I don't know if it was a trick that my mind was playing on me, to keep me from being so homesick.

What kept me going during this time was not religious belief, or thinking about my family or what I would do when I was released, since that was still so far in the future. Instead, I thought about Han and what he must be doing. Was he still living with his family in Beijing, had he become a scientist, had he a wife and children of his own? I hoped, with all of my dark heart, that he had not. I wished him a life as bitter as mine had become. Fortunately, anger is stronger than regret. I do believe that if I had allowed myself to feel pity over my situation, or to miss the outside world, I would have broken down, as many of my fellow inmates did. Instead, my mind remained strong and alert. I have Han to thank for that. But even those thoughts cannot sustain someone forever.

It was in my eighth fall, more than halfway through my prison sentence, when something happened to break the monotony of those years.

The fall was one of the more pleasant times in this region. There had been no snow yet, but you could feel the change of weather in the air, and the dust storms that had blown all summer had died down. The air was very clear and crisp, and it was on one of these days that you could allow yourself to take comfort in the thought that soon another year would be ending. If you looked around yourself, at the yellowing trees and fields, behind which rose towering mountains, you could even think that there was some beauty in this world.

On that day, we were out digging one of those endless ditches when I saw some guards walk by with two men dressed in red robes. I sensed that they were monks, although they did not look like the ones I had seen before in Beijing, who wore yellow or orange robes. These monks were wearing garments that had been dyed a deep, dark red that shimmered richly against the landscape. But I knew they were monks by their shaved heads. As prisoners, our heads, too, were shaved. It was a mystery what the guards were doing with the monks, and why the monks were outside the prison instead of in it. Because, of course, being a monk was also dangerous in these times.

"Who are they and why are they here?" I asked a fellow inmate, who had been imprisoned because he had had the misfortune to have married a foreign woman; now they were divorced.

"They are monks."

"Of course. But they don't look like monks," I said.

"Their Buddhism is not the usual kind. They do not follow *Fo-jiao*. They practice *Lamajiao,* Lama Buddhism from Tibet. They are here to beg for food for the winter." He paused. "Although I don't know how much they will get."

We both thought it ridiculous, funny even, that monks should be begging for food from a place that didn't even have enough to feed the people it was responsible for feeding.

I was amazed at the boldness of these monks, walking through the fields in their bright robes, going up to the guards without any fear. How was it that they had escaped being interned themselves? They had two counts against them: They were religious *and* they were Tibetan. Sure enough, the monks went away empty-handed, but at least they went away free. I watched them as they walked away from the camp, until they were just two red dots that merged into one, and then disappeared against the horizon altogether. I kept that image of them in my mind's eye, and vowed that I would watch for them next year. And that, when I was released, I would go see where they lived.

It was hard for even me to believe, but the day I was released finally came. Fifteen years had gone by, and I was now closer to thirty years of age than twenty. In that time my parents had passed away and my siblings scattered throughout the country. Chou En Lai had died, as had the great Mao Zedong himself, his wife Jiang Qing disgraced, and Deng Xiaoping had instated the policy of reform and opening up to the outside world. I was formally pronounced to have been "reeducated through hard labor" and was allowed to look for work in Xining, which had drastically changed from the last time I had seen it. There were cars and trucks on the road; people owned black-and-white televisions, cassette recorders, radios, refrigerators, sewing machines, and washing machines. I, myself, felt like I had been in a time machine.

Since I had not finished my schooling, I had no real skills to speak of. I had retained my knowledge of English, but I was still wary of revealing to people how much I knew. So I took a job as a groundskeeper at the normal university, where the students were learning to become teachers. In the intervening fifteen years, classes had been reinstated and now a whole other generation was going to school. My generation had been skipped.

At first I was ashamed of admitting where my hometown was. As you know, that is one of the first thing strangers here will ask you, where your *laojia* is. In Xining, if you said you had grown up in another city, particularly one that was large and on the coast and especially if you said Beijing, this indelibly marked you as someone who had not come here by choice, but as a prisoner. However, I soon discovered that many of the other workers at the school—and indeed, people I would meet over the years—had endured the same thing as I had.

That first year was quite difficult. I shared a room with several other men who had been released at the same time as me. We slept on hard bunks, owned very few possessions, and kept to ourselves. We ate our meals cautiously, as though we would never be fortunate enough to have so much food again. It was as if we still lived in the prison.

Soon, it was springtime, and the streets were filled with bits of white fluff that fell from the sky like snow. In the beginning I thought it was due to the sheep shearing that was happening around town, but later discovered that it came from the trees that had been planted along the roads in the past few years. Obviously, I had never seen these trees before. I couldn't help thinking that even though it was spring, and I was free to enjoy it, I still could not feel the warmth of the air. I didn't know how long I could continue like this. I had heard of people who had survived being imprisoned, only to die shortly thereafter from illness or neglect or by their own hand. I did not think I could ever be one of those people, even during my darkest days at the camp, but now I was beginning to wonder.

Then, one day, I saw a monk moving through the crowded market in his red robes. I followed him until he turned down a street that led toward the edge of town and then lost him in the impending dusk. I remembered my vow, to find out where all these monks I had seen over the years had come from. After asking around, I discovered that there was a monastery outside of the city.

This monastery, Ta'er Si, is the one you saw today. It had been spared during the upheaval of the 1950s, perhaps because of its importance in Buddhist history. At that time, the only people who visited there were those who intended to become monks. Therefore, the monks were surprised to see me, a person from town, who did not want to join them. I asked if I could speak to one of the monks who went to beg from the labor camp every year, and was led into one of the buildings.

When my eyes adjusted to the light, I saw I was in a space much smaller than the room I slept in. There were few signs of regular household activity, just a mat to sleep on, a single, battered, metal cooking pot, and a twig broom for the dirt floor. But one wall was taken up by a shrine, behind which hung a tapestry made from colorful scraps of embroidered cloth. This was the focus of the room, not the hearth or the bed. An elderly monk emerged from the shadows and motioned for me to sit down. I told him my name and that I had just been released from the labor camp outside of town, to which he nodded, but otherwise had no other reaction. I watched him as he shuffled about his small room, making tea, which he offered to me. We sat in silence for a long time opposite each other, sipping our tea, saying nothing to acknowledge the other's presence. After an hour had passed, I got up, thanked him for the tea, and left.

This was my first visit with the monk. I went back every few weeks, compelled to see how this man lived in isolation. In my mind, our situations were similar, although he lived this way out of choice. And, of course, he believed in something: his religion, no matter how unfathomable it was to me. He always welcomed me into his home and served me tea. After a while, we began to talk more. I asked him about his background. He was from Tibet proper, where his parents had been very poor, collecting yak dung from the pastures to sell in the village. But they wanted a better life for him, so when he was old enough, they sent him to the monastery, since only monks were educated. He had been in one of the monasteries that had burned down in the 1950s, and afterward had come here.

In turn, I told him about growing up in Beijing, the school I had gone to, my family, the circumstances that had led me to this region. He offered no judgment on any of this. I suppose that by this time it was a familiar story, repeated by the millions across the country. Gradually, our conversations took us outside, and we would walk on the monastery grounds by a small lake. I was reminded of my walks in the park with Mr. Frazier, my missionary teacher from so many years ago. Indeed, there was something about this monk and his quiet bearing that reminded me of Mr. Frazier.

Finally, on one of our walks, I told the monk about my old friend Han. I described how my resentment toward him and the normal life he must be living had kept me warm through the winters at the camp, and how it still burned bright, despite my attempts to smother it. I expected the monk to fault me for harboring such harsh feelings, but instead he just regarded me thoughtfully. He told me that there is a saying from the Buddha, that holding on to your anger is like holding on to a piece of live coal that you intend to throw at someone else. In the end, you are the one who is burned.

I had not thought before that the embers of my anger were what had been keeping me imprisoned. So after that, I tried to let it go. If I thought about Han, I tried to think about the time when we ruled the streets together as Red Guards. I thought about when we were children and played in the courtyard. I remembered the afternoon we had spent at the Summer Palace. To my astonishment, there came a time when I stopped thinking about him altogether.

What also helped was that it became known at the school where I worked that I was an excellent English speaker, and I was called on to help with establishing the very first classes in that language. In this modern age, it was no longer considered taboo to know how to speak in a Western tongue. Soon, I became a full-fledged teacher, achieving my dream in a way I had never thought possible. And then another thing that I thought would never be possible: One day an older colleague invited me home to dinner, and I met his daughter, who became my wife.

Over the years I would go back to the monastery and visit the monk, until his death. I did not feel sad at his passing, as I felt he had probably understood more about life than most. And indeed, so had I. Although I never had the chance to go abroad, as I had talked about in my youth, I have seen and experienced a part of the country that few others have. I have known other people and learned from them without having to leave China. I have been able to rebuild my life here, gaining more than I ever expected. In the end, out of the memory of our friendship, that is what I hoped for your father, too—a family, friends, happiness.

Deep down, that is all I have ever wished for him, ever since we were both boys sitting by the lake at the Summer Palace.

# CHAPTER 12

The three of them sit quietly in the Liaos' living room. The sounds of a fussing baby come from the bedroom, and Ben excuses himself, leaving Liao and Michael alone together. The bottle of grain liquor is almost empty.

"So that's why you wrote my father?" Michael asks.

"I wrote that letter because I was afraid," Liao replies. "If your father was the same boy I once knew so well, he would always remember and feel regret for what he did. But perhaps I was wrong. Perhaps he had completely forgotten about me and no longer cared."

"No," Michael says quietly. "He may not have talked about you to me, or anyone else in my family, but trust me, he didn't forget you." He pauses. "I can't believe you were able to forgive him."

Liao shrugs. "Much time has passed. Perhaps if I had not become a teacher, if I had no family, then I would feel badly toward him. Perhaps if your father was here now instead of you, I would feel that way. But I don't think so. I think I would be happy to see him, and he would be happy to see me."

Michael isn't sure if he understands Liao's reasoning. How can this elderly man, whose life has been ruined by Michael's father, find it in his heart to forgive what had been done to him? Michael himself still can't forgive his own father, and the man has been dead for a year.

"Besides," Liao adds, "I know your father must have suffered too, when he was sent down to the countryside. He must have had to forget about what happened, just as I had."

"He never told me about being sent down," Michael says. "He never told me anything."

Liao glances toward the bedroom, where the fussing seems to have calmed down. "To be truthful, I have not told my son this story before either."

"But why not? What's the point of keeping it all a secret?"

"What is the point of passing something like that on to your children? No, that is not a good parent. A good parent is one who gives his children a bright future, not burdens them with the past." Liao waits a moment. "I do not suppose young people like my son would understand this. They are only interested in making money, in new cell phones and computers and things like that. They do not know what their parents sacrificed in order for them to live so well. But maybe that is for the best. If you knew these things, it would be too heavy of a burden to carry."

The old man could be onto something, Michael thinks. Maybe the people who had the most to forget were better off doing just that. Maybe that was what Michael's father had done, forced himself to ignore the circumstances of his previous life and the unsavory things he had done in it, so that he could go on. Only, Michael didn't know how that could change how he felt about his father.

"I just wish," he says, "that my father would have told me *something*."

"Your father always was—how do you say it?—a man of action and not words. But the fact that you are here today, and that you are the person you are, says much about the kind of man he was. That he was a good son, and a good father."

Michael winces. "I guess."

"You find this hard to believe."

"I mean, look at what he did to you."

"Your father did what he had to, back then, to keep his family together."

A family, Michael thinks, that he was soon sent away from, and whom he eventually abandoned, even if it was through circumstances beyond his control. A family that he never spoke of, not even when he had a wife and children of his own. After everything his father did, the only person who remains from his past is this elderly man in front of Michael, and it's almost by pure chance that Michael has met him at all.

"But *you*," he says to Liao. "You were like a brother to him."

Liao takes off his glasses and wipes them before responding, "Perhaps he knew that I would never try to hurt him or his family in return, that instead I would take my sentence and serve it well. Perhaps he knew that I would forgive him one day, even if he couldn't forgive himself for what he had done."

Looking at Liao's wrinkled face, upon which is written so much, Michael wonders if in the end it is Liao who is the lucky one. After all, he's the one who became the teacher he wanted to be, who is surrounded by his family in his old age, who is able to put the past behind him. He's the one who survived.

"Thank you," Michael finally says.

Liao replaces his glasses and then blinks. "For what?"

"For telling your story and, I guess, for helping me understand who my father was."

Liao nods. "It is his story too."

And now it is his own, Michael realizes, to pass on to whom he chooses. For now, though, he likes that it wholly belongs to him, something he can stick in his back pocket, like the letter that started him on this journey.

It is getting late, and Michael figures he should take his leave. Liao invites him to come back and visit the next time he is in China, and perhaps then he could stay in their house as a guest? Michael wonders where he would sleep in that small apartment with so many occupants already, but thanks Liao for his hospitality. He expresses the same sentiment in return, that Liao and his family are welcome to visit him in the States, before realizing that it would be near impossible for any of the Liaos to get a travel visa. But Liao only smiles and agrees. Both of them know that even though there may be letters exchanged in the future, they are probably never going to see each other again.

"The best thing would have been for me to see your father," Liao says in parting. "But seeing you is next best. You remind me very much of him."

Michael ducks his head, not knowing how to respond to the old man's graciousness.

He thanks Liao's wife and Mary for dinner and declines Ben's offer to drive him back to his hotel. Ben insists on walking him to the front gate of the campus, where white tents are set up by the sides of the streets. Inside these tents, Muslim men in white hats roast skewers of mutton over braziers while customers sit on small stools nearby. The smell of cooking meat is intoxicating, and, despite the lavish meal earlier, Michael's stomach rumbles.

"Would you like to try it?" Ben asks.

Michael holds up a hand. "I'm still full, thanks." But even as he says that, he realizes dinner was several hours—and what feels like several lifetimes—ago.

"Come." Ben gestures toward a stool. "You can't visit Xining without trying this."

They sit down, and a man serves each of them several skewers of meat along with round flat white pieces of bread to soak up the juices. The seasoned chunks of meat are succulent and tender, not at all gamey. It's unlike any mutton Michael has ever tasted before.

"Good, yes?" Ben asks.

"Very good," Michael confirms, and they spend the next few minutes in silence, chewing. He looks around the tent at the other customers, all of whom are men, and blinks when he notices that one of them appears to be digging into a piece of mutton with the fluffy tail still attached. A few of the men sit in pairs, as if they could be couples, although Michael knows they can't be. He remembers how Liao described *tongxinglian* as meaning "the same hearts together." It's an awfully poetic phrase for something that he guesses is still very much forbidden in China.

"This *tongxinglian*." He hopes he's pronouncing it correctly. "How is it viewed here?"

Ben does not blink an eye. "It is still, how do you call it, a taboo. It is thought to be more of a Western idea. It is different in larger cities like Beijing and Shanghai. I have heard of nightclubs there where these people go and nobody bothers them. What are these people called in English?"

"Homosexual. Or gay. And there are other words too. Slang words." Michael decides not to elaborate.

"There are slang words for it here, too. These men, they call one another *tongzhi*. Comrade."

"As in what the Communists called one another?"

"Yes, people here used to call one another comrade too. It is, how do you say—"

"Ironic," Michael supplies.

"Yes," Ben says, smiling.

Looking at the other man in the flickering light from the braziers, Michael wonders how Ben felt earlier, hearing his father tell such personal, incriminating things about himself.. He feels prompted to make a confession in return. "The reason I'm asking, why I'm curious, is because I'm that way too. *Tongxinglian*." The phrase is beginning to sound more natural on his tongue, almost musical. "Do you know what my father said when he found out? He said, 'You are my punishment. You are what I deserve.'"

Michael swallows and sits back, waiting for Ben's reaction. He's never repeated these exact words to anyone, not to Amy the night his father said them, to his sister or mother, or to David. It's as though if he refused to repeat them, they'd lose their power and eventually fade away, like a bruise that turns different shades before vanishing. But it's easy saying them to Ben, who's a virtual stranger to him and whom he'll probably never see again after this night.

Contrary to what he expected, Ben doesn't appear shocked or even surprised. Instead, he says, "Your father meant more than you thought when he said that."

"Only, I didn't know that then." Michael considers that this is probably more than Ben wants to hear, but he continues. "I was sixteen years old, no one else in my life knew this about me. The way my father found out"—okay, Ben doesn't need to know the exact details—"was humiliating and shameful, and on top of that, this is what my father says."

"It is not so bad," Ben says at last.

Michael starts to laugh. "You're right. I could have been put in prison for fifteen years, like *your* father. That puts it all into perspective, doesn't it? But I've spent the past ten years thinking that I was my father's punishment in life, just because of who I am."

"But he is dead—"

"That doesn't make any difference. He'll always be here, in my head, in some way. But I guess I understand more about him now."

That, Michael supposes, is what matters. He may never know exactly what his father was thinking, what emotions he was feeling, that night when he was sixteen. But this explanation is the closest he may ever come to the truth, and, as Ben says, maybe it's not so bad. Maybe it isn't, after all, his fault.

After they finish their midnight snack, Michael and Ben walk out to the road, where Ben flags down a taxi. Ben offers his hand and Michael shakes it, and as the taxi pulls away, he looks back to see Ben waving. He feels a certain affinity for the young man, as if they aren't people who met that morning, or even friends, but somehow related.

As the taxi takes him across town, Michael looks out the window at a city he feels like he knows much better after the past three days. At night it looks more modern, transformed by the lit-up buildings and the bright tents by the side of the road. If he watches the reflection of the red and yellow lights streaming down the inside of the windowpane, he can almost imagine that he's home.

Michael thinks about Liao and his father as teenagers, such close friends they were like brothers, until they were sixteen, and then his father sent his friend to prison. He thinks about how different his own life had been at that age.

A few months after his father had discovered Michael's secret, things appeared to have gone back to normal, at least on the surface. Aside from lecturing him on the importance of applying to the right colleges, his father didn't have much to say to him. He also had a new job that required a longer commute, so Michael was easily able to time it so that they didn't see each other much at all.

Having decided where he wanted to go to college, Michael began to push his boundaries. He stayed out late, smoked pot with Amy, got a fake ID—things he should have done years ago had it not been out of deference to his parents. The one thing he couldn't do with Amy—or in this town, even—was to find someone who would alleviate the frustration that had been building up in him ever since that night his parents had gone out. It was pathetic that the only person he had kissed was his next-door neighbor, and she was a girl.

Then an opportunity presented itself when Emily called to see if Michael was planning to do anything for their parents' anniversary (*Do* they *even know when it is?* he'd replied) and inadvertently revealed that she and Julian were going to be out of town that weekend. Michael tried to convince her to let him stay in their apartment in the West Village.

"I don't understand why you're offering to house-sit," Emily said. "We're only going to be gone overnight."

"Fine, can I please just crash at your place?" Michael pleaded. "There's a party in the city that everyone's going to, and the trains don't run that late."

"What did you tell Mom and Dad?"

"That I needed to go to a friend's house to work on a school project."

"And they're okay with it?"

"Sure." Lying to his sister was as easy as lying to a stranger.

"All right," Emily said. "Just get here by noon on Saturday."

Michael ended up missing his train, so that he was barely able to get the keys from Emily before she and Julian got into their rental car. They appeared to have a lot of luggage for just one night away at a bed-and-breakfast upstate. His sister had always been boring, Michael thought, but this seemed like something a couple who had been married for years would do. Maybe couple's years were like dog's years and aged you before you knew it.

He realized, upon entering their dark, claustrophobic studio apartment, why Emily had sounded so skeptical when he had mentioned house-sitting. There wasn't much to house-sit, not even a plant. The walls where the paint was peeling looked like they had leprosy, and there was a stain vaguely in the shape of Africa above the center of the room. Emily's clothes, in various shades of black and gray, were strewn everywhere, along with Julian's video equipment. They had just moved in earlier that year, but it looked like they had thoroughly entrenched themselves.

Michael found some calcified takeout in the refrigerator and ate it for dinner while standing up, looking through Emily's and Julian's things. The bookshelves contained various law textbooks and massive tomes on film theory, as well as a secondhand copy of *The Kama Sutra*. He flipped through it briefly, trying to get himself worked up, but the couples in the diagrams were maddeningly straight; plus, the poses looked like some form of torture.

When he replaced the book, he knocked it against something in the back, like a loose tooth. It was, he discovered, a jewelry box that contained a diamond so enormous that it seemed like it sucked in the little light that was in the room and refracted it like a giant mirror ball. So Julian was planning to propose to Emily—although obviously not this weekend, unless he'd forgotten the ring. They were what, only twenty-three? Who in their right minds got married that young? His sister's life was truly foreign to him. At the rate he was going, Michael would be lucky if he had a boyfriend by that age.

He was planning to achieve a kind of milestone for himself that night, though. He showered, put on Emily's deodorant, slicked back his hair, and dressed in what he thought of as his smartest outfit: a dark, close-fitting shirt and jeans, which Amy said made him look like an Asian greaser from the fifties, if that wasn't an oxymoron. He made sure he had his fake ID and hit the streets.

Michael knew of the famous pick-up spots, the Ramble in Central Park, certain movie theaters in Chelsea, but he had spent years listening to his mother's warnings about getting, mugged and he didn't want to go somewhere that was too dark. Bars and clubs were a better alternative, but he wasn't comfortable going in there alone. So instead he went to a video store in the Village and loitered in the back section, where you had to be eighteen to enter. Occasionally, the ponytailed man up front would look his way, but then other customers came in and he got distracted.

Michael didn't have to wait long. After about fifteen minutes, a man whose beard hid his age sidled up to him and asked, "Excuse me, have you seen this?" He was holding a video entitled *Anchors Assway,* accompanied by the picture of three sailors in white caps and nothing else, holding anchors over their privates.

"Oh, yeah," Michael replied. "That one's really funny."

"I was thinking," the man said, "maybe you'd want to come home with me and watch it?"

"Sure."

The man said his name was Alex, and that he was a computer programmer. Michael said he was an NYU student in bioengineering. Alex's apartment was only a few blocks away from Emily and Julian's, which Michael considered a good sign. If things went bad, he could just leave and walk home.

Alex's apartment was in a high-rise and did not seem like the residence of a serial killer. Michael had snuck a peek at the stack of mail on the dining room table when they came in, and Alex seemed to be telling the truth about his name. Michael had given his name as Carl Cheung, which was the name of a kid from church.

Alex told Michael to make himself comfortable on the couch and put in the video, and for a second, Michael thought that Alex really meant for them to just watch it. Before the opening credits finished, he turned to Alex, eager to get started.

"Doesn't take much to get you hard, does it?" Alex said, looking at the crotch of Michael's pants and grinning.

Michael wasn't even sure if he found Alex attractive; he was just anxious to get it over with. Alex's beard was scratchy against his mouth, and when Alex removed his shirt, the hair covering his body proved to be equally scratchy. Michael would bet that he'd be covered by a rash by the time they were done. He tried to think about that rather than the fact that Alex must be twice as old as he was, which was more evident when he was unclothed, by the graying hairs on his chest and the sag in his belly.

Michael came almost immediately when Alex took him into his

mouth, and he was afraid Alex would guess that he had never done this before, but Alex just wiped his lips, grinned again, and said, "My turn now."

Alex pushed his head down, and Michael realized, at the same time that it was happening, that he was actually doing it—he had a man's penis in his mouth, and it tasted salty and sour, like regurgitated salt water. Alex grasped him by the sides of the head, tightly but not unkindly, and pushed his face closer. Michael kept his eyes shut and pretended he was sucking on a metal spigot. He couldn't help gagging toward the end.

"You okay, kid?" Alex asked after he was done.

Michael nodded, although he supposed he must have looked rather dazed. Alex handed him a towel to wipe himself off with.

Then Michael said faintly, "I guess I should go."

"Okay," Alex said. "Glad you came over."

He didn't bother to walk Michael to the door, and when Michael looked back, Alex had resumed playing the video.

On the way back to Emily and Julian's apartment, Michael felt oddly light. As sordid as the episode was when he replayed it in his head later, as he was swigging Emily's mouthwash, trying to rid the taste from his mouth, the truth was that he was no longer a complete virgin when it came to sex. He wasn't sure if he would tell anyone about it, not even Amy, but for now, it made him feel pretty damn good.

When he went to college, this became a funny story he would tell, usually while half drunk or half stoned: the story of the hairy man who gave him his first blow job. The girls would feel sorry for him while the boys would be grossed out. Occasionally, with the right boy, it would get him laid.

When he told David a few weeks into their relationship, David said, "So I wasn't the first person who tried to pick you up."

"No," Michael said. "And you probably won't be the last."

In his hotel room, Michael sits on the bed with the ugly orange coverlet, trying to process recent events. It seems like it's been days since he went downstairs to meet Liao and Ben. In the time that

Michael has been away, someone has come in and made his bed, and straightened out his few belongings on the luggage rack.

This is his last night in Xining. The next day he'll catch a train and take another seemingly interminable twenty-four-hour ride in a hard sleeper to Beijing. When he arrives, he'll need to stay a night there before taking the plane back to New York. Fortunately, his flight leaves late in the day, giving him enough time to check out one last place, whose directions he'd gotten from Liao Weishu before he left. His entire trip in China will have taken a week, and most of it will have been spent on a train.

Michael wonders if anyone back home will have noticed that he's been gone for so long. Since he isn't working, there's no employer to keep tabs on him. His mother calls sometimes, but she's used to Michael taking a few days to respond to her messages. His sister rarely checks up on him. David, of course, will be concerned since Michael didn't return any of his messages. He's probably used his key to enter Michael's apartment and discovered his note by now. But even David is accustomed to Michael taking time off from their relationship. Maybe this time he's pushed David so close to the brink that David has given up on him. Michael doesn't want to think of that possibility yet. The fact that it's quite likely no one will have cared that he's been away makes him feel a little uncomfortable, even forlorn. He wouldn't be surprised if things were exactly the same when he returned, with no one being the wiser about where he'd gone or what he'd learned.

Michael isn't sure if he's going to tell Liao's story to his mother and sister, at least not yet. He's not sure if it's even something they need to hear. His mother and sister undoubtedly have questions about his father too, but they'll be different questions, ones that will have to be answered some other way. He knows he will have to eventually tell them, but there are so many much more important things that he hasn't told them. Such as the fact that he's gay.

David had found it unbelievable that Michael's family didn't know. This had come up a couple of months after they had known each other, when David had wanted to introduce Michael to his parents. The Wheelers were in town to see some art exhibit, and

Michael couldn't stomach the thought of walking from one white, well-lit room to another in the company of two strangers who already knew so much about him, including that his father had recently passed away. There would be nowhere to hide from their good intentions.

Besides, Michael knew that he could never reciprocate by asking David to meet his mother and sister. After putting him off with some unconvincing excuses, he'd finally admitted to David that his family knew very little about his personal life.

"Are you serious?" David had said. "What about high school? Didn't they wonder why you weren't dating anyone?"

Michael had explained that Emily hadn't been allowed to date when she was in high school, and neither had the kids of his mother's church friends, so that issue had never come up. There had also been his friendship with Amy, which his mother regarded with suspicion. However, he was sure his mother had never figured out the reason why he never took Amy to the prom or brought home more girls from college.

"I'm sure she never knew. If she did, she'd be telling everyone in church. She can't keep a secret to save her life."

"How about your dad, then?" David asked.

At this point, Michael could have told David what had happened with his father, but he felt strangely protective, especially after his father passed away. He didn't want David to think that his father was a bigot, lumped in with any old Christian fundamentalist you could see railing away on cable TV.

"He doesn't know either," he'd assured David. "It's not that I don't think my family can take the truth, I just don't want them to have another reason to be disappointed in me."

Of course, by saying that, he was dealing David the biggest disappointment of all.

Any reasonable person would have given up after that, but David resolutely stayed with him. Again, Michael wonders with a prickle of apprehension whether this latest stunt of his is the last straw. Suddenly, he wants to know what David has said in his voicemail messages. Maybe he's already dumped Michael, and Michael doesn't know it yet.

Michael picks up the phone by his bed and follows the poorly worded English directions on the accompanying placard to place what must be an astronomically expensive international call to his voice messaging system. The sound of David's voice unexpectedly makes his breath catch, although maybe it's hearing a familiar sound after being in a foreign country for so long. The first couple of messages are apologetic and cajoling—these must have been right after Michael had walked out of his apartment. *It was a joke,* David says once, sounding like it was anything but.

David's next few messages are angry, then pleading, asking Michael to call him back; it's as if he's going through the stages of grief. Michael knows he should call David. But even more than that, he needs to call his mother and, even if he's not quite ready yet to tell her about David, he has to tell her the truth about himself. He knows it's the cowardly way, on the phone instead of face-to-face, from another country altogether, but he knows that if he doesn't do it now, he might lose his nerve.

Looking at the clock, Michael sees that it's past one in the morning, meaning that it's past noon of the same day in New York. His mother should be home from church by now. As the phone rings, he imagines her hurrying into the kitchen to answer it.

"Hello?" comes her voice, distant yet comforting in its familiarity.

"Mom?"

"Michael!" his mother exclaims. "Where are you? Are you in China? Are you okay?"

"Yes, I'm in China and I'm fine." He takes a deep breath. "Mom, I have something I need to tell you."

# CHAPTER 13

Ling had picked up the phone, expecting it to be Beatrice Ma or Pastor Liu on the other end, but when she heard her son's voice, she almost dropped the receiver. Then she had been so flooded with relief upon learning that he was safe that she almost didn't hear the rest of what he had to say. When she finally understood what he was trying to tell her, she blurted out, without thinking how insensitive it must sound, "I know."

"How?" Michael exclaimed. Even through the long-distance hum, his disappointment was clear. Ling knew she should have had a different reaction, maybe pretended she was hearing it for the first time, but it was too late.

"Julian said it, so he must have heard it from Emily."

"But how does Emily know? I never told her anything."

"It doesn't matter," Ling soothed. "What matters is that you're okay."

"Are you? Now that you know?"

Ling's mind raced. To be honest, ever since Julian had spoken the truth, she had kept herself from thinking about the implications of her son's sexual orientation, what it meant for him and what it meant for her prospect of ever having any grandchildren.

She decided to sidestep the question. "Are you in Qinghai, like Emily says?"

"God, how come Emily suddenly knows everything?"

"I think she met your . . ." *Roommate? Boyfriend?*

"Emily met *David?*"

That was his name. "Yes, she met your David."

"But David didn't know I was going to China. Do you know how they met?"

"At your apartment, I think."

"Hope she didn't mess with my stuff."

Ling smiled to herself, remembering how when they were children, Michael would always warn his older sister about going into his room and moving things around. She would prefer that they still had that relationship, with its immature squabbles, rather than nothing at all.

"I have something else to tell you," Michael continued, and Ling felt her heart constrict a little at what else he could possibly reveal. "I was laid off from my job earlier this summer. But I'm fine. I mean, I might have to dip into the money Dad left—"

"That's what it's there for," Ling assured him.

"Just don't tell Emily, okay? I'll talk to her myself."

"If you had called a little earlier, you would have been able to speak to her," Ling said. "She was here for the weekend."

She could tell that on the other end of the phone, Michael was pondering this, exactly what it meant for Emily to be visiting home. "What's been going on since I've been away?"

Well, Ling thought, to begin with, your sister has left her husband, and your mother is in some kind of relationship with her pastor. But that would involve too much explanation, and she was mindful of the international call's cost. "Nothing is going on. How is your trip?"

"It's . . . educational. Everything's really different. I mean, China is different, but this place out west is like twenty years behind the rest of the country or something. People herd *yaks*. I was in a monastery today with sculptures made out of *yak butter*."

"Did you go to Qinghai because of your dad's letter?"

"Guess you know all about that too."

"Not all. I remembered it from when it came in the mail to your dad."

"You never asked him about it?"

Ling felt like she was being interrogated all over again, like with Emily. "No, I didn't ask him about it. There are a lot of things I should have asked your father, but I never did." She paused, thinking there were things she should have asked her son, too. "Who was the letter from?"

"An old friend of Dad's. I met him and his family yesterday. . . . It's a long story. I'll tell you when I get back."

Ling went on to ask Michael what time it was there and if he had eaten yet, then warned him not to try street food and to be careful of pickpockets ("Too late," he interjected). Then she reminded him that the call must be expensive, but just before they hung up, he said, "Wait. I really need to know that you're okay with what I told you."

"Of course I am," she said automatically. "And if your father was alive . . ." She stopped, uncertain of how to continue. "Well, I don't know how your father would feel about it."

"I'm okay with that," Michael replied quickly. "What I want to know is how you feel."

Ling nodded for a few seconds before she realized no one could see her. "Yes," she said. "I'm fine."

After making Michael promise to call her when he got back to the States—*from the moment he landed at the airport*—she hung up the phone. Now that she knew for certain where her son was and that he was safe, she thought she would feel her anxiety lift like a yoke from her shoulders. But instead a nagging worry persisted, just like that night ten years ago when she and Han had gone to dinner at his old boss's house and Michael had disappeared. She'd been so glad to have him back home the next morning that she'd ignored the signs that anything else might have been wrong, especially with her husband. She thought about Michael's second, easier-to-digest revelation, about being laid off from his job. *Like father, like son,* she thought.

One evening about a month after that dinner, Han came home early from work. Ling heard the thump of his briefcase in the hall, and when he came into the kitchen, she thought from the look on his face that someone had passed away.

"Sit down," she said, and he did so, the grooves in his face long. Still, she had the presence of mind to turn off all the burners on the stove and wipe her hands dry before taking a seat across from him at the kitchen table. "What happened?"

"I must be honest with you," Han said.

Immediately, a flurry of possibilities flew through Ling's mind; that her husband was seriously ill, that he was having an affair, that he was leaving her (but *I* stayed, she couldn't help protesting). A small, unforgiveable part of her even wished for the first alternative, that he was sick, because that would mean there was something for the both of them to face together.

"I lost my job," Han said. He said this in Mandarin Chinese, the language that both of them used to talk about serious matters, even after the children were no longer around to hear.

"Oh." *That was it?* "When?"

"Four weeks ago."

That made Ling's mind skip a beat. She thought of his briefcase in the hallway and wondered if she'd imagined hearing it make contact with the floor. "What have you been doing all this time?"

"Walking around. Going to the park. The library. Sitting in the car."

The thought of her husband sitting on a bench in the park or in the library almost made Ling laugh out loud. But looking at the quiet storm of his face, she knew it wasn't funny.

"Do you remember the night at the Averys' house?" That was his boss. Ling nodded. "He told me then. Didn't want me to hear it from someone else there. I guess everyone knew but me."

Her husband sat at the table like a forlorn little boy, his hands folded, his head bent as if the weight of it were too much to carry. Ling almost reached out to touch him, but sensed that if she did, their relationship would never be the same. It was enough that he was allowing her to see this much of his weakness.

"Why didn't you tell me?" she said at last.

His voice was so low that she almost couldn't hear it. But she thought he said, "I can't fail anyone else."

At first Ling thought he meant his boss, which didn't make sense, and then that he was referring to herself and the children. This thoroughly confused her, because as far as she knew, Han was an exemplary husband and father, the kind that provided and supported without complaint. Then it occurred to her that he might be talking about his family on the mainland, of which she knew little about; only that he'd had to leave them behind in the mid-seventies. But compared to whatever must have happened then, this must have been miniscule, a thread in the fabric of history.

In that instant she realized that this was what her husband was most afraid of, what made him so strict with her and the children, this driving fear that they could somehow end up lost to him as well. With this knowledge also came the understanding of just how that she could be stronger than her husband, at this moment and in the future.

"You won't," she said to him. "You haven't. It'll be all right. We don't need to tell anyone else, not even the children."

So they didn't. In the morning, Han left the house before Michael got up to go to school and came home for dinner, although by that time Michael was usually in his room or at the next-door neighbor's. They made the mortgage and car payments, sent in the check for Emily's tuition on time. By the end of the following month, Han had found a new job at a pharmaceuticals company in Trenton, and the next ten years, Ling realized now, were as untroubled as she could have ever hoped for.

Looking at the overgrown backyard from her kitchen window, Ling thought she saw a shadow slink along the fence. Like a ghost, or maybe the white cat that belonged to their neighbor, Mr. Albertson, the one twelve-year-old Emily had mistaken for a stray. That cat couldn't be alive anymore; if so, it would be over twenty years old, and might as well be a ghost. Ling remembered Mr. Albertson calling out the cat's name, Genevieve, and how she had thought he had been calling his wife instead. From what Ling could tell, Genevieve Albertson had been a tough old lady when she was alive, but the thought that her husband yearned for her so had turned her into a romantic figure. At the time, Ling hadn't wondered why Mr. Albertson would draw the neighbors' attention to himself in such a dramatic fashion. But of course a husband would grieve for his wife in this way.

What had Ling done to grieve for her own husband? She gazed at the lawn, the stalks of grass hypnotic as they nodded in the breeze. How silly she was, thinking that if she didn't cut the grass, it would bring her husband back. All through the fall and winter of last year, as the blades had turned brown and snow had fallen in a sweeping white plane, she had looked forward to spring, to when the tender young shoots would break through the crust, indicating a renewal of hope. Of course, what had happened was that the grass had come in quickly and without restraint, and soon it would grow dry and brittle with the coming of fall, and the cycle would start all over again. Unless she did something to alter it.

Ling went upstairs to the bedroom, where in the back of the closet she had kept some of Han's old clothes. Emily and Michael had thought she'd gotten rid of most of their father's things and put the rest in the basement, but there were things that she had forgotten. These clothes of Han's, two patched shirts and a worn pair of khakis, had been at the bottom of a laundry basket that Ling had neglected to empty for weeks. When she'd found them, she'd pressed them to her face. The only scent was a hint of laundry detergent. She couldn't smell her husband at all, which had disappointed her; she didn't even have that to remember him by. So she'd stuffed the clothes as far back into the closet as she could.

Now, Ling drew on one of the shirts and buttoned it, so that the tails hung down to her knees, like a smock. She told herself she was doing it for practical reasons, because she didn't own any proper gardening clothes. After some more digging in her closet, she found a sun hat, probably last used when the family had gone to Florida years ago. Properly armored, she went outside.

In the garage she located the hand mower underneath some gardening tools and dragged it, like a pile of creaky bones, out to the lawn. But where to start? She tried clipping a patch and was amazed at how easily the long blades fell before her. Looking over her shoulder, she saw how crooked the swath was, and remembered how Han always made sure his lines were straight. It was like the way he cut Emily's hair when she was a child. She'd sit on a chair in the kitchen, the bottoms of her bare feet black from the newsprint spread on the floor, while Han cut carefully, stopping often to make sure each side matched in length. Emily would look up, completely trusting, from beneath her bangs.

As Ling pushed the hand mower more confidently through the grass, she understood what Han might have liked about this kind of work. It was slow, methodical, contemplative. She could feel the pull and stretch of the muscles in her shoulders and her calves. At her feet, the blade whirred with purpose. When sweat from her forehead ran into her eyes, she didn't pause to wipe it away. Everything blended together, then and now, the past and present. Here, she was mowing across the sunny patch on the lawn where Emily liked to lay out when she was a teenager, reading and working on her tan, even though Ling told her she'd turn as dark as a peasant. There was the spot where they'd buried Michael's goldfish, the only pet he'd ever been allowed to have and which had died shortly after he turned six. Emily had made a big deal out of it for her little brother, constructing a little cardboard casket and writing a eulogy.

She almost missed the stump of a tree that was hidden in the grass. It took her a moment to remember what it was: a crape myrtle that they'd had for a few years and had blossomed predictably, pink and fluffy like a showgirl. Then last summer it had withered and died, and one afternoon, when Michael was visiting, he and Han had uprooted it while Ling was away at the store. She'd come back to see a peculiarly shaped black trash bag out on the curb, like a hunched old woman. When she'd gone into the backyard, she felt like something was missing but couldn't think of what, as if a trick were being played on her. To confuse her further, her husband and her son were sitting on the porch, not speaking, as was their habit, but at least they were spending some time together. Then, two weeks later, Han had passed away.

When she was done mowing the lawn, Ling stood at its edge and surveyed the work she'd done. She'd had to backtrack in some spots, but for the most part the grass was evenly cropped. She had a blister on the palm of her right hand, and she knew her joints would ache the next day, but for now, she felt like she'd achieved something. This was how, she realized, things were going to be for her from now on, taking pride in small accomplishments.

Gradually, she became aware of someone calling her name. To her horror, she saw Pastor Liu approaching her across the lawn. She knew she must look a fright, wearing her husband's old shirt and, unusual for her, perspiring so much that she could feel the sweat pooling under her collar. The heat pressed against her like another person's body and, feeling like she might swoon, she placed her hand against the rough wood of the fence.

"Are you all right?" Pastor Liu asked. "Please, sit down."

"Thank you," Ling said, sliding into the fence's shade. After a few moments, she was able to collect herself. "What are you doing here?"

Pastor Liu crouched down beside her. "Beatrice Ma called earlier to say that she was wrong about what she told me this morning, that you didn't want to be left alone and would appreciate a visit from me."

Inwardly, Ling shook her head at her friend's meddlesome ways.

"I was worried when I didn't see you at church this morning." Pastor Liu hesitated. "I hope it didn't have anything to do with our conversation last week."

"Not at all," Ling forced herself to say, and grasped at the explanation she had given Beatrice. "I couldn't come because my daughter was visiting."

"She is well? Your children are both well?"

Ling could only shake her head. "My daughter is leaving her husband. And I found out this morning that my son . . . likes other men." That was the closest she could come to expressing it. "I don't mind," she was quick to insist. "I just want him to be happy. But I can't help wondering what my husband would have said, how he would have felt about it. I think he would be upset by it."

"Ling," Pastor Liu said, "I must tell you something, about your husband. I couldn't do it right after he passed away, and I promised myself that I would tell you if you ever wanted to talk to me about him, but—"

"But I never did," Ling finished for him.

"You never did. Han called me one day, about a month before he passed away, and said he needed to see me. We made an appointment, and when we met, he showed me a letter he had recently received from an old friend who lived in China, in—"

"Qinghai Province."

"That's right. So you know about this letter?"

"Not nearly enough. Please go on."

"So he told me about his friend, a man whom he'd grown up with in Beijing, during the Cultural Revolution. Then one terrible day he betrayed this friend, told the authorities that he liked other men, and it sealed his fate. This friend was sent to the labor camps in Qinghai Province for fifteen years."

For a moment, Ling felt a chill of shock at what her husband had done, and then her heart constricted at the thought of him enduring this shameful secret for so long and alone. "And then?"

"The letter was the first time he had heard from his friend since what happened. In it, this friend said he was fine, and he'd forgiven Han for what he had done. But that's not the end of what your husband confessed to me."

"Michael," Ling murmured in realization.

"Han told me that he accidentally found out about your son when he was sixteen. He also said that his reaction was not what it should have been, that he was afraid that he had hurt him. Having received this letter, he wanted to know whether it was too late to save their relationship."

"What did you tell him?"

"I said it was never too late."

When Ling raised her eyes to Pastor Liu, she saw that he meant those words for the two of them too, in this very moment.

"Your husband passed away only a month later. I don't know if he ever had a chance to speak to your son."

"Michael came home two weeks before," Ling recalled. "They spent some time together, but I don't know if anything happened."

"Only Michael can tell us that," Pastor Liu said. "But at least we know that your husband found some kind of peace before he left this Earth."

"Yes," Ling replied. "I suppose so."

"I think," Pastor Liu added, "if I may say so, Ling, that your husband would have wanted you to be happy. And he would want you to be happy by yourself, not because of what your children do, or who they are, or what they might give you."

"I know," she said. She did believe now that everything her husband had done—even when he'd spoken harshly to her when she was eight months pregnant with Emily or when Michael had been sick as a baby—had been, in some roundabout way, to ensure that their family would remain intact, because he knew that was what had given her the most joy in her life. And now that he was gone, and her children were effectively gone, she would have to find a way to make sure of that herself.

A distant rumble of thunder made both Ling and Pastor Liu look up.

"It's going to rain," Ling observed. Already, a thick metallic smell was beginning to come up from the earth, almost palpable in the heat.

"I should go."

As Pastor Liu rose, Ling surprised herself by saying, "Wait. Can you stay for dinner?"

"Are you sure?" Pastor Liu asked.

"Yes," she said with a smile. "After all, it's just dinner."

When they were inside the house, Ling went back to secure the screen door against the coming storm. Through it she looked at her handiwork, the flat expanse of green before her. She thought she could feel a heaviness in the air from the impending rain, like a breath that was finally going to be released. In the moment before she closed the door, she thought she saw her husband standing in the middle of the lawn, waving to her as if from across a green ocean.

# CHAPTER 14

After she left Jean at the corner, Emily walked the few blocks to her next destination. The air had a dusky tinge to it, although she couldn't tell whether it was because it would be getting dark soon or the impending rain. She thought about what she had said to Jean and wondered if her mother had indeed gone on with her life. The house looked like it was being kept up, except for maybe the lawn, but her mother could hardly be expected to do yard work. Other than this morning, it sounded like her mother went to church regularly and saw her friends, including that nosy Beatrice Ma. Emily used to wonder why her mother went to church at all, since she didn't seem to be that devout. But now she was glad that her mother had a reason to get out of the house, a place where she would see other people. It made her feel better that she and Michael didn't go back home as much as they should. After seeing what Jean's house had been like the day before, crowded with friends and relatives, Emily realized just how solitary her mother's existence was without her father.

Which, in turn, made Emily feel her own prospective isolation more keenly. Without Julian, without her job, who would she be? She and Julian had abandoned most of their friends, or their friends had abandoned them, when they'd moved out of the city.

She hadn't taken the time to get to know any of their neighbors, located as far away as they were. Her relationship with Rick had been changed irreparably by a drunken kiss.

That left only her family. They were also the only ones who could provide a place for her to go. However, Emily couldn't stay in her childhood home with her mother. She knew she'd regress in roughly the same amount of time as it had taken to make her bed before she'd left that morning. She had just one other option, Michael's apartment. He'd understand why she would go there instead of the house they had grown up in. But first, she had to get the keys.

The high-rise she stopped in front of was new and nondescript, lacking the charm of a prewar building, the walk-up that she and Julian had lived in, or even Michael's converted tenement. She could see how it might turn someone like her brother off, but at the same time she wondered why Michael insisted on staying in his garret if this was the alternative.

"I'm here to see David Wheeler," she told the doorman.

The doorman gave her a curious look, but he gestured toward the elevator.

David opened the door before she reached the end of the hallway. "I heard you coming," he said.

"Really?" Emily looked down at the carpeted floor.

"Actually, the doorman rang me. Said he thought you looked suspicious."

"He did look at me kind of funny."

"He's just confused. You're not the usual clientele I have up here. Kidding." As if afraid he'd overstepped himself, David quickly opened the door wider.

"Nice place," Emily said, looking around her at the high ceilings, the white walls upon which hung paintings that were made up of solid bands of primary colors, the kind of art she could never understand. Looking at them was like trying to read something in another language. "Do you collect?" she asked.

"Not really," David replied. "I like to try and support young artists here and there. My father did it when I was growing up. None of the artists he bought ever turned out to be anything much."

"Have you seen any of Michael's stuff?"

"I didn't know he painted."

"He doesn't, he draws. At least he used to, as a kid. He might not anymore. I'm surprised he didn't tell you, knowing your interest in art."

"Well, he doesn't tell me everything, apparently," David said. "Do you want to sit down?"

Emily obligingly perched on a hard modernist sofa that made her feel like she was sitting on a doctor's examination table. David appeared to be a little tongue-tied, which surprised her since he hadn't acted that way when they'd first met. For some reason, he'd seemed more comfortable with her in Michael's apartment rather than his own. Maybe he was starting to think of her less as an ally and more like a protective older sister.

"Well, I guess I'll get the keys and be on my way," she said.

"Hold on," David said. "Have you eaten yet?"

Emily laughed. "That sounds like something my mother would say."

"Have you? I've just finished making dinner. . . . It's only pasta, but I'd love for you to stay. We didn't have much of a chance to talk the other night."

"That's true," Emily said.

She expected to be served spaghetti, but instead it was a dish along the lines of something Julian would concoct—deceptively simple, but with carefully chosen ingredients. She'd bet that the tomatoes were fire-roasted, the olive oil supervirgin, the name of the intricately shaped noodles at least five syllables long. The wine, too, was excellent. Although she knew very little about wine, Emily could tell that it was expensive, buttery and smooth. How had her brother ended up with such a sophisticate?

There was no art in the dining space, just one glass wall that framed the glittering traffic down Second Avenue. There were also several photographs scattered on a sideboard, of people who were obviously part of David's family: his genteelly graying parents, a man who looked enough like him to be his brother, a little blond boy. Emily noticed that the same boy appeared twice in some pictures, and then she realized they must be twins.

"Are those your nephews?" she asked.

"Jamie and Tyler," David replied. "My brother's kids."

"They're cute."

"You should have seen them when they were two. Looked like a couple of angels. Absolute terrors on the inside, of course."

"Of course." Emily hesitated. "So you like kids?"

"Sure."

Her ears pricked up at that. Maybe her mother's wish for grandchildren was alive after all. "I mentioned you to my mother," she said.

"Oh?" David let a forkful of fancy pasta fall back on his plate. "What'd she say?"

"Not much." Emily figured it wouldn't help to say that her mother had thought he was Michael's roommate, which was entirely her own fault. "But she seemed pleased that you were a lawyer. A real lawyer, unlike me."

"What kind of law do you practice?"

"Immigration law. That is, I used to. I'm planning to leave it."

"Why?"

Instead of answering the question, she responded, "Why did you want to be a lawyer?"

David looked beyond Emily at their reflections in the window. "Honestly? Because my father was a lawyer. Someone in our family has to continue the tradition, and as the elder son, it was up to me. Can't say it was ever a choice, but at the same time it gives me purpose, makes me feel like I'm fulfilling my duty. Otherwise I might just get fed up with the long hours and unending paperwork." His eyes met those of her double in the glass. "How about you?"

"I guess it's kind of a duty for me too. My father studied biochemisty, but how he came over to this country has a lot to do with why I went into immigration law."

"If it means so much to you, why are you leaving it?"

For the first time, something that she hadn't done with either Julian or her mother, Emily found herself telling David the entire story of Gao Hu, from the moment Jean had stepped into her office to learning of his death the day before. "I know it's unprofessional for me to abandon the case," she said, "but I'm not needed there anymore. My colleague will do a great job without me; he's brilliant. And even if Jean did win millions in damages, it still wouldn't bring back her husband, or Sam his father. Nothing can change that."

"If you don't mind me saying so," David said, "it sounds to me like you just got too involved with that one particular family. It won't be like that with the next case. You'll be more careful."

"There won't be a next case. It's too much for me. Especially since, on top of everything else, I'm leaving my husband. That's why I need the keys to Michael's place." Earlier, when Emily had called David, she hadn't explained why she intended to sleep in Michael's apartment that night, hoping he'd just think she needed to get an early start at work the next morning.

"Really?" David said. "Because I thought you needed the keys for some kind of secret tryst."

"I'm serious," she said. "About the leaving, I mean."

"Of course," David replied. "This colleague of yours, the guy you said you were working with on the case—he's got nothing to do with you leaving your husband?"

Emily stared at David. This, she definitely would never have discussed with members of her own family. "There's nothing going on between us. Okay, yes, we kissed once, but I didn't have an affair with him, and I'm not going to. God, I feel like I'm being cross-examined here."

"Sorry." David grinned. "I *am* a lawyer." Then he turned serious. "But this situation with your husband. Okay, it doesn't have anything to do with this colleague that you kissed once. What does it have to do with?"

Emily supposed she might as well tell him everything, as she'd told him so much about herself already. She started with their move out of the city, her thirty-first birthday dinner, Julian's biological clock and the lack of her own, her and Julian's fight two nights before.

"That's a big difference, wanting kids," David acknowledged when she was done. "You sure that's the way you feel?"

"My mother asked me the exact same thing, and I'll tell you what I told her: How is Michael sure that he's gay? How about you, for that matter?"

"Actually," David said, "I wasn't always certain. I was totally confused in high school, dated a girl whose family went back with mine for ages. But I fell for my lab partner and his long fingers, and she ended up marrying an oil tycoon from Texas. So that didn't work out."

"Meaning?"

"That what you're so sure of when you're eighteen can change. Or when you're twenty-eight or thirty-eight."

"Does that mean you don't know how you'll feel about my brother, say, a year from now?"

"I don't know, but I'm willing to stick around and find out."

"Even when he's miles away, trying his best to make it look like he's left you?"

"He'll come back. He knows where to find me. After all, I'm not going anywhere."

The two of them looked at each other for a moment. Then Emily said, "I think Michael is very lucky to have someone like you. You should make sure he knows it."

"I will," David replied.

Thunder shook the floor-to-ceiling windows, followed by a blast of rain against the glass. Emily and David looked outside to see the traffic lights turn into a neon smear and people rushing for cover on the streets below.

"It's coming down pretty hard," David said. "You want to stay here tonight? I have that spare room."

"No, thanks." Emily was thinking that she would indeed go into the office early the next morning, to clear her desk and figure out what she was going to say to her boss. "I'm afraid that if I stayed, with all this good food and wine, I might get too comfortable and never want to leave."

"At least someone in your family appreciates the merits of this place," David said.

At the door, Emily wasn't sure whether to shake hands with David or give him a hug, as if he were a friend or relative. He wasn't really either, yet. She could tell David was thinking the same thing, and so they both hovered awkwardly at the threshold before finally saying good night, without doing either. Oh well, Emily thought. Perhaps they'd get it right the third time they met, when Michael was there.

With the rain, it took almost as long for Emily to find a parking space downtown near Michael's apartment as it had earlier that afternoon at the diner. Finally, her clothes soaked through, she climbed five flights of stairs to the top of the building. Water streamed down the skylight overhead, hopefully washing away the grime. It took her several tries, but she finally got the key to fit and pushed the door open, giving way to a flood of air that was considerably cooler than she'd remembered it. Aside from that, though, nothing seemed any different, as if David hadn't been there.

She stripped off her wet clothes and looked through the closet for something of Michael's to borrow. Tomorrow she'd need to buy some new clothes, as she'd been wearing the same things for almost the entire weekend. She found a clean T-shirt and sweatpants that, although the legs were too long, fit trimly at the waist. Was her brother really that skinny? She'd always thought of him as a beanpole but couldn't remember. She suddenly had a memory of him, when she was home from college, and he'd been wearing some outfit that Amy Bradley from next door had put together. It'd been a goth-looking concoction of black crushed velvet and leather that could have been appropriate for either a boy or a girl. On her brother it had made him look otherworldly, almost beautiful.

"What's this for?" she had asked.

"I'm going to be a famous fashion designer," Amy said with some difficulty through the latest piercing in her lower lip.

"And I'm going to be her muse," Michael declared.

Emily laughed. "Well, don't let Mom or Dad see you in that," she said.

How old had Michael been then, fourteen or fifteen? She wondered if that had maybe been a tip-off to his sexuality, but at the time she was so involved with herself, her decision to go to law school and to move in with Julian, and whether the first was enough to mitigate the second when her parents found out.

She wondered if she had been a good enough sister to Michael when he was a teenager, if he'd been as confused as David had been in high school. Certainly, with their parents it couldn't have been easy. But she hadn't offered any advice or help, except for that one time when Michael had stayed over at her and Julian's apartment, the weekend they had gone to a bed-and-breakfast upstate, when Julian had intended to propose but had forgotten to bring the ring. Michael was supposed to have gone to some party in the city, but Emily hadn't even asked him where it was or who he was going with. By the time they'd gotten back to their apartment on Sunday, he was gone, without even leaving a note.

Julian had been acting strange all weekend, distracted on the hike they took and the chilly lake swim. Even the sex had not been that enjoyable, although that was partially due to the springs on the bed that seemed to date from the same time period as the Revolutionary War–era headboard. Emily had wondered about Julian's unsettled behavior, since it had been his idea to pry her away from her law books and spend the weekend away.

Then, when they'd arrived home, he had ransacked the bookcase, muttering about something being gone or lost, she wasn't sure which.

"What are you talking about?" Emily had asked him.

"I had it right here. Someone must have taken it."

"Are you accusing my brother of stealing something?" She must have spoken more sharply than she'd realized.

"No, no, of course not. But maybe he had a friend stay here with him?"

"You mean a girlfriend? Michael? You've got to be kidding." What she meant was that she couldn't imagine her seventeen-year-old brother being old enough to date; she still saw him as the twelve-year-old that she'd left behind when she'd gone to college, even though by now he had grown taller than her.

"I don't know, maybe a friend who's involved with drugs or something and needs money?"

Emily stared at Julian. "What exactly is it that you're missing?"

But he wouldn't tell her, and eventually she gave up trying to figure out what he was looking for and started to put away their luggage. Then sheepishly he'd come up with a box that had apparently been filed behind the wrong book. Even before he'd opened it, before he dropped to one knee, Emily knew what he was going to say, and that knowledge did not flood her with a sense of elation. Instead, she felt the rising tide of panic and heard her own voice say yes, she would marry him, but not until she was twenty-five, since that was how old her mother had been when she had gotten married.

Afterward, she supposed it was odd that there had been no one to call with the news. Of course, Julian didn't speak to his parents, and Emily was afraid of her own parents' reaction if she told them. The only family member she could have told was Michael, but he would be on a train on his way home, and Emily didn't know if he would care. As far as she was aware, he didn't spare a thought toward her relationship with Julian.

From that moment, Emily realized, she had been on an inevitable path that had led her to spend countless hours in her office at Lazar and Jenkins in Chinatown, to the converted farmhouse in Westchester, and now to her brother's grotty studio apartment in the East Village. If she reached down far enough, would there be anything left of the person she had been almost ten years ago? Then Emily thought of what David had said earlier, about certainties changing. But what about uncertainties? She had been uncertain then, as she was now, just about different things. Back then, she had been doubtful of a life with Julian; now she was doubtful of one without him.

She went into the bathroom, which was so small someone could sit on the toilet and brush their teeth at the same time, and wrung out her wet clothes. She draped them over the shower curtain rod, noticing the toxic orange stain that the curtain left against the side of the tub. She decided she'd scrub it, and the rest of the bathroom, grateful for any activity that kept her mind occupied. When she opened the medicine cabinet door, she noticed it contained a rusty can of shaving cream, some razor blades, and—ugh—condoms. She quickly shut the cabinet door, not wanting to think about her little brother having any kind of sex.

After she was done with the bathroom as best she could, she continued with the rest of the apartment, her energy starting to return. Yes, she'd clean Michael's place, as a thank-you to him when he got back for letting her stay there, whether he liked it or not. It was the least she could do to keep herself from thinking about what she was doing alone in her brother's apartment at nearly midnight on a Sunday.

When she got to the closet, she reconsidered diving into the clutter of clothes and other items that clearly had to be stored in there because there wasn't space anywhere else. Then she saw a corner of something black and solid, and tugged a leather art portfolio from the jumble. She recognized some of the sketches that spilled out as what must have been exercises from art class—shapes, light-and-dark shadings, portrait blockings. But then there were pictures of people she recognized: her mother, her father, even Amy Bradley at her most rebellious-teenager stage with various facial piercings and spiked hair. The one person Emily did not see was herself. Of course, she thought, Michael must have done most of these sketches in high school, after she had left home. Still, she felt like someone who had peeked into another person's diary, hoping that they had been written about, and finding nothing.

She returned the portfolio to where she had found it, tucking it behind what she recognized as the suit Michael had worn to their father's funeral. She recalled how at the end of that day, she had gone looking for Michael, since Julian was going to drop him off at the train station on his way back home. When she and Michael had asked their mother if she wanted them to stay longer, their mother had refused, but Emily had insisted. She intended to go back to work the next week, even though her coworkers, especially Rick, wanted her to take more time off. But from the moment she had received the call from her mother, Emily had not allowed herself to stop. If she did, she was afraid that she might let everything in her life, not just what had happened recently, catch up to her.

Michael hadn't been upstairs in his room or downstairs in the kitchen. Finally, she found him outside on the porch where she'd seen him retreat earlier that day with Amy Bradley. A faint whiff of something illicit came from his clothes, and she knew what the source of it probably was, but didn't mention it.

"Are you okay?" she asked.

"Yeah. Just tired."

"We all are."

"Really?" Her brother gave her a strange look. "You totally seem in control in things."

"Thanks," Emily replied, even though she wasn't sure whether it was a compliment or not.

Michael looked out into the backyard. "I was thinking that this isn't the first funeral I've been to."

"What do you mean?"

"Remember just after my sixth birthday?"

She followed his gaze out onto the lawn. "You mean when your goldfish died?"

"You wrote a poem or something. About how good goldfish go to the great pond in the sky."

"I can't believe you remembered that."

"Well, it meant a lot, you know, to a little kid."

Emily looked down. Although she'd known what to do when she was twelve, she couldn't do anything for Michael now. The only thing she could think of was to put her hand awkwardly on his shoulder. She could feel the bony point of his shoulder through the fabric of his suit jacket, like what she imagined the joint of a bird's wing to feel like.

"Come on," she said. "Julian's waiting with the car."

Emily thought of the note Michael had left behind, which was still on the table where David had left it on Friday night: "Gone away to take a break. Am fine." In that moment, she saw just how similar she and her brother were. They might not be close in the way that she'd always imagined siblings should be—she may not have even known, at least consciously, that he was gay until two days ago—but they were undeniably alike. They were both running away from people who, for whatever inexplicable reason, loved them. Only Emily hadn't gone as far away as China to do it. Again she thought back to her conversation with David, his unwavering faith in his feelings for her brother. She hoped that faith would be rewarded.

She drew out her cell phone. First, she hit the number for Rick. When he answered, she could hear some kind of commotion in the background, the thumping of feet, splashing water, the querulous voices of children being readied for bed.

"Hold on," Rick said, and she could hear him move down a hallway and close a door. "I can't talk for long. Lisa's going to kill me if I don't get the kids in bed on time."

"I just wanted to say that I'm sorry for what happened yesterday."

Rick lowered his voice. "Me too. I mean, I'm not sorry that it happened—but I'm glad that it didn't go any further." She could hear his breath, as if it were against her cheek. "Lisa and I had a long talk this morning, and I think we've come to some kind of agreement. One that doesn't involve separation." She was quiet for so long that he asked, "Emily? You still there?"

"That's great news. I'm happy for you two."

"Thanks, I appreciate that. You still coming into work tomorrow morning?"

"Yes, I'll be there." She did need to go in, to offer up her resignation and pack up the few personal items in her office. If she explained herself well enough, she knew Mitch Jenkins would let her go without the customary two-weeks' notice. She supposed both she and Michael would be out of work, but they'd manage somehow.

"See you tomorrow, then."

"Good-bye, Rick."

Emily began to get ready for bed. She used Michael's toothpaste, dried her face with his towel. Sliding between his sheets on the futon, she noticed that he slept with his pillow doubled over, just as their father had. Maybe there were ways that she knew him that she hadn't noticed. Then, after turning off the light, she reached for her cell phone again.

"Hello?" came a voice on the other end.

In the brief silence that followed, Emily imagined Julian sitting in the dark by the phone, the vastness of what lay beyond the windows pressing in on him, just as it was on her.

"It's me." She took a deep breath. "I'm ready to talk now."

# CHAPTER 15

Upon Michael's return, Beijing seems bizarrely big and modern, covered in billboards hawking bottled water and electronics, neon lights spelling out the names of Western companies. He stays in the same hotel as when he first arrived, which seems like the Four Seasons compared to where he stayed out west. Since his flight leaves the next afternoon, this is his last night in China.

Michael thinks of what he's returning to: a lack of work, a lack of air-conditioning, a lack of quiet since he suspects David, Emily, and his mother will all want to know what he's seen and done in China. Perhaps he'll make it easier on everyone and have them convene in the same room, which means that his mother will meet David, but perhaps that's unavoidable. Maybe that's even what he intended, by disappearing in such a melodramatic fashion.

What hadn't been dramatic in the least was coming out to his mother. Or, rather, being outed by Emily. He wonders if she knew before. It isn't like they'd been around each other much besides the holidays since she left home to go to college. Also, when she moved away, he'd been a preteen, too distracted with the what and how of hormones to spend much time wondering why. Even when they did see each other, she was always preoccupied with work and her totally bourgeois life with her husband. But maybe it wasn't so bad that Emily had paved the way for his conversation with his mother, softened the blow, and for that he is grateful.

He should, Michael thinks, get both his mother and sister some souvenirs. Maybe he'll have time to do that the next morning, along with the other task he needs to accomplish. But for now, he's intending to make the most of his last night in Beijing.

He decides to have an early dinner at a nearby restaurant that is literally a hole-in-the-wall, a place with concrete floors and folding stools instead of chairs. When people are finished with their food, they push the scraps onto the ground to be swept up later. Even after almost a week in this country Michael still doesn't know what to order, so the waitress brings him two Beijing delicacies: one of shredded and spiced potatoes and the other of eggplant, green peppers, and potatoes cooked together—dishes he's never seen before in the States. He washes everything down with the weak Chinese beer he's grown to like.

Afterward, he takes a long, rambling walk. Apparently, he is in Haidian, the university district. He figures that where there are college students, there must be some kind of entertainment going on. He passes by gates manned by guard stations; these are far more prestigious universities than the one in Qinghai. The air is dense and sticky and permeated with the sound of thousands of cicadas chirping. So far all Michael can see are karaoke bars and more hole-in-the-wall-type restaurants. Nothing that looks like the kind of nightclub that Ben referred to. Michael has to admit that he's curious as to what one looks like. Finally, a taxi driver catches on that he's a foreigner and idles by the side of the street, asking him in serviceable English where he wants to go. "A club," Michael says, without specifying what kind.

"Ka-la-okay?" the driver asks.

"What?" Michael blinks. The driver mimes holding a microphone.

As Michael tries to figure out a way to express himself, a small group of men starts to gather around them, made up of shop owners and a few passersby who look like they are students. One of the shop owners appears to think that he is lost. Another thinks that he's looking for a place to stay and suggests the guesthouse his brother runs. Meanwhile, the taxi driver continues to mention places and different kinds of clubs, each seedier than the last, without hitting on the one that Michael is thinking of. Everyone is trying to be helpful, but in the end it just creates a lot of noise.

Finally one of the students steps forward and says in almost perfect English, "I know where you want to go."

"You do?" Michael stares at the young man. He's wearing tight black jeans and a black T-shirt, with his hair slicked back in a pompadour. Michael is reminded of the image he himself tried to project as a teenager: the Chinese greaser.

The young man smiles and gestures at the three other students with him. "Come with us. We are going to Jiu Ba Jie. Bar Street."

For a moment Michael hesitates. But the boys look harmless, and besides, he is leaving tomorrow. What could happen? There's enough time for one more adventure. So he gets into the passenger seat of the taxi, while his four new friends pile into the back. They are skinny enough that they can fit, laughing as they throw their legs over each other and jab elbows into each other's sides.

Michael watches them through the rearview mirror. The one who had invited him seems to be the leader, and the best-looking out of all of them. There's another whose face is unfortunately pocked with acne, and another who wears thick black-framed glasses. The fourth has hair cut short on the sides, in a rudimentary Mohawk. Something in the easy way that they banter with one another in Mandarin makes them seem younger than college students.

In the mirror Michael catches the eye of the ringleader. "What's your name?" he asks.

"Donny."

"Donny?" Michael almost bursts out laughing.

"It is my English name." Donny introduces his friends, who have Chinese names that Michael immediately forgets.

The taxi is heading southeast on what Michael supposes is a Ring Road, although he isn't sure which one. It looks like any freeway in America, passing by high-rise apartment buildings and even an IKEA. At times bicyclists can be seen peddling down a side street, but for the most part there are only cars and trucks on the road. The taxi takes an exit and immediately gets mired down in a jam of similar red vehicles, all apparently heading toward the same place. After a while, Donny and his friends pile out and motion for Michael to do the same.

Michael starts to hand the driver some bills, but Donny stops him. "It is my treat," he says.

Donny takes the lead down a warren of streets lit by strings of white lights. People sit outside underneath umbrellas bearing the name of some beer company while girls wearing short skirts and T-shirts printed with the same name loiter outside. The clientele appears to be mostly well-dressed, heavily made-up young Chinese women hanging on the arms of much older white men or wealthy-looking Chinese men. Otherwise, sloppily dressed foreigners mill about. Some Chinese and other languages can be heard, but a lot of the dialogue taking place, between the beer girls and their customers, the foreign men and their escorts, is in English.

Down a side street, there is a door from which a thumping bass can be heard. A man who looks too slight to be a bouncer takes more bills from Donny and allows passage into what appears to be a replica of an airplane hangar. Posters from American movies, no matter whether they are military movies or not, hang from the walls: comedies warring with gangster flicks, 1940s musicals with horror films. Fighter-jet propellers are suspended from the ceiling like idle fans. In the middle of the floor is a woman in a leopard-print bikini doing a pole dance; the effect would be sleazy if it weren't so out of place. Everything about this scene is so stereotypically American that it can only be located outside of America.

Michael wonders if he has been taken to the right place. But when his eyes adjust to the dim light and haze of cigarette smoke that casts a pall over everything, he sees that almost all the people in the club are men. Aside from the occasional foreigner, most of them are Chinese. There are couples sitting at the tables on the side. Sometimes they just look like two Chinese men out for a drink, but there are also pairs of older white men with young Chinese men, in a dynamic very similar to the foreign men and Chinese women out on the streets.

"Do you want to dance?" Donny asks, raising his voice to be heard.

Michael shakes his head. "Can we sit down?" he shouts.

Donny finds a table, and a waiter takes their orders. The drinks here, Michael calculates, are as expensive as they are in the States, but when they arrive, appear to be watered down. Michael doesn't even feel a buzz, but the faces of Donny and his friends rapidly turn red. Even though he can't understand what they're saying, being among them makes Michael think of his father and Liao Weishu and their Red Guard friends, although the setting and circumstances couldn't be any more different. What would they think if they could see what Beijing was like forty-five years later, the flash of money and Western influence?

Pock Mark, Glasses, and Mohawk don't seem to know any English and speak to one another, leaving Michael to converse with Donny. He finds out that Donny is from Tianjin, a city a few hours east from Beijing, and that his family owns a department store chain there. He figures that Donny must be pretty well off and doesn't feel so bad that he's let the kid pay for everything thus far.

"Are you in school?" Michael asks.

"I study English at the Beijing Foreign Studies University," Donny replies. "It is my last year."

"What will you do after that?"

Michael anticipates that Donny will want to become an English teacher like Liao, or a tour guide like Liao's son, Ben, but when Donny replies that he wants to work for an international joint venture, he realizes that he's not in Qinghai anymore.

"You are a college student too?" Donny inquires.

"Yes." Michael knows he looks young enough for it to be true. He isn't quite sure why he's just lied, except that he doesn't want to appear like the older foreigner taking advantage of a local.

"What is college life like in America?"

Michael wasn't aware that he'd told Donny where he was from, but he supposes that it's unmistakable, imprinted on him from his face to his clothes. He thinks about how peculiar his own college experience would sound if he tried to explain it to Donny, the night-long cram sessions, the dining hall food fights, the experimentations with booze and drugs and sexual orientation. Donny, with his serious dreams of entrepreneurial life, would not understand.

"It's fun. Kind of like this." He gestures at the noisy club around them.

Donny nods as if the answer is to be expected. "There are many places like this in America, yes?"

"Some."

"And nobody thinks it is strange?"

"There are always people who think it's strange."

Donny's eyes grow wider. "But America is very free. You can go anywhere you want. You can go with anyone you want. I think it must be very wonderful."

"It's not that easy. For example, my parents . . . wouldn't approve of what goes on here."

"My parents would not either. But they do not know I come to this kind of place."

"Mine didn't either," Michael says.

They both look at each other, and then Donny smiles, and for a moment, his face is as open and bright as that of a child. Michael finds himself smiling back.

"Let's dance," Donny says, and Michael allows himself to be led onto the floor.

Michael can't remember the last time he was in a club. David disapproves of such places, says that he's outgrown them, but Michael doubts that David was ever into this kind of scene, even in his avowedly wild postcollegiate days. Michael suspects that this means David once left a restaurant without paying the check, and on a dare. He has actually never seen David dance, or drunk, or dance while drunk, and wonders if that's some kind of flaw in their relationship, not having seen somebody in a situation that contains equal opportunity for silliness and honesty.

In front of him, Donny is acting quite silly, as his style of dancing is more of the electric-shock variety. Sparks should be shooting from his hands and feet, he's so wired. Michael knows that he doesn't move that smoothly himself, so he remains tightly restrained, like a checked box. But as his head begins to spin, either from the watered-down drinks finally catching up to him, or the rush of music, his limbs begin to loosen.

The song that's playing is some disco standard from the 1970s. Michael realizes that nobody in this room, if they were alive back then, would have heard it, since music from the West would have been unavailable at the time. To him, this song is reminiscent of late-night FM radio, awkward junior high school dances, and ironic keg parties. To everyone else here, there's no history; it's just a song to dance to. Michael remembers what Liao Weishu had said about the students dancing at the college, how they want to be unified. There's something unified about everyone dancing here too—in not hiding who they are.

Some time has passed, and both Michael and Donny are sweating as if they're outside in a rainstorm. Then Donny reaches over and places his hand on the back of Michael's neck. He leaves it there for an agonizingly long time, and when Michael is just about to draw away, needing to break the spell if nothing's going to happen, Donny kisses him. His lips are impossibly soft. Michael is first stunned by that sensation, and then the thought that, for once, he is kissing someone who looks just like himself. His own kind.

The song ends, and so does their kiss. Donny says to Michael, "Do you want to go?"

"Where?"

Donny shrugs. "Another club. Or your hotel."

"Let's go."

Back out on the streets, among the swaying throngs of people, the multiple drinks suddenly hit Michael. He stumbles a little, and Donny puts a hand on his arm to steady him, and keeps it there.

"I'm okay," Michael says. "But maybe it should be the hotel and not another club."

Donny hails a cab, and Michael gets in. But he doesn't move over so that Donny can get in next to him. Donny appears confused and then hurt. Michael closes the door between them.

"Good luck with everything," he says to Donny, and tells the taxi driver to go, which the driver can only do slowly because of the crowds, so it isn't a very impressive getaway.

When Michael looks back, he sees Donny gazing after the cab. Then the young man straightens himself and begins to walk back toward the club. He'll find his friends and maybe pick up someone else there, a young Chinese man his age, or, more likely, a foreigner who is impressed with his knowledge of English. This is probably a regular weeknight for him.

The taxi driver is very erratic, and by the time they pull up in front of his hotel, Michael isn't sure he's going to make it. He tosses some bills at the driver, runs into the hotel, and gets to his bathroom just before he throws up. Thank God for modern Western toilets.

He lies down on the bed, fully clothed. Did he really expect to end up in his hotel room that night with Donny? That had to be his intention. You didn't agree to go with someone to a night club and dance with them, even kiss them, in a foreign city without expecting them to go home with you afterward. But what was the point of that? To be able to say to David when he got back to New York, *Oh, not only did I look up my father's old friend, whom he helped send to prison for fifteen years, but I also hooked up with a random college kid?*

Michael already knows what David's reply would be: that it doesn't matter. Everything Michael has done to drive him away— refusing to take the key to his place, not calling him, leaving the country without telling him where he's gone—hasn't worked. David will wait for him, however long it takes for Michael to decide how he feels, because that is who he is. And Michael is beginning to think that, just maybe, he deserves to be with someone like that.

He glances at the digital clock by the bed; it's almost two in the morning. He needs to go to sleep if he wants to get up early enough for his last day in Beijing.

Back in New York, it would be afternoon, and if Michael was there, David would probably have gotten off from work early to meet him. Michael would be at the bar next to David's apartment building, nursing a pint because that's all he can afford, watching the mirror across from him for David to enter. There'd be a businessman or two out for a late lunch, young women looking for an early drink, and then David would flash into view. The sight of him, with his tie loosened, his jacket over one arm, would make Michael catch his breath, as if he'd unexpectedly caught a glimpse of his future.

Michael holds on to this image long enough to drag himself out of his clothes. Then he passes out on top of the coverlet.

The next morning, Michael wakes up, thankfully, without much of a hangover. He finds a cab that will take him to Houhai, the part of Beijing where his father and Liao Weishu grew up. He has on a piece of paper the location of his father's house, which Liao Weishu visited a year and a half ago, which he'd asked Liao to write down before he left Xining. Rather than the highwaylike Ring Road from last night, the cab takes quiet side streets shrouded in a haze that can either come from mist or, more likely, pollution. Occasionally, they pass groups of elderly people doing their morning exercises, or old men sitting outside with their caged birds.

Finally, they stop in front of a gaudily painted gate, and the driver indicates that he can't go any farther. Michael points to the characters on the paper, and in turn the driver points somewhere beyond the entrance, so Michael pays him and gets out. He figures that he can stop and get directions along the way. For now, as he walks down a warren of lanes, he takes in the brick walls, the tiled roofs, the wooden doors, some of which are painted bright red and others which are peeling. These must be the *siheyuans* that Liao had talked about, the compounds that once held families and now are divided up among many unrelated inhabitants. One door is ajar, and he peers through the crack to see a neat courtyard brimming with potted plants. In a corner, two bicycles lean against each other like lovers. There is something timeless about this place, and Michael wonders what it would be like to live or grow up here, in a place that seems so far removed from the rest of the city, if not the entire world.

He hears a rustle from the interior of the courtyard and jerks his head back, as if he were caught spying. What he really needs is to find someone who can tell him if he's heading in the right direction. There are stores along this street, but most of them appear to be souvenir shops, cashing in on the picturesque qualities of the area.

Michael is reminded that he needs to get something for his mother and sister. But when he looks at the wares on display—a certain time period appears to be most popular, judging from the various Mao pins and badges—he thinks of how Liao had said that Michael's grandfather had turned to selling these things, so as to not raise the suspicions of the authorities. Suddenly, the thought of purchasing such an item seems less appealing, and Michael hurries on before the shopkeeper can misinterpret his hesitation as interest.

Abruptly, the lane ends, and Michael finds himself standing in front of a lake that he guesses Houhai takes its name from. But it isn't so much of a sea, as the other side is easily visible, slate roofs rising and dipping in the morning light. As Michael walks along the lake, he imagines Liao passing underneath the same willows with his missionary teacher. He can't be far now; he can feel it. At the corner is a store that appears to be the equivalent of a New York bodega, its front bristling with ads for phone cards and soft drinks, and Michael stops to show the proprietor the piece of paper. The man says something in what Michael knows to be Mandarin, although the Beijing accent makes it sound like a rusty engine. The shopkeeper gestures around the corner and shakes his head, making it seem like he's contradicting himself.

"Can you show me?" Michael asks, pointing at the shopkeeper and then in the direction the man has indicated.

The shopkeeper finally gives in and comes out from around the counter. He's wearing blue plastic slippers from which puffs of dust rise as he leads Michael down the alleyway. Then he stops, and Michael thinks that he must have made a mistake. For in front of him, extending down what seems to be the entire block, are giant piles of rubble. Among them he can make out pieces of gray brick, concrete, and tile, all jumbled together. There are also bits and pieces of household debris: shards of dishes, broken pieces of furniture, torn pages from books—destruction caused not by Red Guards but by modernization.

The man points to a section of wall that miraculously is still standing. "*Chai!*" he barks, then imitates something falling down. "*Chai!*"

On the wall is written a symbol in a circle, what could be an anarchist's symbol, except that it's a Chinese character that looks a little like a tool that's wearing a hat. Michael looks at the piece of paper again, at Liao Weishu's scrawl. He can't believe that in the eighteen months or so since Liao visited this place, it's been torn down. He knows that things must move fast in a modernizing country—villages that disappear overnight in favor of skyscrapers, towns submerged with water from the creation of a dam—but this is unbelievable.

Then Michael thinks about whether his father would feel any regret over what has happened. Somehow, he suspects not. His father made a point of distancing himself from his family and his upbringing. What was the loss of a house, a building of brick and stone, compared to the loss of family members, friends, a history? Now, as his father wished, there's finally nothing left from his past life.

Michael takes a tiny piece of stone from the rubble, folds it in the piece of paper, and puts it in his pocket. He knows it's silly to take such a souvenir, that it might not even be from the right house, but no one aside from himself will know its significance. Then he follows the shopkeeper, who has been watching his actions with a skeptical eye, back to his shop and purchases a soda to thank him for his help. Then he glances at his watch. He still has some time before he needs to go back to the hotel, pack his things, and get to the airport.

He retraces his steps back to the entrance and hails a cab to take him to the Summer Palace, as if he wants to get in as much sightseeing as possible. But in reality he thinks that if he's unable to see his father's and Liao Weishu's old home, he might as well go to the next place that had some meaning in their childhood. The cab heads north, back past Haidian, the university district where Michael's hotel is located, and then west toward the mountains beyond the city.

The haze has burned away, leaving the sky sunny if not entirely blue. Michael is beginning to understand that this is as clear as the weather will get here. With the day advancing, so do the tourists, swarming over the temple grounds, posing for pictures on the graceful arch of the Jade Belt Bridge and boating in Kunming Lake, which really *is* a lake, extending like a vast mirror underneath Longevity Hill. Since he's by himself, Michael feels at distinct odds among the families, foreign tour groups, and packs of students. To escape them, he wanders off down the garden paths until he finds an empty patch of grass by the lakeside. There he sits, closing his eyes to the slender spire of a pagoda on a faraway hill across the lake.

He tries to banish the murmuring voices of the people passing by him, concentrating instead on the sound of the lapping waves and the faint stirring of the wind. He wants to will himself back in time to when two boys were at the Summer Palace forty-five years ago. What did it look like then? Had it been renovated, or did it somehow look more authentic?

Then words in English cut through his musing: "But why doesn't it sink?" It's the voice of a little girl, the words spoken with a British accent, no doubt referring to the famed Marble Boat to the west of the lake. The Empress Cixi restored it in the late nineteenth century, turning it into a symbol of that dynasty's excess and woeful lack of preparation for foreign invaders. Michael wonders why he can't be like the other tourists, concerned about why the Marble Boat doesn't sink, counting the sections in the Long Corridor, bargaining for the best price for a set of ten postcards featuring the Temple of Heaven, which isn't even on the Summer Palace grounds.

He tries to channel a different scene, but the difficulty, he realizes, is that while he's able to picture some random rosy-cheeked boy for Liao Weishu, he can't do the same for his father. He doesn't know what his father looked like as a child; as far as he knows, there are no remaining photographs. He hadn't thought to ask Liao Weishu if he had any pictures, if indeed they had survived his imprisonment, and now that his father's childhood home has been destroyed, there's no hope there either.

So instead he pictures his father the last time he saw him, on a summer day almost a year ago, two weeks before he passed away. Michael was standing in the backyard in the middle of the lawn, since it was the best place to get cell phone reception and also afforded some privacy. As far-fetched as the idea was, he couldn't help thinking that even with his door closed, his parents might overhear him if he were in the house.

That particular afternoon he was talking to David, since he'd finally broken down and decided to call him. Although he'd left the city in a bit of a funk, once he was away and in the middle of the suburban town he had grown up, he'd suddenly needed to hear David's voice. Part of it, he was sure, was that after a night and a morning with his parents, he was beginning to feel like he was a teenager again, sitting at the table while his mother tried to fill his father's usual silence with chatter about her church friends and which of their children were in medical or law school. Uncanny how after seven years, it was as if he'd never left. Even when he talked to his parents, he could feel his speech patterns falling into the familiar cadence of empty reassurance and evasion.

He told his parents that he liked his job and his coworkers. He said that his apartment was spacious and in a safe neighborhood, neglecting to mention he'd had to move recently because his roommate had started a fire and gotten them kicked out. At that point, Michael had decided he couldn't stand another roommate and discovered his very own crawlspace at the top of a five-story walk-up, euphemistically described by the broker as a studio apartment with "penthouselike qualities."

Most of all, he did not say he had just met, and was possibly falling in love, with someone.

That afternoon his mother had gone to the grocery store, and his father had retired upstairs to take a nap, so Michael thought it was safe to go out into the backyard and give David a call. When David answered, Michael listened carefully for any indication that he was outside, possibly in the company of someone else, but the air in the background was dense and still.

"Where are you?" he finally asked.

"Where do you think? Home," David replied.

"What are you doing?"

"What is this, some kind of late-night hotline?" Michael could hear the grin in David's voice. "Should I slip into something more comfortable?"

"Just tell me."

"Okay, I'm getting ready to go out for a run. And I'm wearing a T-shirt and shorts, in case you're wondering."

It was Michael's turn to smile.

"How are your parents?" David asked.

Michael was surprised by how genuinely David seemed to be interested in his parents, asking about them whenever Michael mentioned his mother had called. When Michael said he was planning to visit them that weekend, he almost thought David was going to ask if he could come along. But it was far too early for that; Michael didn't want to think yet where that could lead. He'd be more comfortable with introducing Emily to David first, but he knew a sister wouldn't carry as much weight. He'd told David that his parents were typical immigrant Chinese parents: his mother a conscientious churchgoer who complained to her friends about her lack of grandchildren; his father withdrawn and obsessed with maintenance of nonhuman things, like his lawn.

"They're fine," Michael replied. Unconsciously, he turned toward the house and thought he caught sight of someone standing at a second-story window before the curtain dropped. It could only be his father. Had his father been watching him and had he been able to deduce from that distance who he was talking to?

Michael walked farther away from the house, but he no longer felt comfortable.

"I have to go," he finally said. "My mom's back from the store and I should help her."

"Okay," David said. "Call me when you get in on Sunday?"

"Sure." The things that weren't appropriate yet for them to say to each other lingered in the silence afterward, before they both hung up.

Michael was thinking about this, the things they could have said, when a voice asked, "Who were you talking to?"

He turned around to see his father walking across the lawn to him, in his beat-up slippers that must have once been brown leather but now were so cracked they looked like an old catcher's mitt. His father must have indeed been sleeping, because a lock of graying hair stuck up on the back of his head. Michael had the urge to reach over and smooth it down. He was taller than his father now, and stronger.

"Just a friend," Michael replied.

"Your mother is home?"

His father must have caught the last part of his phone conversation. "I guess not. I thought I heard a car, but it must have been the neighbor's."

"You should get your ears checked," his father said.

And you should get your eyes checked, Michael thought. His father was wearing his usual summer ensemble of an undershirt and pants that he sometimes rolled up when he was seated, making them into de facto shorts. (Michael had always wondered where that custom came from, until he made his trip to Beijing and saw elderly men everywhere sporting the same look.)

"Did you rest well?" he asked, but his father had already moved out of earshot and on to something else.

He was standing by the crape myrtle to the side of the lawn, near the garage, inspecting its bare branches. "Not good," he said.

Michael walked over to join him. He couldn't remember what this tree looked like when it was healthy and in full bloom. "What's wrong with it?"

"*Cercospora fungus.* Causes the leaves to fall off."

Michael thought it sounded like the kind of disease you caught on the bottom of your foot. "Can you do anything about it?"

His father shook his head. "The tree is dead. It'll have to be cut down." He shaded his face against the sun, as if to check how far the day had progressed. "Let's do it now before your mother comes back."

"Do what?" Michael wasn't sure if it was the lazy afternoon or being in the presence of his father that was making his comprehension slower than usual.

"Cut down the tree."

His father went to the garage and came back with a shovel and handsaw, and working side by side they uprooted the tree and cut it down to a manageable size. As he stuffed branches into a black plastic trash bag, Michael considered that this was probably the most time he'd spent with his father in years. His father wasn't the sort to teach him to play baseball or ride a bike when he was a child, or tell him what to expect from girls, as he imagined everyone else's father had. But he had eventually learned to fill those gaps, in his own way.

Michael hauled the trash bag out onto the curb, and when he came back, he saw his father sitting on the top step of the back porch. He went and sat down beside him. Like his father, he looked out to where the tree had been, but since he couldn't say that it had made much of an impression on him before, he couldn't tell whether the backyard looked better or worse without it.

"Too bad we can't go out and get a replacement before your mother comes home, eh?" his father said.

Michael shook his head with a laugh.

"That friend of yours." His father regarded him. "Is it a good friend?"

"Yes," Michael replied. "A very good friend."

"I am glad."

They didn't say anything else, and that was how his mother found them when she came back from the store.

"But I don't *want* to go back to the hotel!" a voice cuts through his memory.

That petulant little British girl again. Michael turns to see her trailing her parents, kicking at the grass. She's six or seven years old, and, to his surprise, she looks Chinese. Michael wonders where her family's from. England, or possibly Hong Kong? What these past few days in China have taught him is that people who look Chinese can be anything.

The little girl continues to declare that she doesn't want to go back to her hotel, but Michael knows he has to go back to his if he wants to catch his flight. He stands up, brushing the dust that permeates Beijing from his clothes. That, he guesses, will be the souvenir he brings back, not a trinket or mass-produced object, but the dirt in the creases of his jeans, the piece of rubble that he picked up that morning in his pocket. These are the only tangible things that are left, and, perhaps, they're enough. For what really matters is the story of his father that's he's bringing back to his mother and sister, and how it's tied into his own story that they never knew, while they were living under the same roof. Even then, it's just a layer to be peeled back, in the hopes of eventually, someday, getting to the person inside.

Then he starts walking down the path after the girl and her parents. It's time for him to go home.

## ACKNOWLEDGMENTS

Many thanks to my editor, Esi Sogah, and my agent, Deborah Schneider. Both of them were wonderful to work with in other capacities, but this is the best working relationship I could have imagined.

I would also like to thank Karen Auerbach, Paula Reedy, Kristine Mills, and the rest of the team at Kensington.

Thanks to The MacDowell Colony and the Corporation of Yaddo for giving me the time and space to write, as well as to my supervisors and colleagues at HarperCollins Publishers who so generously allowed me to attend these residencies and filled in for me while I was there. Much appreciation goes to the crew at Lantern Books for providing me with such a pleasant work environment while I was looking for a home for this book.

I am indebted to those who read this manuscript in its various stages, including Marie Argeris, Katie Chase, Luke Fiske, Kay Kim, Jono Mischkot, Zoraya Nambi, Samuel Park, and Jennifer Pooley. I'm grateful to have spent a year working as an English teacher at Qinghai Normal University in Xining, China, with its amazing staff and students—little did I know that fifteen years later I would be writing about my experiences there in a novel. A special shout-out goes to my fellow teacher Naomi Furnish Yamada, who played the What You Would Be Willing to Pick Up in the Outhouse game with me.

Above all, thank you to my family: my father, James Lee, who came to America at the age of eleven and worked his way up from dishwasher to engineer; my mother, Claire Lee, who passed on to me her love of writing; and my sister, Lydia Lee, who continually inspires me with her own family. Finally, I'd like to thank my husband, Neil Gladstone.

Keep reading for more from Wendy Lee,
including a behind-the-book essay,
a Q&A with the author,
and a reading group guide.

# A Re-education

When I signed up to teach English in China through a volunteer program, I spent hours wondering where I'd be posted. Beijing, the cosmopolitan capital of the country? Ma'anshan, a quaint town on the Yangtze River? Qingdao, the German-influenced coastal city where the beer comes from?

I wound up being posted in Xining, the capital of Qinghai Province, which is located in China's northwest. One of the poorest and most backward provinces in the country, Qinghai became a place where political prisoners were sent for re-education through labor starting from the 1950s, due to its remote location on the edge of the Tibetan Plateau. Xining was once a flourishing trade city on the Silk Route. By the late 1990s, when I was there, it was a dusty, windswept, polluted metropolis of more than a million people.

While Xining wasn't exactly what I expected, I was ready for a challenge. As a recent college graduate, I wanted to experience real life—not just outside of the bubble provided by a suburban upbringing and school but outside of the United States itself.

My college experience in the Bay Area had been filled with literal and metaphorical sunshine. I lived in a vegan co-op where activities included mixing lentil loaf for fifty, line-drying clothes, and holding house meetings where everything was decided by consensus. When chemistry and biology proved too difficult for my nontechnical mind, I took creative writing classes, which left me with few options after graduation. Most of my friends were going to grad school, joining start-ups, or moving into shared houses in San Francisco. I knew I wanted to be a writer but had absolutely nothing to write about.

So, I decided to teach English in China, where at least I would know how to speak the language—that is, conversational Mandarin learned from my parents, which could get me as far as asking for directions and ordering certain foods.

When I told my parents I was going to be spending the following year in Xining, I expected them to be happy that I was returning to their homeland. However, my mother's paranoia kicked into high gear. "They won't know you're an American and you might get deported!" I promised her that I'd always carry my passport with me.

She wasn't reassured. "Don't you know what happened to my uncle in the 1950s?"

My great-uncle was my grandmother's much-younger brother, the sole boy in a well-to-do Shanghai family. He was a pilot and traveled internationally, which led to him meeting his Russian wife. My mother told me that he had to race on a pony across the steppes of Russia to win a rabbit, and thus his bride's hand.

"Isn't that a Mongolian custom?" I asked skeptically. My mother loved to embellish her stories.

In 1949, when the Communists took over the country, my grandmother fled to Taiwan, due to her husband's problematic position in Chiang Kai-shek's Nationalist government. My great-uncle and his family stayed behind on the mainland. During Mao's Anti-Rightist Campaign of the late 1950s, he was one of the thousands of intellectuals sentenced to re-education through labor—exiled to Qinghai Province and ordered to get a divorce. His wife took their four children to Moscow, and it's unlikely he ever saw them again.

Listening to her stories about my great-uncle, I realized why my mother was worried. For many of her relatives, mainland China was a place you escaped from, not where you willingly returned.

Even though I wanted to experience real life, I wasn't quite prepared for what I faced upon arrival in China. In Xining, my status as an outsider was apparent. Within my first few days there, I was pickpocketed. When I tried to order food with my parental-taught, conversational Chinese by asking for *dan chao fan* (eggs and rice), the waitress laughed and said, "You must be from Hong Kong." As a first-time teacher, I floundered in front of my class of thirty students, who were only a little younger than me. Even among the other foreign teachers at the school, I felt different because I wasn't religious.

Loneliness set in. Xining's bleak winters lasted from October to May, which meant that when I wasn't teaching class, I was holed up inside my apartment. Back home, there would have been movies, books, or TV to turn to for solace. Here, the one English-language program on television was state-run news; in other words, pure propaganda. The radio played one pop song in English, the theme from the movie *Titanic* (apparently, the song was as popular in China as it was in America that year). Bereft of anything in a language I could understand, I'd sit for hours next to the hissing radiator in my apartment and look out my window into a bare garden dusted with snow.

The apartments across from me had windows glowing with warmth and life. This was where the other, Chinese teachers lived, often families of several generations crammed into a one-bedroom like my own. Because the school wanted to modernize the foreign teachers' apartments, they had added tubs and sit-down toilets to the bathrooms. A regular Chinese bathroom was just a squat toilet in a closet. Once, I'd asked a Chinese teacher how he bathed. "I go to the bathhouse," he said. Apparently, there was a bathhouse on campus that served everyone who wasn't fortunate enough to have a Western bathroom.

Those families didn't have privacy or first-world comforts, but they spent meals around the table with parents and grandparents, spouses and children. Even if they had to sleep four or five to a room, they didn't have to wake up to an empty apartment. In those times, I'd think about my great-uncle and how lonely he must have felt, separated from his wife and children, sent to what felt like the end of the Earth.

After he had been released from prison in the 1960s, my mother told me, my great-uncle became a teacher in Xining—not at my school, but an agricultural college on the outskirts of town. I wondered whether he was able to relate to his students better than I could. While my class consisted of students who were intending to become English teachers, and they'd been studying English since primary school, I had a hard time understanding them, and vice versa. On my first day of class, a student came up afterward and asked me to speak more "lowly." Had my voice been too loud? Belatedly, I realized that he had asked me to speak more "slowly."

Toward the end of the school year, my mother came out to travel with me to Kashgar, a city on the Silk Road that was even farther west and more remote than Xining. By that time I was a hardened and obnoxious "China Hand" (a foreigner who's become—or thinks they've become—an expert in Chinese culture), embarrassed to be paying for tour guides and taking the soft seat rather than hard seat class on trains. When we ate in restaurants I mentally calculated how many bowls of noodles the cost of our meal could have bought from a street stall.

Before my mother and I left for our trip, we visited the agricultural college where my great-uncle had been a teacher. Visually, this school was pretty much the same as mine, with its nondescript, Soviet-inspired architecture. We visited a dorm, where my mother insisted that she was able to "feel her uncle's spirit."

Later, my mother showed me a picture of my great-uncle that my grandmother had passed on to her. In a faded photograph, he is wearing dark glasses and standing in a garden in a Mao suit, next to a female student. "He loved women," my mother said. So maybe he wasn't quite as lonely as I'd thought.

After nine months, I also wasn't as lonely as I'd once been. By this time I'd gotten to know my neighbors, who invited me over for dinner and to practice their English. I'd also made a few religious and nonreligious friends, both foreign and Chinese.

Most of all, I had learned how to live by myself in a big city, so that I could do it two years later when I moved to New York City to try and become a writer.

# A Q&A with Wendy Lee

*Across a Green Ocean* deals with family secrets and the harm that silence can bring to a family. How much of this is based on your own family?

Some superficial details of the Tang family are similar to that of my own. My parents did meet in New York City and moved to suburban New Jersey after getting married. I have a sister who is five years older than me, which I guess makes me the gay son.

The character of Liao Weishu, Han Tang's friend who is sent to a labor camp in Qinghai Province during the Cultural Revolution, is based on my mother's uncle. He was exiled in the 1950s, so, an earlier time period, but for the similar reason of intellectual persecution. He was married to a Russian woman, and they were forced to get a divorce.

What research did you do about northwestern China and Beijing in the 1960s and '70s, around the time of the Cultural Revolution?

There were two items in particular that contributed to how I chose to write about that time period. The first is the memoir *In Search of My Homeland* by Er Tai Gao, an intellectual who was sent to a labor camp in Gansu Province, which neighbors Qinghai Province, in the 1950s. Although the book describes incredible hardships in an even, matter-of-fact way, there are also moments of surprising humor.

The other is the film *In the Heat of the Sun* directed by Jiang Wen, which is partly based on his own youth as a Red Guard during the Cultural Revolution. The unusual thing about his depiction is that he doesn't focus on the terrible acts that the Red Guards committed or the terror they invoked. Instead, the tone is very nostalgic, and it shows just how much fun these kids had, as would any who suddenly didn't have to go to school, while they navigated the usual teenage territory of first love and newfound freedom.

**The case that Emily Tang works on involves an immigrant who dies in detention under questionable circumstances. Where did you get the idea for that story?**

That is actually based on a real case involving a man named Hiu Lui Ng, who died in a Rhode Island detention facility in 2008. Ng had lived in the United States for almost twenty years, was married to a naturalized citizen, and had two young children, but was arrested on an old deportation order. During his year in detention, he complained of excruciating back pain, but no one believed him. When he was finally allowed to be treated by a doctor, it was discovered that he had a broken back and suffered from liver cancer, which he died from soon after.

I remember thinking when I read the story that this could happen to so many people that I know. Even if you've lived in this country for many years as a productive citizen—you own property, pay taxes, and have a family—you have no rights. Your entire life could be taken away from you in an instant, just because of your immigrant status. You will never feel safe or that you belong. That, to me, is shocking.

**This book and your first book, *Happy Family* (which is about an immigrant woman from China who becomes the nanny to a New York City couple with an adopted Chinese daughter), deal with the notion of what makes a family. Why is this an important theme for you?**

I'm fascinated by the idea that immigrants leave their families to come, often alone, to a new country, where they have to create their own families. How does that affect the rest of their lives? What is the fallout for their children? Even if your parents were immigrants, but you were born in the States, as I was, there is still this thought that your family is not quite normal.

Then, on another level, there are those young people who choose to leave their families to strike out on their own or pursue a dream, which I think is true for a lot of people who come to New

York. There's this continual push and pull of the familiar and the unfamiliar, the wish to be independent and also interdependent, and out of that can come some amazing stories.

**China features prominently in your work. How do you incorporate it into your novels and why?**

I lived in China for three years after college, and it's had an immeasurable impact on the way I see the world. For one thing, I think it's made me appreciate just what my parents gave up to come to this country and create a fairly comfortable life for themselves here. The places where I lived were quite diverse—Xining, in the northwest; Fuzhou, in the southwest; and Beijing—so I've tried to convey just how many different kinds of locations, cultures, and peoples make up the country. I think the typical Western reader probably imagines China as a landscape of mountains bisected by the Great Wall, populated by millions of identical-looking people who work in factories. Whereas it's a very complex, ever-changing country that deserves to be better understood.

**What do you think the future holds for Asian American literature?**

When I worked in trade publishing, I noticed that a lot of successful Asian American novels were set in the past, sort of the "Lisa See" effect. There didn't seem to be as many that had a contemporary setting, even if part of the book was set overseas. And, of course, they were mostly by women, about women. This made me wonder if this is how a mainstream audience prefers to see Asian Americans, as an exotic people from the past as opposed to contemporaries who are undergoing the same issues as them. In the future I'd like to see more Asian American literature that deals with the issues of my (second) generation, not necessarily about immigrants but how to cope with an immigrant legacy; what happens after the American Dream has or hasn't been achieved, or its definition has changed.

**What is the most memorable piece of writing advice someone has given you? That you would give someone?**

When I was getting an MFA in fiction at New York University, my advisor told me to "work hard." I know that sounds like a simple piece of advice, but a lot of people around you won't assume that you're working hard if you're a writer. You're expected to sit down and the words will magically flow from your fingertips. But sometimes even the act of sitting down in a chair for more than an hour will be difficult. And, if you want to get published and your book to be read, the hard work doesn't end after you finish writing the book.

My personal advice, also very common, is not to quit your day job. A lot of writers assume that their lives will change once they get published, mostly having to do with fame and money. Usually, that doesn't happen. Also, having more time to write isn't necessarily conducive to the quality or quantity of your writing. That said, it's good to have a job in which you have some creative energy left over at the end of the day, and where people are sympathetic to your writing endeavors.

**What is your writing process like?**

I wish I were one of those people who wrote every day, but it comes in dribs and drabs for me. For many years, because I had a full-time job in publishing, I would rely on going away to writing residencies for a month or so to get huge chunks of work done. While these were wonderful experiences, they also became a crutch in that I didn't know—and still don't—how to maintain a regular writing regimen. Every time I start something new, there is a moment of terror when I feel like I don't know how to enter the story. But somehow I do.